Praise for Lorraine Brown

'Fresh, charming and wonderfully escapist'
Beth O'Leary

'Utterly charming, you'll be yearning to hotfoot it to Paris!'
Prima

'A magical modern love story, I've fallen head
over heels for Paris again!'
Helly Acton

'A wonderfully engaging tale of love and self-discovery'
Mike Gayle

'A charming, romantic read, which gave me a
real hankering for croissants!'
Sophie Cousens

'The lovely descriptions made me want to take the first
post-lockdown Eurostar to Paris!'
Kate Eberlen

'A gorgeous, romantic book packed full of joy. I mean, who
doesn't need to be whisked away to Paris'
Laura Pearson

'Plotted to perfection and teeming with the
rich sensory romance of Paris'
Kirsty Capes

'With its sliding doors and picture postcard tour through
Paris, *The Paris Connection* is fresh, funny and just the
tonic for dark winter nights'
Zoe Folbigg

Lorraine Brown previously trained as an actress and is about to complete her final year of a postgraduate diploma in psychodynamic counselling. She lives in London with her partner and their eight-year-old son.

Also by Lorraine Brown

The Paris Connection

SORRY I MISSED YOU

Lorraine Brown

ORION

First published in Great Britain in 2022 by Orion Books,
an imprint of The Orion Publishing Group Ltd
Carmelite House, 50 Victoria Embankment
London EC4Y 0DZ

An Hachette UK Company

1 3 5 7 9 10 8 6 4 2

A CIP catalogue record for this book
is available from the British Library.

ISBN (Mass Market Paperback) 978 1 4091 9842 0
ISBN (eBook) 978 1 4091 9 843 7

Typeset by Deltatype Ltd, Birkenhead, Merseyside

Printed in Great Britain by Clays Ltd, Elcograf S.p.A.

www.orionbooks.co.uk

For Robbie and Gabriel, my lockdown loves.

January

I

Rebecca

I was in the bathroom when the buzzer rang, attempting to apply bright red lipstick properly, with a brush, so that it didn't end up smeared ghoulishly across my face by the end of the evening. He was six minutes early, which I thought was *very* inconsiderate. If somebody invited me round for eight, I'd arrive on the dot and not a moment before. Those vital few minutes made all the difference when you were having people over and you wanted everything to be perfect when they arrived.

I gave up on the lipstick and dashed into the bedroom, dousing myself in one more layer of my most expensive perfume and leaving a trail of it behind me as I flitted into the lounge to press play on the Spotify playlist I'd spent literally hours putting together. The melodic beat of London Grammar's 'Hey Now' started up, which I'd thought was a strong first track. Just the right amount of cool without being so hip as to be utterly unbelievable. Tyler might not even be into music and so it wouldn't matter, but I always thought it best to prepare for every eventuality.

I hurtled down the hallway, smoothing down the fabric of my red midi wrap dress, my bare feet sticking slightly on the parquet floor. The latch felt slippery underneath my fingers as I fumbled with the lock and threw open the door.

3

'Oh,' I said.

It wasn't the suave, forty-something New Yorker I'd been expecting, but a different guy with sparkly eyes and broad shoulders and a nose that dominated the otherwise softer features of his face and wavy brown hair that was longer at the front than it was at the sides. He was not suave (or forty) and he was wearing a black jersey long-sleeved T-shirt pushed up to the elbows.

'Hello,' I said, confused.

'Sorry to bother you,' he said.

He seemed a bit stressed, I thought. Now I came to think about it, he did look vaguely familiar, but I couldn't quite place him. Was he one of the Amazon delivery guys? The new boyfriend of my upstairs neighbour? Nope, it wasn't coming to me.

'I'm Jack,' he explained, pointing over his shoulder. 'From the flat opposite.'

I noticed he was wearing black joggers that were too short and showed his ankles and white Adidas trainers with no socks. It was an odd ensemble. Most people would look ridiculous in it, but remarkably he'd sort of managed to pull it off.

'Oh, right,' I said, it finally dawning on me that he was the new guy from across the landing.

'I moved in a few days ago,' he added. 'I'm subletting the flat from a friend for the next six months.'

I knew the friend he meant. Tom something his name was. I'd always thought he was a bit up himself, if I was honest. He had a stunning, waif-like girlfriend with auburn hair and razor-sharp cheekbones who'd wafted up and down the stairs in floaty skirts all summer long, her tan leather sliders clip-clopping noisily on the steps.

'How long have you lived here?' asked Jack. 'Sorry, I didn't catch your name?'

4

'Rebecca,' I said, stroking my cuff with my thumb. He was friendlier than Tom, I'd give him that. 'I've been here a while. A year and a half or so.'

He nodded. 'Ah, I see. You know how it all works, then?'

'Well, the communal hot water *doesn't* work, not really,' I said, immediately warming to my subject. 'So if you want a bath, you'll either have to get up at the crack of dawn or do it after ten. And bin day is Tuesday. And don't slam the lift doors after nine or the woman on the ground floor will kick off. Anything else you need to know?'

He laughed. 'That was a very thorough introduction, thank you.'

'I aim to please.'

The next track on my playlist came on. It must be eight by now.

'Ah, I've got a package for you, haven't I?' I said, remembering there was a reason this Jack was standing on my doorstep.

'You have,' he said, looking relieved. 'Thanks so much for taking it in.'

I went into the kitchen and opened the cupboard under the sink, pulling out all the stuff I'd shoved in there earlier when I'd been flying about trying to make the flat look like a show home. Sweat prickled on my forehead as I riffled through rolls of bin bags and bottles of washing detergent and the kitchen gadgets (the spiraliser, a salad spinner and was that an avocado slicer?) I'd stuffed in there at various points over the last twelve months because I never used them. But there was one thing missing: Jack's parcel.

I stood up again, running my hands through my hair. Where the hell was it?

'Everything all right?' said Jack, tentatively poking his head round the door frame.

I put my hands on my hips, blowing air up into my fringe, as though that was miraculously going to cool me down.

'All fine,' I lied, feeling more flustered by the second.

'Is there a problem?' Jack asked. 'Only I do kind of need it quite urgently.'

'Nope, no problem,' I replied, my heart beginning to hammer against my chest. 'I must have put it in the bedroom for safekeeping.'

Though I absolutely couldn't remember doing that, but it had to be somewhere in the flat. I could remember signing for it and then...nothing. I strode down the hall, determined to find it. This was awful; I hated letting people down. What would my new neighbour think of me? I liked to make a good first impression and this was basically the opposite of that. I could even picture the package, an A4-sized manila envelope with some documents inside, so why couldn't I also picture what the fuck I'd done with it?

'Won't be a sec!' I called, flinging open my wardrobe and rooting through it at speed, pushing all my hangers to one end and then the other, feeling like I wanted to scream. There was no sign of it in here. I slammed the wardrobe doors shut again and then grabbed a tissue from the box on my bedside table to dab my no doubt now-very-shiny face.

'Did you find it?' Jack called, clearly a bit impatient now.

I couldn't imagine what was so important that it couldn't wait until tomorrow. Surely he could see I was in the middle of something?

Trying to compose myself, I walked back out into the hall and stopped dead. Much to my horror, Tyler, dressed in signature head-to-toe Armani, was standing on the doorstep behind a decidedly agitated Jack.

'Rebecca! There you are!'

For some reason, Tyler's booming American voice

6

sounded too big and brash for the stairwell of our very modest block of flats. Perhaps it was just because my nerves were jangled.

'Hello,' I said, feeling my cheeks burning red, just to add to the attractiveness.

Meanwhile, Jack was looking at me expectantly.

'Have you got it, then?' he asked.

I shook my head. 'I'm really sorry, but—'

'Oh for god's sake,' he said under his breath, rubbing the back of his neck.

'Well, if it's that important, you should have made sure you were in to sign for it, shouldn't you?' I snapped at him.

Thanks to his terrible timing and his inability to take responsibility for his own stuff, I was now on the back foot before the evening had even begun.

'Oh, I'm sorry. Was it too much to expect a neighbour to take in a package for me and then to actually be able to find it again?' he replied sarcastically.

'Whoa,' said Tyler. 'What's your problem, man?'

Jack swung around to stare at him and then turned back to me with a face like thunder.

'Listen, if you *do* by some miracle manage to locate it tonight, no matter what time, please drop it in to me, OK?' said Jack, looking as though he was about to spontaneously combust.

'I'm sure I can manage that,' I replied, prickling with self-righteousness but also feeling a tiny bit guilty. I was usually very on top of things like this and it did sound as though it was something quite important.

With an overly dramatic sigh, Jack removed himself from my doorway and sloped the few steps across the landing to his own front door, where he proceeded to fumble around trying to open it, first struggling with the top lock and then

7

the bottom. Meanwhile, Tyler was still on the doorstep, all calm and composed, looking like Richard Gere at the end of *Pretty Woman*. This was so far from the vibe I'd wanted to give off that it was almost comical. I'd wanted to waft to the door in a state of complete serenity, smelling of Jo Malone and with the London Grammar track playingly hauntingly in the background. Now it must be glaringly obvious to him that I wasn't the supremely organised, together person I pretended to be.

'You'd better come in,' I said, ushering Tyler over the threshold, my heart rate slowly returning to something re-sembling normality.

I could do this; I could get things back on track. I would forget about Jack's unexpected interruption and enjoy my evening. A drink would help, I thought, eyeing up the expensive-looking bottle of red Tyler was holding. When he handed it to me, I stared intensely at the label, as though I was some sort of wine connoisseur.

'This looks nice,' I said approvingly.

As I stood aside to let Tyler pass, I caught Jack's eye and quickly looked away. I'd had enough of him for one night. Perhaps it was karma that he was apparently still unable to open his own front door. I tutted as he started throwing himself against it with his shoulder, making a deafening racket that the whole block would probably be able to hear. The doors could be temperamental, but this was absolutely ridiculous.

'Nice neighbours you've got there,' said Tyler, chuckling to himself.

I closed my door and watched him shrug off his black wool three-quarter-length coat and then uncoil his mustard cashmere scarf. He kept his suit jacket on, which made me feel a bit like I was about to be interviewed for a job.

'He's new,' I said, slightly distracted by the banging and crashing outside.

Seriously, what was *wrong* with that guy?

'I love this photograph, by the way,' said Tyler, peering closely at the framed black and white shot of Catherine Deneuve I'd hung on the wall when we (as in me and my ex) had first moved in. Dan – the ex – had hated it, but it had been the one décor-related thing I hadn't caved in on. Everything else was pretty much to his taste, which I regretted now, of course, because here I was, living on my own, stuck with his characterless (he'd say minimalist) white walls and boring IKEA furniture. I ran my finger along the bottom of the frame, remembering how excited I'd been when I'd picked it out; how it had felt like an adventure to be decorating our new home together.

'Can I take your coat?' I asked, remembering I was supposed to be in hostess mode.

The whole thing with Jack had really shaken me up. How inconsiderate of him to get snippy with me when I'd basically done him a massive favour. I could have refused to sign for his stupid parcel, in which case it would have gone straight back to the depot and he wouldn't have had it tonight, anyway. Although, in truth, I wasn't sure he'd be getting it tonight from me either, even if I did find it. I planned to be otherwise engaged.

Tyler waited in the hall while I laid his luxurious clothing items carefully on my bed and then dipped back into the kitchen to grab a box of matches from the cutlery drawer. On the way past, I straightened the two Martini glasses I'd lined up on the side ready, the ingredients carefully placed next to it: tequila, a bottle of triple sec, salt, a bag of limes tipped into a bowl. I hoped it wasn't too try-hard, but I wanted to give the impression that I was the sort of person who

9

casually threw Margaritas together for myself on a Tuesday evening. I mean, there was no reason why I couldn't be. That was the beauty of living on your own: you could do what you liked, when you liked, and there was absolutely nobody around to judge you for it.

'This way,' I said, beckoning Tyler through to the lounge, moving my copy of *Elle Deco* about two centimetres to the left so that it was in line with the arm of the sofa.

I lit a candle, glancing out of the window. It was impossible not to be nosy when you could pretty much see straight into people's homes. The woman in the flat opposite and up a floor was eating her dinner, a later one than usual for her, her laptop open in front of her as she slurped forkfuls of what looked like Chinese takeaway into her mouth.

I liked seeing what other people were doing, the lit-up windows of Marlowe Court stacked one on top of the other, each square frame housing something different, a snapshot of somebody's life. And then, to the right, was the never-ending blackness of Hampstead Heath. The flats on the top floor of our building had panoramic views of the city, apparently, according to my neighbour, Clive, who seemed to know everything about everybody. I made a mental note to ask him what he knew about Jack. He seemed extremely volatile; I wondered whether Tom had got permission to sublet his place. There was a reason landlords vetted their tenants and got references, wasn't there?

'So Hampstead is lovely,' said Tyler, who had picked up the trendy coffee-table book I'd dug out from the back of a cupboard earlier and had positioned in a prime spot. 'All those cool little pubs. And I love your cute cobbled streets.'

I made approving noises to show I agreed with him. I knew I was lucky to be living in such a beautiful, leafy part of London where the average house cost several million pounds and where you passed some actor or musician or other practically every time you popped to the shops. It was crazily pretty Dan used to say, plus he loved telling people at his pretentious city firm that he lived in Hampstead because he thought they'd assume he was loaded. But what I loved about it was all the green, right here on my doorstep. The wildness of the heath that changed with the seasons; the ponds I hadn't yet dared to swim in; the Georgian cottages laced with fragrant, lilac wisteria in the spring.

'Did you get the Northern line up?' I asked.

Tyler laughed, clearly thinking this was an outrageous suggestion. 'I caught a black cab.'

'Don't do the tube, then?'

'I'd rather be above ground. It's not the cleanest down there, right?' he said, turning his nose up.

There was nothing wrong with the tube, nothing at all. I loved rattling along on it, especially if I got a spot standing near the doors and could feel the rush of warm air blasting out of the tunnel and through the windows. Admittedly, it wasn't quite so pleasant at rush hour, but you couldn't have it all. Anyway, we couldn't all afford to jump in taxis whenever we felt like it, could we?

'Can I interest you in a Margarita?' I asked, putting his misguided opinion of the London Underground system aside for now.

He put the book down and moved towards me, sliding his hands over my hips.

I laughed nervously. I'd had too much to drink the first time I'd slept with him a month or so ago, which had meant that for once I'd just let go and had done exactly what I wanted without thinking about the consequences. It felt very different now I was stone-cold sober and in my own living room.

'I really want to kiss you again,' said Tyler.

'You do?' I asked, my voice barely audible.

'I find you so attractive,' he said breathily.

Did he?

I closed my eyes as his lips pressed against mine. From the little I remembered, I'd quite liked it last time.

Just as I was getting into it, an ambulance on its way down the hill to the Royal Free set off its ominous, wailing siren and I flinched. It was something I always did, a sort of primal reaction that took me right back to being seven years old again.

Tyler stopped what he was doing and pulled back, looking worried. He probably thought he'd done something wrong.

'You OK?' he asked.

I nodded reassuringly, kissing him again to avoid any more questions.

Clearly taking this as a sign of my enthusiasm, he propelled me across the room and pressed me up against the wall so that I was wedged in between the bookshelf and the fireplace. Quite turned on by this manly display of confidence, I undid the buttons of his pale pink shirt, helping him take it off. This was good. I was doing what I'd promised myself I would do: I was mostly forgetting about the past and, while I'd been getting ready for my date with Tyler, I had not thought about Dan at all for what felt like the first time since he'd left.

'This is probably a very bad idea,' said Tyler in a gravelly voice, simultaneously untying my dress and sliding it off my shoulders.

'I know it is,' I replied, suspecting that this was precisely what had attracted us to each other in the first place.

It felt good to be doing something I shouldn't for once. In my (slightly biased) opinion, I was one hundred per cent making progress.

2

Jack

I groaned, grappling with the stupid front door which, for some fucking bizarre reason, was refusing to open. God only knows why a third-floor flat in one of the most exclusive areas of London required multiple locks so stiff that you had to use brute force to turn the key.

At last: success!

I flung myself inside, shutting the door behind me with a frustrated flick of my heel. I dropped my bag on the floor and kicked off my trainers, massively pissed off about my run-in with my incompetent, charmless neighbour. How could she lose my package in a flat this size?

I marched barefoot into the bathroom, turning on the hot water, letting it run without the plug in. If Rebecca was right – and, oh, I bet she just *loved* being right – there was probably no chance of a hot bath until much later, but it would be *extremely* satisfying to prove her wrong.

In the bedroom, I tore off my T-shirt, wrinkling up my nose at the stench of stale beer, an unavoidable aroma, unfortunately, when you worked in a pub. I consoled myself by imagining how much worse it would have been back in the days when everyone smoked inside. I'd have been risking my health, basically, and for what? To serve overpriced wine to a bunch of rich twats, that's what.

Just as I pulled my joggers down, I thought I heard something. I stood still, tuning into the tinkling sound, eventually realising it was the faint trill of my phone.

I raced into the hall with my trousers around my ankles, falling dramatically to my knees to unzip my bag and yanking out my phone.

'Shit,' I said, glancing at the caller ID and grappling with the handset; there was no way I could miss this. 'Chad!' I answered, standing up so fast I got protein floaters. I ruffled my hair, trying to get my head together. 'What's up, man?'

For reasons I'd never quite understood, whenever I spoke to Chad, I had that feeling you get when you've been sent to the headmaster's office (which happened fairly often, much to my parents' disgust). You know, that sense of waiting anxiously in a deathly quiet corridor, adrenaline pumping, knowing you're about to get a massive bollocking? I didn't think this was how you were supposed to feel about your theatrical agent – my tutors at drama school had tried to insist that agents worked for us, that *they* needed *us*. It was a nice thought, but for me it had always felt as though the opposite was true. Chad was the ringmaster in our relationship (if you could even call it a relationship) and I was the desperate, sometimes-pathetic puppet.

'There's been a change of venue for your casting tomorrow,' barked Chad, sounding angry at me for presumably absolutely no reason. 'Got a pen?'

'Yep,' I lied, whirling fruitlessly around, as though I was going to find a random pen on the floor of my hallway. I waddled into the bedroom, flinging open the drawer of my bedside table, relieved when my fingers finally closed around the plastic casing of a dodgy-looking biro. I scooped my trousers over my heels and ran back into the hall in my pants, grabbed my script out of my bag and hooked my phone between my shoulder and my ear. 'Ready when you are!' I said, scribbling wildly in the corner of the page until the biro came to life, revealing a blob of scratchy blue ink.

Chad reeled off an address in Soho and I wrote it down, my stomach already churning over how much was at stake tomorrow. This job was a big deal. Not that Chad cared. Pep talks were definitely not his thing. I supposed that was the downside of having a 'superstar' agent: there was a hierarchy amongst Chad's clients and I was clearly right at the bottom of it, which didn't sit particularly well with me. I'd worked out that now and again I actually *did* need some reassurance, although it pained me to say it, because I liked to think of myself as a very un-needy person in general. In any case, there was nothing reassuring about Chad. I had the distinct impression that he thought he was doing me a massive favour by representing me. He had his A-list clients to make him loads of money in commission; he didn't need me for that. In fact, I was pretty sure he didn't think he needed me full stop.

'And don't be late,' sniped Chad. 'They're squeezing you in as it is.'

'When am I ever late for anything?' I said, on the defensive.

I had my faults, but tardiness was *not* one of them. Actually, that wasn't strictly true, I was late for absolutely everything else, but never, ever for a casting. My career had been, and would always be, my number-one priority – when I had an audition, nothing could stop me getting there. Once, I'd had to abandon a gridlocked Uber in Waterloo and sprint full-throttle to London Bridge. I nearly keeled over on arrival, but at least I'd been on time. Naturally, I hadn't got the part; they were after a slick Jamie Dornan type, not some heaving, sweaty mess, but still, you couldn't win them all.

'Did you get the opening scenes I sent?'

I pinched the top of my nose. 'Not yet. I missed the delivery and now my neighbour can't find them.'

I knew Chad was rolling his eyes. He pretty much did that every time I spoke to him, so it was nothing new.

'Well, make sure you get them. I went to great lengths to secure them for you, I'll have you know.'

'Sure.'

Did he *really* need to say that? Since I'd been the one asking if I could get hold of the scenes that came before the one I was reading so that I could put my lines in context, didn't he think I'd do everything I could to get hold of the bloody things? And as far as great lengths go, he'd probably just snapped at his permanently-anxious assistant to sort it out, anyway.

'Wear something that gives an impression of the character,' instructed Chad.

'Yeah, sure, I thought I'd wear the—'

'Are you off page?'

'Um, not quite. Not yet.'

Chad sighed. 'They're seeing some big names for this, Jack, remember that.'

I cleared my throat. 'Like who? Can you say?'

Chad reeled off an intimidating list of actors who were up for the same role.

Fuck. I wished I hadn't bothered asking.

'Great,' I said, swallowing hard. 'I'm on it, Chad. Got a good feeling about this.'

Chad, who'd heard it all before, ended the call without so much as a goodbye and I went into the lounge and flopped onto the sofa in my boxers, feeling all kinds of exhausted. It might have been the eight-hour shift at the pub I'd just done, or the fact I'd been up working on the script until one in the morning. But, most likely, it was because I got like this when I had a casting for a job I desperately wanted. I could actually physically feel the pressure of it building up inside my brain. I put everything I had into every role I went for, obviously, for financial reasons if nothing else, even if it was a crappy commercial for dog food, or that multivitamin ad I did where they'd sprayed me bright orange from head to toe. But this? This was different. This was big time. Netflix. Twelve-episode drama. Recurring role. I'd have money for the first time in my life if I got this job, more money that I'd know what to do with. I'd be in a quality TV series with a brilliant script that could even win awards if it was as good on screen as it looked on the page. I could meet Chad's eye without feeling like a massive failure. And I could chirpily inform my parents that, actually, they'd been wrong about me all along and that – ta-da! – I wasn't the complete fuck-up they thought I was.

I put my hands behind my head, looking up at the ceiling, mesmerised by the way the bulb was swinging backwards and forwards inside its shade. My upstairs neighbour – presumed female, although I'd never actually met her – was dancing around to her Ed Sheeran album again, the jolly piping of 'Galway Girl' filtering through the floorboards. I'd always hated that song with a passion, especially the stupid lyrics about having 'Jamie as a chaser, Jack for the fun'. I already felt like a laughing stock half the time, without smug Sheeran drumming it into me, too.

After a while, I took my script out to the kitchen, deciding I ought to eat despite feeling a bit sick after Chad's call. I'd have an easy dinner, then I'd run my lines a few more times, and then I'd let it go. Trust the work and all that. Focus on staying calm more than anything, because although being nervous could give you the energy required to deliver a decent performance, what was *not* helpful was the sort of debilitating, nausea-inducing variety of nerves I'd had on occasion. Like at my drama school showcase when I'd known Chad was coming specifically to see me. It worked out all right in the end, I supposed, given that Chad had taken me on, but the lead-up to it had been most unpleasant and I'd constantly been on the verge of throwing up for about a week beforehand. I shook the memory away.

I opened the kitchen cupboards, my eyes flicking left and right across shelves bearing items as diverse as Batchelors bacon-flavoured Super Noodles and Waitrose sliced artichoke hearts, trying to work out what – if anything – I fancied or, more importantly, what I could actually conjure up with this mishmash. Eventually giving into the lure of comfort food, I pulled out a tin of baked beans and poured them into a saucepan, turning the ring up to maximum because I was impatient like that.

I laid my script out next to me on the worktop, resting my elbows on the fake-granite surface and mumbling dialogue under my breath, only pausing to glance at the page if I couldn't remember what came next, which appeared to be happening with disturbing regularity. I sighed, telling myself that it would go in eventually. So what if it took me ten times longer than everyone else to learn stuff? As long as I got there in the end, nobody would be any the wiser, would they?

I practised my lines over and over again while my beans bubbled away on the hob. I bet Rebecca was serving up something pretentious and fussy across the hall. She looked like someone who hosted sophisticated, soulless dinner parties and got an ego boost out of impressing her guests with her culinary skills. She probably had a three-course gourmet meal on the go. I reckoned that was her style.

Starter, main and dessert. She wouldn't be making beans on toast, that was for sure, because her smarmy American boyfriend would probably run a mile if she did. And heaven forbid if he spotted a pack of Super Noodles!

I was just about to pop some sourdough in the toaster when I remembered I'd left the water running and legged it into the bathroom. If there had been any hot water in the first place, there wasn't going to be now, was there? At least I hadn't left the bloody plug in and flooded the place.

3

Rebecca

The first thing I noticed when I woke up was one of Tyler's lean, bronzed and unusually hair-free thighs hooked over my left knee. I blinked, trying to get some life into me, rubbing at the corners of my eyes. A chink of blue winter light was twinkling through a gap in my curtains and, realising this wasn't normal, I felt around on my bedside table for my phone, checking the time. It was usually still dark when I woke up.

7.25?! I'd forgotten to set my alarm, which really wasn't like me. But then again, nothing I'd done the night before had been anything like me. For a start, I'd had sex with someone I didn't know very well and was sober enough to remember it this time. Coming out of a long-term relationship, I worried that I wouldn't know what to do any more, that I'd only be able to do it the way Dan and I (occasionally) did it. I was pleased to note that it had all come back very naturally to me and also that I didn't feel all clingy and into him, or have butterflies over whether or not he'd want to see me again, which was what I'd dreaded happening. Instead, I wasn't bothered either way: mission accomplished.

I watched Tyler snoring softly, his lips parted, his eyelids flickering, the beginnings of stubble sprouting out of his jaw, a combination of grey and black and the odd fleck of ginger. I noticed he had tiny, fine lines fanning out from the corner of each eye. If that had been Dan, he would have been slathering on jarfuls of expensive eye cream by now and wearing sunglasses twenty-four/seven to avoid squinting. He hated the idea of getting older and once referred to people over thirty-five as being 'washed up', which I'd vehemently disagreed with. Tyler, on the other hand, seemed perfectly comfortable in his own skin. If anything, I bet he looked better now than he had at thirty.

I eased my leg out from underneath him, relieved he didn't stir when his knee flopped like a dead weight onto the duvet cover. Then I slid sideways out of bed, attempting to keep my body perpendicular to the mattress, before melting onto the floor like a slinky so that I ended up on all fours on the carpet. It wasn't the most elegant manoeuvre, but needs must.

I peeked at Tyler – good, still asleep. I'd make myself look presentable and then I'd wake him – we'd have to leave soon if I wanted to be in the office for nine.

I tiptoed into the bathroom, where I splashed my face with cold water, cleaned my teeth, brushed my hair and put it up in a ponytail because I wouldn't have time to straighten it. I slicked on some lip balm and was tempted to put on the full works, but thought that might be taking it a bit far. I hated feeling like this, that men would be disappointed when they saw me without make-up. Sometimes I wondered about Dan. Whether after sixteen years together I'd stopped making an effort and that was why he'd ended things. Rationally I knew it couldn't have been just that. Rationally I knew a lot of things, but him leaving still felt deeply painful, as though it was my fault, which, in a way, it was, since he'd cited me being emotionally unavailable (even though he understood why, he said) as the excuse for him shagging somebody else. Pushing all thoughts of Dan away, I headed to the kitchen.

I made me and Tyler a coffee. He was vegan, he'd announced last night (I was glad I hadn't bothered cooking) and since nut milk wasn't the sort of thing I had hanging around in my fridge, he was going to have to have it black. I did some frantic tidying, washed up the cocktail glasses, tipped empty husks of lime into the bin. My head was pounding, so I took two paracetamol. Hardly surprising considering we'd drunk three – or was it four? – Margaritas each. What had I been thinking, drinking on a work night? I was usually very strict with myself about stuff like that.

I took our coffees through to the bedroom. I couldn't see Tyler at first because he wasn't in the bed where I'd left him. My initial thought was that he'd got off without saying goodbye, although surely he couldn't have made it past me and out of the front door without me noticing? Then I saw his head bobbing up and down at the side of the bed, which I was relieved about because nobody wanted to think the person they'd spent the night with was so repulsed they'd had to do a runner.

'Morning, beautiful,' he called over his shoulder, his naked body stretched out like a plank, his rock-hard glutes disappearing and then reappearing again.

I put the coffee down on the side.

'You're doing press-ups,' I said, stating the obvious and trying not to stare.

'I have a morning ritual,' he replied, breathing heavily out of his nose after every other word.

'Oh yeah? What's that, then?' I asked, smarting with envy that he had enough willpower to stick to a full-on early-morning exercise regime. I was getting well into my running, but this was a whole different ball game.

'Three sets, each working a different muscle group, and then the same again at night,' he said, still bobbing up and down.

At night? He really did have an impressive work ethic, which probably explained why I could see his shoulder muscles undulating under his skin and his biceps bulging under the weight of his taut body. At forty-five, he was officially the oldest person I'd seen naked, but also undisputedly the fittest. The most Dan had ever managed was a half-hearted jog around the block once a week, after which he'd proceeded to whinge about not having abs like the models on the front of *Men's Health* magazine. That had been him all over, actually: having these big dreams but – unlike Tyler - not being prepared to put in the hard work required to make them happen. My aggressive new neighbour, Jack, looked as though he worked out, from the little I'd seen of him in his strange all-black get-up. He was probably one of those vain types who spent hours preening at the gym and whipping off his top to take photos of himself for Instagram.

I perched on the edge of the bed, listening to Tyler huffing and puffing and feeling guilty and as though I should be doing something more productive. In desperation, I smoothed out the duvet cover and plumped up the pillows.

When Tyler had finished the press-ups, he flipped over onto his back and went into a round of crunches. Yep, those abs were straight out of *Men's Health* magazine.

I picked up my coffee, blowing on the surface of it, watching the way the liquid rippled out from the centre and wondering if I should do some asanas at the end of the bed, or something. I bet that's what the women he dated in New York would have done. Either that, or they'd have been to a spin class and back by now.

'I think I'll go and have a shower, while you're doing that, then,' I said.

If this was what casual sex felt like the morning after, I didn't think I'd been missing out on much. I didn't feel closer to Tyler than I had the night before, or even the last time I'd slept with him; I just felt awkward and as though I wanted this bit to be over with. I'd slept with precisely one other person since Dan had left, and I'd managed to avoid all this because he'd had to get off just after midnight to feed his cat. I'd been relieved about that, because I couldn't see the point of postcoital chit-chat if you had zero intention of seeing each other again.

By the time I got back to the bedroom, Tyler was on his feet. And still naked. He'd opened the curtains and was standing by the window, which seemed a little brazen, considering half the neighbours were probably up by now and could see straight into my flat.

'Is that the famous heath you were telling me about?' asked Tyler, looking out at the treetops and the rolling green grass beyond.

'Yeah. What do you think?'

He nodded slowly. 'It really is something.'

'Towel?' I said hopefully, handing him my nicest, fluffiest one.

I'd handpicked it from the depths of my linen cupboard presuming he'd want a shower. I always kept a pristine set ready in case of visitors.

'You think of everything,' he said, which I was pleased about, because I liked to think I did.

I wondered what he was doing when he started stretching out the towel and holding it taut between his hands. Everything became clear when he suddenly hooked it around my body, pulling me into him. I was dressed already, in a cream

24

silk blouse and my best black cigarette pants. He had sweat running down his temples and I didn't want to stain my top.

I laughed lightly and kissed him gingerly on the mouth.

'Right, then,' I said, wanting to put us both out of our misery, 'we should probably get going.'

Anyway, we did need to leave for work; I was already ten minutes behind schedule. If anything was going to arouse suspicion with my colleagues, it would be me rocking up to the office late. A major incident was likely to be declared if I wasn't pinned to my desk before everyone else got in, and there was no way I could risk anyone finding out what I'd been doing and, more importantly, who I'd been doing it with.

Part of me wanted to see the shock on everyone's faces when they found out, and another part of me thought it would be the most humiliating thing on earth. Would they think I was mad for getting involved with someone like Tyler; someone I worked with? Or would they secretly be impressed that I had it in me? Either way, I was convinced I'd be the talk of the office, and not in a good way. I had a reputation as a very-together-person to upkeep, which, admittedly, had been a bit of a struggle when Dan had moved out practically overnight, but I'd mostly managed to hold it together during office hours and keep the gossip at bay. But if they ever found out about me and Tyler they'd jump all over it, I knew they would.

'Are you sure I can't persuade you?' he asked, inching me closer to him with his towel.

If I got a mark on this blouse, I was not going to be happy. I swatted him away in what I hoped was a playful manner and he finally disappeared off to the shower. I used the time to get my work things together and then I watched him get dressed out of the corner of my eye. Even in the throes of passion, he'd hung his shirt neatly over the back of a chair so that it wouldn't get creased, which made me smile to myself. In a way, he was everything I aspired to be but could never quite manage.

'When did you say you were flying back to New York?' I asked him, grabbing my keys from the side and checking my watch again; we might be able to make up the time.

'Friday evening,' he replied, bending to tie his laces. 'But I'm back towards the end of next week. I'd love to take you out for dinner?'

I carefully zipped up my bag, buying myself some time. Dinner felt like an actual date, which was the very thing I was trying to avoid. We'd had a nice time last night. He was different from anyone else I knew and we'd talked about very grown-up things, like the US property market and art galleries and the predominant themes in the last films we'd watched. What if, when we spent more time together, I started to really like him?

'Sure,' I said, sliding the strap of my bag onto my shoulder. 'Maybe.'

'I'll take you to Nobu. My ex-wife raves about it.'

'Oh, cool. I've never been,' I said, wondering how I'd missed the fact he'd been married. Then again, we hadn't shared anything about our past relationships, which suited me fine. The less of an emotional connection I had with him, the easier it would be to keep myself in check. I wondered if I would be able to carry on like this forever, or whether eventually everyone would – like Dan had – want more than I was capable of giving.

Tyler gathered up his keys and his wallet and I tidied my bedside table and neatened up the curtains. Because I was leaving later than usual, almost everyone had their lights on. One half of the couple whose lounge window faced my bedroom was setting up for the day, opening his Mac Air, a bowl of cereal on the table in front of him. It was funny that I knew what these people ate for breakfast but had no idea what their names were.

'Right,' I said, giving the room a once-over and tinkling my keys.

Tyler followed me along the hallway and out of the flat.

'Oh!' I stopped outside the flat, remembering Jack's package.

I'd found it, finally, on top of the fridge freezer of all places. I'd been on the phone when the courier had knocked and had obviously been distracted or something. I felt a bit bad now, actually. I had no idea what was inside, but he'd seemed disproportionately upset, so it must be something pretty special.

Tyler was already on the next landing down, so I leaned over the railings.

'I'll see you downstairs,' I hissed to him, trying not to wake up those residents of Marlowe Court who had the luxury of getting up at a more reasonable hour.

I went back into the flat, grabbed Jack's package, locked up behind me and knocked on his door.

I took a deep breath, trying to stay calm. I'd apologise, hand over the package and that should hopefully be the end of it. Through the door, I could hear him talking loudly and quite angrily. Seemed to be a bit of a habit for him. Maybe he was on the phone. I bet he was one of those annoying people who made phenomenally loud calls right behind you on the bus.

The door opened and I instinctively took a step back. Jack was in another sporty clothes combo this morning: grey marl joggers and a navy T-shirt. I could see he was a fan of the neutral colour palette.

'Hope I'm not interrupting anything,' I said.

'You're not.'

'Here,' I said, thrusting his package at him.

He sighed. 'Where was it?'

I'd expected a quick thanks, not an interrogation. I cleared my throat. 'On top of the fridge.'

He nodded. 'Right.'

'I didn't find it until gone midnight, so I wasn't going to drop it round then.'

'You should have done. I was still up.'

We stood there awkwardly, neither of us quite knowing what to do next. I supposed I ought to apologise; I hadn't reacted in the most helpful way, in hindsight, but he'd caught me at a bad time. On the other hand, I thought he should be the one to say sorry first – he'd completely overstepped the mark with his condescending tone. No, I was still too wound up to do the whole heartfelt apology thing; there was no point if I didn't mean it.

'Bye, then,' I said, thinking there was no need to keep standing here like an idiot when Tyler – a mature, normal human being – was downstairs waiting for me in the lobby.

'Thanks for dropping it round,' he mumbled after me.

I did some kind of bizarre half-wave thing and turned away as he closed the door.

When I got down to the ground floor, Tyler was busy scrolling through his phone. 'You do realise we're going to have to get the tube into Holborn, don't you?' I said, bustling past him. 'You can't get a cab at this time of day, the traffic's a nightmare.'

'So I'm gonna have to get squished like a sardine on an ancient subway train with no air conditioning, is that what you're telling me, Rebecca?' he replied.

I looked over my shoulder at him, surprised. He wasn't

usually the teasing kind. I wondered whether that was what made things feel uncomfortable between us, the fact that he was quite serious. I wasn't sure he'd made me laugh out loud once. Even Dan had had me cracking up on occasion. Maybe it was a British/American thing; a sense of humour disconnect, although it did make a change to be with someone with a more mature, earnest way of looking at things.

'By the way,' I said, just so it was clear, 'we probably shouldn't walk into the office together.'

'I completely agree,' he replied. 'I can grab a coffee first, then I've got back-to-back meetings. And I need to prep my departmental presentation ready for tomorrow.'

I nodded, relieved. 'Yeah, I saw you were doing that.'

The invitation had been circulated a couple of weeks ago and had been the topic of conversation for days afterwards.

COME AND MEET TYLER MARTIN, CEO OF KINGSLAND MARKETING NYC. FIND OUT HOW HE PLANS TO ELEVATE THE UK OFFICE TO THE NEXT LEVEL AND HELP US TAP INTO THE US MARKET.

There had been great excitement. My friend Freya, who sat at the desk opposite mine, had chirpily informed me that she'd heard he looked like George Clooney (which, I suppose, he did a bit, from a distance and if you squinted).

'It's just that it's kind of a gossipy office,' I said to Tyler now, opening the front door for him because you had to yank the handle a certain way that no visitor could ever manage. 'And there's that promotion coming up. You know, the head of press and marketing position? I'm hoping to get it.'

I didn't tell him that it wasn't something I'd ever really planned, but it was the next step up, and everyone was expecting me to apply, so I felt like I had to.

He followed me outside, looking me up and down as though he was supremely impressed. 'I like your confidence.'

'I did say hoping.'

'And you don't want people saying you got the job because of me, right?' He winked.

I nodded. 'Exactly. I *definitely* do not want that.'

God, that would be the worst. I wanted to get the job because I was the best candidate, not because someone I'd slept with twice had put in a good word for me. Not that I thought he would; he seemed much too professional to blur the boundaries like that.

'My lips are sealed, Rebecca,' he said, slipping on his Ray-Bans, even though it was a freezing-cold January morning and the sun was nowhere to be seen.

4

Jack

I took a sharp left out of Tottenham Court Road tube with the extra scenes that I'd finally got hold of this morning (thanks to Rebecca getting her act together) clutched in my hand. I was pretty much off-page, but I was never completely confident about it. Some casting directors didn't mind you having the script in your hand, anyway, as long as you didn't bury your face in it the entire time; others found it massively unprofessional if you hadn't learned the whole thing off by heart, no matter how many scenes, no matter how little time you'd had to work on it. I was crap at learning lines, as it happened, and it didn't seem to be getting any easier. I tried to be kind to myself. I couldn't help being dyslexic, could I? It was just that nobody really knew that, so whenever I messed up, it probably looked as though I'd been lazy and hadn't bothered to put in the hours. Chad had warned me, very early on, that I should never, ever mention the dyslexia. *They'll think you'll be problematic and cast somebody else*, he'd warned me gravely. I wasn't convinced that this was true, not anymore, but Chad shut me down whenever I tried to bring it up.

My throat was dry, so I stopped at a kiosk, baulking at the fact that a bottle of Volvic cost twice as much here as it did anywhere else because we were in tourist-central. A scrappy piece of paper stuck to the card machine stated that you needed to spend over five pounds for a card transaction. I picked up a packet of crisps that I didn't really want and two Kit-Kats that I did but probably shouldn't have and added them to my haul.

'Five ninety-five,' mumbled the guy behind the counter, digging out a flimsy blue plastic bag.

I tapped my card and waited, trying not to think about the fact that I could have got nearly two whole meal deals for that from Boots.

'Declined,' said the shopkeeper, scooping my stuff up and chucking it behind the counter as though I was going to try to grab it and run.

Highly embarrassed, I skulked off, still thirsty, pulling my coat around myself and feeling utterly fucked off. My finances were in a worse state than I'd realised. At this rate, I'd have to ask for even more shifts at the pub, which would leave even less time for auditioning and potentially rehearsing. It seemed unlikely that Barnaby – the landlord, who had clearly never struggled for cash in his life and who wasn't overly empathetic to my plight as a struggling actor trying to make a living in London – would give me an advance on my wages. He wasn't usually forthcoming about such things, but it was worth a try.

I turned onto Soho Street, looking for the address Chad had given me. After two full circuits of the square, I finally pushed through the revolving glass doors of Lightning Productions, which were so well hidden that you might have thought you were entering MI5 headquarters.

They'd clearly tried to create a certain vibe in the reception area, with soft new-age music piping out of gigantic speakers and a black buddha with water trickling out of its belly button (which was plain weird) taking pride of place in the centre of the foyer. The desk looked as though it had been chiselled out of a rock face and dropped casually into the building. A girl wearing a tailored, grey jacket with what appeared to be nothing underneath was glued to her computer screen.

'Hi,' I said, walking confidently over to her. 'Jack Maxwell for the Lightning Productions casting?'

The girl, who was probably bored stiff and hating on her job, sighed (I wasn't sure why) and began dragging an electric blue fingernail up and down a list of typed names on a piece of paper.

I ripped my coat off, flinging it over my arm. Why was it so hot in here?

'Everything all right?' I asked, concerned that I'd got my timings wrong or that there had been a devastating admin error and Chad had messed up and I wasn't supposed to be here at all. The names were mostly typed, but a few had been scrawled onto the bottom in green felt tip.

'There you are,' she said at last.

I was disappointed to see that I was one of the green additions. In other words, not quite good enough for the main list. This was, I'd realised some time ago, the story of my life.

'Fourth floor,' she said, her eyes pinging back to her screen. 'Somebody will meet you there.'

I crossed the foyer to get to the lifts. A gold plaque detailing all the businesses in the building had been erected proudly on the wall – there were several theatrical agents, a couple of production companies and two casting offices. I took a deep breath, taking in my surroundings; being somewhere like this always made me feel like a proper, working actor. Sufficiently hyped up by that thought, I got into the lift and checked myself out in the mirror. Chad had said to dress with a hint of the character, which I already knew you had to do for TV and film castings and didn't need him to tell me. This didn't mean that if you were auditioning for the part of a doctor, for example, you had to wear a white coat with a stethoscope hung around your neck, but you might wear a shirt and tie.

The role I was up for today was a soldier called Samuel who had returned from Afghanistan with both post-traumatic stress disorder and some vital information on a known terrorist. Luckily for me, Samuel was supposed to be edgy and traumatised, so I could use the fact my stomach was doing somersaults and magnify my real emotions for the scene. That was the theory, anyway. I'd worn a pair of beige cargo pants with a white T-shirt, which was now damp under the arms thanks to the heat blasting out of every orifice of the building. My hair was too long and floppy and I wished I'd followed my instincts and shaved it off. It hardly said military like this, did it?

The lift doors opened with a ping and several pairs of eyes looked furtively in my direction. My heart dropped when I saw that the two guys sitting on the sofa looked like a more attractive version of me. They were in their early thirties like I was, had dark hair (like I did, but theirs was styled to within an inch of its life) and buff bodies (not like me) housed in tight T-shirts. Once they'd realised I didn't pose much of a threat, they went back to whatever it was they'd been doing before I'd arrived.

Seemingly out of nowhere, a girl with a clipboard came bounding up to me like an overexcited Springer Spaniel.

'Jack Maxwell?' she said.

I nodded. 'Yep, that's me.'

'Take a seat,' she instructed. 'We're running pretty much to time, so we shouldn't be long.'

'Great,' I replied, forcing a smile.

I sat down next to a guy I recognised but couldn't think where from. I nodded a hello.

'All right?' said the guy.

His voice was rich and silky and he seemed completely relaxed, as though he was having a beer in a friend's living room and not at an audition for an amazing project that had the potential to change everything.

Samuel was one of the leads; I'd be in every episode if I got the role. This was the kind of thing you read about in the quality Sunday supplements when actors did their first big round of interviews; how it had felt surreal to be offered the part. How I'd known the script was special from the off. How I was still getting used to people asking for my autograph in the street.

I coughed and looked down at my script, reading through my notes.

Samuel is:- secretive, brave, traumatised.
Samuel wants:- to get his life back to normal after 2 years in Afghanistan.
Obstacle:- he has top secret information that the FBI want from him.

'You up for Samuel?' the guy asked.

'Hmmm,' I murmured, looking up again.

I didn't want to engage in small talk, I wanted to sit quietly and go through my lines again, but I could hardly ignore him, could I?

'Same. Have you worked with Lightning Productions much?' he asked.

'No,' I said. And then, when I realised I was expected to elaborate: 'Never. You?'

'Yes. Yeah, I have.'

Course he had.

'So you've not met the casting team?' he continued.

I shook my head.

'They're great. If they like you, they'll get you in for absolutely everything.'

I tried to look suitably impressed whilst simultaneously drying my clammy hands on the legs of my cargo pants.

The perky assistant danced back into the room.

'Jack, right?' she said, pointing at me as though she deserved a medal for remembering my name, which I'd confirmed to her all of about five minutes ago. 'I nearly forgot to tick you off my list. That wouldn't do, would it?'

I smiled and went back to my script. How the fuck was I supposed to concentrate with all these people talking to me non-stop? And then, before I could read a single line, a door opened.

'Good job, Seb,' said a man with a weird transatlantic accent. 'Stay near a phone, OK? They're doing call-backs this week.'

Oh great, just what I needed. It was Seb from drama school and he was the very last person I wanted to see.

I made the mistake of catching his eye as he strode over to the lift.

'Jack, mate!' he crooned, doubling back and coming over. 'You're up for Samuel as well, are you?'

'Uh-huh,' I muttered, sneaking a peek at the casting director, a short guy wearing a navy V–necked jumper, two-day-old stubble and glasses. Trust Seb to be all best buddies with him.

'Look I've got to get to another casting, but we'll catch up soon, yeah?' said Seb. 'Let's get the LAMDA crew together for a drink, shall we?'

'Definitely,' I replied, mustering a minuscule amount of enthusiasm from somewhere. 'Good idea.'

Seb flicked his head towards the open door to the audition room. 'Fingers crossed one of us gets it, eh?'

I crossed my fingers. 'Yeah. Hope so.'

It was all completely fake. Seb was the most competitive person I knew and had been the same all the way through our three-year BA in Acting. If he didn't get the part, there was no way on earth he'd want me to.

'Travis, come on in,' trilled the casting director to the guy next to me. I might have guessed he'd have a name like Travis.

There was lots of back slapping and *how you doings?* and the door shut behind them. How come everyone knew each other? I didn't stand a chance. In fact, I wondered why they'd bothered calling me in at all when they probably already knew who they were going to give it to, anyway.

I took a few deep breaths, trying not to let my confidence disintegrate into a million pieces before I'd even given it a shot. I was here now; all I could do was my best.

I sat back on the sofa and read over my notes until the door opened again and Travis appeared, looking – *quelle surprise* – exceptionally pleased with himself.

'Good to meet you,' he said in his dulcet, silken tones. The lift doors seemed to open automatically for him as he approached and I watched him glide regally inside, oozing self-confidence.

The casting director poked his head around the door. 'Jack?' he said, sounding confused, as though he'd never seen the name Jack before in his life.

'Hi!' I said, jumping up and jogging towards the door. *Be positive*, I chanted in my head like a mantra. *You can do this.*

'I'm Andy Gold,' he replied, holding out his hand. I shook

it, embarrassed about how gross my sweaty palm must feel.

'Thanks for seeing me, Andy,' I said.

'We're going to put you on tape, but keep the script in your hand if you need to.'

I nodded, walking into the centre of the room and standing on a cross fashioned out of grey gaffer tape. There were three people sitting behind a table in front of me and not one of them looked up because they were too busy talking animatedly about a résumé and headshot that clearly weren't mine.

'OK, guys, this is Jack,' said Andy, joining them at the table. 'Jack, this is Pamela McCarthy, executive producer of Project Afghanistan, Kevin Saul, our series director, and Toby Smart, script editor at Lightning Productions.'

They all smiled thinly at me and I smiled back, feeling sick and hot and doubting I'd be able to remember a single thing I'd rehearsed.

'Jack, the project as it stands is pretty top-secret. What I can tell you is that it's in a similar vein to the Emmy-award-winning show *Homeland*, which I'm sure you're familiar with.'

I nodded, rubbing my hand on the back of my neck. Because I was being so closely observed, I was aware of every single thing my body did, every muscle twitch, every blink. I wanted to appear self-assured and relaxed, but I thought I was probably coming across as the complete opposite.

Andy continued, 'It centres around the stories of three men and a woman returning from the front line and the effect it has on their families and their relationships.'

'Sounds absolutely amazing,' I said, meaning it. This was exactly the sort of work I wanted to be doing.

'Any questions?' asked Andy.

'Um,' I said, desperately think of something because it

always made you look that extra bit invested in the project. I'd gone completely blank, of course. 'I don't think so. Thanks.'

'Great, let's get started. I'll read with you,' said Andy.

I brought the pages up, high enough so that I could read them and low enough so that they wouldn't be seen on camera.

'And ... action,' called Andy.

I transported myself out of the stuffy, white windowless studio and into a soulless, grey FBI investigation room in Washington DC. I imagined I was in big trouble and that I was being questioned by my boss.

'*I told you already, I can't remember.*'

Andy responded with the right words but zero emotion; casting directors were notoriously terrible readers.

I looked down at the page and picked up my next line, remembering to look up at the end to really 'deliver' it. And so the scene went on until, with relief, I reached the end without any major fuck-ups. I let myself breathe again and relaxed my shoulders, which I could feel creeping towards my ears.

'OK, Jack, good,' said Andy. 'Let's try to pick up the pace a little. You can keep some of your nice pauses in, that's fine, but it's a fast-paced show in general. And up the stakes a bit – make this mean even more to Samuel.'

I nodded, my mind reeling. Higher stakes. Pace. I chucked my script on the floor – I was going to have to take a risk and go all out.

I performed the scene twice more and by the third attempt I was completely in the moment, in Samuel's head, reacting to the lines as though I was him, feeling myself sprouting sweat that wasn't because I was nervous, but because Samuel was. When I'd finished, I saw the series director nodding his head. Even Andy looked impressed.

'Do you need me to do it again?' I asked hopefully.

It was a funny thing that sometimes an audition was the only chance you got to actually act. I felt that same thrill I got when I was on stage; real people had been watching me and – even better – seemingly enjoying my performance. For once, I had a really good feeling about it.

'I think we've got it,' said Andy, scribbling something in his notebook. 'Your awkwardness actually brought something different to the role, didn't it guys?'

All three of them mumbled enthusiastically in agreement.

I wasn't sure I'd been going for awkward, but if it worked for them, who cared?

'We'll be in touch with your agent by the end of the day,' said Andy. 'Are you free for call-backs later this week?'

'Absolutely,' I said, trying to be positive but remembering I'd heard him say exactly the same thing to Seb.

Still, it couldn't have gone any better. I should be proud of myself for five minutes instead of putting myself in a foul mood because I was already envisioning the worst-case scenario. The thing was, I really, really wanted this job, and if I didn't get it, I knew exactly how painful it was going to be.

5

Rebecca

I snuck into the office, which, thankfully, was still pretty much empty, and slipped into my seat. Foggy-headed from the Margarita-induced hangover, I turned on my computer and scrolled back and forth through the ninety-seven emails in my inbox, most of which I didn't even need to be copied in on, and failed to open any of them. I clearly needed more coffee before I was capable of doing anything constructive.

'Don't tell me you've only just got in!'

I looked up as Freya wafted into the seat opposite me dressed in a floaty maxi skirt and a creased pastel-pink T-shirt. For reasons I hadn't quite got to the bottom of, she regularly wore clothes that were completely inappropriate for the weather, such as a mohair jumper in July and this get-up when it was threatening to snow outside.

'What makes you think that?' I asked, trying to arrange my face so that it looked relaxed and normal.

'You've still got your coat on,' said Freya, eyeing me suspiciously.

Damn.

'Oh,' I said, shrugging it off and stuffing it under my desk.

'Anyway, I'd love to stay and chat,' Freya continued, 'but I've got a meeting with that knob from New York now, haven't I?'

'Have you?' I replied, staring at my keyboard and pretending to focus very hard on typing something.

'You can always count on Americans to call meetings that nobody needs,' Freya moaned. 'It's all work, work, work over there, isn't it?'

'Apparently,' I said.

I was tempted to tell her what had happened, to get her opinion on it, more than anything. Along with what felt like everyone else, she'd been nagging me for months to get out there and meet someone. She reckoned I'd missed out on all the fun of being in my twenties because I'd been with Dan for my entire adult life and that I shouldn't be fucking up my early thirties because of him, too. She was right, of course, but what I didn't need was another relationship. What I needed was a series of casual flings. One-night stands. Inappropriate affairs. Fun without the fear of getting hurt, basically.

'What makes you think he's a knob?' I asked, curious. I mean, I could sort of see why, but I wanted to hear her say it.

'It's obvious, isn't it? You only have to look at him,' said Freya, tearing open a dry-looking cereal bar and stuffing it into her mouth. 'The way he swans around the office in designer clothes, all tanned from his ski trips to Aspen or wherever. And he thinks he's god's gift to women. The admin girls are playing right into his hands, simpering all over him the second he steps over the threshold.'

I felt secretly smug. Unlike half the office, I had not been simpering over him. I probably wouldn't even have given him a second look had we not been thrown together on the roof of a hotel last December.

'You've met him, anyway, haven't you?' said Freya, taking a sip of her foul-smelling herbal tea. 'That night Amanda went AWOL and you had to cover her meeting. What did you think of him?'

I pressed my lips together, thinking about how to describe my first impressions of Tyler Martin. 'He was very charming.'

'Yes, I can see *he* thinks he is very charming,' said Freya.

I laughed. 'He seems nice, honestly.'

'Sure he does. By the way, can I have a look at your ideas for the Been to Bean Coffee campaign?' asked Freya, shuffling papers around her desk. 'In case he asks me for some off the top of my head. I haven't actually had time to think of any.'

'Sure, I'll ping them over now,' I said, even though I'd planned to present them myself at our next departmental meeting. Sometimes it felt as though I was not only doing my own job but half of everyone else's, too. And it wasn't even as though I was particularly passionate about it; I had no real desire to come up with ways to promote yet another coffee company that we really didn't need. I emailed Freya the details anyway and then, checking that nobody could see my screen, opened up my CV, attempting to look at it objectively. They'd finally announced, after months of rumours, that they would be creating a new senior position in the department. Everyone (well, mainly Freya and my friend Val, who worked downstairs in Direct Marketing) assured me I was going to get it and I supposed it was the obvious next move for me. The only person who could possibly put a spanner in the works was the events manager, Amanda Clarke.

Right on cue, she flounced into the office in her Christian Louboutin heels, her Birkin bag clutched in her perfectly manicured hand. At that precise moment, Tyler flung open the door of meeting room four and almost walked straight into her. Amanda, never slow on the uptake when it came to a networking opportunity, made a big drama out of it, laughing loudly enough for the whole floor to hear, her perfect, bouncy hair swishing around her shoulders like something out of a Herbal Essences advert. Credit where credit was due, she did have a talent for getting herself noticed, a skill that, disappointingly, had always evaded me.

'Trust her to be straight in there,' said Freya, tutting. 'I bet she'd shag him if she thought she'd get a promotion out of it.'

I swallowed hard. Clearly nobody could *ever* find out about me and Tyler. I tapped away at my keyboard, watching furtively as Amanda ushered him into a meeting room. She was in full-on flirting mode and I tried to work out if I cared. I thought I probably did a bit, but only because it was her.

Freya crossed her arms huffily. 'I suppose he's going to be late for our meeting, now, after dragging me in at this hour.'

'It is nearly ten,' I said, and then regretted saying anything when I saw Freya's face. 'I'm being a jobsworth again, aren't I?'

'Very much so. We can't all be morning people, Becs.'

The funny thing was, being a morning person had its drawbacks. Sometimes I'd have quite liked to have lounged about in bed until midday, especially when I had a weekend with not much to do and was spending most of it on my own. But there would always be this nagging voice inside my head telling me what a waste of time that would be. And wasting time was something I refused to do. I filled my day with productive things so that at the end of it, I could reassure myself that I'd made the most of it; that if it happened to be my last day on earth, I'd have done something useful with it. I didn't think I'd ever admitted that to anybody and, honestly, it was beginning to feel quite exhausting.

I closed down my CV in case anyone walked past and clocked it on my screen. Mind you, everyone seemed to be assuming I'd go for it, anyway. I'd had fantasies about shocking them all and leaving and doing something else with my life. It had been on my mind quite a lot lately, but I never did anything about it and eventually the thought disappeared and I carried on like I always had. I knew where I was with this job. I had familiarity, structure, a routine, a decent salary; why would I throw all of that away just because I fancied trying something new? Especially when the thing I really wanted to try would mean opening myself up to thinking about the past, which I wasn't sure I'd ever truly be ready for.

My desk phone rang.

'Hello, Kingsland Marketing, Rebecca speaking?'

'It's me,' said Val. 'Can you give me some dates? I zoned out in that planning meeting last week,' she continued.

'What do you need to know?'

She proceeded to reel off a list of upcoming events that she'd conveniently forgotten to write down.

'You on for lunch?' asked Val.

'Can't today. I've got to work on that thing.'

'What thing?'

Val had a memory like a sieve.

'You know ... that application,' I mumbled.

Freya raised her eyebrows at me.

'Oh! The job, sorry, yeah. You know it's a sure thing, right?' said Val.

'You can never be sure, can you?' I replied, glancing at the closed door of the meeting room. 'Lunch tomorrow instead?'

'It's a date.'

The soft, tinkly meditation music Freya played daily and on loop started up. I usually quite liked it; today, I did not.

See, this was what happened when I didn't get my optimum eight hours of undisturbed sleep.

'You look tired,' said Freya, peering at me suspiciously.

'Mmmn, I am a bit,' I said.

She passed me a Rescue Remedy lozenge and I took it, sucking on it wildly.

'Late night?' asked Freya.

'Not particularly,' I replied, trying to throw her off the scent. She definitely knew something was up, but telling her the truth felt far too risky.

'Chatting to someone on Tinder, were you?' she said, not giving up.

'No, I was not,' I said.

I'd already told her that I wasn't into the whole swipe-right thing; it sounded completely humiliating. I didn't want men all over London deciding whether I was attractive enough to bother with based on one measly photo.

'Think I'll go and make a coffee,' I suggested, pushing back my chair. 'Get some caffeine down me.'

In the kitchen, I washed and dried my mug on a stained tea towel and chucked in a teabag. The steam from the kettle fogged up the windows and I smeared a fingertip over the pane, drawing a cloud shape on the glass. I was just about to pour in the water when a pair of large, warm hands suddenly slipped around my waist.

'Well, hello there,' growled someone in my ear.

I recognised Tyler's Manhattan twang immediately.

'Long time no see,' I said, turning to face him.

He glanced over his shoulder and then kissed me hard on the mouth.

I pushed him gently off me with a tinkling laugh. 'We can't do that here.'

46

'Sorry. Couldn't help myself,' he said, letting his hands fall away and grinning at me maniacally.

At that precise moment, Paul from Accounts walked into the kitchen. Of all people. I had history with Paul from Accounts (if you could call a drunken kiss at a Christmas party history) and if I could count on one person in the office to be indiscreet, it would be him. He'd continuously asked me out for lunch after our festive liaison and was very put out when I said no. Dan had only just left and I was a mess and I'd assumed I'd be able to get off with Paul when we were both off our faces on cheap Prosecco and then never mention it again with no repercussions; no awkward conversations. It had been a lesson learned.

'Oh, hello,' said Paul, doing a mock double-take. He looked from me to Tyler and back again, cocking his head as though trying to work something out.

'All right?' I said, swivelling back to my mug, stirring my drink.

'Can anyone tell me where to get a decent coffee around here?' drawled Tyler.

'Um, sure. Here,' I said, flinging open a cupboard and passing him a jar of Nescafé. 'Unless you want to try the vending machine outside, which I wouldn't recommend.'

He looked at the label with disgust.

'There's a Costa over the road, mate,' said Paul. 'I'd steer clear of that cheap crap if I were you.'

Tyler handed the jar back to me. 'I think your friend here is right,' he said to me.

He waved over his shoulder at us as he disappeared out of the room.

'Who's he?' asked Paul, leaning against the counter with his arms crossed.

I picked up my mug, enjoying the heat of it on my hands. 'Tyler Martin, from the New York office.'

I saw him swallow. 'That's him?'

'Yep.'

'I called him mate,' he said, wincing.

'A touch too familiar, in hindsight?'

'He should have introduced himself, shouldn't he?'

I went to leave and Paul moved to the side, flattening himself against the fridge.

'Oh, and Becs?' he called after me.

I stopped, turning to face him with one hand on my hip. 'Yep?'

'If you ever, you know, feel like a chat. Or a drink or something. Well, you know where I am.'

I sighed because I didn't know what else to do and then power-walked back to my desk. Was he ever going to get the message that I categorically was *not* interested?

6

Jack

I got off the bus outside the Royal Free and made my way up East Heath Road. Tom said it got busy around here in the summer, with all the tourists flocking to the heath, but in January it was quieter, the wind swirling leaves around my feet as I passed the pond on my right, people all wrapped up to walk their dogs, kids running wild in their wellies. All I wanted to do was flop on the sofa with a glass of wine and something nice to eat. There was a new recipe I wanted to try, a Mediterranean tray bake, the bonus being that it was all cooked in one dish and therefore would require minimal washing up.

I'd had a pretty productive day all in all – the casting, then I'd popped into the agency to see Chad. I'd reiterated the urgency with which I needed a decent role in something. Didn't matter if it was a theatre run, a TV show or a movie. Obviously a movie would be amazing, but I wasn't in a position to be choosy. Then I'd walked around town for a bit, gone down to the river, over to the South Bank, looked longingly at the National Theatre. Chad had said there might be something coming up there he could get me seen for, a Chekhov, which usually had massive casts and so there was often a chance for someone like me to get a small role with a few decent lines. I could ask casting directors to come and see me, then; they were always impressed when you said you were in something at the National.

Just as I reached the top of the hill and Marlowe Court was in sight, my phone rang. All afternoon I'd literally broken out in a cold sweat every time the phone rang in case it was Chad with good news about the Project Afghanistan recalls. I snatched my phone out of my pocket.

'Hello?'

'It's Barnaby. Can you come in? I'm short-staffed.'

My heart sank. Home was in sight. My sofa was mere metres away. 'What, now?'

'That OK?'

I sighed, thinking about my bank balance. 'Yeah. Give me twenty minutes and I'll be there.'

I ended the call and slouched back down the hill, looking longingly back at my window on the third floor. I popped into M&S by the Royal Free to get a sandwich, because otherwise I'd only end up eating chips and crisps at the pub and if I did get that Netflix job, I'd need to be in the best shape of my life. The guy was a soldier, for god's sake. In fact, I'd start an exercise programme this weekend, in antici-pation of me getting cast in the role. Might as well remain positive until proven otherwise.

As I came out of M&S and headed up past the hospital towards Belsize Park tube, I spotted Rebecca walking to-wards me. She had on a red woollen coat and a grey scarf and grey ankle boots and her nose and cheeks were rosy from the cold. She looked quite sweet like that, all wrapped up like a Russian doll, her cosy-looking outfit belying the fact that she was actually as cold as ice on the inside. Plus it annoyed me that she'd had the foresight to dress sensibly given the threat of snow when all I had on was the thin parka I'd had for years and which had been on the cheap

50

side to begin with and completely inappropriate trainers. I pretended to look busily into shop windows and then timed it so that I caught her eye as she passed, with enough time to acknowledge her without seeming rude, but not so far in advance that it felt weird. After all, the last time we'd spoken on my doorstep had been unbearably awkward, as had the only other time we'd spoken before that, the night she couldn't find my parcel. I supposed I needed to apologise, but I kept putting it off.

'Hi,' she said, giving me a half-smile.

'Oh, hello,' I said, as though I'd only just noticed her.

We both hesitated, unsure whether to stop and chat or just carry on (which I imagined was the preferable option for both of us).

'Coming home from work are you?' I asked in an inspired attempt at conversation not involving mislaid parcels.

'Yeah,' she replied, stamping her feet. 'Can't wait to get out of this cold.'

I blew on my hands, rubbing them together. 'They say it might snow overnight.'

She laughed hollowly. 'Maybe I'll get a snow day, then.'

'Fancy a day off, do you?'

I wasn't sure where that had come from, or why I'd asked her that.

She shrugged.

'Listen,' I said, thinking I might as well get it over with, 'I'm sorry about the other night. I was very stressed out about something and I took it out on you.'

'It's OK,' she said. 'I'd have been annoyed, too, if I were you. I should have found the package for you and dropped it off sooner, even if I did have ... a guest.'

I wondered why she was referring to her boyfriend as 'a

guest' in a mysterious way, as though he was someone out of a period drama.

'We got off on the wrong foot there, didn't we?' I said.

She smiled, the first one I'd seen. It made her look so much friendlier. 'You could say that.'

A gust of icy cold wind cut through my jacket, giving me a chill.

'Anyway, I've got to get to work. Better get going,' I said.

'See you,' she said.

I turned and carried on up the hill and then, after a decent amount of time had passed, I looked back. She was going into M&S too, her bag over her shoulder, her ponytail swishing from side to side as she walked. Even if she didn't seem that enamoured with her job, it must be nice to have a normal routine, to be home at a reasonable hour and know you were getting a pay cheque at the end of the month. I craved that sometimes. Maybe if I'd done better in my GCSEs and not lost confidence in myself at the final hurdle, I could have had options now. Not that I wanted to give up on acting, I loved it too much. But it would be nice to know that there was other stuff I could do if I wanted to.

At the pub, I checked my phone for about the hundredth time that day. Still nothing from Lightning Productions. I sneaked into the staffroom before I started my shift and tried calling Chad to see if he'd heard anything, but his gatekeeper of an assistant informed me that he was currently taking phone calls from LA only and would be unavailable for the rest of the day. Chad had a handful of A-list clients who between them were cast in about ninety per cent of the decent roles on British TV and had mostly broken into Hollywood. This was another downside to having a top agent: they were literally impossible to get hold of.

When I got back out to the bar, a pissed off-looking guy was waving a tenner at me.

'Sorry, mate,' I said. 'What can I get you?'

I pulled his pint of Staropramen, wiped the bar down, refilled the tonic waters, all the while itching to look at my phone again. One call could change everything. I needed one chance, that was all. I could do a brilliant job with Samuel, I knew I could; I'd proved it at the audition.

'Earth to Jack,' said Luke, sidling up behind me. 'What's up?'

Me and Luke had worked together at The Lyndhurst, a decent enough pub 'in the heart of Hampstead Village', since I'd started there three Christmases ago. We'd hit it off right away, despite being different in almost every way possible. He was perfectly happy working in a pub, for example. He had absolutely no ambition to be anything else, and in some ways I envied him that. This relentless feeling that I wanted more, that I *needed* more, meant that I was rarely – if ever – satisfied.

'I haven't heard anything about that casting,' I said, propping up my chin in the heel of my hand. Thankfully, it wasn't a particularly busy night and I couldn't wait for my shift to end.

'How long's it usually take, then?' asked Luke, opening the glass washer and letting out an explosion of steam.

I shrugged. 'Could be an hour, could be a month. You never really know, that's what's so stressful. It's not like you can think: oh well, it's three days since my audition and I haven't heard anything so I can't have got it.'

'Don't they even let you know?' asked Luke, wiping his hands on the front of his straight-cut jeans. He always wore indigo denim and brown desert boots; when he found something he liked, he saw no reason to change it up.

'Nope,' I replied, absent-mindedly polishing the beer tap. 'So you're left hanging?'

'Crap, isn't it?'

That was an understatement. Luke was the only person at The Lyndhurst I'd really talked to about my acting stuff, but even he had his limits. I didn't want to sound miserable all of the time.

Luke reached across me to put some glasses on the shelf. 'You might still be in with a chance, you know. What would the next step be, then? Would you have to go in and do one of those chemistry tests with some hot leading actress?'

I laughed. 'Doubt it.'

'Shame,' said Luke. 'It's a tough industry, dude. I don't envy you, man.'

I shrugged. 'It's what I love doing, though, that's the thing.'

Luke looked dubious. 'You could find something else to love.'

A group of lads came in. They looked like a bunch of estate agents from one of those posh offices on the high street, just finished work by the look of it. I got ready to take their orders.

'It's not as bad as it sounds, you know,' I said, wanting to convince Luke that I wasn't completely nuts. 'The buzz you get from being on stage, the chance to be somebody else for an hour or two, it makes it all seem worth it.'

'I suppose,' he said, conscientiously wiping smears off a wine glass. 'I couldn't do it.'

It was hard for people who weren't actors to understand why you put yourself through it when the odds of success were so low. I wondered for a second what Rebecca did. Whether it was anything creative; whether she'd get it. I didn't think so; I reckoned she had one of those jobs where a ruthless determination to move up the corporate ladder (which I imagined she was very good at) was the only thing that mattered.

I quickly checked my phone again as one of the estate agent lads approached the bar. Nothing. It was nearly seven; I was hardly going to hear now, was I?

7

Rebecca

I paid for my chicken caesar and bacon baguette and found us a seat in the far corner, brushing somebody else's crumbs off the table with the side of my hand and then giving it a once-over with an anti-bac wipe. Val found it hilarious that I carried a packet around with me. I wondered whether we'd be able to hear each other over the drone of about a hundred and fifty other voices all jostling to be heard. Kingsway Pret at 1.30 on a Thursday afternoon had to be one of the noisiest places on earth, but it was close to the office and the sandwiches were nice.

Val slammed her black tray down on the table, falling into the seat opposite.

'I'm starving,' she said, ripping open a packet of crisps. 'I think my stomach's expanded. We went to Mum's last night and I had at least three portions of pepper stew.'

'I so need to taste your mum's cooking again,' I said wistfully, thinking back to Val and Ekon's wedding last year. There had been two weeks of intermittent celebrations, and one of the highlights for me had been the breakfast buffet at Val's mum's the morning after their Nigerian ceremony. Even though I was desperately hung-over, I'd managed to put away two platefuls of akara (which Val had explained was a sort of bean cake), fried yam and plantain. Sitting around a table with other people and enjoying a meal was something I didn't do very often. Mealtimes were quick and functional; something to be got over with, with as little effort as possible. But it had been nice to do it that once at the wedding. And to remember what it had been like when I'd had my own family to do it with.

'Have you seen that shiny American guy swanning round the office?' said Val, digging into her sandwich. 'Talk about polished. I noticed he had these lace-up leather shoes that probably cost more than I earn in a week.'

I laughed softly. Tyler had certainly made an impact; everyone seemed to have an opinion on him. 'I met him at that hotel last month, didn't I?' I reminded her. 'At that place Amanda thought would be perfect for the summer party.'

'It wasn't right for it though, you said?' commented Val in between mouthfuls.

I tore a piece off the end of my baguette, thinking back to that night. It had all been purely professional at first; I'd been covering for Amanda, who had cried off at the last minute, citing a medical emergency. I believed her, actually, since there was no way she'd voluntarily miss out on the chance to suck up to someone more senior than she was.

I'd been waiting for the American CEO upstairs on the roof terrace of the hotel, having navigated the intimidating lobby with its resident DJ and pretentious staff dressed entirely in white linen. It was marginally less fake-holistic on the roof and admittedly the view was spectacular. The Shard stood shimmering in the distance; to the right was the London Eye and, below us, the rooftops of the National Gallery. Chilled-out dance music pumped out of the speakers, although I couldn't imagine who would want to sit up here in December. It'd be lovely in the summer, though, I could see that.

'Excuse me? Rebecca?'

I turned towards the smooth American voice and smiled. The man standing next to me was tall and handsome. Film-star handsome. Everything about him oozed money and confidence and he was immaculately groomed – he had the designer suit, the cropped salt-and-pepper hair, teeth that dazzled, even in this half-light.

I shook his hand. 'Really lovely to meet you, Mr Martin.'

'Please, call me Tyler.'

He moved in next to me and whistled in admiration. 'Nice view,' he said.

He smelled clean and expensive, a woody, spicy fragrance that was probably something by Tom Ford. He seemed like a Tom Ford kind of guy. I, on the other hand, felt massively scruffy in my black jeans and cream polo-neck jumper combo; if I'd known about the meeting in advance, I could have worn my Reiss trouser suit, the smartest (and most expensive) item I owned.

'Apologies for the weather,' I said, as a particularly sharp gust of wind plastered my hair across my face. I scraped it off again, ramming it behind my ears.

Tyler laughed. 'That's England for you, huh? Anyhow, New York is under a foot of snow. I was lucky to get a flight out.'

We turned back to the view. Surely he'd be impressed by the London skyline if nothing else. It always took my breath away, even though I'd lived here all my life.

'What's that super-old building?' he asked, pointing at a church across the square.

'Um, St Martin-in-the Fields, I think,' I said, squinting to make it out. 'It's really beautiful inside, you should see it. It dates all the way back to the seventeen hundreds, I think.'

'See, this is what I love about London,' said Tyler, shaking his head, seemingly in awe. 'All that history, everywhere you look.'

I smiled across at him. Americans were always impressed by stuff like that. I'd felt similarly in awe when Dan and I had gone to New York for our tenth anniversary. It had permanently felt as if we were on a set, coming across location after location we recognised from film and TV. I'd taken rolls of photos. Not that I'd looked at them since Dan had left. I couldn't bear to see how happy we'd been then.

'So, on first impressions, what are your thoughts on having the summer party up here?' I asked, keen to get out of my own head. 'There are lots of cosy spaces for people to sit and chat. And we could do the awards ceremony over there, with the London Eye as a backdrop. What dates were you thinking of? July or August, presumably, although, of course, we can't count on the weather even then.'

He hesitated. 'Can I be honest with you, Rebecca?'

'Of course.'

I mentally prepared myself. What was he going to say?

'I don't like it,' he said, looking sideways at me. 'It's trying too hard to be cool. The ridiculous lighting, the pseudo-trendy music – it wasn't what I envisaged, and I'm kinda disappointed. Was this place your idea?'

Tempting as it was, I wasn't about to throw Amanda under the bus, even if she had totally dropped me in it. It was my own fault for agreeing to cover for her; I needed to learn to say no once in a while. 'Not entirely,' I said, choosing my words carefully. 'It was a joint effort. But Amanda has exquisite taste and is extremely knowledgeable about the industry. I can see why she thought this would be perfect.'

'It's not right,' he said, shaking his head.

If Tyler went away unhappy, it would reflect badly on

the whole UK office. I forced my mind to focus, wondering what I could do to make things right.

'What don't you like about it?' I asked, buying myself some time.

'The guest list is going to be very exclusive,' he explained. 'Winning accounts with these companies could earn us tens of thousands of dollars. It could harm our brand to host an event in a hotel that favours style over substance.'

I winced, flicking through the notes I'd scribbled on the bus, desperate to find something I could use. 'Were you thinking of something more traditional, then? Something classy and discreet?'

'Exactly,' he said.

'What about The Savoy? They've had a refurbishment relatively recently, and Gordon Ramsay has a restaurant there, which might appeal from a catering point of view. And we could even do a drinks reception in the American Bar, which might be a nice touch for your US contacts.'

'Carry on,' he said with a hint of a smile

My mind was whirling with ideas now. 'Or if you want to go more contemporary, there's a lovely restaurant in The Shard,' I said, pointing it out, 'with a glass atrium and spectacular 360-degree views. It's always fun to go up there, even for people who live in London. We're not as used to being up high as you are in New York,' I joked, trying to lighten the mood.

Tyler nodded. 'That's more like it.' He took out his phone and tapped something into it. 'I was thinking about a signature cocktail. We could call it The Kingsland and it has to taste out of this world.'

'Right ... of course. Good idea,' I replied, scribbling it down. I could feel a cocktail-tasting session with Val coming on. Sometimes the job had its perks.

Tyler gestured towards the lifts. 'Shall we go? I think I've seen enough. I'm back in London early next month, we should meet again then.'

'Amanda will probably take over from here on in,' I told him, heading towards the lifts and pressing the call button.

'Actually, I'd like to continue working with you,' he said, touching the top of my arm lightly, 'if that would be all right? I feel like we're on the same page, here.'

I bit my lip, thrown off guard. 'I'd have to speak to Amanda first,' I replied.

It was flattering that he wanted to work with me, but I also didn't want to step on Amanda's toes – it wasn't fair. She was highly competitive (*Worse that you!* Val had once very untactfully stated) and would go into overdrive if she thought I was some kind of threat to her position.

'Listen,' he said, looking at his huge gold and leather watch. 'Would you have time for dinner? My PA booked me a table at The Wolseley. It would be great to have some company.'

I looked at him, biting my lip. I'd always wanted to go to The Wolseley. The alternative would be another night in the flat on my own, and hadn't I had enough of those?

'Sure,' I said. 'I have time for dinner.'

I took a sip of my drink, looking sheepishly at Val. I was going to have to tell her.

'I've got a confession to make,' I said.

I knew I could trust her and I probably should have told her as soon as it happened. It was just that I didn't want her getting all overexcited about nothing.

Val tipped the last of her crisps into her mouth straight from the packet. 'Go on.'

I cleared my throat. 'I've kind of been sleeping with him,'

I said, looking her straight in the eye. I had nothing to be ashamed of.

'Who?' she asked, looking genuinely confused.

'Tyler Martin.'

It took her a moment to register what I'd said and then she pushed her chair back from the table as though she'd been hit by a bolt of lightning, her mouth hanging open. Her reaction was so over the top that I burst out laughing.

'Since when?' she spluttered.

'Since we went for dinner after the meeting at the hotel.'

'This was just after Christmas?'

'Uh-huh.'

She clutched her chest dramatically. 'I can't believe you've left it this long to tell me.'

I groaned. 'I know, I know. But I've only just got my head round it myself. Plus I asked him not to mention it to anyone because I don't want people in the office to find out. And then I thought I could hardly ask him to keep it quiet if I wasn't going to do the same.'

'I suppose,' said Val, who still looked shocked.

I pushed my baguette aside. 'Anyway, I've only seen him a couple of times. He came to mine on Tuesday and stayed the night. We're supposed to be going out again, but then presumably he's back in New York for the long haul so that will be that.'

Val pulled her chair back in and put her elbows on the table, resting her chin on the back of her hands. 'He flies back and forth a lot, doesn't he? So why can't you carry on seeing him?'

The thought of it made me feel panicky. That was never what this was about. 'He's probably got loads of women on the go in New York, hasn't he?' I said. 'That's what they do over there. I'll be one of many.'

I waited to see if I felt even a twinge of jealousy at the thought of it. Nope. Nothing.

'You like him?' asked Val.

Did I?

'He says all the right things,' I replied. 'And he's very cultured and all that.'

'What about the sex?'

'What about it?'

'Any good?'

I hesitated. 'Yes?'

Val frowned. 'I've seen you more enthusiastic about a large glass of wine.'

I thought it might take me some time to get used to having sex with someone other than Dan, that was all. They were very different, after all. And then, for some reason, I thought about Jack and his jersey top; the way the fabric had been stretched taut across his chest, all tight and smooth. I shook my head, wanting to remove the image from my mind as soon as possible. What was I thinking about him for? I hadn't seen him since we bumped into each other outside M&S the other day, which had been only marginally less uncomfortable than our previous two encounters.

'So where do you go from here?' asked Val. 'It could get *very* interesting if everyone finds out. You know what they'll say when you get the promotion.'

'If I get it.'

She waved her hand as if to indicate that it was a done deal.

'Has he asked you to visit him in New York?' asked Val.

I laughed. 'God, no.'

Val went all dramatic again, staring dreamily into space. 'I can see it now, the two of you dining out at The Four

Seasons. Running together in Central Park at dawn, watching the sun rise across the Hudson River.'

'OK, don't get carried away,' I warned her.

Val looked at me earnestly. 'Just be careful, OK?'

'That's exactly what I'm being.'

'You deserve to have a good time,' said Val. 'But mixing work with pleasure … I dunno. It rarely ends well, does it?'

'It's not going to get that complicated, Val,' I assured her.

I couldn't quite bring myself to tell her that I was only with him precisely *because* I knew it couldn't go anywhere. That conversation would be best saved for another time. I thought one bombshell of information was all Val could take for one lunch hour.

I checked my watch. 'On that note, I should get back. I need to get something finished before Tyler's presentation at three.'

'I won't be able to keep a straight face at the meeting now, you do know that, don't you?' said Val.

'Val …'

'I'm joking.'

The two of us stood up.

'Oh, I meant to ask, are you still thinking of moving out?' asked Val. 'Only one of Ekon's colleagues is looking for a place in North London. I could arrange for him to come and have a look round, if you like?'

When I'd stayed on in the flat after Dan had left, my intention had been to move somewhere cheaper. The rent had been fine with the two of us splitting bills, but it was hoovering up well over half of my salary now I was there on my own.

'I keep putting it off,' I admitted, getting up to chuck my leftovers in the bin.

'How come?' asked Vic, pulling on her coat. 'I thought you were skint.'

I wrapped my scarf around my neck. 'I'm happy there, Val.'

I'd got used to being on my own and couldn't imagine living in a house-share, not now. I wanted my own space, a place where I didn't have to put on a show for anyone, or appear to be more organised/a better cook/tidier than I actually was. Sometimes I didn't do washing for days and my laundry basket was practically overflowing and there was nobody to see it but me. I thought everyone at work might be shocked if they knew.

'You'd better get that promotion, then,' said Val, nudging me in the side.

I did up my coat. 'Yeah. That would help, wouldn't it?'

I dug my hands into my pockets as we stepped out onto Kingsway. The road was gridlocked for some reason and when I looked up towards the tube, there was an ambulance parked up with its doors wide open. I immediately felt the blood draining out of my face.

'Actually, you know what? I need to pop to the bank,' I said, trying not to panic.

'Shall I come with you?' asked Val, completely oblivious to my change of mood.

'No need,' I replied, already backing away. I could see them working on somebody, lifting some poor person onto a trolley. 'It's on The Strand, so a bit out of the way. I'll see you back in the office, OK?'

'Keep me posted on the Tyler situation!' shouted Val after me.

I waved and walked in the opposite direction. The ambulance's siren started up and I upped my pace until I was too far away to hear it.

8

Jack

It was nearly 5.30 by the time I got home. I couldn't be bothered to stop at the supermarket, so I was going to have to cobble something together out of whatever I had in the fridge. Maybe I'd do a pasta puttanesca, my classic can't-be-bothered dish. I walked around the already-familiar curved driveway of Marlowe Court and up the front steps of the middle block, holding the door open for Dave from the first floor, who was a plumber and had been very helpful when I'd just moved in and I couldn't get the boiler to work. There had been a few days between Tom moving out and me moving in and it had been like an icebox inside the flat when I'd arrived.

The block's foyer was like a faded kickback to the 1920s, with terrazzo flooring and a giant mirror along one wall. I bypassed the tiny, rickety lift, which I hadn't yet been brave enough to use, and started up the stairs. On the second floor, a door swung open with a creak and a familiar face appeared.

'Is that you, Jack?'

I came to a stop. 'Everything all right, Clive?'

Clive was the beaming, elderly man I'd met the day I'd moved in. He'd watched me from his doorway, cheering me on as I'd lugged my two huge suitcases up the stairs (the lift

– which I would have used on that occasion, actually – had been out of action, which Clive said was par for the course).

'Could you do me a favour and open this damn thing for me?' he said, handing me a jar of strawberry jam with a quivering hand. I took it from him, smiling.

'Course I can,' I said, opening it easily with one turn, but then leaving my hand on it, pretending I was finding it more of a struggle than I actually was. I didn't want to make him feel bad; he was over eighty now, but at six-foot and broad, he'd probably been twice as strong as me, once. I thought it must be hard to lose that; to think back to what your body had once been able to do.

'Thank you, Jack,' he said, taking it from me. 'It's very nice to have such helpful neighbours.'

'Any time,' I replied. 'So how's things? Have you been making any of that rum punch you were telling me about?'

Clive threw his head back and laughed, a gravelly rumble that always made me feel like joining in, whatever my mood. His big, booming voice with a Jamaican lilt echoed pleasantly around the stairwell. 'I'm out of Guinness,' he said. 'Once I pop to the shop again, I'm going to make another batch.'

'I'll pick some up for you tomorrow,' I offered. 'I'll drop it in after my shift.'

'That's very kind of you,' he replied, his face lighting up.

We both looked round as the front door slammed shut and footsteps started up the stairs. There was something fascinating about the comings and goings of the block; I found it comforting to know I was surrounded by people on all sides, residents from different walks of life and cultures and family dynamics – students, single mums, young professionals, all living in close proximity to each other, mostly getting along, from what Clive had told me. I felt like maybe I could be myself here in a way that I hadn't been able to be in my last house-share, which had been full of other actors who all seemed to be doing better than I was. In that respect, it had felt no different from being at home, where it had been my golden-child brother, Dom, I was always trying to keep up with. Except I could never compete with his straight A grades and his captaincy of the football team and his successful Oxbridge applications. It had been a relief when I'd discovered acting in sixth form – I'd only joined the drama club because one of my mates was but then it turned out that acting was something I was quite good at. Really good, actually, if the teacher's constant praise was anything to go by, and for once, my dyslexia hadn't held me back.

The footsteps came to a stop as Rebecca appeared at the top of the stairs. She had her shoulder bag in one hand and a Tesco carrier in the other.

'Hello, love,' boomed Clive.

'Hi Clive,' she replied.

She was ever so slightly out of breath.

'Hello,' I said.

'All right?' she said, putting her bags down and brushing her hair out of her eyes.

'Do you need any help with those? They look heavy,' commented Clive.

'I'm fine, thanks,' she said. 'It's my own fault for getting carried away in Tesco.'

I could see a four-pack of Heinz Baked Beans peeking out of the top of the bag. Maybe she slummed it with beans on toast like the rest of us when American Boy wasn't around, then.

'Right. Better get all this in,' she added, picking up her shopping and brushing past me up the stairs. 'See you soon, Clive!'

'Lovely girl,' stage-whispered Clive when she was out of sight.

I heard her putting her key in her front door on the floor above, then the door slamming shut behind her. The wind seemed to catch them on our floor, I'd noticed, and I had to go to great lengths to close mine quietly when I came home from a late shift.

'Yeah, she seems all right,' I replied. 'A bit schoolmarm-ish, maybe,' I added. 'I constantly feel like she's going to tell me off.'

Clive tutted at me. 'No, no, no, you've got it all wrong.'

I laughed. 'Probably,' I said.

I didn't really know her, did I? So what if I'd had one run-in with her, or two if you counted our first couple of ex-changes, it didn't mean she wasn't a nice person underneath that arsey exterior of hers.

'She was very unhappy for a while because her young man moved out,' said Clive conspiratorially. 'I remember it was around Christmas when it happened. Not the one just gone, the one before. She didn't even get a tree that year and I said she should because it would make her feel better.'

I was interested all of a sudden. I lapped up stories about other people's disastrous love lives because it made me feel much better about not having one of my own. In fact, I'd go one step further and say that it was evidence that I was doing the right thing by steering clear of all that. I had enough to worry about without adding relationships into the mix. What did I have to offer someone, anyway? I was working what felt like 24/7, I had no money and even though I was thirty now, I had a pathological fear of having to 'settle down' in case it interfered with my ability to travel guilt-free to wherever the next acting job might be. I was hardly a catch, was I?

'What happened?' I asked, unable to resist the Marlowe Court gossip mill that Clive appeared to be at the helm of. I glanced up to check that Rebecca was still safely behind a closed door. I didn't imagine she'd take kindly to her neighbours swapping stories about her. I mean, who would?

Clive shuffled closer, lowering his voice. 'I don't know all the details,' he began, 'but that girl looked sad for months. Barely smiled. Worked all hours. I told her she mustn't work so hard.'

'Blimey,' I said, wondering what had gone so wrong. It must have been quite gutting for her if they were actually living together.

'She's much better now. Always smiling.'

I nodded politely, but the truth was, I thought she seemed very serious. She hadn't even seen the funny side of her not being able to find my package, for example, judging by the way she'd been storming about looking for it with a face like thunder. Mind you, neither had I at the time. And she was a vast improvement on my last neighbour, who had been a miserable middle-aged man who banged on the wall with a broom handle whenever we dared to put the TV on. He particularly hated it when my old housemate, Gideon, who did musical theatre, was rehearsing his repertoire with his tinny backing track on full blast.

'Anyway, better go and make myself some dinner,' I said, starting up the stairs. 'Let me know if you need anything else, Clive, yeah?'

'If you make any more of that banana bread, I'd really appreciate a slice,' he called after me.

I gave him a thumbs-up. I'd tried a new recipe at the weekend and had dropped a couple of wedges down for him.

'And don't you work too hard either,' shouted Clive. 'Hollywood not calling yet, then?'

I looked over my shoulder, grimacing at him. 'Don't ask.'

Clive pointed his finger at me. 'Don't you go giving up now.'

I waved him off. I wasn't quite there yet and was holding onto the tiniest bit of hope that something might happen with the Lightning thing. And until I heard for sure, I was going to attempt to remain hopeful.

9

Rebecca

I stood outside the entrance to Greenhill Lodge and rang the bell, waiting for one of the office staff to buzz me in.

'Morning,' I said, putting the bunch of yellow tulips I'd brought with me on the desk and signing myself in.

'Hello, love,' replied Barbara, one of the care assistants. She bent down to sniff at the flowers, inhaling deeply. 'Your nan's doing ever so well. She even came down to play bingo last night. Won herself a box of Quality Street.'

I raised my eyebrows. 'No way!'

'She had a whale of time,' said Barbara, handing me a visitor's lanyard. 'I've never heard her laugh so much.'

'She used to love it back in the day,' I commented, thinking back to my childhood, when next-door's teenaged daughter would come and babysit every other Saturday night so that Nan could go out. She'd get all dressed up, usually in something bright, glittery and adorned with sequins.

'She was telling me she had a big win, once,' said Barbara.

I nodded enthusiastically. 'Five hundred pounds, I think it was. It was more money that we'd ever seen in our lives.'

An image popped into my head of Nan counting out her wodge of notes the following morning, shaking her head in disbelief. She'd treated me to a new doll from the expensive shop on the high street and I'd treasured it for years. Still had it somewhere.

'I could do with winning five hundred pounds,' said Barbara wistfully.

'I know the feeling,' I agreed, hooking the lanyard Barbara had passed me around my neck. 'Am I OK to go straight down?'

'Course, love,' she smiled.

I headed off through the reception area, waving at a couple of the residents I'd got to know as I passed the entrance to the dining room. They were involved in a heated card game, by the looks of it, so I left them to it and made my way down the brightly lit carpeted corridor of Marigold Wing, knocking softly on the door of Room 31. When there was no answer, I poked my head inside.

'It's only me, Nan,' I said.

'Hello, love,' she answered, her voice not carrying as far as it used to. 'Come on in.'

She was sitting in the armchair by the window, looking out at the garden. The lawn was covered in a sparkly white frost and I wondered whether she was longing for spring, when she could sit out on her favourite bench again and boss the gardeners around. Even at eighty-two she had a feisty spirit.

'Here,' I said, passing her the flowers. 'Thought these would look nice on your windowsill.'

'Ooh, lovely,' she cooed, taking my hand and squeezing it.

I kissed her on the cheek and then shrugged off my coat, laying it on the end of the bed.

'How's things?' I asked her.

'Oh, you know. Not bad,' she said.

The care assistants had helped get her dressed and she was wearing one of her neat, cream blouses with the Peter

Pan collar, tucked into a pair of shapeless peach trousers. She had a blanket thrown over her knees, and on the trolley table next to her was a glass of water, the TV remote and a vial with various pills in it. She was on medication for all sorts of things and it felt as though I was in a constant battle with her GP about whether they were all strictly necessary or whether one simply cancelled out the other.

'I hear you've been playing bingo,' I said, opening up the cupboard under the TV and getting out the vase she'd brought with her when she moved in. It had been a wedding gift, she told me, and was over sixty years old. I held it carefully; I'd always dreaded breaking it, I knew she'd be devastated if I did.

'I have indeed.'

She'd been reluctant to join in with any of the on-site activities when she'd first moved into the home eighteen months ago. The manager had told me that was perfectly normal, that it took some time for people to adjust to having some of their independence taken away. Nan had lived in the same house for fifty years, and it had been all tied up with memories of my grandad, of my mum, and me, as a child and then a teenager and then an adult, right up until I left for uni in Sheffield when I was eighteen. Her tiny, terraced house had been the social hub of the street once – she and Grandad would be the ones organising barbecues for the neighbours in the summer and Christmas parties in their front room. I remembered our house being jam-packed with half-drunk revellers and the frenzied plucking of cheese and pineapple on sticks out of a foil-covered potato and the clinking of glasses of cheap, sparkling wine. I'd usually watch the action from the top of the stairs, straining to see through the banisters, too cool to join in, but fascinated by the increasingly erratic behaviour of my neighbours – who had all seemed so old to me then – who would get merrier and merrier, before cramming themselves onto the makeshift dance floor (which was basically the middle of the lounge when the sofas had been pushed back) and swaying their hips to Nan's *Soul Classics* CD. If Nan spotted me on the stairs, she'd come and drag me down and make me dance with her. Then Grandad would whirl me around the room as though we were doing some kind of funky Viennese waltz and I'd be laughing so hard I was nearly sick.

'Work all right is it?' asked Nan.

I shrugged. 'Same as always.'

Nan looked at me, her glasses reflecting the light from the bay window. 'You said you'd look for something else, Beccy. You ought to, you know, if your heart's not in it.'

Apart from my parents, she was the only person who'd ever called me Beccy. It made me sad that once Nan had gone, that particular nickname would be gone forever, too.

I glanced at Nan's bedside table, which was peppered with pictures of my mum, the odd photo of the three of us, all in different-sized frames, the ceramic one I'd brought Nan back from Greece years ago taking pride of place. There was only one picture of me on my own: I must have been two or three and was sitting on a beach bashing a bucket with a spade. I didn't know where we were, but Mum and Dad would have been nearby, just out of shot, waiting to take me for a swim in the sea or fishing for crabs in a rock pool.

'Yeah,' I said. 'I've been looking around.'

'You deserve more,' said Nan. 'You shouldn't put things off – you know that better than anyone.'

She was right, I shouldn't, but it wasn't that easy to start over, not after I'd spent over a decade building a place for myself at Kingsland. I'd fallen into marketing after uni be-cause I needed a job and that seemed as good a one as any. I'd worked hard and had moved up the ranks pretty quickly and had enjoyed the feeling of being successful and well respected. I'd realised lately, though, that something was missing. Nan was forever asking me what it was, but I found it difficult to explain. I supposed it was that I didn't much like the feeling of earning a multimillion-pound business even more money. That part of my job – working out how best to persuade people to buy our clients' products – felt fake and, at times, dishonest. I wanted to help people, I'd always thought that, but I couldn't seem to get off the corporate treadmill for long enough to take the time to work out exactly how.

'I've applied for a promotion at work,' I said, wanting to make it sound more exciting than it felt. 'Head of press and marketing. I think I'm in with a good chance of getting it.'

Nan nodded slowly. 'More money, is it?'

'Yeah,' I replied, nicking one of Nan's Quality Streets and passing her a strawberry delight. 'That's not the only reason I'm going for it, though. It would be the next step up in my career. I'd be on the senior management team, all that.'

'You'd get to make all the decisions, then,' said Nan.

She reached out for her glass of water, struggling to hold its weight as she brought it to her lips. I helped her put it down again.

'Not quite,' I said. 'I would have a whole team under me, though.'

Nan looked at my suspiciously. She had a way of seeing through me, of knowing when there was something bubbling away under the surface that I wasn't admitting to. The thing was, half the time it was just a feeling. Something I couldn't quite make sense of. Or didn't want to make sense of, more like.

'And what about the flat?' asked Nan. 'Are you managing on your own?'

I topped up Nan's water from a plastic jug on the table. 'Course I am. I'm actually quite enjoying being on my own.'

Nan looked at me. 'Don't forget, I know how lonely it is living by yourself.'

Nan hadn't done so well after Grandad died. She'd kind of gone into herself, had pretty much lost her spark overnight. And then when she'd had a bad fall, things had got even worse. It had taken her a while, though, to admit that she might need a bit of extra help. In that respect, I could see lots of myself in her and understood her determination to do it all on her own. It had taken a lot for her to move in here, but I was glad she had, and I thought she was, too, in a way. She was being sociable again for the first time in years, for a start, which was lovely to see, but I knew it was still a struggle for her. She missed her home and my grandad every day – I did, too.

'I'm not in much during the week, anyway,' I told her. 'And the neighbours are nice. Friendly. A new guy's moved in across the corridor. I'm not sure about him, actually. I think he might have anger issues. And there's that old guy downstairs, you know, the one who likes to chat?'

'A new neighbour, you say ...' said Nan, perking up. 'Good-looking, is he?'

I rolled my eyes at her. 'Don't go getting any ideas, Nan.'

I almost told her about Tyler. He was my type: well dressed, polite, polished, charming. Not someone who lounged about in tracksuits and shouted at strangers about missing packages, although I supposed he had apologised.

Dipping my hand into the box of Quality Streets again, I pulled out my favourite: the green triangle. 'Right,' I said, with a mouthful of chocolate. 'I'll make us a cup of tea, shall I? And fill up your vase so I can arrange the flowers. Oh, and look,' I added, pulling a box of Mr Kipling's Fondant

Fancies out of my bag with a flourish. 'I got us a treat. Your favourite.'

10

Jack

I pulled on a pair of boxers and stared at myself in the bathroom mirror, turning to the right and then the left, sucking in my stomach and then letting it fall out again. Fuck. Was this what I had to look forward to now I was thirty? Was it really all downhill from here like they said in the magazine articles I'd read about sluggish metabolisms? I groaned, looking over my shoulder to see how I looked from behind. Not great, I concluded. Not great at all.

I heard a door slam opposite and the slapping of multiple pairs of feet on the stairs. Feeling uncharacteristically nosy, I went into the lounge and looked out of the window, hiding my half-naked body behind the curtain. The front door clicked and Rebecca sprang down the front steps, simultaneously doing some kind of over-arm stretch. She looked like every other north London woman I'd seen, in her black leggings with a gaudy pattern down the side and a matching tight-fitting vest that were probably from the phenomenally overpriced gym-wear shop on Heath Street. She looked fit, though, I had to admit, like a proper runner and I absent-mindedly ran my hand across my decidedly less-ripped-than-they-used-to-be abs.

Taking another peek, I watched her doing some warm-up lunges, her ponytail swishing around between her shoulder blades. And next to her was the same up-himself, slick guy with the booming American voice I'd seen her with last week. He was definitely her boyfriend, then. Women liked blokes like him, probably, with his nice suits and his mature attitude and his perma-tan. He had it all together in a way that I – clearly – did not. I tutted to myself as he started lunging, too; I could see his quads bulging even from this distance. Then they both jogged off. Rebecca was fiddling with her phone which was strapped to her arm and he was skipping sideways, first with one foot leading and then the other, like I'd seen footballers do when they were warming up at the side of the pitch. Seriously, who did these two think they were, David and Victoria Beckham?

I looked at my watch: 7.05 a.m. If I was serious about getting into shape, I would actually have to get out there and do something about it at some point. If I went for a run now, I'd have to shower again, but that felt like a crap excuse not to do it. I'd have plenty of time to have my second shower of the day and still make it to the pub on time for my lunch shift. If I wanted leading man roles, I was going to have to suck it up and push myself, even if what I really wanted to do was to make myself three slices of buttery toast, maybe even put some peanut butter on it, then slump in front of *Good Morning Britain*. The competition at castings was getting fiercer and fiercer and if I could get the upper hand in any way at all, I had to try.

Before I could talk myself out of it, I pulled on a pair of jersey tracksuit bottoms, fished a black T-shirt out of the washing basket and put on my running shoes, which I noticed were still looking vaguely new, probably because I could count on one hand the number of times I'd actually been out running in them. I downed a glass of water, grabbed my headphones and forced myself out of the door.

Outside on the driveway, I did a few half-hearted stretches myself (blatantly copying what I'd just seen Rebecca do) before setting off with relative enthusiasm. Rebecca and American boy had gone left, probably heading through the woods and onto the heath, so if I went right and round towards Kenwood House, I should be able to avoid them altogether.

Twenty minutes later, I staggered back into the driveway of Marlowe Court, probably bright red and sprouting sweat from every pore. I hadn't taken any water with me, which I'd used as a convenient excuse to cut my run short and head home. Dehydration was extremely dangerous, after all; it would have been reckless of me to carry on without being suitably hydrated.

I stopped dead when I saw Rebecca about to put her key in the front door, her boyfriend doing hamstring stretches behind her. Damn, I'd thought they'd be out for at least an hour. Wasn't that what people like them did? A mini-marathon of a morning?

I looked over my shoulder, wondering whether I should reverse back out of the driveway and hide down the road a bit until they'd gone in, but if they caught me doing it, I'd seem like a weirdo. The other option was to brazen it out because, after all, why did I care what they thought of me? So what if I was sweating profusely – wasn't that what you were supposed to do when you exercised? Anyway, as far as they were concerned, I could have run 10K; there was absolutely no reason for them to know I'd only made it halfway to Bishop's Avenue and back.

In the end, I went for the second option, walking confidently up to the front door and doing pointless side stretches as I went. I pretended I hadn't seen them until the last minute. Mind you, American boy didn't appear to have noticed me anyway and barged through the front door the second Rebecca got it open. She was just about to slam it in my face when she saw me standing there like a knob.

'Oh, sorry,' she said, putting her foot in the door to stop it closing.

Bar a stray hair falling across her face and a smear of sweat on her upper lip, she didn't look as though she'd exerted herself in the slightest. In fact, she had the air of someone who'd taken a leisurely walk to the corner shop and back. This was, allegedly, what happened when you really got into running, or so I'd been told. It became easier the more you did it. Rebecca should be pushing herself harder, really. I felt inordinately smug then – maybe I was doing something right after all (i.e. exercising to the point of exhaustion).

'Thanks,' I said, grabbing the door.

'Been for a run, too?' she asked as I followed her inside the foyer.

'Yep,' I replied, wiping my face on the arm of my hoodie to stem the flow. 'I really went for it this morning.'

'How far did you go?'

I followed her up the first flight of stairs. 'Um, not sure, actually. I didn't track my route today.'

What was I talking about, 'tracking my route'? What even was that, and if I wanted to pretend I was the sort of person who 'tracked my route', why wouldn't I have 'tracked' it today?

'What about you?' I asked, trying to talk normally and as though I wasn't desperately in need of oxygen. This made it worse, and by the time I got up the next flight of stairs, I felt as though my chest was about to explode.

'Only 4K today,' she answered, taking the stairs two at a time.

'Not bad,' I said, struggling to keep up, gutted that I'd only managed half that distance.

She shrugged. 'I actually like cardio. I'm one of those annoying people who hogs the treadmill for an hour at the gym.'

I bet she was.

We reached our floor at last and not a second too soon because I seriously thought I might be about to pass out. Her boyfriend was leaning against the wall with his ripped arms crossed. I acknowledged him with a tight smile – I thought I ought to – and he gave me a flick of the head back.

'Bye, then,' I said breathlessly to Rebecca.

'See you,' she said.

There was a lot of jangling about of keys all round as we both let ourselves in. They were probably off to NutriBullet a protein shake, or something. I, on the other hand, thought I deserved a treat after all that exertion and so I made myself the biggest bowl of Rice Krispies known to man and slumped on the sofa, flicking on the TV. I didn't fancy the news, so I flicked on BBC iPlayer and went for something familiar and comforting: re-runs of *Doctors*, which reminded me of being a drama student when I'd watch daytime TV for hours on end. Only in the holidays, mind you. Drama school wasn't the sort of set-up where you popped in for lectures now and again and had loads of free time to go to the library/sleep. It was full on, 9–5 every day, often running over into the evenings if you were working on a play. I realised that since I'd left nearly ten years ago, my life hadn't got any less full on. That was the thing: when you wanted to be an actor, it took over your entire life. There wasn't time for anything else, what with having to factor in making some actual money.

I zoned out in front of the TV, slurping cold milk into my mouth, gripped by a scene where a boy gets knocked off his bike and the driver doesn't stop and races off in a blind panic. *Wait a minute*, I thought: I recognised the driver. I leaned forward, squinting at the screen, fumbling around for the remote to rewind it. It was definitely him: Charlie Mathers-Thompson from the year above me at LAMDA. I put my cereal down half eaten. It was a good role. Charlie became an integral part of the episode; turned out his character knew the boy he'd mowed off the road and had done it on purpose. There was a very dramatic scene where he snuck into the hospital ward and was caught twiddling with dials on the life support machine, trying to finish the boy off.

I rewound it, watching it again and again, working out how I would have done it differently, muttering the words under my breath, as though I was practising for an audition. I could have got this part if they'd called me in for it, I knew I could. Then I fast-forwarded ahead to the credits and noted down the name of the casting director. Ah. I'd auditioned for her once before, for an *EastEnders* spin-off. I made a mental note to ask Chad to send her my résumé and headshot again, remind her who I was. Since I still hadn't heard anything about Project Afghanistan, I couldn't let the ball drop. I had to keep pushing forward, even if it meant annoying Chad in the process.

A text pinged and I glanced down at it. It was Luke.

You working today?

Course I was working, I was always bloody working.

I sighed, covering my face with my hands. When was I going to catch a break? Because I knew this wasn't how my life was supposed to be. I was an actor, a good one, but the way things were going, it felt like I'd be stuck behind a bar earning minimum wage forever.

II

Rebecca

My thighs were burning after sprinting full throttle up East Heath Road, which in hindsight had been a tad over-ambitious. I bent double at the waist, struggling to catch my breath and simultaneously scrolling through my Fitbit: 5K in thirty-one minutes. Not my best time by any stretch of the imagination. It didn't help that I'd been distracted by thoughts of work and promotions and interviews, all whirring about in my head as I ran. I should be going into this new phase of my career with confidence; full of passion about taking that next step up. Instead, I felt kind of dead inside. Every time I read through the job spec for the head of press and marketing (which I'd done A LOT, hoping something would suddenly click), I felt completely numb. I didn't usually do numb, much as I would have liked to at times. I filled the void with stuff – with school, with work, with running, with Dan, with whatever would keep my mind off the inevitable.

I made myself do some hamstring stretches because that was where I usually ached most the next day, but my heart wasn't in it. I fished around in the pocket of my leggings for my keys and was just about to put them in the lock when the front door flew open and Jack nearly slammed straight into me. Rattled, I took a step back, smoothing my hand over my windswept hair.

'Hi,' he said, clutching his chest. 'Sorry!'

'No worries,' I replied, wondering whether there was a reason he was charging around like a bull in a china shop.

'Been for a run again, have you?' he asked, holding the door open for me.

I'd noticed that since our row over the parcel had blown over, all we seemed to talk about was running. It was as though we'd hooked into the one thing we had in common.

I slipped past him. 'If you can call it that,' I said.

He looked surprised. 'What do you mean?'

I shook my head. 'It just wasn't a very good session, that was all.'

He leaned against the door with his hands in his pockets. 'It is fine to have an off day, you know,' he said.

I nodded, pretending I completely agreed with him. 'Sure. Course it is.'

I'd never felt like it was OK, though, that was the problem. One slip, one wrong move and it felt like everything could potentially come crashing down around me, no matter how many times I tried to rationalise it. In any case, this conversation was veering into unchartered territory. Best to end it now before one of us said something to annoy the other.

I jangled my keys in my hand. 'Have a good day, then,' I said, noticing he was all in black again. I started springing up the stairs, my breath coming in rapid bursts.

'You, too,' he called after me.

I still didn't know what he did or where he went every day. He'd been right when he'd said he was hardly ever in, but there seemed to be no particular rhythm to it. Some days, he'd be up early and then back late, past midnight sometimes. Other times, I heard him clattering about all day and then he'd go out at teatime. He often had his TV on really loudly, I knew that much; sometimes I could hear it from the landing below. Once, I'd heard him coming up the stairs behind me and as he got closer, obviously not realising I was there, he'd been talking to himself, mumbling something fast and incoherent under his breath. I wondered what that meant, if he had some kind of condition. That was the thing in London: you knew your neighbours to say hello to. Knew what kind of clothes they wore, the take-aways they liked, their supermarket of choice. You knew if they recycled or not, how often they ordered from Amazon. Sometimes you knew what kind of music they were into if they played it loud enough. And then you made up the rest, pigeonholing them into whatever archetype you'd decided they fell into based on the very little information you had. If I was to guess, I'd say Jack worked in some trendy industry, like music or advertising. That he had as many women on the go as he had packages delivered (not that I'd seen any women, admittedly). That he hated cooking and that his flat was a mess. That he was privileged (hence the need to get his own way) and had very likely been to private school. I mean, I was making a lot of assumptions here, but I was pretty convinced I was right about most of it.

Once I'd showered and changed, I made myself a normal tea and Tyler a camomile one. It had been the only herbal tea I could find and had been stuffed at the back of my cupboard behind the jar of decaf coffee I also never used. I had the sneaking suspicion it was past its sell-by date, but surely dried herbs didn't go off? Anyway, I hadn't been sure I was going to see him again after I'd turned down his offer of dinner at Nobu. In hindsight, perhaps I should have stocked up my cupboards with health freak/vegan-friendly things just in case.

I walked into the lounge and put the drinks down next to Tyler, who was typing frantically away on his laptop.

'How was your run?' he asked.

I flung myself on the sofa next to him. 'Terrible. I couldn't get going.'

He looked up, surprised. 'How so?'

'Dunno,' I said. 'Just wasn't feeling it.'

He frowned. 'Those are the times we need to push hardest, right?'

'Right,' I replied, turning my head away and surreptitiously rolling my eyes.

As if it was that easy. It seemed he mistakenly thought I was as fit and dedicated to exercise as he was and he found it impossible to imagine that I – or anyone else for that matter – might have an 'off day', as Jack had put it.

'I'm gonna to have to get a flight back to New York tonight,' he said.

'OK,' I said, rearranging the coasters on the coffee table so that they were just as I liked them.

He reached over and tucked a hair behind my ear. 'Sorry, sweetheart. I'll be back in a few weeks.'

'It's fine,' I said. 'Really.'

It was better, in fact, but I didn't tell him that. We'd been spending too much time together anyway, and although part of me was enjoying the fact we were doing things like running together and ordering takeaways, the kind of stuff I hadn't done with another person for over a year now, I knew it wasn't because he had any particular feelings for me; he'd alluded to dating a couple of women at home in New York, and I was clearly nothing more to him than a London-based distraction. It would be easier all round when he was back in the States and I could resume my usual, solitary existence.

I watched him swipe his tea off the table and go over to the window. He said it reminded him of home, the fact that you could see right into other people's apartments.

'Amanda's upped her game,' he commented.

This was strange. He'd never spoken about her before, or anyone else at work, for that matter.

'In what way?' I asked him.

It was just like her to actually start doing some work when the promotion was around the corner. She was the sort of person to swan in, do a great job for about five minutes and swipe the promotion I'd been working steadily towards for the last couple of years out from under my nose. I pushed down the part of me that said maybe that would be a good thing. That maybe then I'd be forced to do something different and wouldn't actually have to make the decision myself.

Tyler looked around. 'I mean, she's good, right? She's not afraid to say what she wants. Her ideas are on point.'

I put my hair into a bun, fumbling with the band. 'Sure. She knows what she's doing.'

Amanda brought out the worst in me, which wasn't really fair because she actually hadn't done anything except be her (albeit annoying) self. That and the fact she was one of those girls who always seemed to fall on her feet. I'd always felt a bit resentful towards people like that, who had seemingly cruised through life.

'Are you going in the shower first or shall I?' asked Tyler, coming over and kissing me lightly on the top of my head. I hooked my hand around his neck, pulling him in for a proper kiss.

'I will,' I said, jumping up and grabbing the empty plates and mugs that were scattered around the room, still a little confused about why he'd brought Amanda up. 'Ready to leave for work in thirty minutes?'

'Sure,' replied Tyler, flopping on the sofa and putting his bare feet up on the coffee table.

I bit my lip, resisting the urge to ask him to take them right back off again. After all, he was going back to America soon and I'd have the place to myself, which was just as I liked it.

12

Jack

I legged it into the pub, sweating in too many layers and wishing I'd left the flat earlier so that I hadn't had to run all the way here. I'd made the mistake of putting on a film and had got all engrossed in it. I'd kept promising myself ten more minutes, five more minutes, until I was so close to the end that it would have ruined the whole thing to have stopped it and gone back to it later.

'Sorry, mate,' I said to Luke as I dashed behind the bar, slinging my coat into a corner. I ran my hands through my hair. 'Right, what needs doing?'

The pub had been open for just over an hour and was already filling up with the usual slew of punters. There were all sorts of offices around here: solicitors and dance studios and property management companies; you never knew who was going to come in. It was a decent pub with a mix of loaded, bohemian clientele from Hampstead and Belsize Park and a more discerning bunch who came up from Kentish Town and Camden.

'Tut, tut,' replied Luke, tapping his watch. 'I should put you on a disciplinary for this.'

'Yeah, right,' I said, laughing.

Luke had already commandeered the sound system and had put Oasis' *Definitely Maybe* on for the one hundred and fiftieth time. Despite being sick of this (admittedly very good) album, I hummed along to 'Cigarettes & Alcohol' while I rearranged packets of crisps in a bowl.

'Since I'm now a duty manager now and all,' continued Luke, smiling smugly at me.

I did a double-take. 'You're a what?'

'Yep,' said Luke, tapping a navy blue badge attached to the lapel of his too-big shirt. Now he came to mention it, he did look a lot smarter than usual. 'Barnaby finally promoted me.'

I leaned against the bar for support. Luke had worked here off and on for twelve years; this was big news.

'What brought that on?' I asked, fanning myself and pretending to be overwhelmed.

'God knows,' replied Luke. 'I just said yes before he could change his mind.'

Still in shock, I slapped him on the shoulder, which was the closest we ever got to a hug. 'I'm pleased for you, mate. Honestly I am. Now, about that disciplinary …'

'You can wash all those glasses as penance,' said Luke. 'I've got some paperwork to do,' he added grandly, picking up a clipboard and disappearing off into the staff area.

I looked around the all-too-familiar bar with its psychedelic patterned carpet and dark wood chairs and tables and the screen we occasionally played big sporting events on; they were particularly keen on Wimbledon around here. Was I, too, destined to work here for over a decade? Would I be promoted to duty manager in ten years' time, at which point I'd be nearly forty-fucking-one?

Before I could contemplate that distressing thought any longer, the door swung open and a group of guys of about my age strutted in. I recognised one of them immediately: Seb. How could you bump into someone this often in a city of eight million people?

'Oh hello again, Jack,' he said, directing his friends to a table in the corner and approaching me in that cocksure way he'd permanently adopted. He hadn't been like that on his first day at LAMDA. I remembered it vividly; he'd been so nervous when we'd had to perform our audition monologues to our new classmates that I'd been worried he was going to pass out mid-scene. He winked at me. 'Still working here, then, are you?'

'Looks like it. What can I get you?'

'Two rum and Cokes, a pint of Red Stripe and a bottle of Becks. Oh, and throw in four packets of crisps, will you? Any flavour will do.'

I busied myself pouring the beer; measuring out the spirits.

'Heard from Lightning about the Netflix gig?' asked Seb, clearly fishing for information.

I glanced up, trying to tell from his facial expression whether he'd got the job and wanted to brag about it or whether he was as much in the dark as I was. I decided on the latter; for somebody who was quite a good actor, he was crap at hiding his emotions in real life. He'd never been able to keep his competitiveness a secret, that was for sure, and I'd seen him seething with envy in his seat on numerous occasions when I'd got a particularly good piece of feedback or a role in the end-of-term play that he'd earmarked for himself. To make it worse, quite often we were up for the same parts. Unlike me, though, Seb had got a couple of big jobs lately that were pushing his career into a whole new playing field. I didn't suppose he was having to slog it out in a pub to make his rent.

'Not yet,' I replied. 'Bit surprised, actually. Thought I'd at least have got a call-back.'

Mind you, I always thought I deserved a call-back and

nine times out of ten I didn't get one, but you had to believe in yourself, didn't you, otherwise what was the point?

'What about you?' I asked him, sliding the rum and Cokes across the bar.

He picked up one in each hand. 'Nah, nothing yet either.'

I nodded, momentarily united in disappointment with a fellow actor who was waiting for news, too. If we stopped trying to get one up on each other, we might actually be able to be friends. Although, saying that, he was a bit of a twat. He'd dated half our year at LAMDA at one point or another, and according to some of the girls he'd been out with, he'd been a complete nightmare. I'd never understood what they all saw in him in the first place, or why he felt the need to complicate everything by shagging girls from his own proverbial front doorstep. Life was so much easier when you steered clear of all that. I'd learned my lesson the hard way when I'd got involved with Nathalie, who had at least been in the year above.

'What's your next gig, then?' asked Seb. 'Got anything lined up?

I leaned across the bar, casually, as though talking about my career was not something I was desperate to avoid at all costs. 'I'm waiting to hear about a couple of projects,' I lied. 'A director I worked with at the Donmar is doing something in the West End in the autumn, so I'll be hearing from her any day now, probably.'

Seb raised his eyebrows, impressed.

'You?' I asked, despite really, really not wanting to know.

I finished pouring the Red Stripe and plonked it in front of him, frothy beer dripping all over my fingers.

'One sec,' said Seb, taking the rum and Cokes over to his mates and then coming back for the rest. 'Things are going great, man. Since I got back from LA, especially.'

I swallowed. 'Oh yeah, I heard you went out there. Good was it?'

I only asked to be polite and I now desperately wished I hadn't. If you went out to LA it wasn't usually for a bit-part, was it?

Seb nodded earnestly, his hands in the prayer position. 'Have you done pilot season?'

I shook my head. 'I'd love to. But, you know, haven't managed to fit it in.'

Couldn't afford it, more like. I was always reading articles about Brits who'd made it big in Hollywood, but the idea of cobbling together the money to do it felt more and more unlikely with each year that passed.

'You have to go, man,' said Seb, in the style of one of those new-agers who'd been brainwashed on a meditation retreat. 'I can't rave about it enough. I was getting seen twice a day out there,' he went on. 'HBO had me in, then I got that BBC period drama thing off the back of a workshop I did. I came back super geared up and ready to work.'

'Sounds amazing,' I replied, my breath coming a little faster. How was I supposed to compete with people who'd be out to LA and done all that? I'd heard you could be auditioning every day if you were lucky, not once a month like you were here.

'Seriously, Jack, get yourself out there. You're getting frustrated, losing confidence in yourself, I can see it in your eyes. I was the same before LA. It was the best move I ever made.'

I nodded, mortified that Seb seemed to be able to see right through the I'm-quietly-confident façade I usually very successfully presented to the world.

He grabbed his crisps and the rest of his drinks. 'Do it, mate. You won't regret it.'

'Thanks for the heads-up,' I called after him.

The exertion of giving the illusion that I wasn't panicking about the state of my career, my finances and pretty much everything else in my life had made my head spin. It was exhausting pretending to be OK when you weren't.

'D'you need me out here?' said Luke, appearing beside me, still clutching his beloved clipboard.

'Not really,' I replied, deep in thought. 'Hey, Luke? Since you're my line manager now, is it you I ask for an advance on my wages?'

Luke looked chuffed to have any responsibility whatsoever. 'I suppose I am. What is it you need?'

'Check this out,' I said, searching on my phone and finding the class timetable for the Actors Centre in Covent Garden. 'There's a class I really want to do, with the casting director on one of the big American soap operas. They must be looking for British actors, otherwise why would they bother coming over?'

Luke frowned. 'Aren't there any British actors where he's from? Los Angeles or whatever?'

I shrugged. 'That's not the point though, is it? The point is, if I can make him love me, he'll keep me in mind for future roles, won't he? Imagine that ... moving to the States. Earning thousands of dollars an episode.'

'That does sound good,' admitted Luke. 'How much do you need, then?'

'Well, the class is forty quid,' I said, marvelling at the fact I could never have had this conversation with Barnaby. There were definitely some advantages to having your mate as your boss.

'Right,' said Luke, looking all official and writing it down. In for a penny, literally...'And then I sort of haven't got any money to eat. So maybe another fifty quid to tide me over until payday?'

Luke gave me a look. 'How long are you going to go on like this?' he asked me. 'I'm worried about you, mate.'

'In what way?' I asked, grabbing a cloth and frantically polishing a spot on the bar. *Worried about me?* This was very embarrassing. The last thing I wanted was people feeling sorry for me.

Luke put his clipboard down. 'Don't you want some normality in your life? A regular job? So you know what money you've got coming in every month, so you're not scraping around to pay the bills?'

Reluctantly I put my cloth down. 'Sometimes, yeah. There's this girl,' I said, for some reason thinking of Rebecca. 'She lives opposite me and she's got this sorted life: 9–5 job, nice clothes, nice boyfriend, always looks well put together.'

'Nice-looking?' asked Luke.

I nodded. 'Yeah. She'd be even prettier if she wasn't such hard work. But my point is, watching her come home at the same time every night, knowing she's got the whole evening free to do whatever she pleases, knowing she's got the cash to buy whatever she wants within reason … it looks appealing sometimes, I have to say.'

Luke poured himself some water and downed it, slamming his glass down in the sink. 'Sounds like you quite like her,' he said.

I groaned. What had I started? 'She's really not my type.'

'Why, what's your type?'

I tutted. 'I don't know. But not her. She takes herself too seriously. I bet she only dates guys who've got money, anyway.'

I couldn't help but compare myself to her glamorous American boyfriend who probably spent hours preening himself in front of the mirror, mesmerised by how good he looked.

Luke put his hands on his hips. Bizarrely, he seemed somewhat irritated. 'You don't know that, though, do you? You're making all these assumptions about someone you've only had – what – a couple of conversations with?'

'Look, it's not just her. I'm not interested in seeing anyone, you know that.'

I wasn't sure how we'd even got onto this subject.

Luke looked at me, more earnestly than ever before. I thought this duty manager business might have gone to his head. 'So basically, you're pushing people away before you've given them a chance?'

I served one of the locals another pint of Carlsberg. Annoyingly, Luke waited, hovering over me. He wasn't going to let me off the hook with this one, I could tell.

'Give them a chance to do what?' I asked Luke, once I'd given the man his change. 'Add a whole load of hassle to my already massively busy life? I need to focus on my career, mate. Making a success of that is all that matters at the moment. I'm nearly there, my big break is just around the corner, I can feel it.'

Well I could, vaguely.

Luke tutted. 'Maybe. But that doesn't mean you should put everything else on hold. Why can't you have both?'

'It doesn't work like that.' Although, admittedly, other actors seemed to manage it. 'Anyway, you're only saying this because you're practically married,' I snapped.

Honestly, these people in serious relationships had some sort of superiority complex, didn't they, with their trips to IKEA and their Sunday-morning brunches on Columbia Road and their matching towel sets?

'I live with someone I love,' replied Luke. 'I get to see her face every day. You should try it sometime.'

He stomped off, clearly having had enough of me, the keys to the till clinking against the buckle of his belt. So much for getting that advance.

13

Rebecca

I did up my trainers up, checked my hair in the mirror, strapped my phone to my arm and hung my headphones around my neck. I was going to push myself this evening, add in some hill sprints or something.

Hesitating, I picked up the Amazon package I'd left on top of the microwave. Jack might not be in, but I'd try anyway, on my way out.

I opened the door and took the two steps required to reach Jack's door, knocking on it softly. After a few seconds, I heard the clattering of something on the hob and then the patter of footsteps coming down the hall. He coughed softly before opening the door. I ran my thumb along the corrugated cardboard edge of the parcel.

'Hi,' I said, brandishing the package in his direction the second he appeared in the doorway. 'This came for you.'

He was barefoot, his feet a bright white in contrast to the elasticated hem of his navy joggers. I could see dark hairs just above his ankles, in the gap before his trousers started.

'Ah, yes,' he said, opening the door wide. 'I got one of those "Sorry I Missed You" cards yesterday. This is becoming a bit of a regular occurrence, isn't it?'

'You could say that.'

This was at least the fifth package since he'd moved in, not that I was counting.

'The problem is, I tend to be out a lot,' he added. 'So you might get a few of these, I'm afraid.'

'Really?'

'So sorry. If you do.'

I wondered why he kept ordering stuff online, if his riotous social life meant he was never going to be in to sign for them. Bit selfish, I thought, expecting everyone else to keep getting up and down to answer the door, to take in parcels that took up too much space in their miniscule galley kitchens. This particular time, for example, I'd been in the bath when the doorbell rang and I'd jumped out, thrown on my dressing gown and had stood dripping water all over the hallway floor while I spoke into the intercom and directed the courier up to the third floor.

'What are all these parcels you get, anyway?' I asked, trying not to sound snippy. I was interested to know what he needed to order all the time, and why perhaps he couldn't buy it in an actual shop.

He looked taken aback. 'Um, nothing mysterious. Books, mainly. I read a lot. Sometimes I buy plays, if I'm auditioning for something. Or box sets, if I want to familiarise myself with a particular show before a casting.'

I raised my eyebrows. 'Oh, right. You're an actor, then?'

That explained why I was always hearing him muttering to himself; he was probably running lines. It also explained why he strutted around the block in his monochrome jersey lounge pants as though he owned the place. That's what they all wore, wasn't it, these pretentious theatre types?

'I thought I'd mentioned it,' he said.

I shook my head. 'Nope, don't think so.'

We'd barely had a conversation, had we, except for a bit of

small talk about running times? Plus he probably imagined it was just oozing out of him, that I should have just looked at him and thought: *He's definitely an actor.* Knowing my luck, he was really well known and I'd made a fool of myself by not realising. I was desperate to ask whether I would have seen him in anything, but I'd once read that it was the worst question you could possibly ask. Because if you had to ask, you probably hadn't 'seen them in anything'. And also, weren't they out of work eighty per cent of the time anyway? I didn't want to rub it in, it seemed soul-destroying enough as it was.

'I just auditioned for a big Netflix show, actually,' he said, leaning against the door frame.

'Did you?' I asked. 'What kind of thing was it?'

He stretched the sleeves of his top over his hands. 'Like a military drama. Messed-up soldiers with PTSD. Secrets and lies. You know the kind of thing.'

I nodded. '*Homeland*-style.'

'Yeah. Yep, exactly.'

'How did it go?' I asked, genuinely curious.

'Good,' he said. And then he screwed up his nose so that it went all crinkly. 'I probably won't get it, though.'

'Why do you think that?'

He shrugged. 'I think they'll probably go with a bigger name.'

I nodded, thinking how confident he must be to even put himself out there in the first place. I'd tried acting once, when I was at school and had had such extreme stage fright that I'd begged Nan to call and tell them I was sick (which, of course, she refused to do).

'Is it as hard as they say, then? Constant rejection and all that?' I asked.

I handed him the package, wondering why I was still holding it.

He took it, putting it under his arm, laughing softly. 'It's tough, yeah. But the thing is, when it goes well, when you actually get the part and you're up there on stage in front of a couple of hundred people – twenty people, even – it's the most amazing job on earth.'

'That's why you keep doing it,' I said, understanding. I got what it was like to crave recognition for your work, although in my case it was on a much smaller, subtler scale.

'It's the unpredictability of it that gets you,' he added, drumming his fingers on his parcel. 'I mean, I could never afford to live somewhere like this usually,' he said, waving his arm around the stairwell. 'I'm only here because Tom wants to keep the flat on while he's in New York and he's charging me a token rent. Otherwise I'd be back living in a crappy house-share.'

'I know the feeling,' I said. I tightened my ponytail thinking I ought to get going on my run because as the minutes passed, I felt more and more like sacking it off.

He looked doubtful. 'You do?'

'Why did you look at me like that?' I asked him, narrowing my eyes.

'Like what?' he said, all innocently.

'Like you don't believe I know the feeling.'

He looked sheepish. 'Well, you've probably got a nice stable job, haven't you? So I just thought you probably don't have to worry about making the rent.'

I hung my mouth open in mock outrage. 'I'll have you know that I rented the place with my ex-boyfriend, so everything was split two ways. And then when he moved out, my intention was to move out too, because I couldn't afford it on my own.'

What had I mentioned Dan for? Not that Jack would necessarily care, but I was still smarting from the humiliation of moving in with someone I thought I was going to spend the rest of my life with and then having them move out six months later.

'Sorry to hear about that,' said Jack. 'And I apologise for making assumptions about your finances. It's not cheap to live round here, is it?'

'You can say that again. Mind you, it's nice in Hampstead, isn't it?'

'Yeah,' replied Jack, looking over his shoulder as an appliance beeped in his kitchen. 'Even if I am surrounded by rich people 24/7.'

I smiled. 'I can't decide if I find it aspirational or if I'm just insanely jealous.'

He looked up at the ceiling, pretending to consider it. 'If you're anything like me, I would suggest insanely jealous?'

I fiddled with my Fitbit strap, rotating it back and forth. He was probably exaggerating about his financial status, anyway. I could tell by his voice that he was one of those middle-class boys who'd had everything handed to him on a plate and couldn't quite get his head round the fact that the one thing he wanted more than anything – i.e. an acting job – was permanently evading him. There were loads of them round here, guys wearing beanie hats and tracksuits because they wanted to look all street and then going back to their parents' five-storey family home for Sunday lunch. His parents were probably paying his rent on this place anyway, however 'token' he'd declared it.

'Sorry, I've just realised I haven't asked you a single question about yourself,' said Jack.

'A self-obsessed actor? Shocker,' I teased.

We both laughed, which felt nice. He was actually quite easy to talk to when he wasn't ranting at me about something.

'We're not all like that, you know.'

'If you say so.'

'What have you got against actors?'

'Nothing,' I said. 'I've never even met one before.'

'Well there's Tom,' he said.

'Oh, yeah.'

Obviously I could hardly start slagging off his friend, but I had the feeling that even Jack could see that Tom was exactly the sort of luvvie type that most people would find irritating. His cocky, resonant voice would ring out across the landing at all hours and his too-cool-for-school attitude meant that he appeared permanently aloof. I didn't suppose it was fair to tar all actors with the same brush, but Tom was all I had to go on.

'Tell me something about yourself, then,' said Jack, 'and I'll prove to you that I *can* actually be interested in other people.'

'Don't worry about it,' I replied, putting one of my earbuds in. 'There's nothing much to tell.'

'Well, what's your job?' he asked, obviously feeling bad. 'That's a good place to start.'

'I work for a marketing company,' I said. 'In the city. See? Bet you wished you hadn't asked.'

He made a big show of looking impressed. 'No, not at all. I've always thought that world sounds very glamorous. Are you always out wining and dining clients over boozy lunches at The Chiltern Firehouse?'

'I think those days are long gone, sadly,' I replied. 'Although there is this bar downstairs from work where we sometimes take clients. It's not at all fancy, but it can be boozy.'

'I knew it!' he said. 'See, you get to do normal things like spend your lunch hours drinking and your afternoons gossiping with people by the water cooler. Now I'm insanely jealous of you.'

'Yeah, but you're doing something you love, so there's that.'

He shrugged. 'Swings and roundabouts, eh?'

I smiled at him, thinking I might have been wrong about him. He didn't appear to be quite as full of himself as I'd thought. 'Well. Better get going,' I said, 'or else I'm going to talk myself out of this run.'

'You don't go out on the heath too late, do you?' he asked, looking worried. 'Only it's getting dark already.'

'I stick to the residential streets in the evenings, mainly. Might go up to Highgate Village, do a bit of a circuit through Archway, come back up by the Royal Free.'

'Impressive,' he said. 'You're well into your exercise, aren't you?'

Dan had said the same thing. It annoyed him, he said once; accused me of being obsessed with running. It wasn't that I was a health freak or anything. It was just that when my heart was pumping, when sweat was pouring down my back, I felt alive and I felt in control and I felt as though I could achieve anything I wanted to achieve. I didn't often feel those things when I was just on my own doing nothing. Those were the worst times; when it was quiet and I'd do the same old replaying of stuff in my head.

'That wasn't a criticism, by the way,' Jack added quickly, as though he could read my mind. 'I meant it as a compliment.'

'Thanks,' I said, not sure how to take it.

'I appreciate you dropping this in,' he said, tapping his fingers on the package.

I nodded and turned to jog down the stairs, not looking back, although I guessed Jack was still standing there because I hadn't heard his door shut. Between the first and second floors, I bumped into Clive, who was struggling up the stairs with a shopping bag in each hand.

I whipped my earpods out. 'Are you OK there, Clive?' I asked.

He looked up, out of breath. 'That bloody lift is out of service again,' he said. I detected a wheeze in his voice.

'Here. Let me take these bags up for you,' I said.

'You can't manage them,' he said.

'Course I can. Come on, hand them over.'

Once his hands were free, he grabbed hold of the banister, hauling himself up the stairs behind me. I walked slowly so as not to make him feel as though he had to rush to keep up with me, and also because the bags were actually really heavy – I had no idea how he'd made it down from the village with them.

'You should get your groceries delivered, you know,' I suggested. 'I can set it up for you if you like? Have you got a PC or a laptop?'

'No, but I have got a smartphone,' he said, his voice still strained. 'Will that do?'

I waited for him on his floor. 'Yes, that's perfect. Shall I pop in later this week, show you how to do it?'

He smiled at me, rubbing my arm. 'I'd like that, thank you, Rebecca.'

'Want me to take these inside for you?' I asked, pointing at the shopping.

'No, no, you leave them here on the doorstep. I can see you're on your way out, I don't want to keep you.'

I hesitated. 'You're sure you can manage?'

He waved me off. 'I'll be fine. You go and enjoy yourself now.'

'I'm going for a run, Clive. Hardly riveting. But thanks,' I said, starting off down the stairs again.

I looked up to see him bending down, hooking the handle of a bag over one frail wrist, bracing himself on the door frame just so that he could straighten up again. I had a mixture of emotions when I saw elderly people. I used to feel resentful sometimes, that they'd lived to be eighty or ninety and other people hadn't. But the older I got myself, the less I felt like that. In fact, I looked up to these people who had survived a whole lifetime and had lived through events that we could only imagine and continued on in spite of it all.

Outside, it had started raining, but not badly enough to give me an excuse not to go. I pulled up my hood and set off at a slow jog, warming up my limbs. I couldn't stop thinking about Clive, hoping he was managing on his own, wondering whether I should have helped him unpack his bags. Next time I was at Greenhill Lodge, I'd pick him up a brochure. I knew the older generation found it hard to have to give up their independence, their homes, but he might like it there, hosting poker nights in the games room, or whatever. Getting involved with all the activities. And Nan would love him.

February

14

Jack

I popped into Le Pain Quotidien on the corner and treated myself to two chocolate croissants. I clearly wasn't going to get a Tom Hardy-esque body if I kept eating like this, but it was one of those days when I thought: *Fuck it, I need junk food.*

Just as I'd stuffed a fistful of flaky pastry into my mouth, my phone rang. I chewed manically, wiping my hands on my jeans.

'Hello?' I said, swallowing hard because it was Chad calling and that could only mean one thing, surely. Good news. Otherwise why would he bother? He didn't usually.

'Jack, it's Chad. I got your voicemail.'

'Yeah?'

'And your emails.'

I winced. 'OK. Yeah, I just … I thought it went really well at the casting and I was just wondering whether I—'

'You didn't get a recall.'

I stopped dead, right there in the street. 'What?'

Chad was doing that thing where he was typing an email to somebody else at the same time as having a conversation with me. I knew that whatever I said, he'd only be half listening.

'What did they say?' I asked.

It was always best to know, that was my policy. However hard it was to hear at the time, however demoralising, you might be able to take something away from it. All that learning lines and staying up to think about character and rewatching endless hours of Middle-East-set dramas wouldn't have been for nothing.

'They said they really liked you and thought you did an excellent job with the script, but they went with a name in the end. They're going to keep you in mind for something else.'

I pinched the top of my nose. 'So that's it, then?'

'No need to sound so miserable, Jack. I think it all sounds very positive.'

This was not Chad trying to soften the blow, this was him trying to get out of having a maudlin conversation with me about why my career had stalled. Not once had he ever been sympathetic or kind or any of the other things I'd naively thought a theatrical agent might be.

'I'm getting a bit desperate here, Chad, to tell you the truth.'

'Sorry, Jack, I've got another call coming through. I'll let you know when something else comes in,' he said, hanging up.

I stared at my phone, gripping it hard, feeling so badly like launching it onto the pavement and smashing it into a million pieces. Fuck Chad. Maybe I needed a new agent, how about that? Somebody who actually thought I was worth fighting for. And fuck Lightning Productions, too. Why hadn't they just offered it to a big name in the first place, then, and saved everyone else the trouble of believing they were actually in with a chance?

I chucked my croissants in the nearest bin, I couldn't stomach them now, and carried on up the hill, slightly bent at the waist, like I was battling my way through a storm. What I really wanted to do was turn around and go home, drink a bottle of wine, even if it was only five o'clock in the afternoon, and fall asleep on the sofa with *The Chase* on in the background.

When I got to the pub ten minutes later, I was feeling even worse if anything. The whole way there, I'd been replaying the audition in my mind. Deconstructing everything I'd said, every comment they'd made. Mumbling the lines – which I still remembered and would for a while – under my breath, imagining how they'd come out, whether I should have done them differently, whether that might have made them want to take a chance on someone like me.

'You're two minutes late, mate!' said Luke as I pushed through the door, which felt like a huge effort for some reason.

'Whatever,' I replied, avoiding looking him in the eye. I couldn't deal with his ridiculous manager routine today.

Keeping my head down, I went straight to the staffroom, dumped my stuff, took a swig of my water and tried to pull myself together. How was I going to get through my shift if I could barely muster the energy to speak? It was going to be a nightmare.

I took a deep breath and went out to the bar. Luke was opening a bottle of wine, looking sheepish.

'I was only joking,' he said.

I shrugged, taking my place at the bar. It was filling up already, what with it being a Friday evening. Staff from the hospital, teachers from the schools. The locals came later – the couples from the Victorian conversions that surrounded the pub who earned god knows how much even though they were probably younger than I was.

'Everything all right?' asked Luke, sliding over. 'You seem a little … upset.'

I still couldn't look at him. I had that dead-inside feeling that was all too familiar. 'I didn't get that Netflix series.'

Luke sighed. 'Shit. Sorry about that. I know you thought it went well.'

'It did go well. But, as usual, they've gone for someone who already has an amazing career going on. A "name", they call it.'

'Do you know who?'

I shook my head. 'Richard Madden probably. He's in everything at the moment. I suppose they think it'll be a guaranteed hit with him attached to it.'

Luke had seen me like this loads of times. He was actually the one person I didn't have to pretend to be all right in front of.

'You'll feel better in a few days,' said Luke. 'I know it's tough now, but you'll pick yourself up, do another casting, get another job. You always do.'

'I know,' I replied. 'It's just that you take the time to live with these characters, and almost become them in your head. And then, when you don't get a chance to actually play that part … it feels like a kind of grief in a way. I know that sounds pretentious, but that's how it is.'

Luke poured me a sneaky whisky and slid it to me under the bar. 'Get that down you,' he said.

I knocked it back before anyone saw.

'Thanks for not thinking I'm pathetic,' I said to him.

Luke patted my back reassuringly. 'Never, mate. I can't pretend to understand, not really, but the whole acting world feels messed up to me. At least you're putting yourself out there in the first place.'

And I, for possibly the first time, felt a pang of envy for

Luke's simple life. For his lack of ambition, for the happiness he gleaned from being duty manager of a pub, for his loved-up life with his childhood sweetheart of a girlfriend.

It was gone ten when she came in, the girl with the red jumper and the dangly earrings. She was with a couple of friends, sat at the corner table drinking JD and Cokes. She made a beeline for me when she came to get their third round. I hoped she wasn't going to make me talk, because although I felt marginally better, I wasn't up for anything more than very basic conversation.

'Hiya,' she said, all chirpy. She had a northern accent; Manchester, maybe.

'What can I get you?' I asked, keeping it professional.

Under normal circumstances, it tended to make your shift go faster if you chatted to the patrons. Not if they were too drunk, though, because then they'd go on and on and you'd have to pretend to go and change a barrel or something just to get away. But I'd met some nice people at work. People who were easier to talk to and seemingly more interested in my life than my actual blood relatives were.

'Can you do cocktails?' she asked.

'Um, yeah,' I said, thinking: *Please don't order cocktails.* They required the kind of effort and panache that I did not possess this evening.

'In that case, three Cosmopolitans, please,' she said in an annoyingly cheerful manner, as though she thought she was doing me a favour.

I smiled tightly.

It took me ages to find the cocktail shaker, that's how rarely we used it.

'Do you work here a lot, then?' she asked, leaning on the bar.

'Um, now and again,' I replied, glancing up.

'What else do you do?'

I poured six double shots of vodka into the shaker. 'I'm an actor,' I said.

Her face lit up. 'Nice! Would I have seen you in anything?'

I nearly said: I don't know, would you?

'Not sure,' I said. 'Possibly not, unless you go to the theatre a lot. Or you're a *Holby City* superfan and have watched the two episodes I happen to have been in.'

She screwed up her face. 'I'm a medical student, so that's the last thing I want to watch when I have time off. Also, it's not at all realistic.'

I chucked in a glug of cranberry juice. 'That's TV for you.'

'You look like an actor,' she said.

'What does an actor look like?'

'You know …'

I didn't.

'What's your name?' she asked.

'Jack.'

I chucked in the ice, closed the lid and began to shake. Everyone looked over, as though I was performing some kind of show. Doing a Tom Cruise in *Cocktail*. I felt pressure to chuck up the shaker and catch it behind my back or something.

'What's yours?' I asked, pouring the mixture evenly between three wine glasses. I couldn't be bothered to find proper cocktail ones.

'Ishanvi,' she said.

'Nice name,' I replied.

'It's Indian.'

I nodded, sliding her the drinks.

'What time do you finish?' she asked.

I looked at her. She was pretty. Tiny and fragile-looking,

with big eyes and lips painted ruby red to match her jumper.

'I'll be here until midnight,' I said.

She picked up all three drinks, the stems slotting between her fingers. 'If I'm still around, we should do something after,' she suggested. 'If you want.'

I hesitated. I was desperate to get home so I could wallow in self-pity and chuck a Tesco Value pizza in the oven. But then again, here she was, giving me another option. Was there a chance that hooking up with someone I didn't know might help me forget about my shitty acting career for a minute, possibly longer?

'Maybe,' I said, non-committally.

One-night stands were fine; it was all the other stuff I couldn't be bothered to get into.

Later, me and Ishanvi walked through the backstreets of the village together, past the Anglican church on Downshire Hill, and the huge Freemasons Arms pub, which had just closed for the night, too.

'You must be doing all right to live around here,' remarked Ishanvi, seemingly impressed.

'It's only temporary,' I replied, pulling my scarf tighter around my neck.

'Still,' she said.

'Yeah. Still.'

We turned left up East Heath Road. I pointed out the pond glittering in the moonlight; she said it looked romantic.

'Are you all right with this?' I asked her.

'All right with what?'

This was the awkward bit. I should probably have said all of this when we were still at the pub, so she'd have had the option to say no and go back to her friends.

'With this just being one night,' I said.

I knew it wasn't generally what women wanted to hear, but I'd always thought it was best to be honest from the start. To not mislead anyone.

She laughed. 'Why wouldn't I be?'

'So you don't mind, then?' I asked, surprised.

'Nope,' she said, looking up at me. She was at least a foot shorter than I was. 'Do you know how many hours us student doctors have to work?'

'So you don't have time for relationships either, is that what you're saying?'

'Yes, Jack, that's exactly what I'm saying.'

'Phew,' I said, laughing lightly, relieved.

She reached for my hand and squeezed it. 'You're a strange one, aren't you?'

I decided she meant strange in a nice way and took it as a compliment.

15

Rebecca

It was half-twelve and I was still up, not at all tired and enjoying the Negroni I'd made for myself. I was perfecting the recipe before I offered it to anyone else and reckoned I'd nailed it on the second attempt, having achieved the perfect ratio of Campari to Martini Rosso to gin. I'd watched TV and listened to music for a bit and I'd had a nice bath, but mostly I'd laid on my sofa and looked out of the window. People were beginning to go to bed, and one after the other I watched lounge lights switch off and imagined bedside lamps being flicked on. The couple diagonally opposite were up, I'd just seen her smoking a cigarette out of the window. The guy in the apartment one floor below them had his laptop open and kept stopping what he was doing to take a swig from what looked like a bottle of beer. I'd often wondered what he did; he was always out before I got up and home before I got in. At weekends, he disappeared altogether.

When I went to wash up my glass, I heard voices. A man and a woman with a sunny, young-sounding voice. I plastered my cheek to my front door, being as quiet as I could. It took me a few seconds to make anything out, and I smeared my thumb across the spyhole because I could barely see out of it and then realised it was dirty on the other side.

Jack was outside. I could see the top of his head, and his

shaggy brown hair and the bridge of his nose. His back was pressed up against his door, his head was bent and tilted to the side and he was kissing someone. I could only see the back of her head – she was tiny and was wearing a black puffa jacket with a red scarf. Jack had his hands cupped around her face, his fingers laced through her long, black hair.

I took a step back from the door. I could hear them, still – she was moaning loudly (which I thought was a bit unnecessary given she was in a public place), but he was silent except for the sound of him fishing about for his keys.

I let myself have one last look. They'd switched around now and she had her back against the door. She was standing on tiptoes and had her hands hooked around his neck. He had a hoodie on, one I'd seen him in before; it was a bit too short for him, as though it had shrunk in the wash. His jeans were sitting low on his hips. He had one hand on her waist, and his key was in the other. Why didn't he just hurry up and let them in for god's sake, instead of making a scene on the landing?

I dragged myself away, even though part of me wanted to keep watching. Was this what my life had become: sneakily observing the sex lives of my neighbours?

My glass slipped out of my hand, crashing into the sink. I froze for a second or two, hoping Jack hadn't heard, which he feasibly could have done if he was still in his hallway. I reassured myself that he was probably far too caught up in what he was doing to notice.

Already regretting drinking this late at night, thinking that it wasn't going to do my running any good if I kept having hangovers and sacking it off, I poured myself a glass of water.

I couldn't resist one more glance through the spyhole on the way back to the lounge, just out of interest, of course. The door was closed and there was no one to be seen. I could hear music, though, and could just about make out the familiar chords of Massive Attack's 'Unfinished Sympathy'. He had decent taste in music, then, not that it mattered. I wondered if she was his girlfriend, although I'd never seen her before. I wasn't sure how he'd find time to have a relationship, given he was allegedly out all the time. Perhaps now he'd be in to receive his packages instead of expecting everyone else to do it for him.

Back in the lounge, I picked up my phone. Tyler had been back in New York over a week and we'd barely been in contact, which, of course, was what I'd wanted all along and yet somehow, tonight, I thought it might have been quite nice to know he'd been thinking about me. I'd texted him to see how his flight had been and he'd replied to say New York was freezing; that he'd enjoyed his trip to London, that he'd see me next time. But there had been no mention of when the next time might be.

My thumb hovered over the open message key. Should I contact him? Was I only tempted because I felt a bit lonely, suddenly? Although, rationally, I knew that I had no right to feel sorry for myself when there were millions of other people in the world who didn't have anyone either. It was just that when Dan had gone, it had felt doubly bad, because I'd naively assumed he was the one person who could be relied upon not to leave me. Just shows you, you can never really know someone, can you?

I flicked through my phone contacts, pausing when I got to the 'D's. I hadn't spoken to Dan for months and had unfriended him on Facebook so that I didn't have to be subjected to photos of him having a whale of a time with his new girlfriend, a woman from his office who I'd met twice and had foolishly thought was lovely.

Worried I was about to do something stupid, I texted Val instead. She was one of those people who went to bed late and got up early and was fully functioning no matter how little sleep she'd had. She rarely called it a night before 1 a.m., which I'd always thought would be a brilliant way to get things done. All those extra hours! She read at least a book a week and had memorised the most film trivia of anyone I knew.

Are you still up?

I pressed send and waited, looking out at the flats opposite. Almost every window was in darkness now, except for one on the second floor. I thought students might live there; I'd seen three or four young guys coming in and out, wearing V-neck jumpers and Eastpak backpacks, which seemed to be prerequisites for students studying in London.

My phone rang.

'What are you doing up?' said Val.

'Watching *Real Housewives of Beverly Hills* on loop. You?'

'Had a late dinner. Started a film but didn't finish it. Ekon's knackered, so he's gone to bed, but I'm not tired yet.'

'You must have too much going on in that head of yours,' I replied.

I wondered whether part of Val's inability to sleep was about her not being able to switch off. She seemed to think she could solve the problems of the world at two o'clock in the morning.

'Yeah. Maybe,' she said.

I curled my feet up underneath me.

'You OK?' I asked.

She didn't sound her usual upbeat self, although, given the time, I supposed it was hardly surprising. I didn't think

I'd ever spoken to her on the phone this late before, not because she wasn't up, but because I wasn't.

'Just tired,' she said.

I frowned. 'But you said you weren't tired a second ago.'

'Oh, I don't know then,' she muttered.

I undid the strap of my watch, putting it on the coffee table.

'You sound a bit flat, Val?'

I heard rustling her end, which I thought was probably her closing the gorgeous teal velvet curtains she had in her lounge. I loved her house; it was vibrant and warm and colourful, just like she was. If my flat was a reflection of my personality, I dreaded to think what would it say about me. It still felt half empty, I thought, or half full, depending on which way you looked at it, I supposed. In the summer, the whiteness of the walls and the lack of clutter had made it feel cool and clean and I'd convinced myself I liked it like that. But now it was winter again, I felt as though it didn't give a sense of who I was, the things I was into, or even the person I wanted to be. I was stuck in the past, which was pretty much how I felt all round.

'I'm fine, Becs, honestly. I'd tell you if I wasn't, wouldn't I?'

I wasn't convinced, but she clearly didn't want me to push the point, so I backed off.

'So the reason I texted you was that I was about to message Dan and wanted you to tell me not to,' I said.

'Absolutely do not text Dan. No good can come of it.'

'Would there really be any harm in it, though? You know, a casual *how's things?*'

I heard Val take a drink of something. 'What would be the point, though? You don't want him thinking you're still pining for him, which I don't think you are, anyway, judging by your recent dalliance with a certain shiny American?'

I took my earrings out and put them next to my watch.

'Do you think he misses me?'

'Probably. Let him.'

'Yeah,' I said, inspecting the badly applied red varnish on my toes. 'He's probably out with her anyway, isn't he? He'll have taken her to some romantic, luxurious restaurant in town, all expenses paid.'

'He was never one to splash money around, from what I remember,' remarked Val.

'He might be different with her,' I said.

I heard the front door slam downstairs and wondered who was coming in this late and thought it was probably the girl on the top floor whose name I couldn't remember and who was a nurse and worked all hours.

'I mean, maybe it's time to close that door for good now, Becs,' said Val tentatively.

She knew how hard it had been for me, but she also knew that tonight was just a blip, that usually I was fine without him.

'I'm trying,' I replied.

'I know you are.'

'Anyway, I'll let you get some sleep,' I said.

'Yeah. I should probably try,' said Val. 'We're off to Ekon's parents for the weekend. I'll have to do non-stop talking for forty-eight hours.'

'And that's a problem for you because …?' I joked.

We said goodbye and then I turned my phone off and hid it under a cushion to avoid doing anything stupid in a moment of madness.

When I went to get another glass of water from the kitchen, I could still hear music coming from Jack's. Lately, strangely, I'd been consoling myself with the fact that he was spending every night on his own, too, and that he seemed perfectly happy about it. But not even he was alone tonight.

16

Jack

I should have got off at Waterloo, it would have been quicker in hindsight. Instead, I was having to leg it over the bridge at Embankment, my head down, barely noticing the view, the London Eye spinning on its axis to my right, the buses sliding back and forth across Waterloo Bridge to my left.

I charged down the steps on the other side, hugging the river as I ran past Giraffe and the Royal Festival Hall. The National Theatre on the South Bank was one of my favourite places in the world. I'd hung out here when I was a kid, when, admittedly, I'd been slightly more interested in the skatepark under the arches, but I'd always been fascinated by this great big hulk of a seventies building and the enticing posters I'd seen outside, inviting you to go and see performances of *Hamlet* or *The Cherry Tree* or some mysterious-sounding Greek tragedy.

I popped open the buttons of my coat, wondering if I ought to have worn something smarter than the black T-shirt and grey hoodie combo I had on. In my defence, I'd come straight from the pub. The thing was, I knew my brother would be in one of his sharp work suits and that everyone would think I looked a state in comparison, but that just wasn't my style and they'd have to take me as I'd come.

Following signs for the Olivier Theatre, I flicked my wrist to check my watch: 7.25. I'd made it. Just.

I showed the usher my ticket and she directed me to a seat near the front, two rows back and right in the middle. Dom clearly hadn't skimped on seats, they must be the most expensive in the house, but then my brother didn't do things by half.

I walked down the steps of the aisle, breathing in the atmosphere, wishing I was behind the curtain waiting to go on stage instead of in the audience. I loved peering out at the auditorium just before the curtain went up. The clinking of glasses, the smell of the glossy pages of the programmes, the hushed chatter. Now I got a waft of expensive perfume as I made my way to the front. I hoped nobody would notice I had my oldest trainers on.

Mum spotted me and started waving frantically. I half waved back, saying 'excuse me' to the stuck-up couple sitting on the end of the row who gave me daggers, as though I'd suggested they kill someone when I asked if I could please get past.

'Sorry,' I mumbled reluctantly, squeezing past their knees.

I made it to my seat next to Dom, who, of course, was all suited up and smarmily holding a glass of champagne, smirking at me.

'You made it, then,' he said.

'Sorry, yeah. I was working,' I replied, unravelling my scarf, stuffing everything under my seat, wishing to god I'd had time to get a drink. I grabbed Dom's out of his hand and took a massive mouthful before he could protest. 'Hi, Mum,' I whispered, leaning forward. 'Happy birthday.'

'We didn't think you were going to make it,' she hissed.

I grimaced and apologised for about the fifth time in sixty seconds.

My dad nodded briefly in my direction and then pretended to be mesmerised by the stage with absolutely nobody on it. I didn't bother trying to get any more out of him, he'd only ignore me to make a point. I supposed I was going to get a lecture in the interval.

The orchestra struck up and everyone shuffled in their seats, that wonderful loaded silence rippling through the audience.

At the interval, we traipsed out into the bar. Dad had pre-ordered drinks for everyone except me.

'I didn't know what you'd want,' he said, which was a lie, because he was really into his red wine and it had rubbed off on me and he knew it had.

I joined the massive queue for the bar, simmering with re-sentment and feeling like I'd pissed everyone off, which was how I always felt with my family anyway. By the time I'd been served, there were only about ten minutes left until the second half started. I rummaged in my coat, pulling out the present I'd wrapped at work in the post-lunchtime lull. I was pleased with myself because I'd popped into Waterstones on the high street and had bought a sheet of the world's most expensive wrapping paper. I thought the shimmery fern print elevated the gift, which in itself wasn't that impressive, but it was something I thought Mum would like.

'This is a surprise,' remarked Mum, putting her glass down on a nearby ledge and pulling ineffectively at the paper; I'd got carried away and had used too much Sellotape. When she finally prised it open, she smiled kindly at me. 'I've heard good things about this,' she said, turning over the latest Margaret Atwood and skimming the synopsis on the back. 'Thank you.'

I shrugged. 'Sorry it's not much.'

'Still skint, are you?' said Dom, ever tactful.

I should have thanked him for the tickets, but I couldn't bear the gushing from Mum and Dad that was bound to ensue if I mentioned it. Sure, he'd bought Mum tickets to see *Follies* – she loved musicals – and splashed his cash around as usual and his reputation as son-of-the-decade was fully intact. I just wasn't going to give him yet another chance to act out our tiresome family dynamic, starring Dom as the good boy and me as the bad. I'd text him later instead.

'Um, things are OK,' I said, not wanting to give him the pleasure of gloating about how much money he earned and how little I did. Although I'd rather be skint and happy any day, doing what I loved rather than stuck in a soulless office surrounded by wankers and piles of boring legal papers. Nobody ever seemed to mention the fact that he'd once announced he'd rather die than do corporate law, but that that was precisely what he'd ended up doing. 'How's things with you?' I asked him. 'Work OK?'

'Busy,' he replied, stuffing a handful of pistachio nuts into his mouth.

'Any interesting cases?' I asked, pretty convinced that there wouldn't be. His job didn't make for the most riveting anecdotes.

'Really important case,' he said, chomping loudly. 'It's been all over the press, you've probably heard about it. Big firm in the City being sued by the family of one of their employees after he topped himself in his lunch hour.'

'Jesus,' I said, gulping at my wine. I looked over my shoulder at the queue – I might have to get another to take in with me.

'What do you make of the show?' piped up Dad. 'What's your expert opinion, then?'

'It's a very slick production,' I commented. 'They must have had a massive budget. The size of the cast!'

'Do you remember when you were on stage here once, Jack?' said Mum. 'Shakespeare, wasn't it?'

I nodded, thinking wistfully back to the first big thing I'd been cast in when I'd left drama school. It had been the most exciting experience of my life. Getting ready in the backstage warren of dressing rooms. Hearing the names of famous actors being called to the stage. Hanging out in the bar afterwards. I'd thought that had been the start of something really, really big, but instead, my role at the National Theatre seven years ago was possibly still the most impressive thing on my CV.

'I don't remember that,' said Dad.

'You didn't come and see it, that's why,' I said, trying not to sound bitter.

He'd been working late, apparently, and hadn't turned up; I still remembered it. And despite it being a three-month run, Dad hadn't found the time to come and watch me another time. It pretty much summed up our relationship, really.

'Got any acting work coming up, then?' asked Dad, flicking through the programme, only half listening.

He'd always hated me being into drama and acting. I'd once overheard him telling Mum that I was 'wet' and complaining about me not wanting to play football like Dom. At one point, he threatened to make me join the Army Cadets; I thought he was afraid for my masculinity, as though being an actor didn't match up to his neanderthal opinion of what a real man should be like. If earning loads of money in a job you hated, drinking excessively and spending the majority of your time schmoozing at the golf club were prerequisites for being a 'real man', I'd rather not bother.

'Things are going pretty well, actually,' I told him. 'I'm thinking of going to LA for a bit.' That wasn't strictly a lie – I was *thinking* about it.

Dom snorted into his drink. 'LA? What do you want to go there for?'

I looked at him in disbelief. What disparaging thing could he possibly have to say about that?

'It's where the big money is, isn't it?' I suggested, using a currency I knew they'd relate to. 'I'm doing a class at the Actors Centre later this month – they've got a casting director over from the States. You never know, do you?' I said, looking pointedly at Dom.

Sometimes I suspected that the tiniest, most hidden part of him was envious of my lifestyle, of my freedom to do whatever I wanted. When you didn't have any money to begin with, you couldn't be frightened of losing it. The opposite was true of Dom; he had it all: the six-figure salary, the doting girlfriend, the mortgage on a cool, industrial two-bed apartment in King's Cross. He had more to lose, but I wondered if he ever felt trapped. Whether there was part of him that might want some of what I had. If there was, he didn't show it.

'You're working at that pub full time now, are you?' asked Dad, smoothing down his tie.

'Not full time, no,' I said.

It might feel like I was sometimes, but no, I definitely wasn't.

The bell rang for the second half.

'Anyone want another drink?' I asked, hoping they'd say no, because then I'd have to bung it on my credit card.

'Get me another large glass of the Malbec, will you?' said Dad.

'Same,' piped Dom. 'Now where's the loo?'

'Mum?' I asked, biting my lip. I hoped my card went through, otherwise my humiliation for the evening would be complete.

'I'm fine,' she said, clutching the book to her chest. 'And thanks for this, it was very thoughtful of you.'

I kissed her on the cheek. 'Glad you've had a nice birthday.'

As the foyer emptied out and everyone took their seats, I dived over to the bar before they pulled the shutter down.

17

Rebecca

I pushed through the fogged-up glass doors of Bar Monaco, immediately slipping off my coat and draping it over my arm. It felt comfortingly familiar in here with the smell of sweet sticky cocktails that had been carelessly spilt on the floor and the baskets of salty frites everyone ordered for dinner because they were cheap and they couldn't be bothered to stop and eat something proper. I'd always thought of it as a sort of extension of the Kingsland Marketing staffroom and every time I stepped through the doors, I could guarantee there'd be someone I knew inside. I liked that. The idea that I had a local, that Bar Monaco was sort of my equivalent of the Queen Vic (usually without the massive rows and slipping-out of devastating family secrets).

'Becs!'

I spun around looking for Val, trying to place where her voice had come from. The wooden dance floor was already packed full with the usual hordes of City workers flailing their arms around, half-drunk pints of beer swinging precariously in their hands. There was always at least one smashed glass on the floor by the end of the evening and occasionally – just once or twice – it had been mine. Saying that, I tended to watch what I drank after work these days, mainly because I got slaughtered very easily if I hadn't eaten and, more often than not, made a complete fool of myself. By far the worst time had been the year I'd started at Kingsland, when I'd got off with a seventeen-year-old from goods-in and had been too embarrassed to go down for the post for weeks afterwards.

I finally spotted Val and the others waving frantically at me from across the room.

Twisting my body left and right to avoid bumping into anyone, I crossed the dance floor. Atomic Kitten's 'Whole Again' was blaring out from giant speakers; the one downside of this place was that the music was crap.

'Hi, everyone,' I said, approaching the table. 'Sorry I'm late. And happy birthday, Val!'

'Aaargh, you're freezing,' she said, laughing when I hugged her.

I pressed a present and a card into her hands. 'Here you go – just a little something. I meant to give it to you earlier, but I've been in meetings all day.'

We'd been buying each other birthday gifts for the last ten years, since we'd started our new jobs on the same day and had had to sit through an excruciatingly dull health and safety training session. We'd hit it off instantly, giving each other sneaky, bored eye-rolls like teenagers, her childlike exuberance an antidote to my more conscientious, less out-there personality. She brought out the fun in me and, according to her, I stopped her going completely mental. Not that she was like that so much these days. Marriage had calmed her down. I thought that's what probably happened when you hit your thirties and did the requisite 'settling down' thing. I wondered what happened to thirty-somethings who didn't 'settle down'. Should we carry on acting like we were twenty-five forevermore, going to clubs until the doorman told us we were too old to get in, the hangovers getting worse and worse with each decade that passed?

'God, I feel old,' groaned Val.

'You're a baby,' I replied, laughing.

'I'm thirty-four. Thirty bloody four,' said Val, squashing her cheeks dramatically between her hands.

I shook my head. 'Stop worrying, will you? You know you look about ten years younger than you actually are.'

Val sighed, slumping into her seat. 'I may look it, but I certainly don't feel it,' she said. 'Anyway, enough about me and my decrepit, aging body. Sit down, Becs, get a drink down you.'

Paul from Accounts moved up to make a space, patting the bench next to him. Great.

'Why are you so late, anyway?' asked Val.

'I had a press release to finish,' I explained, reluctantly taking a seat next to Paul.

'You work too hard,' said Val, tutting and turning my present on its side, shaking it next to her ear. 'If you don't get that promotion, it'll be a complete travesty. Oooh, what is it?'

'Nothing breakable, luckily.'

Paul pushed an empty wine glass in my direction, plucked a bottle of white from an ice bucket and poured me a glass. I liked the way this happened with ease and grace, everything moving into its proper place like a Viennese waltz.

Val ripped the wrapping paper open, barely registering the beautiful embossed design I'd spent ages choosing – it had little chandeliers on it, each one sparkly and rough when you ran your thumb across it. I was always touched when someone gave me a beautifully wrapped gift, or a card that had some sort of special significance. Val, on the other hand, couldn't have cared less about presentation and I might as well have wrapped it in plain, brown parcel paper.

'Oh my God, I love them,' shrieked Val, holding up the

Oliver Bonas 'V' charm necklace and palm-tree print scarf for everyone to coo over. 'Roll on summer!'

We hugged again and Paul tried to pour Val a glass of rosé, but she put her hand over the top of her glass.

'I'm fine,' she told him. 'I'm pacing myself.'

I gave her a funny look, making a mental note to ask her about it later. She wasn't usually one to hold back when it came to wine consumption, especially on her birthday.

'How's things?' asked Paul, his trouser leg scuffing against my thigh.

'Fine, thanks.'

'I heard a rumour about you,' said Paul, raking his fingers through his strangely voluminous head of hair.

I looked across at Val who was busy mauling another present, slicing open a box wrapped in red, shiny paper.

'Oh yeah? What's that then?' I replied.

He winked. 'Someone said they saw you and that wanky American CEO guy getting very cosy.'

I stared at Val, hoping she'd somehow pick up on the vibes that I needed her, but she was too busy with her present. I concentrated on remaining calm, on appearing nonplussed and talking in a very casual way, as though his comment meant nothing to me.

'That's the most ridiculous thing I've ever heard,' I said, carefully taking a sip of wine, resisting the urge to down it in one. 'Who on earth told you that?'

Paul smirked. 'Oh, I couldn't possibly reveal my source.'

I tutted. 'Well, whoever it was needs to get their facts straight. We're working together on a project, that's all.'

Paul reached for the wine bottle again and topped up my glass, slopping it over the rim so that it pooled on the table. He flicked at it with the edge of his hand, leaving a shiny smear.

'I've heard he's a massive player, just to warn you,' said Paul. 'Apparently you're not the only Kingsland employee he's been seen getting close to. Wouldn't want to see you get hurt or anything.'

I laughed airily. 'Course you wouldn't,' I said, knowing that nothing would give him more pleasure. I imagined that hearing rumours I'd been linked with one of the CEOs had been yet another devastating blow to his clearly very fragile ego.

'Just be careful,' warned Paul, swilling wine around his mouth before swallowing it so hard I saw his Adam's apple move.

It had rattled me, though, what he'd said about Tyler. I was aware that he was probably a player back in New York, but surely he wouldn't want the hassle of having two women on the go in the same company in London? I wanted to know who Paul was talking about, which other 'employee' he was referring to, but I was absolutely not going to give him the satisfaction of asking. Anyway, this was what I'd wanted, wasn't it, something casual? A fling with someone there was no danger of me actually falling for?

'What are you two whispering about?' asked Val loudly, her present-opening marathon clearly completed.

'Nothing much,' I said.

'Actually,' piped up Paul, 'we were talking about the rumours doing the rounds. About our Rebecca here and the George-Clooney lookalike from the New York office.'

Of course, the DJ had chosen that precise moment to cock up his set and in the second or so of silence, Paul's booming voice reached the other end of the table. The girls down there instantly perked up, looking at me like a magpie might eye up a piece of silver.

'Oh! I heard about that,' trilled Violet, the reception

manager. 'You were covering for Amanda when you met him at that posh hotel, weren't you?'

She was squeezed between Abi and Martine from Direct Marketing, the three of them looking all cliquey and brittle, poised delicately on the edge of their seats like exotic birds on the branch of a tree.

'On the pull at a work-related meeting, tut, tut,' said Paul.

'I wasn't on the pull,' I protested. 'I was extremely focused on my work, actually. It was a very stressful—'

'Are you seeing him, then?' screamed Martine, just in case the entire bar wanted to know about the whys and wherefores of my love life.

'No, I'm not *seeing* him,' I replied, convincing myself that it wasn't exactly a lie. God, this was awful.

'More wine, anyone?' asked Val, finally noticing I needed assistance.

Everyone nodded enthusiastically, moving – to my great relief – on to a different topic.

I escaped to the loos, wondering how word had got out already when we'd been so careful. To be honest, I wouldn't be surprised if Paul had started the rumour himself.

I locked myself in the cubicle, listening to the comings and goings in the bathrooms. As was always the case in Bar Monaco, it was the equivalent of the kitchen at a house party, the place where the most sensitive/interesting conversations happened under the cover of fluorescent lighting and the shimmer of Bayliss & Harding handwash. I was just about to flush the loo when I thought I heard my name. My hand dropped to my side.

'Amanda's got it in the bag, don't you think?' said a voice that sounded suspiciously like Violet's.

Working on reception was clearly the perfect job for her, since she was privy to everyone's business as well as their diaries and she used this knowledge to exert a sort of power over people. If you traced back any office gossip, it was almost guaranteed to have originated from Violet's desk.

'You don't think Rebecca's in with a chance?' That was Abi, her Liverpool accent was easy to identify.

I leaned against the door of the cubicle.

'No way,' said Violet with absolute conviction. 'She tries hard, though. She's always in the office, for a start, isn't she?'

Abi laughed. 'Hasn't she got much of a social life or something?'

I winced. Didn't they say that if you listened in on people talking about you, you were bound to hear something you wished you hadn't? But short of opening the door and confronting them, I was stuck in here, and they had no idea I could hear every single word they were saying.

'Well, her boyfriend dumped her, didn't he, so she's probably got nothing else to do?' replied Violet. 'I reckon she thinks the job's hers, but I've seen Amanda's presentation and it's *amazing*. Really exciting and dynamic and all of that.'

'Don't imagine Rebecca's will be anything out of the ordinary, do you?' said Abi.

'Rebecca's a grafter,' said Violet, 'but in my opinion, and obviously it's not up to me, but Amanda's got that special something. She'd bring something really different to the role, I reckon.'

I heard the hand dryers go on. Abi said something in reply, but her voice was drowned out by the roar of hot air. The door opened and creaked shut again and then there was silence.

I let myself out of the cubicle and looked in the mirror, wiping smudged liner from under my eye with my thumb. Was that really what people thought of me, that I was some lonely, pitiful spinster past her sell-by date? Anger swirled inside me as I washed my hands, ripping a paper towel out of the holder, then rolling it into a ball and lobbing it into the bin. Weirdly, the anger was more to do with their perception of me than it was about the prospect of me losing out on the job. I realised I didn't want it anyway. There: I'd said it. I did not want to be head of press and marketing at Kingsland Marketing, I wanted to do something with my life that would make me feel fulfilled, in a role where I could actually do something to make other people's lives better. Maybe I could work for a charity, or something like that? Mum had been a social worker, and a brilliant one, but I didn't think I could cope with that. I felt fired up, suddenly. I was going to start researching careers as soon as I got home. If only Abi and Violet knew that their bitchy gossiping session about me was exactly what I'd needed to hear.

18

Jack

I locked the front door behind me, crouching down to check the weather out of the stairwell window. It was grey and cloudy again, which wasn't unusual for late February, and at least it wasn't raining.

As I started down the stairs, I heard voices on the landing below.

'I'll pick it up on my way home from work,' I heard someone saying.

I thought it sounded like Rebecca.

'Although it won't be until seven-ish. Is that OK? It's not too late?'

'Whatever time you get home is fine. Don't be going out of your way for me, all right?' boomed Clive's voice. 'Promise me?'

I checked my watch, suddenly in a panic. No, I was all right, it was just gone 7.30 like I'd thought. It's just that I wasn't expecting to see so many people up and about this early. Saying that, I wasn't usually out of the flat at this time, myself – maybe it was always like this.

'Morning,' I said as I reached the bottom of the steps.

Rebecca turned around to look at me. She was wearing a satin shirt tucked into skinny trousers. The top few buttons had been left open, revealing quite a lot of skin given the weather; a smart red coat was slung over her arm. She had sparkly earrings on, little drops.

'You look nice,' I said.

'I've got a meeting at work,' she replied, looking a bit flustered. 'I don't usually get this dressed up.'

I laughed. 'You've got the power suit on.'

She smiled. 'Yeah, exactly.'

I looked down at my own clothes – black jeans and a grey sweatshirt – and wondered whether I should have made more of an effort, too. I wanted the casting director to notice me, didn't I, and so perhaps I should have thought a bit more about how to make an impact from the off? It was too late now; I'd just have to wow him with my acting skills instead.

'Where are you off to so early, young man?' asked Clive.

'I've got an acting class,' I said, my eyes flicking to Rebecca, who raised her eyebrows.

'Where's that, then?' she asked.

'The Actors Centre. It's in Covent Garden.'

She nodded. 'I think I've been past it. Near Seven Dials, isn't it?'

I got a little buzz from the fact she'd noticed it; I wasn't quite sure why.

'That's it,' I said. 'It's with some American guy who casts one of the big soaps over there.'

'Oh, right. What, would you move out there, then?' asked Rebecca, twiddling her earring between her finger and thumb.

I shrugged. 'I mean, I'd love to.'

'Don't you go leaving us already,' said Clive. 'You've only just got here!'

'I can pretty much guarantee I won't be going any time soon, Clive,' I replied, glancing at Rebecca. 'Anyway, I should go. Enjoy your meeting.'

Which was probably the wrong thing to say, because what could possibly be enjoyable about a work meeting?

I squeezed past her, carrying on down the stairs.

'Break a leg at your acting class,' shouted Clive, probably waking up half the neighbours, but it made me smile.

There was a layer of frost on the ground when I stepped outside. Traffic was already building up on East Heath Road with commuters making their way into town and mums in 4x4s taking their kids to whichever outrageously expensive private school they were at.

I cut down Well Walk, past the beautiful homes that were set back from the road, each of which must have been worth several million, their owners' Range Rovers parked in the narrow street outside, both sides, so that I imagined it must be impossible to drive along this road without scraping a really expensive vehicle. My favourite house was the one with the fenced-off roof terrace. I imagined myself up there, entertaining all my friends, soaking up the sun while reading my next brilliant script and fielding calls from Chad (or perhaps I'd have got myself a new agent). That's what life could be like if my class went well today. In a few months' time, I could be wandering through the streets of Beverly Hills, looking up at palm trees and blue skies instead of craggy treetops and near-freezing temperatures. I'd always thought I'd do better in LA. Even Chad had alluded to the fact I had a good look for the US market. Not that he'd ever done anything about it, mind you. You'd think he might have suggested I go out there if that was the case.

I ducked along Flask Walk, past the flower shop that was just opening up and the place selling antique bric-a-brac and turned right onto the high street for the tube, excited for what lay ahead.

*

Stuffing my script into my bag, I pushed through the glass door of the Actors Centre on Tower Street. I'd spent the walk up from Leicester Square tube mumbling the lines under my breath, only occasionally glancing down at the page, which I'd been organised enough to photocopy onto coloured paper at Snappy Snaps in the village because it helped with my dyslexia. I'd felt confident last night when I'd done a speed run in the shower, but now when I tried to remember them, I kept getting stuck on one (I thought not particularly well-written) line. Sometimes when I tried to work out the meaning of a line but couldn't because it made no sense, it was practically impossible for me to remember it. My brain just wouldn't take it in. I just had to hope that, by some miracle, it would all fall into place when I needed it.

I signed in and made my way to Studio 2, which was downstairs and through the bar. Actors were scattered everywhere, downing cappuccinos, sifting through head-shots, making important-looking phone calls in the corner. I shrugged off my coat, already too hot.

When I stepped through the doorway of Studio 2, the barrage of urgent whispers I'd heard from the hallway in-creased in volume. I felt a prickle of self-doubt; at least a couple of the guys had the kind of look that was perfect for American soaps, where handsome people had affairs with other incredibly attractive people and then it all went badly wrong. What I really wanted was to be cast in projects with integrity, work I really believed in. I could see myself in a Steve McQueen movie, for example, or a big-budget Emmy Award-winning drama like *Breaking Bad* or *Stranger Things*. Soaps weren't really my thing, but there was no way I could afford to be fussy.

'Jack!'

I looked up, scanning the row of seats running along the

far wall. It wasn't unusual to see someone I knew at these classes; often it was more fun that way. You had someone familiar to chat to at coffee time, for example. Occasionally, though, depending on who it was, my competitive streak kicked in and I spent the entire session comparing my feedback to theirs. No matter how many times I told myself this was pointless and destructive, it didn't seem to be a habit I could break.

'Over here!' said the voice.

My heart sank. Seb was sitting right at the end of the row and there was an empty seat next to him, which he was patting furiously. For god's sake. What was he doing here? He was like my shadow lately, going up for the same roles, the same classes.

'Hey!' I said, shuffling over.

I shoved my coat and bag under my seat and sat down with my script on my knee.

'Managed to get a day off from the pub, then?' asked Seb.

I noticed that his biceps were bulging out of the cap sleeve of his Breton-striped T-shirt. He must have been working out hard. I supposed he'd gone all 'LA' after his trip out there.

'Yep,' I replied lightly. 'Should be a nice change from pulling pints.'

'Who do you reckon we'll be paired up with?' asked Seb, leaning forward and scanning the row, no doubt working out which attractive but not-too-talented actress would be best placed to showcase his talents.

The piece we'd been given was an intimate scene between a husband and wife. The female character had just found out that her husband was having an affair with her best friend, and there was an intense soap-opera-style showdown.

'Not sure,' I said, disinterested.

Who my scene partner might be was the least of my worries. Why couldn't I remember that bloody fourth line?

The ripple of chatter and laughter subsided as a small man wearing a checked shirt and a cap bounded into view. Everyone stared at him, shifting in their seats with palpable anticipation. In the world of acting, casting directors pretty much had rock star status (and they knew it).

'Hey guys!' he said, pulling up a stool and leaping nimbly onto it. 'My name is Dax Delano and I am the associate casting director on *Days of Our Lives*.'

There was a chorus of half-hearted hellos.

'You all got the sides, right?' asked Dax.

Seb waved his script around enthusiastically, highlighting the fact that, yes, we were all indeed competent enough to open an email and print out a script for a class we'd paid to do.

Dax pulled the peak of his cap off his face. 'You'll come up, perform your scene in pairs, and I will give feedback. I'll then throw it open to the rest of the class. At the end of the session, I'll name two guys and two girls who, had this been a real audition situation in Los Angeles, I would have called back to read for the producers. Is that clear?'

Seb nudged me hard in the ribs. I wasn't sure whether this was a sign of solidarity or competitiveness, but either way I was pretty sure I'd have a bruise tomorrow.

'First up will be ... Imogen McKintree and Jack Maxwell.'

Typical. I hated going first and hadn't even had a chance to have one last surreptitious glance over the script.

'Let's get started, guys,' said Dax, sliding off his stool and taking a seat stage left.

I took a deep breath, shot up and took my place on the floor.

'First off, introduce yourselves,' instructed Dax. 'Let's find out a bit about who you are.'

Dax was in his thirties, short, unshaven and strangely pale, as though he never saw daylight. Not exactly the Hollywood look I'd expected.

My scene partner, Imogen, a plummy blonde wearing a pair of denim dungarees and bright yellow ballet pumps, was busy bigging herself up and I could tell from the credits she was dropping – *Sex Education*, *The Crown* – that she'd done a lot more TV than I had. That was supposed to be a good thing, according to my tutors at drama school. I should use her experience to enhance my own performance, let her push me to the next level.

Imogen finally stopped talking and everyone looked expectantly at me.

I rolled out my usual patter.

'Hi, everyone, I'm Jack Maxwell. I'm thirty and represented by Chad at Star Management. My credits include *Romeo and Juliet* at the National Theatre, *A Streetcar Named Desire* at the Donmar Warehouse and a guest-star role in *Holby City*, which is a British medical drama, in case you don't know it,' I said to Dax, hoping to dazzle him with my British charm.

'Great. Let's get going,' replied Dax, only looking semi-impressed. 'I know it's difficult going first, guys, but an audition situation would be even tougher. When you're ready.'

I turned to Imogen, who was already in character, or at least I hoped she was, as she was already looking moodily down at the floor. She lifted her head and caught my eye, her face twisted with disgust, her arms folded, her shoulders hunched, and then she flew at me with her first line before I'd even had a chance to think.

'*How could you do this to me, you bastard?*' she screeched through gritted teeth.

I remembered my character objective and came back at her with my line, hoping the work I'd done at home would shine through. At one point, though, I became aware of the audience in my peripheral vision, which was never a good sign; it meant I wasn't properly 'in the moment'. I also felt physically stuck, as though my feet were submerged in two feet of thick mud, and I seemed unable to do anything except just stand there while Imogen flew around me like a banshee, her arms outstretched, her mouth open wide like a chorister. She was dominating the scene, rushing through it like a bulldozer, crushing all the subtle moments I'd planned. At one point, Imogen grabbed me and I managed to push her backwards (not too hard, obviously), which I thought might have looked good, but, in truth, I was struggling to get a hold on it.

At the end, everyone clapped politely and, as I waited for my feedback, I noticed that I was slightly out of breath, which might convince everyone I'd really gone for it. It was one of those times I wished I could have said, stop, this is crap, I need to start again.

'OK. Imogen, great job,' enthused Dax. 'You started the scene with a strong objective and carried the intensity and energy through to the end of the scene. I like the moment when you grabbed him and I think perhaps you could have played the scene more physically all the way through. Jack ...' Dax pulled his cap over his eyes. 'There were some very nice moments.'

'OK ...' I said, waiting for the 'but.'

'You reacted well to Imogen. I got a definite sense of you trying to control the situation and shut her down and I could tell your backstory had been well developed. I think you could have moved more, made it more dynamic, you know? But good job.'

I listened intently, attempting to look grateful for the feedback.

'Anybody else have comments?' asked Dax.

An auburn-haired girl wearing rectangular glasses and a black polo neck stuck her hand up. Could she *try* any harder to look arty and serious?

'I think you were taken by surprise, Jack, at the beginning of the scene,' she said. 'It was like you weren't ready for it to start, and I actually saw you switch into character, which, I'll be honest with you, was a little off-putting.'

For fuck's sake. What happened to classmates being supportive?

'Anybody else feel that?' asked Dax, and I was pleased to note that most people either shrugged or shook their heads. 'Hope you found that useful, guys,' he said chirpily.

I nodded enthusiastically. 'Shall we go again?'

That was usually how classes worked – you did your scene, you got notes and then you had a chance to redeem yourself by doing a second run.

'No time, I'm afraid,' said Dax. 'We have a very full class today.'

I couldn't believe this. What was the point in giving us feedback if we couldn't use it to do a better job the second time around? Even in an actual audition – since that was seemingly what Dax was trying to replicate – they let you do it two or three times.

I sloped off back to my seat. My eyes felt wide and bright. I clearly hadn't done enough to make Dax want to cast me in *Days Of Our Lives* so that was one more avenue to success ruined.

'Good job,' said Seb as I sat back down.

I smiled tightly across at him, pretending I was too caught up in watching the next pair introduce themselves to

149

respond. It would have been marginally less humiliating if he hadn't been here to witness the whole thing.

Seb was last to be called and was paired with the annoying auburn-haired girl, who I secretly hoped was terrible. However, as soon as Seb and his partner, who was called Saoirse (of course she was) started the scene, it became apparent that she was, in fact, really good. And so, to my extreme irritation, was Seb. The scene played out completely differently from the others: more intense, less shouty. They were reacting and not acting, as my acting tutor at LAMDA had repeated over and over again. At the end of their scene, they actually got full-on applause and even I had to join in.

'At last!' boomed Dax, jumping up and joining them on the stage. 'Someone has taken a risk and it has totally paid off. Great job, guys. Powerful, subtle, perfectly pitched for television. I loved it. What did everyone else think?'

Shouts of 'excellent' and 'moving' rang out.

I felt like there was a hole where my stomach should be. I was used to being the best in my year at drama school and now suddenly I wasn't even the best of a group of twelve. I didn't know what had changed. I thought it might be the fact that I'd been acting (or doing voice or movement or singing or whatever) all day, every day for three years at drama school. I'd been at the top of my game, totally focused with absolutely no distractions. I'd done a few shifts a week in a nearby pub, but other than that I'd lived and breathed acting. As time went on, I felt less and less 'ready'. There was such a long gap between auditions that I often felt rusty. I'd do classes every day if I could, but, of course, they all cost money that I just didn't have and now it seemed as if I was just getting further and further from my dream.

'I didn't think it was that good, did you?' said the girl next to me snippily.

I shrugged, resisting the urge to bitch just because I was insanely jealous. Anyway, there was nothing negative to say. It had been great, and that was the end of it.

When Seb came back, I said, 'Excellent, mate' and he gave me the smug, knowing smile I'd seen myriad times before.

I sighed, watching Dax drag his stool centre stage and leap onto it again.

'Nice job, all of you,' he began, looking at his watch as though he couldn't wait to leave. 'Some of you are almost there; some of you have a lot of work to do. But the four people who impressed me most, and who would be getting a call-back are Seb, Saoirse, Imogen and Isaiah.'

The four chosen ones beamed. I clapped reluctantly.

'Oh, and if I was feeling generous, also Jack Maxwell.'

Generosity or not, I perked up, my heart pumping. I hadn't completely fucked it up then. My mind began ticking over. At the end of the session, I'd cruise casually past and ask for his card. Then I'd get Chad to drop him a follow-up email; maybe we could even arrange a trip to LA. Things were suddenly looking up.

19

Rebecca

Holborn tube was closed due to overcrowding and so when I saw a number 168 bus trundling up Kingsway, I jumped on it without hesitation. It was raining, so I'd rather be on a rammed bus than waiting in the cold and wet, even it was travelling agonisingly slowly.

I found a window seat on the top deck and got out my phone, flicking through it absent-mindedly. The bus juddered on, stopping and starting, stopping and starting. I smeared my hand across the fogged-up window so I could see out. It was tipping it down now, puddles already forming in the dips in the roads, car wheels churning up water, commuters dashing across the road, headlights flaring. I rested my head against the window, watching sparkling raindrops run down the pane.

We pulled into the concrete plaza otherwise known as Euston Station, which looked bleaker than ever tonight. When I looked down, there was a sea of umbrellas bobbing about on the pavement. The driver made an announcement that there were seats free upstairs, which meant that downstairs it was heaving. Sure enough, up piled about thirty soaking-wet passengers, the largest of whom – a six-foot-something guy in an enormous puffa jacket – threw himself down next to me, almost bouncing me off my seat. His drenched sleeve pressed against my elbow and I shimmied as far as I could to the right, attempting to get away from his soggy, quilted polyester, but to no avail.

Since the journey was already pretty unpleasant, for some bizarre reason I thought I'd add insult to injury by looking back at my last few message exchanges with Dan. It had been over a year now since he'd moved out, but I hadn't forgotten anything about the moment it happened. It kept playing over and over again in my mind. I wanted to learn from it or, more precisely, make sure it never happened again.

I'd been home from work nearly an hour that evening in December and had been in the kitchen when he arrived home. He'd texted to say he was running late, and so I'd lit a candle, opened a bottle of wine and had laid out two glasses on the coffee table in the lounge. He could get tetchy after a long day in the office, a City job that made him quite a lot of money but not one of those massive six-figure sums you read about. He drove a BMW and he wore nice suits and he'd treated me to a couple of city breaks. Rome had been lovely, and Seville the summer before. He was – in some ways – a proper grown-up; a 'real man' as my Aunty Carol had once described him. As opposed to what, I'd always been tempted to ask her?

He'd let himself through the door, looking paler than usual, his face all drawn, and I'd thought it must just be because he was exhausted. He kissed me like he always did and I pulled him close to me.

'Everything OK?' I asked, looking into his eyes.

He nodded, shifting his gaze to the chopping board.

'Homemade moussaka and salad,' I said, waving my hand at the aubergines on the chopping board. I was making an effort to cook more and was starting to quite enjoy it.

'There's wine open in the lounge. Looks like you could do with a glass.'

'Can we talk, Becs?' he said.

I picked up a tea towel to wipe my hands.

'Sure,' I said. 'But then I need to get the cheese sauce on.'

He took my hand and led me into the lounge, kicking off his shoes. His coat was still on, which seemed odd, as though he wasn't planning to stay.

We sat on the sofa and I started to feel a bit sick. I got the overwhelming sense that whatever he was about to say, it wasn't going to be good. He kept hold of my hand and put it on his knee, placing both of his hands over it. Was it something to do with work? Had he been fired? Made redundant? He'd said they were having to get rid of people. Whatever it was, we'd cope. I could cover the rent for a bit, just about, he didn't need to be worried about telling me.

'What is it?' I asked him gently.

He hung his head. 'I don't know how to say this.'

'Tell me.'

He pulled his hands away, raking them through his hair. 'You know Karen?'

'Yes.'

Karen was his new-ish work colleague. They'd clashed at first, but then they'd had a couple of work nights out and he'd said she wasn't as bad as he'd first thought. I'd met her myself – once when I popped into the office to drop off some papers we needed to sign to secure the flat and once at somebody's birthday drinks. She was Australian – sporty-looking, confident. I'd warmed to her immediately.

'What about her?' I asked him.

A light popped on in the apartment opposite. The guy who lived there had just got in from work. I watched him take his jacket off, turn on the TV.

'I've been talking to her a bit recently,' said Dan.

I laughed, I didn't know why. Nerves, I supposed.

'We've been going out for lunch a bit. Spending some time together.'

I poured us both a glass of wine, noticing how my hand was shaking so much I slopped it over the side. 'And?'

He groaned. 'I feel so fucking bad about all of this, Becs, honestly I do.'

I looked up at the ceiling, willing myself not to cry because I knew what was coming, of course I did. 'Bad about what, Dan?'

'We slept together. Twice. And it's not just sex, Becs. I really like her.'

I felt a sort of dull thudding inside my chest. When I swallowed it was so loud, I thought he must have heard it.

'Right,' I said, my voice barely more than a whisper.

'And the thing is, it's come out of the blue. I wasn't looking for anything like that. I was happy here, with you, Becs.'

I threw the tea towel I was still clutching across the room and stood up.

'So what changed?' I said, raising my voice. 'Did you get bored of me, was that it? You could have talked to me about it, Dan. It's not easy, is it, when you've been together as long as we have. The excitement goes, I get that.'

'It didn't, though,' protested Dan in a wobbly voice. 'I never thought that, not until I met Karen.' He started crying, then, his shoulders shaking. 'The last thing I wanted to do was hurt you, after everything you've been through.'

I went over to the window, looking out at the view I loved so much, wondering what would become of the life I'd started to build for myself here. In actual fact, I couldn't imagine my life without Dan in it at all. Sixteen years we'd spent together and he was throwing it all away for a woman he'd known a matter of weeks.

'What does she give you that I don't then?'

He shook his head. 'Don't do this.'

'I want to know,' I demanded.

He put his head in his hands. 'She's ... uncomplicated, I suppose. Easy-going. Fun. Open about her feelings. I've never had that before. I thought that the way we were – you and I – not talking about anything, burying everything under the carpet, was normal. But it's not, Becs, or at least it's not normal for me. I don't want to live like that anymore.'

I wiped my nose on my sleeve, determined not to let him see how much he'd hurt me.

'So you're going to leave me, then, are you?' I asked him.

He came to stand next to me, his eyes red, his cheeks tear-stained. 'Yes, I think I am. I'm sorry, Becs. I'm so, so sorry.'

I got off the bus at South End Green, stepping out into the cold evening air, grateful that the heavy rain had turned to drizzle. I put my head down and walked up towards the heath, stopping at the newsagent by the overground station to buy a bottle of Shiraz and then carrying on up the hill. Dan's words were ringing in my ears, even after all this time. I knew I didn't talk about feelings, but that's because they were too painful to think about half the time, so why would I? It had always been easier for me to keep stuff to myself, and I'd thought it would be easier for everyone else, too. But what if it wasn't?

When I let myself into Marlowe Court and reached the third floor, Jack was there. He was crouched on his doormat with tools spread out all around him.

I pushed my matted, wet hair off my face instinctively. 'Hello,' I said.

He dropped a spanner on the floor with a clatter and looked round.

I picked it up for him. 'Sorry if I made you jump.'

20

Jack

Rebecca was standing over me looking wet and a bit sad.

I took the spanner from her. 'Thanks.'

'What are you doing, then?' she asked.

'Attempting to fix my door. It makes a really loud creaking noise every time you open or close it and it's doing my head in, so I can only imagine what it's doing to everyone else's.'

She smiled. 'Ah, yes. I had noticed that.'

I grimaced. 'Sorry. Hope it didn't wake you up or anything. It can be quite late by the time I get in from my shifts at the pub.'

She shrugged. 'Don't worry, I'm quite a heavy sleeper. Once I'm off, nothing can wake me.'

I laughed. 'I'm the same.'

'Well. Good luck,' she said, walking over to her door, her hand dipping into her pocket for her keys.

I noticed the wine in her hand. 'Looks like you've got an exciting night planned,' I said.

She looked down at it as though she'd only just remembered she'd got it. 'Oh, right,' she replied. 'Not really.'

Her boyfriend was probably coming round, although I hadn't seen him much lately. I reckoned he had the kind of job that spanned several time zones. He was probably away in Hong Kong or wherever it was these business types went.

'Don't suppose you fancy a glass?' she asked.

I ran my fingers through the front of my hair, surprised. Although things were easier between us now, we'd never really got past the awkward small-talk stage. This was definitely the friendliest she'd ever been. 'Um, yeah. Sure. Why not?'

'Back in a sec,' she said, letting herself into her flat and closing the door softly behind her.

I could hear cupboards being opened and shut, the clink of glasses knocking together.

Turning my attention back to my door, I picked up the can of oil I'd found under the sink and applied it generously to the hinges. Someone upstairs turned their music up and I could hear bass-heavy dance music. Presumably it wasn't Ed Sheeran girl. Anyway, somebody was having a good time up there. I was surrounded by people who had an actual life, or at least some semblance of one. I made a mental note to reconnect with some of my old mates from drama school – there was a group of them who always used to be out on a weekend and I'd join them on the odd occasion I had enough money to buy a round. And then because I kept not turning up, because I was working, or whatever, they stopped asking me. It had made me feel a bit shit, to tell you the truth, as though I'd been very easily forgotten about. I still didn't have any money, but it would be good to catch up with them once in a while.

I tried the door – no squeak. Mission accomplished. I packed all my tools away and waited, unsure what to do. Maybe Rebecca had had a change of heart and realised she didn't want to have a drink with the sad case across the landing. Then, suddenly, her door popped open and she was standing there holding two tumblers of red wine. She'd taken off her coat and was wearing a black pinafore dress over a camel polo neck. She'd put her wet hair up into a ponytail.

'Here,' she said. 'It's only from the corner shop, I'm afraid, so I'm not sure how nice it'll be.'

I took a large mouthful. 'Hmmm,' I said. 'Shiraz, right?'

She nodded, seemingly impressed. 'Do you know a lot about wine, then?'

I leaned against my door frame, swilling the wine around in my glass. 'A fair bit. My dad's really into it. He brings all these vintage wines up from the cellar on special occasions and we all have to "ooh" and "aah" about how amazing they taste and pretend it's not ridiculous that he's spent two hundred and fifty quid on a bottle of drink that'll be gone in half an hour.'

'Wow,' replied Rebecca, pushing up her sleeves one by one, swapping her glass from one hand to the other. 'A wine cellar, eh? Very nice.'

I took another mouthful. I knew how that must make me sound, but it was the kind of thing that didn't even register when I told my actor mates. Nothing I said about private school or skiing holidays or having had an au pair from the age of twelve months ever landed, because it was what everyone did in the circles I hung out in. It was refreshing to see Rebecca's reaction and to realise that this was not, in fact, normal.

'It's more of a giant wine rack, really,' I said, trying to play it down, 'and we call it a cellar because it just happens to be in our basement.'

'Still,' she said.

'Yeah. Still. Sounds a bit flash, doesn't it?

I noticed how she'd begun to mirror me, how she was leaning against the frame of her door, too, her hip bone jutting out to the side.

'How was your acting class the other day, then?' she asked.

I tapped my fingertips on the base of the glass. 'Not bad. Didn't get the impression the casting director was blown away by my performance or anything, but I got his card, so you never know.'

She'd nearly finished her wine and her eyes looked brighter than they had when she'd first come up the stairs. I wanted to ask her if anything was wrong, but I didn't feel like I knew her well enough yet.

'I'm sure it was fine,' she said. 'I bet you're just being critical of yourself.'

I laughed softly to myself, self-conscious, suddenly. 'I dunno. I struggle sometimes, in auditions.'

'Do you?' she asked.

I probably seemed very confident to her, everyone said that when they first met me. And I usually let them carry on believing that, because what was the alternative? Admit to being anxious a lot of the time? I didn't think people had much sympathy for actors in the first place; they probably thought I should stop moaning and go and get a proper job like everyone else.

'I'm dyslexic,' I said, surprising myself. I didn't usually volunteer this particular nugget of information, especially so soon after meeting somebody. 'So it takes me ages to learn my lines. And then sometimes, what they do is they ask you to add lines in, or move scenes around, and it messes with my brain.'

She picked up the wine bottle from the doorway and topped up my glass.

'That sounds really tough.'

I shrugged. 'It can be, yeah.'

'If you ever need any help running lines, give me a shout,' she said.

'Thanks,' I replied, burying my nose in my glass to hide the fact that I was actually quite touched. Nobody had ever offered to help me like that before. 'I'm getting notes of cinnamon and blackberries, see? You try,' I said, nodding at her glass.

She stuck her nose inside the rim, sniffing delicately.

'Oh, yes,' she agreed, her eyes wide. 'I'd never have picked up on that if you hadn't said.'

I smiled. 'At least my dad's good for something.'

She looked at my quizzically. 'You don't get on?'

I took a sip of my wine. 'Not really.'

For some reason, I felt bad saying it, as though I was betraying my dad by admitting how difficult things were between us. I knew that he was doing as much as he was capable of and also that some people had it a lot worse.

'Shame,' she said.

'Yeah. It is.'

'Right,' said Rebecca. 'Better go and get some dinner on.'

I didn't know why I'd mentioned my dad, it was a bit of a mood kill. No wonder she was keen to get away.

I handed her my empty glass. 'What are you having?'

She looked embarrassed. 'A ready meal. Thai green curry, I think.'

'Nothing wrong with a microwaveable meal once in a while.'

She was probably knackered after work and couldn't be bothered to cook; we'd all been there.

'I suppose,' she said, backing away. 'See you around, then.'

I nodded enthusiastically. 'Sure. And thanks for the wine.'

She smiled and closed the door behind her.

I thought her boyfriend probably wasn't coming over tonight, then; Armani suits and ready meals didn't really go. I went back inside my flat, shoved the tools in the kitchen and grabbed a beer. I had a taste for wine now but didn't have any, so Red Stripe it was.

Slumping in front of the TV, I flicked aimlessly through about 250 channels. I was still avoiding anything war-related as it reminded me of the Netflix audition and of Samuel, who now I'd never get to play.

My mobile rang.

'Hey.'

'It's Luke.'

'I know.'

Luke could not seem to grasp the concept that caller ID was a thing that everyone had and therefore he no longer needed to announce himself as though he was making a telephone call circa 1974.

'What's up?' I said.

He was at the pub; I could hear the chatter and clink of glasses coming from the kitchen.

'What are you doing tomorrow night?' he asked.

'Working. As you well know, because you did the rota,' I replied, sinking about half a can of beer in one.

'You're only working till six,' said Luke. 'So afterwards, come to mine for dinner. Donna's invited a few people round.'

'As long as these friends of Donna's don't include anyone she's trying to fix me up with,' I warned him.

I knew what the pair of them were like. Their hearts were in the right place, but honestly, I hated it when they tried to play matchmaker.

'Well there is someone,' said Luke, sounding sheepish.

I rolled my eyes. I knew it.

'This friend of hers. Her name's Janine. She saw you on TV apparently and thinks you're fit.'

'She hasn't seen me in real life, has she? She might change her mind then.'

And when she realised I was less TV star and more jobbing actor.

'She's very pretty,' added Luke. 'She's a primary school teacher. You know, nice and stable. She'd be good for you.'

I carried on flicking through Netflix, only half listening.

'And Donna's going to put a nice spread on,' said Luke. 'Lots of Cava to go with it. Come on, it'll be a laugh.'

I sighed. It did actually sound quite nice. Donna and Luke were always good company – there was never any drama with those two, they just accepted each other for what they were, limitations and all. In my experience, the relationships I ended up in weren't like that. I never quite knew how to be myself – sometimes it felt as though I was putting on a show, playing the part of whoever it was I thought they'd want me to be. Luke said I just hadn't met the right person yet, but it was difficult to imagine that this 'right person' even existed.

My last girlfriend (not that I'd really call her that, since we'd never made it official) of any note was in my second year at drama school. Nathalie had been in the year above and had basically treated me more like a lackey than a boyfriend, which I'd pathetically gone along with for ages before coming to my senses and ending it, at which point she professed to be heartbroken. It had a been a nightmare, and a distraction I'd vowed never to repeat, especially not when I was paying a small fortune to be there. I thought that perhaps, because I was one of the only students whose parents weren't dolling out the money for fees, living expenses and anything else their little darlings required, the stakes seemed a little bit higher for me than they were for most other people. And when it came down to it, acting was more important to me than a relationship. Certainly, back then, and there'd been nothing to change my opinion on that thus far.

'OK, I'll come,' I said. 'But I do not, and I repeat DO NOT, want to be fixed up with anyone.'

I was up for a bit of fun, it wasn't like I didn't like women, but I felt much more comfortable if I was in the sort of relationship that wasn't really a relationship. Then it didn't matter so much what they thought of me, did it? I didn't feel that intense pressure to please them, which was a dynamic that took me right back to trying to please my dad, a pointless and exhausting pursuit.

There was silence on the other end of the line.

'Are you still there?' I asked. It wasn't like Luke to be stuck for something to say.

'I know I'm starting to sound a bit repetitive, but I'm worried about you, Jack,' he said quietly.

This was dangerously emotional territory for Luke, and for me, too – the closest we'd got to opening up to each other was when we'd drunk half a bottle of whisky each and had confided in one another about how disappointed our parents were in us. We hadn't gone into great detail, mind you, but there'd been a mutual understanding that we'd had to work things out for ourselves. Or, more accurately, Luke had worked things out for himself and I still had a lot to learn.

I finished my beer. It went down the wrong way and I coughed and spluttered for a bit, holding my phone away from me.

'Sorry,' I said eventually, coming back on the line. 'What exactly are you worried about?'

'I can't see how you're ever going to be happy if you don't let people in.'

'I let people in!' I protested.

'Like who?'

'Well what are we doing now? I'm being honest with you, aren't I?'

'To a point,' said Luke.

I heard voices. Luke told someone he'd be there in a second.

'Damn, do you have to go?' I asked sarcastically.

'Some dodgy-looking blokes have just walked in, apparently, so yeah, you're off the hook. But I mean it, Jack. Something's got to give.'

'Lecture over?' I said.

'Lecture over.'

'Great. I'll see you tomorrow,' I replied.

Who'd made up this rule that you had to get married and have kids, anyway? Why? Lots of people didn't. Look at Clive downstairs, he seemed happy enough and as far as I knew he'd been single all his life. And I would have used George Clooney as an example, but he'd gone and ruined it for single blokes everywhere by marrying Amal and having twins. Twins!

'Oh, and thank Donna for the invite,' I said, hanging up.

I picked up the remote, deciding that an episode of *Ozark* might suit my mood. But I couldn't relax because Luke's words kept buzzing around in my head. Were people really that concerned about me? I seriously needed to get an acting job and fast – not only would it sort out all my money problems, but it would get everyone off my back. After all, how could I possibly commit to a relationship when I was busy with work and zipping around the globe to shoot Oscar-winning movies in exotic locations? That, people would understand, I was sure of it.

21

Rebecca

I checked my monitor: 5.35 p.m. Officially time to stop replying to emails and leave the office. Looking over my shoulder to make sure nobody was watching me, I opened the Word document containing the application form for the head of press and marketing position. It had taken me hours – literally hours – to complete. I didn't know why you couldn't just submit a CV and covering letter, like you used to. For anyone who didn't get invited for interview the form added insult to injury, didn't it, because you'd basically wasted several days of your life filling it out?

The Kingsland Marketing HR department was comprised of two women who had been in the job for twenty years apiece and to say they played it by the book was an understatement. Personally, I thought human resources was a terrible name for the department, since they didn't appear to take actual human feelings into account. When there'd been a spate of redundancies a few years back, for example, the people unlucky enough to lose their jobs had had to pack up their desks and vacate the office in under an hour. The security guard from downstairs had been hovering over them as though they were going to smuggle out top-secret information on Kingsland Marketing and sell it to the *Daily Mail*. Maybe that's what people did when they were angry and desperate. Perhaps I'd even feel like that if they gave the job to Amanda. I didn't think so. Anyway, it was now glaringly obvious that I didn't really want it, but it felt like a huge step not to apply. I'd be admitting to myself and everyone else that I wanted something to change and then there would be no going back, would there?

My phone rang. Strangely it was Val.

'What on earth are you still doing here?' I demanded.

Val was usually out of the door on the dot of 5.30 because she said she refused to give the company a minute of her time for free. I admired this attitude, but I also couldn't really get my head round it. I was obsessed with not getting complacent, by being at the top of my game all of the time and making myself completely indispensable. I didn't know what kind of disaster I imagined was going to befall me if I left on time once in a while or – god forbid – took a day off sick.

'I could ask you the same thing,' said Val. 'Let me guess, you're looking over your application for the twenty-fifth time.'

I laughed. 'You know me too well.'

'Step away from the application,' instructed Val.

'I'm nearly done,' I insisted.

'Got time for a drink in Bar Monaco?' she asked.

I always had time for that.

'See you in there at six,' I said, replacing the receiver.

One more look through the application and then I would force myself to press send.

Val put our drinks on the table and took a seat, waving over at Freya, who was with the art department at a table on the other side of the dance floor.

'I hope you're going to tell me you sent that application?'

said Val. 'Enough with the procrastinating. The job's yours and you know it.'

I sighed, resting my chin in the heel of my hand. 'I told you what I heard in the loos the other night.'

Val tutted. 'Abi and Violet haven't got a clue what they're talking about. They're just up Amanda's arse because she got them on the guest list at Mahiki a few weeks ago.'

'Is that place still going?' I said, thinking back to all the celebrity photos I'd seen of people stumbling out of the door of the Mayfair club what seemed like decades ago.

'Apparently,' replied Val, who had much cooler taste in music than I did and would not be seen dead at such an establishment.

I took a deep breath. I had to tell someone. 'So I'm thinking about not applying for the job.'

Val stopped sucking her drink through a straw and frowned at me. She widened her eyes. 'Since when?'

I sighed. 'I don't know, really. A couple of weeks? I've been going over and over it in my head, and something doesn't feel right about it. I've got this feeling that I want to try something different and if I take the promotion, I'm stuck here for another couple of years at least, aren't I?'

Val looked shocked. 'I had no idea you felt stuck, Becs.'

'Well, I've only just worked it out for myself, to be fair.'

Val nodded. 'So what else would you want to do?'

I took a sip of my own drink. Someone turned the music up and Dua Lipa's 'Physical' blasted out so loud that I had to raise my voice by about a decibel so that Val could hear me.

'I've seen a job,' I said. 'And it sounds perfect.'

'Go on,' said Val, nodding with encouragement.

'It's a marketing director role for Children in Crisis. So a step up, but the pay would be the same because, well, it's a charity, isn't it?'

'What do they do?'

I bit my lip. This was the part I wasn't sure about. 'They work with children who have lost parents or siblings. Offer them bereavement counselling, organise days out, match them with another child going through something similar. I remember feeling really lonely when it happened to me. I felt like I couldn't talk to anyone else because you didn't want to upset them and because I didn't think they'd really get it, anyway.'

Val took my hands and squeezed them. 'It sounds great, Becs. But why now, do you think?'

I thought about it and Jack popped into my head. I'd only known him a couple of months, but seeing him talk about his acting, realising what he was prepared to sacrifice to go after his dream, had triggered something inside me. And he believed he was good enough to make it, that was the thing that stuck with me. Was I staying at Kingsland because I didn't quite believe I had the talent to do anything else? Did I really want to spend the rest of my life doing a job I didn't love because I was too scared to try something new?

'I think it's that I feel ready to do something like this, finally,' I said to Val by way of explanation.

It was true, I did, I just missed out the bit about Jack. I'd tell her at some point, but she'd only jump to conclusions if I mentioned him now and would go off on one of her matchmaking crusades. Jack was lovely to talk to and also, admittedly, very nice to look at, but he was the very last person I was going to get involved with, even if there was a chance he'd be interested in someone like me. It would be asking for trouble to fall for an actor who could get his big break at any second and disappear off to Hollywood. Plus he was my neighbour. Marlowe Court was where I was happiest – if anything was to happen between us (which obviously

I didn't want it to, but just say it did) and it went wrong, then him living opposite me could ruin everything.

Val beamed at me. 'Well I'm proud of you,' she said.

I beamed back, feeling a bit choked up.

'It's going to be awful at Kingsland without you,' she moaned. 'How am I going to cope? Who am I going to have wine-fuelled lunches with?'

'I'm not going anywhere yet, am I?' I said, laughing. Trust Val to run ahead of herself.

22

Jack

I checked my phone: 10.27. Chad had said to meet him outside the agency at 10.30. If I was even one minute late, I knew he'd use it as an excuse not to stick around and I was not going to let him worm out of this one.

I waited on the pavement outside Star Management, gearing myself up for the conversation I should have had with him months ago. Years, even. There was always lots of activity around the agency. I watched as somebody got out of an Addison Lee car, a cap pulled down over their face, sunglasses on, and I wondered which big name client was going inside. I hadn't even been granted a proper meeting. Chad had told me he could spare ten minutes while he was walking from the office to a brunch meeting at the Charlotte Street Hotel. Since I really wanted to talk to him, I'd had no choice but to agree.

For the hundredth time, I questioned my decision to sign with a huge agent like him, who had barely any time for clients who weren't being seen for leading roles, who weren't quite living up to the promise they'd shown when they'd been top of their year at drama school. But then again, how could I have turned him down? Everyone had wanted Chad to represent them and I'd felt special on the night of my graduation showcase because it had been only me he picked out.

I scrolled through my phone, my head flicking up and down as the door to the agency opened and closed, opened and closed. Delivery guys drove up on their motorbikes, assistants ran out to fetch coffee. A girl I didn't recognise was buzzed through the door, a Lily James type who was bound to get cast in the next BBC period drama. And finally Chad, looking like he always did, as though it was 1985 and he'd just stepped out of a an aerobics class at Equinox Hollywood: black Lycra cycling shorts, electric blue vest, cap, mirrored sunglasses. Expensive trainers. Sustainable water bottle.

I waved and jogged over to him.

'Chad!' I shouted as he strutted off down Broadwick Street, blatantly having forgotten I was meeting him at all.

'Chad!' I said, trying again, lengthening my stride.

He looked over his shoulder and showed a flicker of recognition. 'Oh, hey Jack.'

I fell into step beside him. 'How's things?' I asked, making the obligatory small talk before launching into my well-rehearsed tirade about my future in the acting business.

'Manic,' said Chad.

Whilst he ploughed through oncoming pedestrians, letting them part ways for him, I was constantly hopping right and left, twisting my body to avoid slamming into people coming the other way. Chad moved as though he had a right to walk in a straight line and perfect strangers, seemingly understanding that, simply glided out of his way. I wondered whether that kind of attitude was something I could pull off, whether that was what I was doing wrong. After all, if the doubts and insecurities I felt inside were also obvious from the outside, nobody was going to give me a job, were they?

'So what can I do for you?' asked Chad. 'You said you needed to talk.'

I cleared my throat. 'I'm going to level with you, Chad. I'm struggling here.'

He gave me a sideways look, which felt like a warning: was I going to dare to complain? What could I possibly have to moan about when I was represented by the agent all young actors dreamed of being signed by?

'How so?' he said.

I'd noticed, lately, that because he spent so much time on the phone to LA, he'd developed a subtle West Coast twang. And he was always juicing and had recently gone vegan, which I'd only realised when I'd given him a box of Rococo chocolates (which had cost me a fortune, by the way) for Christmas and he'd told me that he didn't do dairy or any other ingredients from an animal source. Sheepishly, I'd taken the chocolates back and had regifted them to my mum, who had been altogether more pleased with them.

'I need something stable,' I began as we walked up the steps on Ramillies Street and onto a heaving Oxford Street. 'A series regular, I mean. Could you get me in to see the guys at *Holby* again? I'd even consider a soap.'

Chad chugged on his water as we darted between buses and bikes and crossed the road. 'You need to build your résumé,' he said. 'And we need to get some casting directors in to see you. Remember what I said about doing some fringe? If we can get you something at one of the more prestigious venues – Edinburgh, maybe – you'd be surprised how willing they are to come out and see stuff.'

I nodded enthusiastically. 'Cool, cool. I do need to make some actual money as well, though,' I added, hoping he'd understand.

It was just that I'd been out of drama school for nearly a decade now. I'd been acting a long time and I felt as though I deserved to be paid a decent wage for it. I had a sudden pang of longing for how simple life had been when I'd started acting at school. When I'd been at my after-school drama club, I hadn't been the outsider anymore, the boy who wasn't particularly academic and who was excellent at sport, but not quite good enough to make up for all the other stuff. I made new friends who liked the same things I did and my life had begun to revolve around rehearsals, where I could be myself and actually feel good about it.

'So what you're saying is, you want a series regular role given to you on a plate? That you're not prepared to put in the hard work?'

He clearly hadn't understood, then. 'I do work hard,' I said, quickly losing my patience. Why did he have to be such a wanker all the time? 'And I don't think ten years of walk-on roles and theatre is "expecting it on a plate". I'm ready to ramp my career up a notch and I think I deserve it and I think I'm good enough.'

Chad looked surprised at my sudden outburst. He was probably expecting the meeker, more submissive version of Jack, but I was done with him. If I wanted to make something of myself, then I was going to have to push hard for it. No one else was going to fight my corner, not even my agent, it seemed.

'I'll see what I can do. I'm meeting Jen from *Accident & Emergency* for dinner tonight, I'll try to lever you into the conversation,' he said.

'That would be great,' I replied, pleased that he seemed to be taking me seriously for once.

'But, as a pay-off, I want you to do the fringe. I'll get my assistant to put some feelers out, see what's coming up.'

I swerved, narrowly avoiding walking straight into a bin. 'OK. But it would have to be a short run. I can't afford to takes weeks off for rehearsals either.'

The candy-striped awnings of the Charlotte Street Hotel popped into view. This, I knew, meant that our 'meeting' was coming to an end, but at least I'd put my point across and if Chad did what he said he was going to do, it could lead to something.

'Thanks for seeing me,' I said to Chad, slowing my pace. 'And I really appreciate your help. It's just, I'm thirty now, you know? You think, don't you, about the future? About money, all that.'

Chad gave me a look I couldn't quite read. Disappointment, probably. 'I'll be in touch,' he said, before swinging onto the terrace of the hotel, waltzing through the entrance as a doorman in a black suit scrabbled to hold the door open for him leaving me outside on the street watching on.

March

23

Rebecca

I'd taken a different route this morning, finishing up my run at the pond near Jack Straw's Castle. The water shimmered ominously behind the reeds which were beginning to grow around the perimeter of it now spring was coming. With a layer of mist hanging on the surface of it, you could almost imagine it hundreds of years ago, when there would have been just the grassland of the heath around it: no roads, no gridlocked lines of cars making their way into central London.

As I walked along the driveway of Marlowe Court, my body cooling down, my breathing returning to normal, I saw the front door to our block open and a tall man, stooped, with a black scarf wrapped tightly around his face and neck, coming out.

'Clive?' I said as I got closer.

He pulled the scarf down off his face, his breath fogging in the cold air.

'Hello, my dear,' he replied, stamping his feet to keep warm.

'This is an early walk for you,' I noted, taking out my earbuds so I could hear him properly.

'It is,' he said, very enthusiastically, given the time. 'I'm out of milk, so it's a good excuse to get me out and about at a decent hour. I have to walk every day, otherwise everything will seize up. That's what happens when you get old!'

I smiled at him. 'Well, enjoy,' I said. 'I reckon it's about to rain, though, so don't stay out too long.' I pointed up at the sky. It was only just getting light and there was no sign that it was going to be anything other than grey and wet all day.

'Ah, don't worry about me,' he replied. 'I'm stronger than I look, young lady.'

I laughed. 'I don't doubt it,' I said, letting myself through the door.

I'd just started up the stairs and was thinking about whether to have a yoghurt or a couple of slices of toast for breakfast when I heard shouting, followed by the elongated beeping of a horn. I looked out of the window on the first floor, forever nosy about what was going on with the neighbours. Pressing my nose against the glass, I tried to work out what was happening. Had somebody blocked somebody else in? I was glad I didn't drive, actually, because I couldn't imagine anything more frustrating than being in a hurry to get somewhere and not being able to get your car out because some idiot had parked badly.

I could see a black BMW in the driveway, the young guy from the Turkish family on the ground floor was pacing around at the back of it with his hands over his mouth. When I looked on the ground, I could see the sleeve of a coat and what I thought was a hand. My stomach lurched, adrenaline surging through me. It was Clive, I knew it was.

I flew back down the stairs, flinging open the front door, running outside.

'What's going on?' I shouted as I approached the car.

The young guy, whose name I didn't know, was wide-eyed and completely mute and his phone was hanging limply in his hand.

I looked down.

'Clive!' I said, throwing myself to the ground next to him. His eyes were closed and his limbs were twisted in different directions, so that his body was shaped like a zigzag. 'What happened?' I screamed, looking up at the guy.

'I didn't see him,' he said. 'I was reversing out of the drive and I didn't see him. Is he dead?'

'It's all right, Clive,' I said, ignoring the question. He couldn't be. He wasn't. 'You'll be all right, stay with me, OK?' I soothed, stroking Clive's arm.

My heart was thumping in my chest and I thought I might be about to throw up. My brain wasn't working properly, just when I needed to think more clearly than ever – what should I do? Every second I didn't take action could cost Clive his life.

'Call an ambulance!' I said to the guy, who was now crouching down next to me, whimpering.

I pulled off my tracksuit top with shaking hands, laying it over Clive's chest.

'Clive? Clive, can you hear me?' I asked, bending to talk into his ear.

The BMWs hazard lights were flashing on and off, and when they illuminated Clive's face, his lips looked very pale and I didn't think that was good. I had to act quickly.

'Call a fucking ambulance,' I said to the driver, who was still staring at me blankly.

If neither of us was going to be able to help, we'd have to find somebody who could.

'Help!' I shouted, in the hope that somebody would hear me and look out of the window. Surely somebody must have noticed what was going on. 'There's an emergency, help!'

I put my cheek next to Clive's face, to feel whether or not I could detect even the slightest breath. I couldn't. Tears filmed over my eyes. Not again; this couldn't happen to me again.

'What's happened?' said a breathy voice.

When I looked up, Jack was there and I didn't think I'd ever been more relieved to see someone in my life.

'He's been knocked over,' I said. 'I don't think he's breathing.'

Jack knelt down next to me.

'Do you know CPR?' I asked him, panicked now.

With every second that passed, the more unlikely it was that we had any chance of saving Clive.

'I was taught it for a scene I did on *Holby*,' replied Jack, pushing my top aside, ripping open Clive's coat and then his shirt. 'It was a while ago. I need to remember what they said.'

'I'll call an ambulance,' I said, pulling out my phone, dialling 999 with fingers that suddenly felt too big and clumsy for the keypad.

I watched Jack laying his hands on the centre of Clive's chest, feeling around for the bottom of his breastbone, concentrating hard. I reeled off the details of the accident to the operator on the other end of the phone, watching Clive's face for the tiniest sign of life, for a glimmer of hope. Jack had locked his hands together and was pushing down hard on Clive's chest, counting under his breath. I gave the operator our postcode.

'Tell them to hurry,' shouted Jack, putting his mouth over Clive's and blowing air into it, once and then once more.

Blood was pumping so hard in my temples that I thought I might keel over myself.

'It's on its way,' I said, kneeling back down next to Jack, taking Clive's cold hand and clutching it in mine.

24

Jack

I straightened my arms, found my spot and did another twenty compressions, humming 'Stayin' Alive' by the Bee Gees under my breath because that was what the resident doctor on *Holby* had told me would be a nice touch for the scene I'd played. He said it was what people were taught on first-aid courses. If I'd known I'd need to do it for real a couple of years later, I'd have paid more fucking attention to the detail. Was it twenty or thirty compressions? Two breaths, or three?

A siren blasted in the distance; surely that was for us. The Royal Free was literally a minute's drive away.

'Keep going,' said Rebecca quietly. 'You're doing brilliantly.'

She slid her top under Clive's head, stroking his forehead gently.

'You're in good hands with Jack here, Clive,' she said, glancing at me. 'We've got an ambulance on its way for you and everything. We're lucky to have Jack as our neighbour, aren't we?'

Rebecca looked very pale and was sweating now herself. I hoped she wasn't about to faint or something, because there's no way I'd be able to sort her out as well.

I did two more breaths, watching to see whether Clive's

chest rose and fell. It did. Surely that was a good sign. If I could just keep oxygen pumping around his body, he might be in with a chance once the paramedics took over.

The sirens were getting louder. I saw a blue light flashing through the trees and then, seconds later, the ambulance pulled into the driveway. Two paramedics got out and ran over. One had a defibrillator and told us to stand back. A couple of the other neighbours had come outside by this point and were standing around gawping. The woman from the ground floor was in her dressing gown and was sobbing loudly into a tissue and the young guy who I presume had knocked Clive over was sitting on the kerb with his head between his knees. The paramedics checked Clive's pulse, listened for any signs of breathing and then put the pads on his chest.

Rebecca bent over, as though she was trying to catch her breath. Only hesitating for a second, I reached out and rubbed her lower back.

'Are you OK?' I asked, which was a ridiculous question. Of course she wasn't OK. I wasn't sure I was, either.

The first round of defib didn't work. I said a silent prayer, asking for Clive to make it, although given I never prayed and hadn't been to church since I was about eight, I hardly thought God was going to be listening now.

The paramedics fiddled with the machine and then did another round. This time, I saw Clive's lips move the tiniest bit, a flicker of his eyelids. I clamped my hand over my mouth. This had to mean that there were at least some signs of life, didn't it? The paramedics did some more checks and then very carefully began to ease him onto a stretcher. One of them mentioned a broken hip. Fuck, poor Clive.

I picked up Rebecca's top and put it around her shoulders because I could see her shaking.

One of the paramedics turned to face us. 'Do either of you know this gentleman?'

'He's our neighbour,' I said.

'You won't be able to come in the ambulance with him, then. But you can meet us down at the hospital if you like.'

I looked at Rebecca, who looked terrified and was now a very greyish green, although it might have been the light.

'I'll follow you down,' I offered. It was the least I could do. If Clive was going to die, there was no way I was going to let him be alone when he did, not that I wanted to think about that at this stage.

'Are you sure you're OK to go?' said Rebecca, her voice all croaky.

'Course,' I replied, not that I was feeling as confident as I sounded. I'd never had to deal with anything like this before and it had been awful seeing Clive lying there, completely helpless. I was surprised that I'd managed to remember a thing about the CPR.

She slipped her arms into her top.

I watched the paramedics shut the ambulance door, feeling my throat swell as I caught a glimpse of Clive being rigged up to various wires and a tube being put down his throat to help him breathe.

Please let him live, I thought to myself. He was such a nice man, he didn't deserve this.

Tentatively, I put my arm around Rebecca. I could feel her shaking and pulled her closer to me, hoping the warmth of my body might help. She'd been for a run and had hardly any clothes on, which probably wasn't helping.

The engine started up and we watched as they took a left out of the driveway, roaring down East Heath Road towards the hospital.

'I'll go and lock up and then I'll head down there,' I said. 'Do you want to come with me?'

Rebecca shook her head. 'I don't think I can. I've … um, I've got to get to work.'

I dropped my arm, gently. She looked in no fit state to go to work, but I didn't like to say. She probably just needed a hot drink or something – wasn't that good for shock?

'There's probably no point both of us being there, anyway,' I said, not wanting her to feel bad.

She fumbled around in her pocket for her keys. I found mine instead, opening the door for her. I had a quick glance over my shoulder to check that the bloke with the BMW was all right; he must be shocked, too, and I thought I'd heard the paramedics say the police were on their way. The woman in the dressing gown was sitting with him now, so that was something. I followed Rebecca inside and we stumbled silently up the stairs, my head fried by everything that had gone on. When we got to our landing, she stood there on the doorstep for what felt like ages, as though she couldn't think properly either.

'Let me know how he is, won't you?' she said over her shoulder.

Before I'd had a chance to reply, she'd opened the door and disappeared inside.

25

Rebecca

I was twenty minutes late to my meeting and for the first time in my life I couldn't have cared less. I'd felt like not coming in at all, to be honest, but, of course, my need to do the right thing (for everyone else, that is) had prevailed. I'd got dressed on autopilot and had made my way in on the tube, although I couldn't tell you anything about the journey. All I could think about was Clive lying on the pavement. Was he dead, or had they managed to bring him round? It felt like the not knowing was worse, even if it turned out to be bad news.

I knocked on the conference room door and went in without waiting for an answer.

'Sorry,' I said, slumping into the one empty seat next to Amanda.

Mike Walbeck, who was notoriously a stickler for time, gave me a look as though he was desperate to make some sarcastic comment, but then probably saw my face and thought better of it.

It felt like everyone was starting at me, actually, so god knows what I must look like. I needed to pull myself together, really, otherwise I might as well have stayed at home, but I couldn't seem to stop shaking. When I tried to get my notebook and pen out of my bag, it took me ages to get hold of them.

'Right. Where were we?' said Mike Walbeck, going off on one about budgets and social media campaigns and other things I had absolutely no interest in hearing about.

I caught Amanda's eye at one point, and she gave me one of her condescending smiles. I tapped my pen on my desk, trying not to let my mind run away with me, but it was full of images of blue lights and bodies lying on the ground and sirens wailing in the distance.

'Amanda, can you give us a heads-up on the summer party event?' said Mike. 'Tyler Martin has been in touch to say that he wants to start sending out invitations within the month.'

'With pleasure,' replied Amanda, sitting back in her chair and crossing her legs. 'As you know, Tyler came to the UK at the beginning of the year. I showed him a few different venues in London and together we decided that The Savoy was the perfect choice for us. It's quintessentially English, has great food and comes with that air of British luxury that he was after. He particularly loved the idea of a drinks reception in The American Bar.'

I bit my lip. Trust her to pass The Savoy idea off as her own, even rolling out the exact same phrases I'd used with Tyler myself. She wasn't even acknowledging that I'd had anything to do with it. I felt a flicker of frustration, but Amanda and her petty one-upmanship were the least of my worries. All I cared about was whether or not Clive was OK. I wondered where he was now. Were they operating on him, perhaps, if they'd managed to get him breathing again, trying to fix his hip? Was Jack there with him, telling him everything would be all right?

'Excellent work, Amanda,' said Mike, doing a sort of

mock applause. 'He's not an easy man to please, so kudos for giving him exactly what he wants.'

'Yes,' simpered Amanda. 'He was very specific. He's got an exceptionally clear vision for how he wants things to be.'

Sweat popped on my forehead and I wished I could open a window. I just had to get through this meeting and then I would be able to calm myself down.

I felt better when I got back to my desk and I could pretend to be too busy to do anything except stare morosely at my screen. I sipped at a glass of water and blew my nose, opening a document for effect, although I wasn't planning to do anything with it.

I could feel Freya's eyes boring into me and realised I was going to have to tell her. It was obvious that I wasn't myself, and I couldn't really pretend to be.

'Is something wrong?' she asked, looking concerned.

I sighed. 'You could say that. My elderly neighbour, Clive, got knocked down by a car outside our flats. I had to call an ambulance. My other neighbour had to do CPR right there in the car park.'

Freya's jaw dropped. 'Oh my goodness. Is he …?'

I shook my head. 'I don't know.'

Freya shoved a whole bottle of Rescue Remedy at me. 'You poor thing,' she said. 'Here, take as much of this as you need.'

I tipped about half a bottle of the liquid down my throat, not caring what the side effects might be (I doubted there would be any, since I suspected the whole Bach remedies thing was a placebo, anyway).

'It's Clive I feel sorry for,' I said, an image of him lying there motionless popping into my mind's eye.

I remembered how traumatic it had been for Nan when

she'd fallen down the stairs, never mind all the other stuff that must be happening to Clive. His heart had stopped beating. Could he really recover from that? Had we been quick enough? If Jack hadn't been there, it would have been too late, I knew that for sure. I wouldn't have been able to save him.

'Good job your neighbour knew CPR,' commented Freya, taking the Rescue Remedy back and downing the other half of the bottle herself.

'I'm so glad he was there because I was completely useless.'

'I'm sure you weren't,' said Freya, kindly.

'I was. I just sort of froze.'

'Well, it's understandable, isn't it?'

I shrugged. It had actually made me see Jack in a whole new light. So much for me being the organised, efficient one – he'd really stepped up when I could barely even dial 999. If Clive did survive, it would all be down to him.

'Let me go and make you a drink,' offered Freya, shooting out of her seat. 'You look very pale, Becs.'

I nodded gratefully, resting my head in my hands.

When I got home that evening, the first thing I did was knock on Jack's door.

'Oh, hey,' he said, answering the door with a tea towel in his hand.

'I wanted to see if there was any news on Clive,' I said, putting my bag down on Jack's doormat. 'Did he pull through?'

'Yeah, I was going to knock round later. He's out of the coronary care unit,' explained Jack. 'And they've operated on his hip. They seem to think he'll make a good recovery. It'll take time of course, but it looks like he's going to be OK.'

'Oh thank god,' I said, feeling a rush of emotion. I

swallowed hard, willing myself not to start balling on his doorstep. 'That's amazing news.'

Jack looked down at his feet and then back up at me again. 'Were you all right this morning?' he asked.

'Um, yeah, course. It was a shock finding him lying there, that was all. I'd only spoken to him about thirty seconds before. He was off for a walk and I was coming back from a run.'

Jack nodded, but I could tell he thought there was more to it.

'Anyway, I should be asking you the same thing,' I said. 'How are you feeling about saving someone's life?'

He laughed. 'I think the paramedics and the doctors did that.'

I looked at him dubiously. 'You do know that it would have been too late by the time they got there, right?'

Jack shifted from one foot to the other. 'Maybe.'

I couldn't believe how much Jack was squirming. 'Is it difficult for you to take a compliment or something?' I asked him.

'I mean, not usually,' he replied.

'So what, then?'

He flicked his tea towel onto his shoulder. 'I don't know. I feel like anyone would have done the same thing. If I hadn't been there, somebody else would have cobbled together some CPR. It's what you do in those situations, isn't it?'

'Well I couldn't have done it,' I said.

'You could.'

I shook my head. 'No. My mind went completely blank. I was no use whatsoever.'

He pushed his hair back off his face with the heel of his hand. 'Anyway, it doesn't matter who did what, the main thing is he's going to make it. I was going to go and visit him tomorrow, once he's settled onto the rehabilitation ward.'

I knew what was coming next and I tried to prepare myself, my mind whirring with possible excuses.

'You could come with me if you want?' said Jack.

I closed my eyes for a second or two, calming myself. It was a perfectly reasonable suggestion. Why wouldn't I want to go and visit Clive? He'd very nearly died. Of course I should want to go and see him.

'Let me think about it,' I replied, busying myself picking up my bag and walking backwards towards the safety of my flat. 'I'm pretty full on at work at the moment, but I'll definitely try to make it. What time were you thinking?'

'Six-ish, probably ...' he said in a strange voice, as though he was trying to work out what the hell was wrong with me. 'It's just that he's got no family, has he? The hospital were saying they have no next of kin on record. So if we don't go, he'll be all on his own.'

I turned to open my door, practically falling into the hall-way in my eagerness to get inside.

'I'll let you know,' I said breezily, as though I wasn't be-having strangely at all. 'But I will definitely try to make it.'

He was still standing in the doorway, looking at me with his head cocked to the side.

I shut the door, leaning against the wall, my head resting against Catherine Deneuve. And then I let the tears come. I let them soak my cheeks and when I felt a sob building up in my throat, I went into the bathroom and shut the door. There was no way Jack could hear me from there.

26

Jack

My dad was waiting at a table in the middle of the restaurant. He'd fitted me in between meetings, he'd said. I'd been half tempted not to show up because I had a bad feeling about what he wanted to see me about. I didn't imagine he wanted a cosy chat; I could count on one hand the number of times Dad and I had voluntarily been out for lunch or a drink together.

He was on the phone when I arrived, barking something about court dates and missing papers to some poor person on the other end of the line. I sat down and poured myself a glass of water, knocking it back.

'Sorry about that,' said Dad, slipping his phone into the inside pocket of his jacket.

'No worries,' I replied, trying to hide my surprise. I didn't think I'd ever heard him apologise for anything before.

'Drink?' asked Dad.

I nodded, scanning the menu. A waiter wearing a pressed white shirt and a smart, black apron appeared beside me. It was the sort of trendy, stylistic place my dad liked to conduct his work-related meetings – I suspected it was probably because he thought it made him look relevant and interesting, which maybe it did. I ordered a cappuccino and a sparkling water; Dad went for a double espresso.

'So,' I said, putting the menu down and looking at Dad. 'To what do I owe this pleasure?'

Dad laughed softly. 'What, can't I meet my own son for coffee, now?'

I looked at him, frowning. I was pretty sure he hadn't been overcome by a sudden desire to spend time with me. 'Was there anything in particular you wanted to talk about?' I asked, determined to get it out of him.

There would be something – there always was. I didn't think I'd done anything wrong this time; nothing I could think of, anyway. As far as I knew, everyone was well. Although Mum had mentioned that Dom seemed very stressed, but surely that was par for the course when you were earning a six-figure salary? That was probably it: Dad was going to ask me to talk to my brother, to subtly find out if everything was all right. The thing was, though, I wouldn't really know, would I? It wasn't like we ever confided in each other, and if I had a problem, he'd be the last person I'd want to talk to about it. In fact, that was probably about the only similarity between us, the fact that we liked to keep our feelings to ourselves. I couldn't speak for Dom, but personally I channelled all my emotion through my characters – I could express anything, then. At times, it was very cathartic. I had the feeling Dom's emotions were all pent up and waiting to explode.

Dad shifted in his seat. 'One of my clients is a governor at a boarding school in Surrey,' he said.

'Oh, yeah?' I had no idea where he was going with this. 'What does he need a lawyer for, then?'

'Obviously I can't say,' replied Dad.

'Oh go on,' I teased.

He gave me a look.

'He said they're looking to recruit a drama teacher,' continued Dad.

194

'Ah,' I said.

The waiter brought our drinks. I stirred a spoon around and around in the froth at the top of my coffee.

'How did you get onto *that* subject? Small talk at the vending machine in court, was it?'

Dad downed his espresso in three short, sharp mouthfuls. I heard his throat contracting and opening again. 'I can't remember how it came up,' he replied.

I looked around the restaurant, which was just off Covent Garden piazza and had a sister restaurant in New York. I didn't know, because I'd never been, but I didn't imagine the Manhattan branch was full of middle-aged suits wooing clients over too-early bottles of expensive wine and eggs Benedict. I was surprised Dad wasn't drinking, actually, he didn't usually hold back.

'What are you thinking, then?' I asked him, although I was pretty sure by now where this conversation was going.

'I was telling him that you're a decent actor, by all ac-counts, but that you can't catch a break. Like you said, all the jobs are going to a handful of actors, aren't they? You lot aren't getting a look in.'

I wrenched open the top of my water and it promptly fizzed out like a volcano, dripping down my hands and soak-ing the poncy white tablecloth. I tutted, wiping my hands on a carefully folded linen napkin.

'That's going to change, though,' I said. 'I just need to keep going.'

'For how long, though, Jack?' asked Dad.

He took off his jacket and hung it carefully over the back of his chair. The massive sweat rings under his arms indicated that he was finding this conversation as difficult as I was.

'As long as it takes, I suppose,' I said.

I was sick to death of repeating myself. Why was I

constantly having to justify my career choice to people, including my own family? For people who weren't actors or some other kind of creative, I didn't suppose they understood what it was like to love doing something so much that you couldn't imagine giving it up, even if you never made enough money for a mortgage and a mini SUV and luxury holidays and all those other materialistic things that everyone (my family, in particular) seemed hung up on.

'My client said he could put in a good word for you. It's a big school. Excellent facilities, he said: a purpose-built theatre. They want to put on a couple of big plays a year.'

I massaged my temples, trying to stay calm.

'I don't think so, Dad,' I said, preparing myself for the onslaught of anger and outrage.

On the odd occasion Dad bothered to give me advice, he expected me to take it. And because I was so used to Dad having a go at me, it was like my body was primed and ready for attack whenever I was with him. Although when I say 'primed and ready', what I actually tended to do was retreat as quickly as was humanly possible.

'I want you to think about it,' he said, summoning the waiter and ordering a glass of Pinot Noir. I knew he wouldn't be able to resist. 'We're worried about you.'

I actually laughed out loud. Not another one? 'Worried about what?'

'That you're not going to make anything of yourself.'

I snapped then. 'Like Dom, you mean? That's the benchmark, really, isn't it? If I'm not a lawyer and I'm not throwing my cash around, I must be a complete and utter failure.'

'Keep your voice down,' hissed Dad, looking furtively around. 'I've got a client coming in a minute.'

'I don't want to be a teacher, Dad,' I said quietly, losing the will to fight over this again.

He sighed. 'They're paying over forty grand a year, Jack. And you wouldn't need to go in every day; he said they might agree to three days a week. He reckons he could easily get you the job. He runs the place, basically.'

I tried not to look impressed by the idea of forty thousand pounds a year. Compared to what I earned at the pub, that felt like a phenomenal amount of money. But I'd be stuck, then, wouldn't I? I'd be committed. What if an audition came up? It wasn't like you could say to a casting director: Oh, I'm working that day, could I come in next Monday instead? They'd laugh in your face.

'I'm not ready to give up on it yet,' I said to Dad, knowing he wouldn't understand.

'Give up on what?' he snorted. 'Scrabbling around for jobs and being permanently on the poverty line?'

I rubbed my hand over my mouth. Was that really what they thought of me? Had he forgotten about my role at the National, my part of one of the biggest serial dramas in the country? 'The thing is, though, if I was to take a teaching job, I wouldn't feel like a proper actor anymore.' Although, admittedly, the idea of having the finances of a proper adult was hugely appealing.

'It's up to you, Jack,' said Dad, chugging on his wine as soon as it arrived at the table. 'But you might not get a chance like this again. A decent job in a highly regarded school. Maybe you could think about passing some of your talent on to the next generation. Give something back.' As though Dad's job – getting rich people out of trouble, basically – was 'giving something back'.

'Actually, I saved someone's life the other day, so there's that.'

I wasn't sure where that came from, but it was as if I needed to prove to him that I wasn't entirely pathetic.

Dad looked confused. 'What? When?'

'My neighbour, Clive, got knocked down by a car. Stopped breathing and everything. I had to do CPR until the ambulance came.'

I could tell Dad didn't know how to respond. That he was secretly impressed by the idea that his feeble son *could* actually step up when required.

'Where did you learn how to do that, then?' asked Dad, opening the top button of his shirt.

'I had to do it in a scene once. For *Holby*. We got proper lessons from a real-life doctor so that it looked authentic.'

I felt slightly odd bragging about something like this when poor Clive was still flat on his back in hospital, but I was actually proud of myself for once and I didn't think there was any harm in telling my dad about it. Most people would, wouldn't they?

'Well good for you,' said Dad, clearing his throat.

I sighed, picking up my bag. Was that the best he could do?

'Do you want some money for the drinks?' I asked, getting up out of my seat.

Dad waved me away. 'Course not.'

'See you later, then,' I said.

'I won't give him a definite no on the job, yet,' called Dad after me.

The idea of admitting defeat and trying something new terrified me. Look at Rebecca with her marketing job. I didn't know for sure, but it seemed a bit as though she was going through the motions. When she talked about work, she seemed almost embarrassed about it. I didn't blame her, actually, and I'd put her 'making rich people richer' job in a similar category to my dad's (although presumably her clients hadn't actually broken the law). And, in her defence, she didn't exactly seem comfortable with it. In any case, I wasn't ready to become one of the thousands of failed actors out there. I was good enough to make it, I knew I was.

As I crossed the piazza and headed back up towards Long Acre, I gave myself my own, personal agenda: if I didn't start to make more money, if I didn't get a regular on a series, or something in a long-running play in the next twelve months, I'd consider retraining. But this was a decision I'd make on my own, not something to be forced on me by my parents, who had never supported me being an actor, anyway. Mum had been less vocal about her disappointment, but only because she'd been too caught up in her own career revival to care. I'd even paid for drama school myself, with loans and part-time jobs. They'd begrudgingly offered to cover the course fees, but I hadn't wanted to feel indebted to them, or to be under pressure to make enough money to pay them back (which was just as well now and possibly the best decision I'd ever made).

No, I was much better on my own, carving my own path and doing what I thought was best for me at the time, even if it turned out not to be in the end. I only had myself to blame, then, didn't I?

27

Rebecca

I paced around outside the entrance to the ward, trying to psych myself up. Already my whole body was on high alert, my senses heightened to within an inch of their lives, my brain frazzled. Everything jarred with me: the squeak of someone's shoe on the shiny floor, the visitors arriving, talking in hushed voices, clutching bags of snacks and magazines. The nurses whizzing down the corridor holding ominous-looking silver petri dishes. The smell of disinfectant and the remnants of lunch – some kind of meat and mashed potato, I imagined.

I took a deep breath and wished I hadn't because the smell was now lodged in my throat. I swigged wildly at my bottle of water. It had taken me about twenty minutes to get this far, in fact I'd stood outside the main entrance to the hospital for so long that a taxi driver had pulled up to ask if I needed a lift.

Two more senior-looking nurses walked past me talking about blood results and ECGs. I pulled my cardigan tightly around myself, trying to stay calm. Clive needed me, I told myself. He didn't have any family, Jack had said, which had been the thing that had made me come. Imagine if I'd been like Clive, if I hadn't had my nan and grandad to come and visit me when I was in hospital. Nothing bad was going to happen to me if I went inside the ward. And I wasn't about to have a heart attack even if my pulse was so fast it felt like I might although, if I did, I was in the right place.

'Rebecca?'

I jumped at the sound of my name. Jack was strolling up the corridor towards me, all relaxed, as though this wasn't the absolute worst place on earth.

'You came!' he said, beaming at me. He pressed the button on the door to the ward so that it opened automatically. 'After you,' he added, ushering me through.

Shit. What now? I wasn't ready for this, not yet.

'Um, I'll be there in a sec,' I said, fishing about in my bag for my phone. 'I just need to make a quick phone call and then I'll be right with you.'

Jack looked at me strangely, moving away from the door so that it shut again. 'Are you OK?' he asked. 'You look a bit clammy.'

I put my hand on my forehead. I did feel a bit feverish now he came to mention it. If I was ill, I definitely shouldn't be going in, should I?

'I'm fine,' I said, smiling weakly. I was just making excuses now. 'It's just ... hospitals aren't exactly my favourite place.'

This was a massive understatement.

He frowned. 'Oh, right.'

'In fact, you could say I've got a pathological fear of them,' I admitted.

Damn. I hadn't meant to say all that. I'd not told anyone about my phobia (I supposed that's what it was) for a long time. It hadn't come up, and it wasn't something I announced for the sake of it.

'I see,' said Jack, leaning against the wall. 'Do you know why?'

I pressed myself against the window as two porters pushed

a (thankfully empty) stretcher through the doors to the ward. There was something about the rattle of the wheels that sounded familiar. I'd been on one, apparently, when I was being transferred from one hospital to another, but I'd blocked all of that out. My memory seemed to come back in flashes, that was how it worked.

'It's a long story,' I replied.

And one that I didn't just like to throw at people. They never knew what to say, anyway, and then I felt bad for them, so I'd found it easiest not to bother.

'Is there anything I can do to help?' asked Jack. 'Shall I get you a coffee from downstairs or something?'

I shook my head. 'Thanks, though.'

Jack nodded.

'It's just a feeling I have,' I said. 'It's hard to explain.'

If I tried to pinpoint the symptoms, they might look something like a panic attack: racing heart, sweating, tight chest.

Jack moved out of the way to let a pair of doctors pass. Their white coats sent shivers through me all over again.

'Why don't you try?' he suggested. 'It might help to talk about it.'

He looked so worried about me that I almost told him. Did he really want to know, or was he saying it to be polite?

'I'll be fine in a minute,' I said, deciding baring my soul to a relative stranger whilst blocking the only doorway to the ward probably wasn't the best idea. 'Let's go in. It's not really about me, is it? I'm here to see Clive.'

Jack gave me an encouraging smile and pressed the button again and we walked together into the ward, which felt much better than having to do it on my own.

'If it all gets too much and you need to leave, let me know, OK?' he said.

I nodded, concentrating on taking deep breaths in and long, slow breaths out.

There were rooms leading off to either side of the corridor, each with several beds in. The hum of subdued conversation and the beeping of equipment and the serious-looking gaggle of nurses poring over someone's notes almost finished me off.

'OK?' asked Jack, looking concerned.

I gave him a thumbs-up, seemingly not able to summon the energy required to speak. Some visitor I was going to be – I was hardly going to cheer Clive up behaving like this.

'Through here,' said Jack, putting his hand on the small of my back to guide me into the last room on the left.

I surveyed the scene. An empty bed to my right, a lady watching an ancient TV opposite her. In the far corner was an old man in proper old-fashioned pyjamas with a woman sitting by his bed holding his hand. Clive was in the opposite corner.

I lagged a few steps behind Jack, summoning my resolve. I wouldn't have to stay long. I wanted Clive to know I cared, that was all. And then I could leave and go and have a shower and try to erase all thoughts of hospitals from my mind.

'Clive, mate,' said Jack, pulling up two chairs. 'Look who's come to see you.'

Clive, who was propped up on several pillows, turned his head to look at me. I was glad to note he looked a hundred times better than the last time I'd seen him.

I went closer to the bed and gave him an awkward kiss on the cheek. Mind you, it was hard not to be awkward when I was worried about dislodging a canula or another vital piece of equipment. There were wires everywhere. A heart monitor flashed red at the end of his bed. If I were him, I'd be looking at it constantly, wondering why some peaks were higher than others, worrying that it would go flat again.

'Hey, Clive. How are you feeling?' I asked him, perching gingerly on the edge of a plastic grey chair.

'Alive, thanks to you,' said Clive, taking my hand. I noticed how bony his was and wondered whether it would always have felt this fragile in mine, even before the accident.

'I didn't really do anything,' I replied, embarrassed.

'You were the one who called for help, weren't you?' said Jack. 'Called the ambulance, all that?'

'I'd be dead if it wasn't for the both of you,' said Clive, patting my hand with his free hand. 'I will never be able to thank you enough.'

I glanced at Jack.

'I'm just glad I could help,' I said, squeezing Clive's hand. 'And that you're on the road to recovery. You were right when you told me you're stronger than you look.'

Clive laughed, although it was a more subdued version of his usual, hearty one.

'So how are you coping in here?' I asked him, keen to do my visitor's duty so that I could make my excuses and go.

He grumbled. 'They say I can't get out of here any time soon. I'm stuck here and I don't seem to have any say in the matter.'

'Well you need to make sure you're completely better,' I said. 'That was quite a major accident you had there. Your body needs time to recover, doesn't it?'

I flinched as a machine beeped and a flurry of nurses came rushing over to the man opposite.

'What's happening?' I asked, turning to Jack for reassurance, trying to sound less anxious than I felt.

One of the nurses whipped the curtains closed so we couldn't see what was going on.

'Second time today that's happened,' said Clive.

'Seriously?' I said, shocked.

Was that what it was like in here? At any given moment, someone in the next bed, who hours earlier had been sipping tea and doing a word search, could cark it right in front of you?

'We're in a hospital, my dear,' replied Clive. 'Anything could happen.'

'Don't say that, Clive,' said Jack, glancing nervously at me. Perhaps I'd gone pale again. 'We're here to cheer you up, aren't we?'

'Oh, I got you these,' I said to Clive, pulling a punnet of grapes out of my bag and putting them on his bedside table.

'Mind if I open them?' asked Jack. 'I'm starving.' Clive nodded and Jack ripped off a small bunch for himself. 'I'm supposed to be on a health kick,' he said to me.

'How come?' I asked.

'Trying to up my game a bit. I plan on going up for lead roles, so I need to be fit,' he explained, his mouth full of crushed fruit.

'You look pretty fit to me,' I said, immediately cringing. 'What I mean is, you look like you work out.'

I felt my cheeks burning and pretended to check something on my phone so I didn't have to look at anybody. What had I gone and said that for?

When I thought the coast was clear and glanced up, Jack was grinning at me. I'd played right into his hands by rubbing his ego and telling him how good he looked.

'When you're a big time A-list actor in Hollywood you can get one of those personal trainers,' suggested Clive.

'Yeah. Not sure that's going to happen any time soon,' replied Jack, leaning back in his chair. 'How's your job going, anyway?' he asked me. 'Must be nice not to have to hustle for work all the time.'

'I was just thinking the opposite. That it must be nice to do something you're really passionate about. No two days are the same for you, are they?' I said, smiling across at him.

He shrugged. 'I used to think that. But after a while, the uncertainty gets less and less appealing. These days, it's not so much: *when will I get my next job* as *will I ever get another job in my entire life?*'

I thought he was only saying that to make me feel better. I'd seen what a great time he had, always out, dropping into cool-sounding acting classes, kissing girls on the doorstep. Although I couldn't help but notice there hadn't been anyone since that tiny girl in the black puffa coat earlier that month.

'I'm going to have to make a move soon,' I said, looking nervously across as the curtains opened and a decidedly unwell-looking elderly man was wheeled out, his tearful wife walking alongside him. 'I've got an interview next week, so I need to start on some prep.'

Jack raised his eyebrows. 'Oh I didn't realise you were looking for a new job. What is it?'

'Same company,' I said. 'But a more senior role.'

'Reckon you're in with a chance?' he asked.

I put my bag on my lap, getting ready to leave.

'I think so,' I replied, almost telling him that I wasn't sure if I wanted it.

'We wish you all the luck in the world, don't we, Jack?' said Clive, whose bunch of grapes was already looking barren.

'Of course we do,' Jack agreed, smiling at me as I stood up. 'Best of luck.'

'Come and see me again soon, won't you?' boomed Clive, so loudly that all the other visitors looked over at us.

I nodded enthusiastically.

Jack stood up. 'Shall I walk you out?'

'Oh no,' I said. 'You stay with Clive.'

I gave them both a wave and headed for the exit, holding my breath as I passed a food trolley with several silver domes on it. I could just imagine the horrors lurking underneath.

Later that evening, I was slumped in front of the TV watching *The Bachelorette*. It was one of those shows I got completely hooked into, even though I knew that most of it was fake and that there was no way twenty-five guys could be madly in love with a girl they'd known for all of a fortnight. I was particularly fascinated when they professed to be heartbroken and cried their eyes out in the back of a limo after getting sent home. I was pretty sure that what they were really upset about was the fact that their five minutes of fame was over and that they'd been humiliated on national television. And yet, there was something about watching other people being rejected that made me feel much better about my own life. It happened to everyone, didn't it? Even beautiful girls who'd been crowned Miss Arizona 2016 or whatever. Nobody got everything they wanted.

And another lesson I'd learned from *The Bachelorette* (yes, I took it that seriously) was that no matter how hard you tried, you couldn't make somebody fall in love with you. And it's often nothing you've done. You're just not right for them and they're not the one for you and there's nothing you can do about it. I thought briefly of Dan and how little had changed for me one year on. I wasn't heartbroken like I had been before, admittedly. But what had I learned from the break-up? How had I used it to change my outlook on the world? I was beginning to feel different, stronger now, and I was a bit clearer about what I wanted from my life. But it still felt as though I hadn't actually done anything about it.

My phone rang; it was my Aunty Carol.

'Hello,' I said, getting comfortable and pausing the TV. She could talk for England.

'How's everything with you, then?' she asked.

'Good. Working hard, the usual.'

I almost told her I'd been to the hospital to visit Clive but realised in the nick of time that it probably wouldn't go down too well. My aunt didn't wish anyone harm, but I also thought she felt envious of anyone who'd had an accident and had survived it, or who'd recovered from a life-threatening illness. I'd seen it in her eyes when she'd told me about Debbie who lived across the road from her, for example, who was in remission from Stage IV breast cancer. I knew she was thinking: why her? Why did she get to live? And I knew she felt bad about it, but you couldn't help how you felt, could you? Val reckoned it was 'unresolved grief'. At least I think that's what she'd called it. She was full of jargon because she'd been in therapy for years and considered herself somewhat of an expert on all things psychology-related.

'How's Uncle Steve?' I asked.

She sighed. 'He can't seem to sit still for five minutes. I'm not sure he's cut out for retirement.'

My uncle had given up his job as an electrician last year because Aunty Carol had nagged him into it and had persuaded him that he shouldn't be going up and down ladders and working with electrics at his age (seventy). She had a point, but the thing was, he'd always kept himself busy. For as long as I could remember, he worked all hours, and on his weekends off he'd either be doing stuff around their house or for Nan and me, or helping out the neighbours by doing odd jobs. I thought it had probably been his way of carrying on, and now that had been taken away from him, he clearly had no idea what to do with himself.

'How's that new man of yours?' asked Aunty Carol.

For a moment or two I couldn't think who she was talking about, but then I remembered I'd stupidly mentioned Tyler in passing on one of our last phone calls. What had possessed me? She'd never let that one go, now.

'Oh, he's back in New York,' I said vaguely.

'Ooh, a long-distance relationship,' chirped Aunty Carol hopefully.

Hardly, I thought. 'Not really,' I replied. 'It was only a casual thing.'

We chatted for a few more minutes about banal topics such as the fruit cake she'd made that had sunk in the middle, my upcoming interview and whether or not I thought she'd ever be able to persuade Uncle Steve to go on a cruise and then I ended the call and went out to the kitchen to see which delights I could conjure up for dinner. I hadn't been able to face M&S after leaving the hospital, so I was resigned to cobbling together whatever I could find in the fridge. I might possibly be able to rustle up a bowl of pasta with grated cheese.

As I passed the front door, I heard voices outside and couldn't resist a little peek through the spyhole. A tall guy in an anorak was standing on Jack's doorstep. Beyond him, I could see Jack. He had no top on and a towel wrapped around his waist. His hair was wet and his skin was glistening with soap suds and water. He was laughing, letting his friend inside. I couldn't help noticing how toned his stomach was, how he had actual *Men's Health* abs, just as I'd suspected that first night I'd met him.

I pulled back, shaking my head, going into the kitchen. What was I looking at him like that for? He wasn't my type at all, even if he had been very kind when I'd almost had a meltdown at the hospital. I got a pan out, filled it with water and put it on the hob, trying to erase all thoughts of a half-naked Jack from my mind.

28

Jack

I scanned the audition room, relieved that there was no one around I knew. It made it easier if I only had my own performance to concentrate on instead of second-guessing which one of us they were going to prefer.

I sat on the floor because all the chairs were taken. Experience had taught me that this meant I was in for a long wait. That by the time I was called in to read, in about an hour and a half's time, I'd have zero energy and would have lost the will to live. I massaged my temples, closing my eyes. I had to go in with the right attitude, or it was a waste of a time me being here. The casting was at the Jerwood Space, a modern, vibrant and very arty venue near London Bridge. The show itself, though, was going to be at the Soho Theatre, which was infinitely more impressive than a dusty old church hall in the back end of Bethnal Green, which had been the venue for my first fringe 'job'.

I pulled the script out of my bag, scanning through my lines, which I thought I knew. There weren't that many of them, thankfully, since it wasn't the lead I was reading for. I'd baulked at this, initially, to be honest – couldn't I even get the lead in a fringe show with no budget? But then I'd realised the lead character was supposed to be sixty-five, so it was out of my hands. It was a new play, written and directed by a guy who'd had a massive hit at the Edinburgh festival last year.

The room was swathed with the sort of industrious silence I was used to: the rustle of scripts, the odd cough, the murmur of actors attempting small talk. I flicked through Instagram, Twitter and TikTok, wondering if I should warn Luke I was probably going to be late for my shift.

'Hi,' I said, walking confidently into the room one hour and fifty-seven minutes after my allotted audition time. 'I'm Jack Maxwell.'

'Nice to meet you, Jack,' replied a young guy in ripped jeans and a red T-shirt. He had hair that was shaved at the sides, was wearing a nose ring and looked about twenty-one. 'I'm Joe and this is my assistant director, Raven,' he nodded at the girl sitting moodily next to him, who also looked fucked off to be running almost two hours late.

Joe proceeded to tell me a bit about the play, which was about a man with early-onset dementia and how the lines between fantasy and reality were becoming blurred. I was up for the role of his son-in-law, who was, by all accounts, a money-grabbing arsehole. I often got seen for these kinds of roles and wondered if that was how I came across in real life: a dick with a massive ego.

'Let's hear you read,' said Joe, ushering me back.

I dropped my script to my side, confident that I could remember the lines, imagining myself into the suburban living room of my wife's dad.

Joe began to read and I responded, owning the space and delivering what I thought was a pretty good performance. I thought that because the stakes weren't so high (there was no money involved, for a start), I was able to give my all and make my own choices without trying to work out what I thought it was they were looking for.

'That was great,' said Joe, looking surprised.

I saw him and Raven exchange glances. This was very positive; I'd clearly impressed them.

'Can we hear you sing?' he asked. 'Acapella is fine.'

I raised my eyebrows. 'Sing?'

'That's right,' confirmed Joe, looking at me eagerly. 'There are a couple of musical numbers in the play. Some movement, a few routines. I haven't asked *everyone* to sing, so ...' he said, by way of a warning. What he was basically saying was that I'd done well, but that if I seemed difficult to work with, if I was underprepared, then the role would go to somebody else. There would always been somebody waiting to snatch the job right out from underneath you in this business.

'Um, I haven't actually prepared anything,' I said, 'but sure. No problem.'

If they wanted you to do something like sing, they should give you prior warning, for fuck's sake. Musical theatre wasn't something I did: it wasn't like I had a repertoire of numbers up my sleeve that I could pull out at random for any occasion.

'We just want to get a sense of your voice,' explained Joe. 'Sing anything. A nursery rhyme if you want, I don't care. We just want to make sure you can hold a tune.'

I'd have to do the number I had learnt at LAMDA, the one I'd been told to practise every now and again because you never knew when you might need it, which, luckily for me, I'd diligently done. I took my place on the floor.

'I'll do "One Song Glory" from *Rent*,' I said, making some attempt to get into character, running through the lyrics and the melody in my mind. I'd just have to go for it.

Anyway, this guy was so young, he'd probably never seen *Rent*. Hopefully he'd have no idea how it was supposed to sound, I could improvise if I had to.

I took a deep breath.

'One song glory, one song before I go ...' I sang. *'Glory, one song to leave behind ...'*

Thankfully the words came. I kept it short, just a few bars, although to tell you the truth, I could have carried on. It was a great song and it was actually very freeing to belt it out at full volume, which I could never do when I was rehearsing at home in my flat because I was too self-conscious about my neighbours hearing me. Although with Ed Sheeran blasting out from above, they probably wouldn't hear, anyway.

'Perfect,' Joe said enthusiastically. 'Sorry we caught you on the hop there, but it was great, Jack, really.'

I nodded, feeling unusually pleased with myself. Maybe doing some theatre again would be good for me. And Chad was right, the Soho Theatre, plus this hotshot director, would be great incentives for casting directors to come.

'We'll be in touch,' said Raven, who seemed slightly less sullen than she had when I first walked in. I took that to be a good sign.

Outside, I felt buoyant for the first time in ages. I'd forgotten what it was like to have something go well. High on life, I walked past a couple stumbling out of a bar under the arches. They were talking loudly, probably drunk, and kept stopping to kiss passionately right in the middle of the pavement. I tutted, about to navigate my way around them when I did a double-take: it was my brother. And that was *not* his girlfriend, Theresa.

I stopped, not sure what to do, and almost caused a pile-up in the street in the process. Shit, what was he doing? Should

I pretend I hadn't noticed and walk on past? But then, why should I? Was it bad that I wanted to see him try to worm his way out of this one? Plus, I actually felt some sense of loyalty to Theresa – she was lovely and I'd always secretly thought she was too good for him. According to Mum, they were the perfect couple. Yin and yang. His life was complete with her in it, that's the impression he'd given us all. Clearly all was not as it seemed.

The girl – whoever she was – had walked off now, waving at Dom over her shoulder, leaving him, drunkenly swaying, alone. This was my chance.

I sidled up to him, touching him lightly on the elbow. I thought I'd play it neutral – I wouldn't lie about having seen what happened, but I wouldn't make it my opening gambit, either.

'Hey,' I said quietly.

He whipped round, his eyes glassy.

'It's only me,' I added, holding out my hands, taking a step back. Bloody hell, what was wrong with him?

He squinted, as though he couldn't quite believe that I was there. That was the thing with London, you quite often bumped into people you knew in the most unexpected places and scenarios. I'd seen my old voice tutor from LAMDA drinking a can of Guinness on the back of a night bus once. I'd even bumped into my dad in an itsu in City Road.

Dom put his hands over his mouth, breathing heavily into the palms of his hands.

'You OK?' I asked, worried now. Was he having some kind of psychotic episode?

Then he dropped his hands, brushed down his suit and smiled at me. 'Wow, Jack. Didn't expect to see you here.'

'So it seems,' I said.

We both looked in the direction the girl had staggered

off in, although she'd seemingly disappeared into the tube already, out of sight.

'Who was that?' I asked him.

'What?' said Dom, looking as though I'd just crawled out from a hole. 'Oh, you mean *her*? Just someone from work. No one special.'

'That's why you were kissing her, then, was it?' I said, stepping to the side so that I wasn't blocking the thoroughfare.

Dom laughed hollowly. 'Just being friendly, that was all.'

This was ridiculous, I wasn't blind and I wasn't going to let it go like I knew he wanted me to.

'So Theresa wouldn't be bothered if she knew, then?' I asked.

'Mind your own business, Jack,' said Dom, straightening his jacket. 'What are you so interested for, anyway?'

I shrugged. 'No reason. I was just thinking that if you are shagging around, you might just want to be a bit more subtle about it. Anyone could have seen you; you're right by a busy train station.'

'You know what, Jack?' said Dom, walking off. 'Why don't you try taking a look at your own life first, yeah? When are you going to get a relationship of your own, eh, instead of constantly interfering in mine?'

I crossed my arms, looking at him, fascinated. He really was an arsehole. And in some small way, it made me feel better that I'd witnessed that, that I'd seen for myself that his life wasn't the bed of roses he made out it was. I felt sorry for Theresa, of course, but she was a smart girl, she'd eventually work out what he was like, if she hadn't already.

'You going to Mum and Dad's at the weekend?' I shouted after him, unable to resist the opportunity to wind him up even more.

He waved his hand in response, refusing to look at me.

He had the air of someone who'd been caught doing something he shouldn't have been. Of a man who'd showed a side of himself he'd previously pretty successfully kept hidden. And all of a sudden it dawned on me why it made me feel so weird: I'd seen Dad like that before, all cagey, like he was covering something up. And it felt familiar and it felt wrong and it was clear to me now why Dom and I clashed all the time: he and Dad were too alike. And although it was a terrible thing to say about your own flesh and blood, I didn't particularly like either of them.

29

Rebecca

My chest was burning as I ran up the slope, away from the lake. If I could just make it to the top, I'd have done my 7K. My thighs felt as though they were going to explode as I staggered the last few metres up the hill, pumping my arms to help my body along.

I checked my Fitbit: 39 minutes. Not bad. Three minutes faster than I'd run the same distance on Sunday.

I flopped down on the grass, lying flat out, dandelions tickling the back of my neck. Above me, the sky was blue with fluffy clouds, like when you drew a picture of a house when you were a kid. My imaginary abode had always been square, detached, with a front garden full of flowers, a curved path and smoke chugging out of its chimney. In other words, nothing like my actual house, which had been in the middle of a slightly shabby row of terraced houses with no front garden in a suburban town. I didn't remember ever seeing flowers in our little patch of garden at the back.

I sat up, resting my chin on my knees, hugging my shins. It was gorgeous here. To my left was Kenwood House in all its creamy, dramatic Georgian glory and in front of it the lake and the white bridge, which looked like the most romantic setting on earth from this angle but was in reality a replica and couldn't actually be walked across. I let my imagination run away with me, picturing myself as a lovestruck heroine in a Jane Austen novel. In order to do justice to this image, however, I had to work hard to block out the family with five noisy children behind me, the lively group of octogenarians playing boules to my left and the man teaching his dog to catch a manky tennis ball in its mouth to my right.

The hairs on my arms stood on end now that I was cooling down and I pulled at the tracksuit top I'd tied around my waist, slipping it on. When I looked up, I spotted somebody thundering diagonally up the hill. I was glad he was struggling as much as I'd been because that meant that it wasn't so much my lack of fitness that was the problem as the steep incline. I had another sneaky look: I recognised that black-on-black ensemble, the T-shirt with some sort of hip-hop slogan on it, the three-quarter length joggers. Jack.

Possibly sensing me eyeballing him, he spotted me, too, and came to a stop, bending double to catch his breath and then walking towards me.

'You OK there?' I said.

His face was bright red and there were rivulets of sweat streaming down his face. 'Just about,' he replied, taking a deep breath in and then blowing it noisily out again through his mouth. 'God, that hill is tough.'

I nodded empathetically, dabbing at my forehead with the sleeve of my jacket. 'I know. I'm going to be aching big time tomorrow.'

'How was your run?' he asked.

Because the sun was behind him, it was like I was viewing him in silhouette, the features of his face almost too dark to make out.

'Not bad,' I said. 'I wasn't really up for it, but you always feel better afterwards, don't you?'

I watched him stretch his quads, flipping his heel up

behind him, holding onto his foot. He had excellent balance; if that had been me, especially if I'd had an audience, I'd have been flailing my arms about all over the place.

'Have you seen any more of Clive?' I asked him.

He crouched down in front of me. 'Popped in last night. Physically he's doing really well,' he said. 'The hip operation was a success, as far as they can tell. Obviously they're still monitoring him and all that. They got him out of bed for the first time earlier in the week. He managed a few steps, the nurses said.'

I'd knocked to ask Jack about him once or twice, and each time there was this kind of unsaid mystery surrounding it. I could tell he was wondering what my hospital phobia was all about.

'It's his mental health I'm worried about,' added Jack, flopping down on the grass next to me, his legs splayed out in front of him.

'Oh, really?' I said, surprised. Clive had always seemed so strong. So independent, so capable of dealing with anything life might throw at him.

Jack sighed. 'He's lonely, isn't he? I think I underestimated how important it is for him to see us all, even if it's only to say a quick hello to as we go up and down the stairs.'

I pulled blades of grass out of the ground. 'That's sad.'

Jack leaned back on his elbows. 'He was telling me how he's lived this really solitary life and how that suited him for a long time. He liked being able to please himself. But now they're talking about him going into a home.'

The wind picked up and I tucked a stray hair behind my ear.

'My nan's in Greenhill Lodge, not far from here.'

Jack raised his eyebrows. 'Does she like it there?'

I nodded. 'She's definitely starting to. She's like Clive,

really sociable, so it's nice that she's got people to talk to all the time. Although she still thinks all the other residents are much older than she is and that she's far too young and spritely to be in a place like that!'

Jack laughed.

'I could mention it to Clive,' I said. 'Next time I visit,' I added, looking off into the distance.

Jack looked out at the lake, then back at me again. 'Can I ask you something?'

I swallowed, knowing what he was going to say. 'Sure.'

Jack leaned forward, re-tying one of his shoe laces. 'How come you're scared of hospitals? I mean, I don't want to pry, and feel free to tell me to mind my own business. It's just … I thought it might help to say it out loud.'

I knew this would happen. It always did when you started to get closer to someone and they told you stuff about their lives and you found it impossible to talk about your child-hood or your past without mentioning the thing that had changed everything, that had affected every part of it.

I picked a daisy out of the grass and started pulling off its petals one by one.

'My parents died,' I told him. 'Just before my eighth birthday.'

Jack didn't say anything for what felt like ages.

'Shit,' he said eventually. 'I'm so sorry.'

I nodded. It was apt that I should be telling him while we were sitting on the heath. I only had odd memories of my mum and dad: the night it happened, and a picnic here on the heath the summer before. Dad had played frisbee with me; Mum had been sunbathing with her straps down. We'd had cheese sandwiches and crisps and Dad had found a kiosk somewhere and had bought us all an ice-cream.

'Thanks,' I said.

After all these years, I still wasn't sure how best to respond when someone offered their sympathy. Thanks for what? For a while I used to say *it's okay* because I didn't want the person to feel awkward, but then I realised that actually it wasn't okay, so why was I saying it was?

'What happened?' asked Jack, looking across at me. His bare arm was brushing against the sleeve of my tracksuit. Perhaps it had been there all along and I hadn't noticed.

'There was a car accident,' I said. 'Black ice on the road. I was in the car with them, but I got off lightly in comparison: bruising and concussion and a broken collarbone. I was in hospital for a while myself, so I didn't know what had happened straight away. I can't remember it, but apparently my nan was the one to tell me. Our car had hit a tree and my parents had taken most of the impact. They'd both died instantly, the police said.'

Jack pinched the top of his nose. 'Fucking hell.'

'So yeah, I went to live with my nan and grandad after that. My mum's parents. And my mum's sister, Aunty Carol, was just round the corner. So I had people. I always felt very loved and they did their best to give me a good life. But, you know ... it was never the same after.'

Jack took my hand and squeezed it really tight. 'I wish there was something I could say to make it better,' he said, looking out at the lake.

He let go of my hand and undid the top of his water bottle and took several mouthfuls.

'Sorry to depress you,' I said. 'I bet you weren't expecting that.'

I stood up, rotating my shoulders.

He shielded his eyes from the sun. 'I'm glad you told me. And I understand now,' he replied. 'About the hospital. It must bring everything back.'

'Yeah,' I admitted. 'Even though I've got no memory of the accident itself, sometimes I get flashbacks, just these weird, disjointed images. It's triggered by sound usually. Ambulance sirens are the worst.'

'I guess that's because of the trauma,' remarked Jack.

I'd heard that word bandied about over the years, but had never known what to do with it. How was someone supposed to get over a trauma? It was always going to be there, wasn't it?

'I should get back to my run,' I said.

'I thought you'd finished?' said Jack, looking confused.

'Feel like doing a couple more kilometres,' I replied.

Exercise helped. After the accident, Nan had signed me up for as many clubs as she could afford – swimming and netball and gymnastics – because she wanted me to live as normal a life as possible, to be joyful again and to spend time around other children. It worked on and off. Of course, you couldn't be completely joyful when you'd suddenly lost the two people you'd loved most in the world.

Jack nodded, observing me quietly.

'If you ever want to talk about it,' he began, 'I'd like to hear more. I know it's probably difficult to put into words. But you could try. If you like?'

I smiled at him. Nobody had ever said anything like that to me before, not even Dan. I think people assumed it would be too painful for me to talk about and so avoided mentioning it altogether. Their intentions were coming from a good place, I got that, but it always made me feel ten times more alone with it all.

I hesitated before I turned to jog down the hill, back towards the lake.

30

Jack

The windows of the club on Dean Street were all steamed up and I didn't realise how packed it was until I pushed my way inside. The place was a heaving mass of actors and staff from the agency and industry people, all drunk and sweating and talking loudly (about themselves, no doubt). I should have listened to my instincts and taken an extra shift at the pub when Luke had offered it to me. The DJ was playing hip-hop so loud I could feel it pulsating through my bones.

I strained my neck, looking for Chad. I planned to have a casual chat with him while he was possibly inebriated and in a good mood, but if he was on one of his health kicks, he wouldn't be drinking at all. Surely even Chad was capable of having a good time at a party.

'There you are, mate. I was wondering if you were going to make it,' said Seb, dancing up to me, swivelling his hips in time to the music, his eyes glassy, his dark curls wet with sweat.

I had no idea why he was here, he wasn't even represented by Star Management.

'Wouldn't miss this, would I?' I lied. 'Seen Chad?'

Seb was now dancing with Chad's assistant, grinding his crotch against her thigh. 'He's around somewhere,' he shouted over his shoulder.

I looked around, my eyes searching the room, eventually spotting Chad, who was ordering a sparkling water at the bar. Oh god. I'd been hoping that tonight there would be a chance for me to get on a level with Chad, to see whether we could salvage something. It had been better between us at the beginning. I'd actually thought he liked me, then, and he had at least shown a modicum of enthusiasm about my work and had (a tiny amount of) time for me. We used to have actual conversations about stuff other than the very perfunctory details of my next audition. It was becoming clear now that I needed a new agent, but the thought absolutely terrified me. Could I really give up everything that Star Management represented? Would I be better off at a smaller, boutique agency where they might not have the contacts Chad had, but they could see my potential for what it was? I had longevity, I had passion and I was prepared to work hard. And if Chad couldn't see that, then it was time to move on.

'Excuse me? Jack, isn't it?'

I whirled round. A man in smart grey trousers, a white pinstriped shirt that was open at the neck and rectangular glasses was standing next to me.

'That's right,' I replied, smiling. You never knew who you might meet at these sorts of things.

'I'm Alistair Kemp,' he said. 'From Hargreaves & Kemp.'

'Hi!' I said, recognising the name immediately.

I'd written to him years ago, when I was about to leave drama school and was looking for an agent, but then I'd been swept up in the Star Management machine.

'Wasn't expecting to see any other agents at a Star event,' I commented.

Alistair laughed. 'My brother-in-law's on the board of

directors,' he explained. 'Fancied a night out, so thought I'd gatecrash.'

'Don't blame you,' I said, grabbing a strange-looking canapé from a passing waitress.

Alistair did the same, peering at it.

'What do you think it is?' he said, sniffing it with suspicion.

I shrugged. 'No idea. We're just going to have to be brave and go for it.'

We simultaneously popped them into our mouths making appreciative noises. I still had no clue what was in it.

'I enjoyed your performance on *Holby City* last year,' said Alistair.

I forced my last mouthful of canapé down my throat. 'You did?'

Immediately I wished I'd made more of an effort. I was wearing the exact same outfit I wore for every single networking event, opening night party or family function: black jeans and a black French Connection shirt that I'd once bought for an audition. I'd baulked at the price at the time, but if you worked out the price per wear, it had been a veritable bargain.

'You went to LAMDA, didn't you? I vaguely remember your showcase. I was about to ask if you wanted to come in for a chat when I heard you'd signed with Star.'

'Oh right,' I said, grabbing two glasses of Champagne from a passing waiter and handing one to Alistair. 'That feels like a long time ago now.'

Alistair laughed. 'So how's it going with Chad?'

I looked nervously around. Could I really do this now?

'Um … it's fine,' I replied. 'I mean, he's very busy.'

'The life of a superstar agent, eh?' said Alistair.

I nodded, taking another furtive look around. Chad was

now schmoozing with some guy in a suit. I didn't trust him anymore, I realised. I wasn't convinced he wanted the best for me and, honestly, I didn't know why he hadn't dumped me by now.

'Obviously it wouldn't be appropriate for me to poach Star Management's actors at their own party,' continued Alistair. 'But if you ever feel like a change, you know where I am.'

I swept my eyes around the bar, glad to see that Seb was still otherwise engaged on the dance floor. I didn't want him putting two and two together and gossiping about it.

'It's definitely something I'm thinking about,' I said, lowering my voice. Just saying it out loud made me feel more powerful than I had in years. My future didn't have to hinge on Chad and whether or not he deemed me important enough to find work for. Alistair was here and he thought I was good enough. I still had it. I *was* talented and I *hadn't* been deluding myself all these years.

Alistair surreptitiously gave me his card and I said I'd drop him a line.

All night I had a sort of excitement buzzing around inside me. It felt good to take control of my own future and for someone to believe in me. Oddly, when I was thinking about what I should do and who I could talk to about it, who might understand, my mind immediately went to Rebecca.

31

Rebecca

I didn't usually get the lift because it felt lazy, but I'd gone a bit mad in Tesco in the village and badly regretted it now that the handles of the cheap plastic bags you had to pay for the privilege of using were cutting into my fingers so sharply that the tips were white, with angry red stripes gouged through the middle of my flesh. This was a regular occurrence; I always seemed to buy more than I needed and then wondered why it was such a struggle to get home.

I dropped the bags by the lift doors, shaking out my hands to get the circulation going again and pressed the call button. Nothing. I pressed it again. For fuck's sake. What were the chances, the one time I needed to use it? I'd heard residents complaining about its unreliability before, but I'd never experienced the frustration of it myself and therefore had only ever made empathetic noises in commiseration. Now I knew exactly why it manifested such fury.

I stomped up the stairs, stopping at each landing to catch my breath and to give my fingers a break. What had possessed me to buy a four-pack of chopped tomatoes and a six-pack of mineral water in the same trip? Never again.

When I reached my floor, the culprit of the missing lift was staring me right in the face: some idiot had left the door open. Everybody knew that if you left the door open, it wouldn't work. And, according to Clive, it was often someone on the sixth floor who'd failed to close it, meaning that somebody had to climb about a hundred stairs to rectify somebody else's mistake/selfish act. To be fair, it was sometimes visitors who left it open, and perhaps they didn't realise, but still.

I'd gone from being sympathetic but unmoved by the affairs of the lift to absolutely incensed by them. I reached out and yanked the lift door, intending to pull it shut, but it didn't budge. I tried again, jarring my shoulder in the process. It appeared to be stuck, which meant that nobody would be able to use the lift until further notice, which meant that if, for example, the lady with the baby on the fifth floor was still out, she was going to have to lug her pushchair up five flights of stairs.

Without thinking too much about, it I knocked on Jack's door. The second I'd done it, I realised it might not be the best idea. It was as though I wanted someone to vent to and just because he was the closest, he was about to be the unhappy recipient. Since Clive's accident we'd been chatting more, which was nice. It felt good to have a friendly face just across the hall and also very useful at times like this. Of course, I should probably have had a go at fixing the lift myself first, but it was too late now.

Jack's door opened. There he was, in another odd ensemble of a zipped-up tracksuit top and white football shorts. For the first time, I noticed that he wasn't as tall as I'd thought – 5'10, maybe 5'11. If I wore my highest (only) pair of heels, we'd be about the same height. Not that we'd ever be going out together, especially not with me in heels. I glanced into his flat. There were three pairs of trainers lined up in the corridor, two white and one black.

'Um, I just wondered if you were any good at fixing lifts?' I said.

He stuck his head out into the hallway and looked at it. 'What's up with it?'

'The door's stuck halfway across, so no one can use it.'

He glanced at my two bulging bags of shopping and grimaced. 'You had to walk up, did you?'

'Yep,' I replied, trying to hide my frustration. It wasn't his fault. Unless he'd had a visitor who'd used the lift, in which case …

'Let me get my tools,' he said, disappearing down the corridor. 'Come in for a sec if you like.'

Unsure what to do, I followed him inside, not wanting to seem rude. Also, I'd never actually seen the inside of any of the other flats except Clive's and I couldn't miss this opportunity to see how different they were, particularly the ones on this side of the building. Would his be identical to mine in layout? Would his decor give the space a whole different vibe?

I slipped off my shoes, leaving the front door open, and headed into the hall.

'I'm in the lounge,' I heard him call.

My lounge was second on the right, so assuming his was, too, I made my way there.

'Wow,' I said, looking around. 'This is lovely.'

I immediately felt a pang of jealousy at how cosy and lived-in the room looked. A *Bosh* recipe book was open on the coffee table and there was an issue of *Equity* magazine on the arm of the sofa. A couple of dirty coffee cups and a pile of scripts had been discarded on the twirly multicoloured rug. The bookshelves were full to brimming and there were all sorts of bits and bobs above the fireplace: old theatre tickets, framed photos, a couple of houseplants that were flourishing and healthy (something I'd annoyingly always failed to achieve with my own plants). I immediately got a sense of who he was. And I thought that if somebody came to my flat, they probably wouldn't get any sense of me at all.

'Won't be a sec,' said Jack, who was scrabbling in a drawer. 'Sit down if you want.'

I perched on the edge of the sofa. When I looked behind me out of the window, I noticed his view was completely different to mine, of course. He looked out over East Heath Road and to the multimillion-pound houses that had back gardens the size of small parks. The whole of Hampstead Village was laid out in front of him, curling upwards to the peak of the hill where the tube station was.

'Lovely view,' I said.

He looked around. 'What's yours like, then?'

'The heath off to the side. And then other people's flats, mainly.'

'You can see into them?'

I nodded. 'Yeah.'

He laughed. 'I'd love that, to be honest.'

'It's perfect if you're quite nosy like I am,' I admitted. 'You can gather information on these people that you've never actually met, except perhaps to say hello to if you happen to take the rubbish out at the same time. It would be good for you, being an actor.'

'It would,' he agreed. 'I'll have to come over and observe when I'm in need of character inspiration.'

I laughed, pushing the strangely alluring thought of him coming into my flat to the back of my mind.

Jack suddenly pounced on something in the drawer and brandished a screwdriver at me dramatically. 'I knew it was in there somewhere,' he said.

My eye caught a programme for *Romeo and Juliet* at the National Theatre on the mantelpiece.

'Were you in that?' I asked him, going over.

He nodded, looking pleased I'd noticed. 'Yeah,' he said, picking it up. 'I was Benvolio,' he added, flicking wistfully through the glossy pages. 'Look, here's a picture, the scene where I tell Romeo to run away or he'll be put to death.'

I looked over his shoulder at the photo. He looked like a completely different person in the picture. He was drenched with sweat, bare chested and with much longer hair pulled back in a small bun. His face was contorted with anger, an expression I couldn't imagine him doing in real life.

'Do you like going to the theatre?' he asked me.

'Sure,' I said. In theory, although I rarely went. 'I'm not massively keen on musicals though.' And then I looked around the room, panicked that he was actually a musical theatre aficionado and I'd hugely insulted him. Mind you, there were no copies of the *Les Mis* soundtrack that I could see; no *Starlight Express* memorabilia.

'I'm not a big fan, either,' he said.

I smiled, relieved. 'Oh good.'

'I did an audition the other day and they made me sing for the first time in ages,' he said, grimacing.

'You don't like singing?'

'I mean, it's not my favourite thing,' he replied. 'You?'

'God, no. Not even in the shower.'

'You should let loose in the shower,' he said. 'I do.'

I had a flashback to seeing him standing on his doorstep half-naked and laughed to hide my embarrassment. Thankfully he seemed keen to crack on with the lift job and was heading towards the door. I followed him out of the room and back into the hallway, grabbing my shoes on the way.

'So, yeah,' I said, pulling at the handle of the lift. 'It's not budging at all, see?'

'Let's have a look,' he said, leaning in closer so that our

cheeks were almost touching. I was very aware of him being inches away from me, and of trying to act as though this felt completely normal. I was breathing so hard that I could see my chest rising and falling in my peripheral vision.

Jack started fiddling with the hinge, twisting a bolt with his screwdriver, one at the top and one at the bottom. When he tried the door, it slid effortlessly open and did the same when it closed.

'There we go!' he said, looking pleased with himself.

I took a step back and admired his handiwork.

'You're good at fixing things, aren't you?' I said.

He put his tools in his back pocket. 'Apparently so. It's one of those things I didn't know I could do until I was forced to try.'

'I guess the same could be said for most things,' I replied, unlocking my door and dragging my shopping into my hall-way. 'Anyway. I've got that interview tomorrow, so ...'

He looked at me through his too-long, floppy fringe. 'Are you nervous?' he asked.

I nodded. 'Partly because I'm not sure if I even want the job.'

He looked confused. 'I thought you said it was the same sort of thing but a step up?'

'Yeah, it is,' I said. 'I'm just a bit sick of the industry I'm in. It's not really me.'

'What do you reckon is "you", then?'

I bit my lip. 'I've applied for something, actually. It's still a marketing role, but at a charity working with children who have been bereaved.'

Jack nodded enthusiastically 'Sounds great. Is that some-thing you've always wanted to do? Because of what happened to you?'

'It is,' I replied. 'But I was too scared for a long time. In case it was too painful, or something, which I suppose is a bit selfish. I mean, if I can help other children like me, I should, right?'

Jack thought about it. 'I don't think there's a "should". You have to do what feels right for you.'

I smiled. 'Hard to know, though, isn't it?'

'Don't get me started,' he said, smiling back.

I put my hand on the door handle. 'Thanks for sorting the lift,' I said.

'Any time,' he replied, grinning. 'It's one way for me to make up for all those packages coming your way.'

I rolled my eyes. 'Yes, well,' I said, pretending I minded. Now I'd got to know him a bit, I didn't so much. You could hardly do normal working hours when you were an actor, could you?

I closed my door and leaned my back against it, thinking about his eyes for some reason. How they'd lit up when he was telling me about his part in *Romeo and Juliet*. About the tops of his arms, his pale wrists. And then I shook myself out of it and started unpacking my dinner. There was no way I could afford to get close to someone again, no matter how easy they were to talk to.

32

Jack

A few days later, when I left the flat to get to my shift at the pub, Rebecca was coming home from work.

'Hey,' I said, waiting on the landing to let her pass. 'How was your interview the other day?'

She slid her bag off her shoulder so that it was dangling from one hand. 'I didn't do it,' she replied. 'Told them I wasn't sure it was the best move for me.'

'Blimey,' I said, pleasantly surprised. 'That must have taken guts. Good for you.'

'They were a bit shocked,' she said, laughing. 'I think they see me as being welded to my desk. I don't think they'd imagined for a second that I might want to leave.'

'When will you hear about that charity job?'

'Not sure,' she said. 'I might not even be what they're looking for.'

'I bet you are,' I replied, crossing my fingers. She crossed them back. 'Anyway, better get to work,' I said, tripping down the stairs.

I heard her get her keys out and then, because it popped into my brain and I didn't give myself the time to filter it out, to think of all the reasons I shouldn't say it, I ran back up to our landing. She looked surprised to see me.

'Um, you said you like theatre, didn't you?'

She hesitated. 'Sure.'

I put my hands on my hips, slightly out of breath. 'I've got a spare ticket for something at the Park Theatre tomorrow night. A friend of mine's in it. You wouldn't fancy coming, would you?'

'Um …'

'You're probably busy,' I backtracked, silently kicking myself. 'Don't worry, I know it's short notice.'

'No, that sounds good, actually,' she replied, jangling her keys.

'Great,' I said, still not sure why I'd asked her in the first place. I went to the theatre on my own all the time. Plus, since Nathalie, my ex, was in it, it might be awkward. It had just seemed a shame to waste the ticket. 'Shall we meet in the bar on the ground floor?'

She nodded. 'What time?'

'Can you get there for about seven?'

She let herself into her flat. 'Sure,' she said, turning to look at me with those almond-shaped, brown eyes that I always pictured when I thought about her. 'See you there.'

'Here we go,' I said, nabbing a spot out on the pavement in front of the theatre.

I put our drinks down on the shiny, silver table and promptly watched them nearly slide off the edge because the leg was wonky. I caught them just in time and then crouched down, shoving my copy of the *Evening Standard* under one of the legs to steady it.

'Large Sauvignon Blanc, right?' I said.

'Perfect,' she replied, sitting down and tucking herself into the table. 'I'll get the interval drinks.'

I pulled my coat around myself. It had been a lovely bright

day earlier, but it was pitch black out now and too cold to be sitting outside, really.

'We can stand inside if you prefer?' I suggested, noticing that she was rubbing the tops of her arms. 'There's not much room, but we can find a corner somewhere.'

'It's fine,' she said, shaking her head. 'I like it out here.'

I caught the tail end of a conversation happening at the table next to ours. I reckoned they were actors, too, because they were talking about a friend of theirs who was putting something on at the Kings Head. I strained to hear; you never knew when this kind of information might prove useful. Sometimes I thought it might be nice to take a night off from being an actor.

I took a sip of my pint. 'That's better,' I said.

'Tough day?' she asked.

'I worked the lunch shift at the pub, then had a casting for a toothpaste advert in the afternoon.'

She laughed. 'Did you have to pretend to clean your teeth in front of a row of brand executives?'

I grimaced. 'How did you know?'

She looked different tonight. Her hair was down, falling over her shoulder in soft curls. And there was something different about her make-up, although I couldn't tell you what. She wore quite a lot of make-up, I'd noticed, but in a way that looked natural rather than over the top. I liked the way her lips were always painted a sort of matte plum. In any case, she looked lovely. And I'd been excited to see her, an emotion I hadn't felt in years (if ever). Luke kept telling me that he thought my life would be fuller if I opened myself up to the idea of a relationship, but I couldn't make myself like someone, could I? Like Donna's friend, the one he'd tried to set me up with at the dinner party; she'd been nice enough, but there just wasn't any chemistry on my part, so what would have been the point in pursuing it? And I was sick of dating actresses, of moving in those same circles all the time. When I'd got tangled up with girls from drama school, it had never worked and had become a terrible sort of competition as to who had the upper hand and whose career was going better. With Rebecca it was easy. I didn't have to pretend to be something I wasn't because this was not in any way a relationship, other than a friendly one that friendly neighbours have. It had crossed my mind that Rebecca might think I was asking her out on a date, but then I came to my senses and realised that she wouldn't think that because I was pretty sure her dates didn't involve wobbly table legs and studio theatre in Finsbury Park. She was probably used to being wined and dined in the capital's most exclusive restaurants. I could imagine American boy splashing his cash on a dinner that cost more than my weekly rent.

'So what does your boyfriend do?' I asked her. 'I haven't seen him around for a while, does he work away?'

She stared into her drink, running her finger around and around the rim of the glass. 'I don't have a boyfriend,' she replied, looking up.

'Oh,' I said, frowning. 'I thought you were with that American guy …'

She shook her head, looking embarrassed. 'We were seeing each other for a while, but it was nothing serious. He's gone back to New York now, anyway.'

'Oh, I see.'

I wasn't sure why, but I felt a sort of relief. I thought it was probably because I couldn't imagine her with someone like him now that I'd got to know her better.

'So are you seeing anyone else?' I asked.

Oh god, what was wrong with me? I was making it sound as though I was interested in her and that wasn't it at all.

'Not really,' she said, fiddling with the hoop in her right ear.

'How come?'

She tilted her head to the side, propping it in her hand. 'This is probably a bit deep, but I don't really want to put myself out there anymore. I can't stand the thought of loving someone and then losing them again.'

'I imagine that's partly because of your parents, right?' I said, settling back in my seat.

I thought about what she'd told me a lot. I mean, my feelings towards my own family were complicated, but I couldn't imagine losing them, let alone when I'd been a child.

She nodded. 'It must be, I suppose. But then I met my ex-boyfriend, Dan, when I was really young. We were sixteen when we started going out.'

I took a sip of wine, trying not to look shocked. I was barely functioning at sixteen, let alone starting a serious relationship. 'So you were with him for a while?'

'Well I'm thirty-two now, so …'

I shook my head, still reeling. 'Sixteen years …'

She smiled. 'Half my life, so yeah, I guess it was a long time.'

I felt panicky just thinking about it. Sixteen years with the same person, making sacrifices, having to take their wants and needs into account, only for them to get off and leave you at the drop of a hat. No thanks.

She twisted her wine glass around by the stem. 'What about you? Seeing anyone?'

I shook my head, a bit too vigorously. 'Nope. Too busy.'

She gave me a strange look.

'I'm focusing on my work.'

She nodded, looking at me suspiciously, as though she thought I was hiding something.

'Oh, I grabbed us a programme,' I said, changing the subject. I plucked it out of my bag, sliding it across the table.

Rebecca opened it up, flicking through the actors' head-shots and bios.

'Who is it you know?' she asked.

'Here,' I said, prodding my finger at a glossy shot of a black girl in her early thirties. 'Nathalie. She's great. She was in the year above me at drama school. It was obvious she was going to do well. We went out for a bit, actually.'

Where had that come from? I'd specifically decided not to tell Rebecca about my history with Nathalie.

'Oh, did you?' she said, peering closely at Nathalie's head-shot. 'was it serious?'

'Not really. I think she just liked having me around as a sort of trophy boyfriend. She wheeled me out whenever she wanted a plus-one, and then barely spoke to me the rest of the time. Eventually I lost interest, which I don't think she was best pleased about.'

'What were you like at drama school, then?' asked Rebecca, going in closer to read the text. 'Did you get the best parts, too?'

'Sometimes. Usually.'

She looked up. 'You're good, then?'

I swilled my drink around in my glass. 'You'll have to come and watch me sometime. Make up your own mind.'

An announcement informed us the performance was about to start and that we should please take our seats. I stood up, scraping back my chair. Rebecca grabbed both our drinks and followed me into the auditorium. Inside, it was dark and still, a small studio theatre with four of five rows in the stalls where we were sitting and two or three rows up on the balcony. Enviously, I imagined the actors behind the set, earnestly doing their warm-up exercises. Running lines under their breath. Arranging to meet for post-performance drinks.

'This is us,' I said, shrugging off my coat and stuffing it under my seat. Rebecca did the same, revealing a black shirt tucked into skinny blue jeans. It seemed like a different look for her; less buttoned-up than the stuff she usually wore to work. Actually, the more time I spent with her, the more I enjoyed her company. She was grounded in a way I wasn't used to. And she was super smart and intuitive – I felt like she got what I was trying to say, even if she didn't know much about the acting world herself. I found it funny, now, that we'd got off on the wrong foot and that I'd made these assumptions about her based only on that.

'Do you wish you were on the stage?' she whispered in my ear, as though she could see what was inside my head.

I shrugged and then nodded. 'Sort of.'

And then the lights went down and the play began.

At one point I felt like I was going to get cramp and I stretched my right leg out in front of me. My thigh pressed against Rebecca's and I gently pulled it away, feeling self-conscious in case she thought I'd done it on purpose. It took me a few seconds to concentrate on the play again after that. Worryingly, it had felt quite nice.

33

Rebecca

The play was set in Brooklyn in the 1950s and was about the dynamics between members of an Italian/American family who were struggling with life and love. Jack's ex, Nathalie, was brilliant and during the curtain call she winked at Jack and he whooped and I felt part of something, as though I suddenly had exclusive access to a secret world. I could see why Jack loved it so much, and how rewarding it must be to give such an amazing performance that the audience gave you a standing ovation afterwards.

'What did you reckon?' asked Jack, sitting back down in his seat and turning to me.

I pulled my bag onto my lap, picking my empty wine glass up off the floor. The audience were talking in hushed voices sprinkled with the tinkle of laughter and I noticed people looking longingly at the stage as though they didn't want to leave this make-believe world they'd been part of for the last two and a half hours.

'I loved it,' I said. 'The cast were so good. I don't know how you lot do it!'

I'd forgotten how seeing a play could toy with your emotions like that; how it could make you see something in a different way. The world of corporate marketing felt dry and soulless in comparison – I wasn't about to run off and be an artist or anything, but I could definitely see the appeal.

'Have you got any jobs coming up yourself?' I asked him.

He nodded, looking at me, his face probably the closest to mine it had ever been. He had lovely smooth skin and the most perfect eyebrows. 'I got offered a part in a fringe play today, actually,' he said.

'Congratulations,' I said. 'Are you pleased?'

'Yeah. I think so. Also, I got approached by another agent the other night. I think I might set up a meeting.'

I watched the last of the remaining audience members leave the auditorium. We were completely alone now, the air thick with silence, a contrast to the explosion of music and sound and dialogue that had dominated the space for most of the evening.

'What's wrong with your current agent?'

Jack rubbed his jaw. 'He's at the top of his game. Represents half of Hollywood.'

'Isn't that a good thing?'

'That's what I thought initially. But then I realised that it means he basically has no time for people like me.'

'Ah,' I said. 'It's a small fish in a big pond type of thing?'

Jack laughed. 'Thanks for branding me a small fish.'

I looked down at the glass in my lap. 'Sorry.'

That had come out all wrong. I just meant that's how he must feel, not that he was an actual small fish. From what he'd told me, it sounded like he was very good and just needed a break.

'It's fine,' he said, nudging me in the ribs.

The air around us suddenly became even stiller, the only sound being the chatter from the bar, the faraway clinking of wine glasses.

'We should go, I suppose,' he said.

'Yeah,' I replied, spotting the ushers hovering with black bags, ready to clear up.

'It's been ... nice to get to know you a bit,' he said, looking out at the stage.

'Definitely,' I agreed.

'Fancy a quick drink at the bar?' he asked.

'Sure,' I said. 'Why not?'

The two of us stood up and Jack steered me towards the exit, his hand placed lightly on my back again, which felt surprisingly comforting. I was having such a good time. It was doing me good to get out of the flat, to not think about the things my mind was usually preoccupied with, like was my nan OK, had not interviewing for the job been a massive mistake, had Tyler ever been remotely interested in me for anything other than sex, and if not, did it really matter anyway? The play had taken me out of myself; for a brief time, I'd been caught up in somebody else's (albeit fictional) life instead and conversation with Jack flowed so easily that I hadn't thought about anything else except having a nice time here, with him.

'Jack, mate!' said a guy appearing beside us. He slapped Jack really hard on the back, which I thought must have hurt.

'Rory, dude. Good to see you,' said Jack, not giving anything away if it had.

Rory clocked me and looked confused. My insecurity kicked in and I immediately decided it must be because I didn't look like the type of person Jack would usually hang out with. I imagined those girls to be exceptionally beautiful, probably blonde, somewhat privileged and massively full of themselves. The sort of girls who could wear a pair of boyfriend jeans and a white vest and look amazing.

'Rory, this is my neighbour, Rebecca,' said Jack. 'Rory and I were at drama school together,' Jack explained to me.

'Oh right,' I said. 'Nice to meet you, Rory.'

Rory pumped my hand several times. 'Fraternising with the neighbours, eh? That's what I like to see.'

Jack and I looked at each other. It did sound weird when you put it like that; I couldn't imagine myself going out for the evening with anyone else from Marlowe Court, not even Clive, as lovely as he was.

'Oh here's Nathalie,' announced Jack with a flourish, gesturing towards a door that presumably led up from backstage.

The cast were piling out, looking all pumped up and pleased with themselves as though they were high on adrenaline. Practically everyone in the bar turned to look at them and I thought it must be impossible not to have a huge ego with all that day in day out. They looked completely different off-stage – the way they were dressed, their hair loose, their skin free of make-up. I had to admit there was something thrilling about the fact they were heading in my direction. Although of course, it was really Jack and Rory's direction.

Nathalie hugged them both and there was more exaggerated laughter and congratulations, and although she didn't get her back slapped, she might as well have done. She was doing a good job of being humble about it, in that quietly confident, semi-fake way you might have cultivated if you were used to being brilliant on stage and to everyone raving about your performance afterwards.

'Nathalie, this is Rebecca,' said Jack as Rory headed off to the bar.

Nathalie did a sort of arsey double-take once she finally noticed I was there.

I put out my hand. 'Nice to meet you,' I said. 'And congratulations on your performance.'

She took my hand and shook it limply, giving me a subtle sweeping look up and down.

'And how do you two know each other again…?' asked Nathalie, looking from one of us to the other, her head swinging like a pendulum.

'We live opposite each other,' explained Jack.

'Oh right,' said Nathalie, snatching a glass of Prosecco from Rory, who had just arrived back from the bar. 'You're in Tom's old place?'

'Yep,' said Jack. 'Apparently he's doing pretty well out in New York.'

Nathalie tutted. 'This is coming from him, though, right?'

I looked at Jack, who shrugged non-committally. Was this what it was like with them, all trying to get one up on each other? Couldn't they actually be happy when one of their friends got a job? Although Jack had seemed genuinely pleased for Nathalie and proud of her performance, so maybe it was just Nathalie with the envy issues.

'And what do you do, Rebecca?' asked Nathalie, in the style of someone who couldn't be less interested in the answer.

'I work in marketing,' I said.

That usually killed the conversation.

Sure enough, Nathalie turned to Jack. 'What have you been up to since I saw you last? Tell me all,' she said, touching his arm lightly.

I only half listened as Jack rattled off the things he'd been doing over the last few months. I wondered whether this was something actors had to do, recite a list of their most impressive credits at every opportunity.

As Jack, Rory and Nathalie proceeded to talk over each other about which casting directors loved them and whether their agent was getting them seen for the new *Line of Duty* season, I let my eyes wander around the bar, taking in the groups of cool, arty-looking people talking about the 'themes' of the play in too-loud, half-drunk voices. I hoped nobody was going to ask me for my thoughts on the play. What kind of insightful, intelligent stuff could I say about it if they did? I didn't think *it was great* would cut it.

When Jack checked I was OK a few minutes later, it was the perfect opportunity to make my excuses and leave.

'I think I'll make a move, actually,' I said.

As much as I'd enjoyed spending time with Jack, and the play itself, this clearly wasn't my world and I didn't have enough energy to pretend it was.

I saw a flash of disappointment on his face. 'Oh, really? I was about to get us another drink.'

I smiled politely. 'It's just that I've got a few things I need to do before work tomorrow.'

'Oh, sure. OK. Will you be all right getting home?'

I put my empty glass on a nearby table and pulled on my coat. 'Course.'

Rory, whose voice was getting louder and more boisterous as time went on, tried to drag Jack into some sort of debate he was having with Nathalie about who had directed some obscure foreign film and Jack held up his finger to indicate he'd be a minute.

'I'll walk you out,' he said.

I said goodbye to Rory and Nathalie, who barely stopped ranting long enough to acknowledge me, and followed Jack out of the bar and onto the street, where lots of people were gathered for post-performance drinks, despite the cold. I wrapped my coat around myself.

'Thanks so much for the ticket,' I said. 'It was lovely to do something different.'

He nodded. 'If I get any more freebies I'll definitely let you know.'

'OK.'

'Not that it needs to be free. I mean, we could just pay for a ticket like normal people.'

I laughed.

Jack pushed his hair off his face with the heel of his hand. 'How are you going to get back?'

I nodded my head towards the entrance to Finsbury Park underground. 'I'll jump on the tube, I think. It's too cold to hang around waiting for buses.'

A gust of wind sent my hair flying across my face and Jack reached out and tucked it behind my ear, so that for a few, delicious seconds he was almost cradling my face in his hand. It was so unexpected that I didn't know how to react. Part of me wanted to put my hand over his and keep him there, but then I knew that if I did that we'd have crossed a line and that things couldn't go back to the nice, safe, uncomplicated way they had been before.

Jack dropped his arms to his sides, as though he'd realised the same thing; that this wasn't what we did. Good, we were on the same page. It was better this way, for both of us. Desperate to get back to some sort of normality, I flicked my eyes away and looked through the window into the bar. Nathalie was looking in our direction, glaring at us with a face like thunder.

'Nathalie seems nice,' I said, although I didn't really mean that, so I didn't know why I'd said it.

'She can be,' he replied.

I got the sense that she was still interested in Jack, although maybe it was just her competitive streak coming out. Not that she needed to feel threatened by me.

'Listen, were you serious about helping me with my lines?' said Jack. 'Only, rehearsals for the play start in a couple of weeks and I want to get on top of things. Go in really prepared. I really feel like this could be a turning point for me.'

'Of course. Any time. Just let me know.'

I meant it, too. When it was just the two of us it was fun and easy and I was always happy to help an actor in need.

He nodded. 'Great. Well, then. Have a safe journey home.'

My feet didn't seem to want to move. In a way, I could have stayed there all night, chatting in the cold, but what would that have achieved? I felt around in my pocket for my Oyster card.

'See you soon,' I said, giving him a half-wave over my shoulder as I forced myself to put one foot in front of the other and walk in the direction of the tube.

34

Jack

Clive pointed to the busy terrace overlooking Pond Street, seemingly the only outdoor space in the entire hospital. It wasn't exactly picturesque, with buses hissing to a stop on the road alongside us and patients in varying degrees of undress, from pyjamas to gaping operating gowns, all trying to enjoy a tiny bit of fresh (if you could call it fresh) air. Lots of them were smoking, too, even some of the ones hooked up to drips. For some reason, that depressed me more than anything else.

'Over there, man,' said Clive.

I pushed his wheelchair into a corner by the stairwell, just above the drop-off point for A&E. Pushing a grown man in a wheelchair was far more difficult than I'd imagined.

'This will do,' Clive instructed me.

After some faffing about trying to find it, I managed to put the brake on. It was the warmest day of the year so far, according to Clive, and I was dripping with the exertion of getting him down from the ward and also because I was wearing a long-sleeved sweatshirt with a fleece lining, which had been an unfortunate choice, in hindsight.

'Sit,' said Clive, pointing to a low wall.

'You're bossy today,' I replied good-naturedly.

Clive sighed. 'I feel like I have no say in what I do up on

the ward. I'm told to do this, eat that, walk there, take this tablet, that tablet. So when I get a chance to tell someone else what to do for a change, I'm going to take it.'

I nodded. 'Understood. Feel free to tell me what to do. By all accounts, I could do with some direction.'

Clive raised his eyebrows at me. 'What makes you say that, young man?'

I pulled a packet of Jaffa Cakes out of my bag and offered one to Clive, who promptly took two and stuffed them both in his mouth at once as if he'd not eaten for a week. I couldn't imagine Jaffa Cakes were on the NHS menu.

'I don't know. Things are actually going all right at the moment and I'm not used to it. Feels like I'm going to do something to mess it up,' I said.

Clive swiped another Jaffa Cake out of the packet. 'What things are going right?'

I rubbed my jaw. 'I've got a part in a play – no money, but a decent production with a director there's a lot of buzz about.'

'What else?' asked Clive. 'You're not talking about women, are you?'

I shook my head. 'I don't need all that hassle. I've told you that before.'

Clive slapped his hand on his thigh as though he was angry. 'You can't close yourself off to finding love. I won't have it.'

I looked at him, worried. What had I started? When he got wound up about something, there was no stopping him.

'Take it from someone who knows,' Clive went on. 'Do you want to end up all bitter and twisted like I am?'

'Um …'

'Do you?'

'I didn't realise you *were* bitter and twisted,' I said, wanting to keep him calm. It couldn't be good for his blood pressure to get all het up like this.

'Do you think I want to spend every night sitting in front of the television set with nobody to talk to? I've lived on my own my whole bloody life and I regret some of the decisions I've made and I can't do anything about it now, can I?'

We both looked up as a family came tumbling over to sit near us, the little boy full of energy, the woman looking as though she would imminently be giving birth to baby number two.

'Well I can't force it, can I?' I said.

Clive shifted in his chair. 'But you're putting obstacles up, aren't you? All this nonsense about not having enough time. I see you around and it's not like you're never in.'

I rubbed my mouth. 'That's a bit harsh, Clive.'

'I'm saying this for your own good.'

If I'd known he was going to be like this, I wouldn't have come. As it was, I'd had to miss my run because it would have made me late to visit him and then even later to my shift at the pub. I was going to be on stage in a few weeks' time, I had to be in shape.

'What about that neighbour of ours? Rebecca?'

I watched the pregnant woman levering herself down onto a wall. 'What about her?' I said.

Although, I had to admit, I had been thinking about her a lot since we'd gone to the theatre. I kept replaying the moment when we'd been standing outside afterwards and she'd had strands of hair all over her face and I'd brushed it off for her without even thinking. I'd felt something, no matter how much I'd tried to tell myself I hadn't. But was it just friendship, was that what I was feeling? It was just that she was quite a good laugh and also she looked very hot when she wasn't all buttoned up for work. She also had very nice lips, I'd noticed when I'd looked at her in profile in the auditorium. And she smelt divine, like frankincense; sort of Christmassy, even though it was March.

'You two seem to get on well,' said Clive, looking at me with a penetrating glare.

Seriously, Clive needed to chill out today.

'She's nice, Clive, yeah.'

I'd even found myself taking the bins out on purpose the other day. I'd seen her coming out of hers with the recycling and had left it a couple of minutes before taking mine down so as not to look like a stalker. I hadn't thought too much about it. I was pretty sure I wasn't her type, anyway. She clearly had a penchant for guys who wore nice suits and had got their shit together. It was just nice to have somebody to talk to now and again. When I wasn't in a play, when I wasn't hanging out with the rest of the cast, it could feel kind of lonely living on your own. She'd made that better. It didn't mean I wanted to take it any further.

'So if she's nice, why don't you ask her on a date?' said Clive, clearly not prepared to let it slide.

I looked at my watch, wondering how soon I could leave without seeming rude. The poor guy hadn't been outside in weeks, I should probably give him a few more minutes. Just then, Clive had a coughing fit and I watched his hands shake as he took a glug of water. I patted him gently on the shoulder.

'Are you all right there?'

He nodded, screwing the cap back on his bottle. When he spoke again, his voice was all husky. 'It is possible to have a job and someone to love, you know,' he said, dabbing at his eyes with a screwed-up tissue.

'Maybe,' I replied, more gently now. He was only trying to help. 'It's just that when you're part of a company, when you're rehearsing, putting a play on together, you become really close. Like a family. And it's like you don't need anyone else.'

Once I'd started rehearsals, I'd feel more like myself again. I wouldn't be craving Rebecca's attention or anyone else's.

Clive looked at me, frowning. 'But it's temporary, isn't it? These people probably have actual families.'

'Not always.'

'What about your actual family, then?'

I frowned at him, confused. 'What, you mean my parents? What about them?'

'You never talk about them.'

I pulled the cuffs of my sweatshirt over my wrists. 'There's not much to say, Clive. I see them once in a while for dinner. They're not particularly interested in my life; I don't think they get it.'

'Don't get what?' said Clive.

Talking about my parents made me squirm. 'They think I should give it all up, get a proper job. My brother's a lawyer. Apparently we're all supposed to be lawyers.'

Clive patted my knee with his hand. 'You do what you want to do. You don't let anybody tell you otherwise.'

I stood up and stretched. Clive could be quite intense sometimes. 'Come on, we'd better get you inside. It's nearly supper time, isn't it?'

As I went to push Clive's wheelchair back towards the hospital entrance, he put his hand over mine. 'Don't shut yourself off to love, Jack. That feeling … you can't get it anywhere else. And your acting friends won't be there when you're my age, you know that, don't you? Promise me you'll try.'

'I promise,' I said, patting his hand back, not sure if I meant it or not. Personally, I thought I was fine as I was. I was thirty, not eighty, I didn't need to be thinking about a companion for my twilight years just yet.

As I pushed Clive back through the car park towards the ward, I wondered whether Rebecca would get this same grilling next time she came to visit. Nathalie had been all weird with me after Rebecca had left the theatre the other night, winding me up about there being a spark between us, but I reckoned she was only saying that to test the waters. She still couldn't bear the fact I'd been the one to end things with her and clearly she never wanted me to be happy with anybody else. I didn't think she'd actually seen a spark. I mean, I'd felt something, but it wasn't dramatic enough that I needed to do anything about it. Tom would be back from LA in a couple of months, anyway, and then I'd be moving out and I'd probably never see Rebecca again. It wasn't as though I was likely to bump into her because we moved in completely different circles. I was glad, actually. It would bring things to a natural end without either of us getting hurt.

April

34

Rebecca

I was still thinking about the theatre trip when I waltzed into the photocopier room holding a pile of shredding and humming loudly to myself, stopping abruptly when I saw a man bending over the machine, prodding at buttons. I didn't recognise him from behind.

'Well, hello there,' said Tyler, turning round and giving me one of his dazzling, film-star smiles.

'Oh,' I said. 'Hello.'

I'd had absolutely no idea he was in town and felt quite put out by the fact he hadn't told me. Nobody wanted to be thrown off guard like this at work. Mind you, in truth, I hadn't really thought about him much since he'd been away.

'I wasn't expecting to see you,' I commented.

'I should have let you know,' he said, ripping off his jacket and throwing it on top of the spare boxes of copy paper. 'But it was very last-minute. I got on a flight last night and haven't stopped since.'

I nodded, putting my own photocopying down on the side. 'So how have you been?'

God, this small talk thing was awful. Nobody would guess we'd spent three nights together. Any intimacy we'd built up had well and truly vanished.

'You know, I'd love to stop and chat, but I've got to get

these papers copied before the senior management meeting. That secretary on reception …'

'Violet?'

'Yeah, Violet. She's at lunch, apparently, so I'm having to do the goddam thing myself.'

He turned back to the machine.

'Want a hand?' I said, although part of me wanted to watch him struggle, since he clearly thought doing his own photocopying was beneath him.

He stepped aside. 'I thought you'd never ask.'

'Twelve copies should be enough,' I said, pressing one button. I didn't know what he was making such a fuss about.

The machine began to groan as it worked its magic and noisily started to spew paper out into the side tray.

'How's the summer party looking?' I asked, searching around for something to say. 'Did you get that event plan I sent over?'

I'd been working really hard on it. Amanda had asked me to put it together and I'd been bristling at first, since she was supposed to be taking the lead and had already taken the credit for my ideas about the venue. But now that I'd decided to leave, it didn't bother me half as much.

'I did, it was great. I said to Amanda that I'd like you on the team permanently, but she seemed to think you were tied up elsewhere.'

I half laughed. 'Did she, now?' I said, passing him his copies.

He took them, hesitating. 'We could do dinner later in the week,' he suggested. 'If you've got some time in your schedule?'

Of course Amanda chose that precise moment to fling open the door. She stood there, backlit, beautiful, one hand on her hip. 'Sorry to interrupt,' she said, a fake smile plastered to her face. 'Tyler, I wondered if I could have a quick word?'

And then something came over me. I wanted to annoy Amanda and also I'd been thinking too much about Jack and needed to rein myself in. Since I was leaving anyway, it didn't matter anymore if people found out about me and Tyler. In fact, I almost couldn't wait to see their faces when they did.

'Dinner sometime would be lovely,' I said to Tyler. 'Call me?'

And then I turned back to the photocopier, pushing buttons indiscriminately, imagining Amanda standing there open-mouthed. Neither of them spoke, but I heard them leave the room, the door clicking shut behind them.

After they'd gone, I did my photocopying and went back to my desk. I scrolled through my work emails and then, once I'd checked nobody was looking, opened up my Gmail. One message in particular caught my eye. I took a deep breath and opened it.

Interview: Marketing Director, Children in Crisis

I clicked into it, my heart beating a little bit faster. They were inviting me for an interview a week on Tuesday. I had to prepare a presentation, it said, about what I understood the ethos of the charity to be and what I thought I could bring to the role from both a personal and a professional perspective. My heart sank; I hated presentations. It had been fine when I'd had to do them here at Kingsland because I knew the company like the back of my hand and I knew exactly what they'd be looking for. But this was different. I'd never wanted a job this much. I was going to have to bring my A-game, not least because I knew I didn't belong at Kingsland anymore, if I ever had.

36

Jack

I saw her as soon as I walked up the steps from the platform at Hampstead tube. I followed her and about twenty other people into lift 4. We all stood in silence as the lift began to move, whisking us up to street level. I tried to catch Rebecca's eye, but she was reading something on her phone, frowning as she strained to see in the dim light.

The lift doors opened and everybody filed out, Oyster cards at the ready, buzzing themselves through the barriers. When we got out onto the street, I lengthened my stride, catching up with her in a matter of seconds, not caring that I'd meant to pop to Tesco on the way home.

'Hey,' I said, falling into line with her.

'Oh, hi,' she said, clicking off her phone and sliding it into her bag. 'How are you?'

'Great, actually,' I replied, grinning.

She laughed; a pretty, tinkling sound. 'What's going on?'

'I got a guest spot on *Accident & Emergency*.'

Interesting that Chad had finally pulled this off just as I was seriously considering signing with Alistair. Don't get me wrong, it was great to finally be working, but it didn't change the fact that my relationship with Chad was long past its sell-by date.

'No way!' shrieked Rebecca, almost as excited as I was.

I followed her left down Flask Walk, pulling my hoodie out of my bag and slipping it on. The wind had picked up while I'd been underground and it felt much chillier now.

'What's the part?' she asked.

'I'm playing a teacher who takes his class on a school trip and one of them nearly drowns and then the parents blame me.'

I'd already started my character work; it was just the sort of role I could get stuck into and make my own.

'Juicy!' she said. 'When do you start shooting?'

'Next week,' I said, holding out my palms because I thought I felt a drop of rain.

I heard the tinkling noise of a fairground ride, which must have carried over from the East Heath car park, where I'd spotted them setting up this morning.

'Can you hear that?' I said. 'Do you like fairground rides?'

I thought of a particularly scary-looking ride involving a tilted cage I'd spotted earlier. 'I'm a bit of a wuss when it comes to things like that. My brother, Dom, used to get annoyed with me when we went to Thorpe Park for a day out and I refused to go on anything except the log flume.'

'I'm the same,' she said. 'No way I want to put my life in the hands of a machine that's only been put up the night before and may or may not have been properly checked.'

'My thought exactly,' I said.

'How old is your brother?' she asked.

I'd thought about Dom off and on since I'd seen him at London Bridge. He hadn't turned up for dinner at Mum and Dad's that weekend, avoiding me, no doubt.

'He's thirty-three next month,' I said.

'Do you get on well?'

I shook my head. 'Not really. Actually, I bumped into him in town recently and he was kissing a woman. Which

261

would be fine if it had been Theresa, his girlfriend. They live together,' I explained. 'So I guess he's having an affair or something, I don't know.'

I instantly regretted bringing this up in case it triggered something for Rebecca – for all I knew, her douche of an ex-boyfriend had done the same thing to her.

I looked across at her. 'You probably don't want to know all this.'

She shrugged. 'It's fine. So go on, how did he react when he realised he'd been caught out?'

I sighed. 'Typical Dom. He's a lawyer, remember, so basically he denied it and then tried to twist it to look like I'd imagined the whole thing.'

Rebecca rolled her eyes.

'We're quite different,' I said.

'Sounds like it.'

It was beginning to feel like there was a sort of understanding between us. That we could say anything to each other and it wouldn't matter what. I'd never really had that before. There was always part of myself I held back from other people, but the more I got to know Rebecca, the more I felt comfortable showing her who I really was.

'Actually,' I said, changing tack, 'I could do with running through my lines for *Accident & Emergency* if you'd have time. It can be stressful on set as it is, and then it's even harder to remember things.'

'Sure,' she said. 'We can do it now, if you like?'

It had suddenly gone very dark and the fine drops of rain I'd felt a few moments before had turned into a full-on torrential shower.

'Oh no!' said Rebecca, looking for her umbrella.

We were right by the Wells Tavern and it seemed like as good a place as any to take shelter.

'Fancy a quick drink?' I shouted over the din of the rain now slamming onto tarmac and car roofs and through the huge linden trees that lined the street.

'Yes!' she replied, running ahead and through the doors to the pub.

We stood shivering on the mat, laughing.

'You get a seat and I'll grab the drinks. What are you having?' I asked.

She'd found a seat in the corner and had already laid the script I'd handed her out on the table. As I took a seat next to her, I checked out the Andy Warhol-style screen prints on the wall – possibly of local or once-local celebrities: Jamie Oliver, Boy George, Melvyn Bragg. I could see a George Michael one over near the sofas.

The sash window nearest us had been left open and I could still hear the gushing rain, which felt much more relaxing now that we weren't actually out in it. If I'd closed my eyes, I could have imagined us away somewhere warm and tropical. We'd be sheltering in a straw-roofed beach bar before deciding to brave the rain to for a swim, running hand in hand laughing into the water. I cleared my throat. What was I doing?

'So you're playing Peter Walsh?' said Rebecca, flipping through the pages.

'Yep. So if you could read everyone else, that would be great.'

Jesus. I needed to concentrate on this rather than getting carried away with bizarre thoughts about frolicking in the sand with Rebecca.

She laughed softly. 'Hope you're not expecting much. Acting's not really my thing.'

'Honestly, whatever you do it'll be better than most casting directors manage,' I said, wanting to put her at ease. 'You should see them in auditions, mumbling their way through the lines, completely devoid of emotion.'

'That makes me feel better,' she replied, picking up the script and holding it with a vice-like grip. 'Right,' she said. 'Let's give it a go. Shall I start with the scene when they're about to get on the coach outside the school?'

I nodded, taking a deep breath. 'Yep. Go for it.'

'*Sir? How long is going to take us to get there?*

Rebecca began to read the part of Julie, the girl who would eventually nearly die in a reservoir. She was putting some emotion into it, I could see her really trying to get into character, and I thought it was the sweetest thing I'd ever seen and actually quite good.

I responded with my line and so we carried on until we'd read all of my scenes twice through. I didn't even care that the guy on the next table to us kept looking round. Not to sound arrogant, but I was used to that sort of thing. I could see that Rebecca had felt a bit self-conscious, but it hadn't stopped her.

'You're word-perfect,' she said, sounding impressed.

'Well, I was up half the night learning them,' I confessed.

'I can totally see you in this part,' she said, looking down at the paper, which was highlighted in several different colours. 'Do they always send it on orange paper?'

I shook my head. 'I printed it that way myself. It helps if you're dyslexic. Something to do with minimising visual stress.'

'Oh, I see.'

'You're a good reader,' I said.

She laughed. 'I wish. I've got to do a presentation for a job interview. That charity job I told you about. I'm dreading it.'

I took a mouthful of my beer. One of the bar staff delivered a delicious-looking steak frites to the couple on the sofa and I wished I could suggest staying for dinner but couldn't face the will it/won't it go through credit card drama.

'I can help you with your presentation if you like,' I said. 'Return the favour.'

She put her head in her hands, groaning. 'I don't think I could do it in front of you.'

I tutted softly. 'Why not? I bet it's brilliant, anyway. You know your stuff, don't you?'

Her hands were still over her eyes and I reached out to pull them gently away. She let them fall to her lap and we sat there looking at each other for what felt like ages, smiling like idiots. It suddenly felt very warm in the bar. I needed to take my hoodie off, but I didn't want to break the moment, even though I wasn't entirely sure what the moment was about.

The rain had slowed to a gentle shower and I could just about make out the sound of raindrops pinging off the window ledge. In the background were the muted sounds of a busy bar: the chiming of glasses, soft bursts of laughter, the bell to indicate something was ready in the kitchen. And I didn't know why, but because of all of that, it felt right to kiss Rebecca. I reached out and rubbed my thumb across her cheek. She leaned into me so that the tips of our noses brushed together. I could feel her breath on my face, her knee pressing against mine. And then suddenly I was kissing her, softly at first. When I closed my eyes and stopped overthinking things, it felt nice. More than nice. Perfect. I cupped the back of her head in my hands and kissed her harder. A cool breeze blew in through the window and licked my cheek and ruffled her hair.

She pulled back.

'What are we doing?' she whispered.

'I don't know,' I said, not wanting to stop.

She sat back in her seat and I did the same, all sorts of emotions rushing through me. It seemed like a bad idea, but it had felt like a good one.

'Sorry,' I said.

She tidied her hair, pulling at her ponytail. 'It's fine. I wasn't exactly complaining, was I?'

'Not exactly,' I replied.

We both laughed. Good, we could see the funny side. No damage had been done. We'd just carry on as we had been before. Neighbours. Lift repairman. Scene partner. We were lots of things to each other, but just not *that*.

'The rain's easing up,' she said, looking out of the window. 'Shall we head off?'

'Yep, good idea,' I agreed, getting casually to my feet, trying to act as though nothing out of the ordinary had happened. I strode off ahead, out of the pub, as though I was on some sort of cross-country hike. 'We'll be home in five minutes!'

37

Rebecca

Val was already sitting in the corner table in Pennethorne's when I got there, the one near the wine wall. I looked at it longingly.

'Yes, I know you want a house with a wine wall,' said Val, having witnessed me lusting over it many times before.

I slumped into my seat. Val had already ordered me a large red and it appeared as if by magic.

'Didn't fancy a large?' I asked her, looking pointedly at her miniscule glass.

'Not really,' she said, taking a tiny sip of her drink. 'Trying to cut back.'

I picked up the food menu, scanning through it, although I pretty much knew it off by heart.

Val coughed lightly. 'We've been trying for a baby for a while now, if you must know.'

I put the menu down, my mouth dropping open. This was huge.

'That's brilliant news!' I said. 'I hadn't realised, otherwise I wouldn't have kept trying to ply you with alcohol.'

I knew Val wanted kids, but she'd always been adamant that she wasn't planning to get pregnant until she was at least thirty-eight. She and Ekon wanted to travel the world first, she'd said.

She sighed. 'It's not exactly going to plan, to be honest.'

I slipped off my cardigan, looking around the bar. It was a gastropub in the middle of Somerset House, and you generally saw the same faces, mostly from the creative businesses that worked out of the upstairs rooms. I'd earwigged on literary agents having lunch with authors, music producers having drinks with their artists and, at Christmas, they'd be joined by tourists warming up after an afternoon on the pretty outdoor skating rink.

'How do you mean?' I asked.

'I thought I was pregnant just before Christmas, even though I was on the pill. Remember when I threw up that time, after I'd had that weird-looking sushi for lunch?'

'Yes,' I said, remembering how relieved I'd been that I'd gone for a simple chicken and salad focaccia at that particular restaurant.

'So my period was late that month and I thought the pill had failed.'

'Right ... but it hadn't?'

Val shook her head. 'But in those few days until I did the test, I felt sort of excited. And when I found out I wasn't pregnant, we both felt disappointed.'

Somebody came over to ask if we wanted any food and we said that we'd order some in a bit.

'So you've been trying since then?' I asked.

'Four months,' said Val, with the confidence of someone who'd been tracking her cycle. 'And nothing's happened. So I've been to the GP and they're going to run some tests.'

I reached over and rubbed her arm reassuringly. 'I'm sure there won't be anything wrong. It can take years, can't it? The average time it takes to get pregnant is longer than you think.'

Val nodded but didn't look convinced. 'In the meantime,

I thought I'd at least try to sort my health out. I've cut down on alcohol and caffeine. Started doing a bit of yoga, that sort of thing.'

'Blimey,' I said. 'Hardcore.'

We laughed.

'Val?'

'Yes?'

'I'm really happy for you.'

She hesitated. 'There's nothing to be happy about, not yet. But thanks.'

I couldn't stop smiling. Val was going to make an amazing mum.

'And don't worry,' she said, 'I'm not suddenly going to be obsessed with talking about ovulation cycles and nothing *but* ovulation cycles.'

'It's fine if you are.'

'Anyway, enough about me,' said Val, still being impressively restrained with the wine. I reckoned she could make one small glass last all night. I made a concerted effort to slow down so that she didn't feel like she was missing out. 'What's going on with you and our extremely attractive American CEO?'

I groaned. 'God knows. I agreed to go for dinner with him, but I just don't think I'm that into it. But then – and I probably should have told you this before – that was kind of what attracted me to him in the first place.'

'It was?' said Val.

I looked at her sheepishly. 'I might have thought it was the perfect way to get everyone off my back about dating. I thought someone like Tyler, who I couldn't imagine actually falling for, and who lives thousands of miles away, would be the perfect way for me to stay in control of my feelings. A sort of no-risk dating situation.'

Val gave me one of her knowing looks. 'You know what my therapist would say?'

I shook my head. 'No, Val, please don't.'

'She would say,' said Val, ploughing on, 'that you were attracted to him precisely *because* you knew it would never work. That you're displaying avoidant tendencies because of your past and sabotaging your chances of finding real love.'

'Would she now?'

Val took a furtive sip of wine. 'You don't think there's some truth to that?'

I pushed back my chair. 'Maybe,' I said, resigned to the fact that Val was onto me. 'Look, I really need the loo.'

'Don't think you're getting out of having this conversation by physically removing yourself from it,' said Val too loudly as I bolted for the bathrooms. 'That's what avoidant people do!'

When I walked out of the ladies' and into the bar it was absolutely rammed, what with it being 7 p.m. on a Thursday, the perfect evening for after-work drinks because even if you were hung-over the next day, you only had eight hours of work to get through.

As I squeezed past a group of girls at the bar, I felt a hand resting lightly on my waist.

'Hello,' said someone in my ear.

I was about to remove said hand and unleash at whoever it belonged to when I looked up and saw Jack standing there looking smarter than normal – he had a shirt on, albeit a black one – and there were two drinks on the bar next to him: a beer and what looked like a G&T.

'Fancy seeing you here,' I said, in that too-enthusiastic tone I used when I bumped into someone I didn't particularly want to see but I wanted them to think I was ecstatic about it. I reckoned he'd been avoiding me since our drink at the pub. Who was I kidding? Since our kiss, more like. I'd been playing it over and over in my head, which annoyed me, because it had been nothing really, just a silly moment. I blamed the stormy weather – it did funny things to you, wasn't that what they said?

'You look nice,' he said.

I looked down at my pale pink blouse and faux leather pencil skirt and was glad I'd made an effort this morning. I fiddled with the top button of my blouse.

'I work on Kingsway,' I explained. 'This is one of our regular haunts. Well, the regular haunt we go to when we want to talk without being interrupted by cheesy nineties pop and a constant stream of people from the office.'

'Ha!' he said. 'I see.'

'What about you, what brings you here?'

Jack picked up the drinks from the bar. 'I'm here with Nathalie, actually. She's got some project she wants me to get involved with. A show she's hoping to take to Edinburgh next year.'

'That sounds interesting,' I replied, spotting Nathalie waiting at a table in the corner. Maybe that explained why he'd felt weird about kissing me; he was probably in the process of getting back with her. 'I should get back to my friend,' I said, nodding in Val's direction.

Val, I noticed, had perked up like a meerkat and was watching us with great energy and interest.

'OK,' said Jack. 'And listen, I meant to pop round to go through that presentation with you, but I've been flat out with the *Accident & Emergency* thing and the pub. If I'm not back from Elstree too late on Monday, I'll call in, if you like? Tell you how the job went. And you can show me your presentation.'

'Sure. But don't put yourself out.'

'I wouldn't be.'

'You always wear black,' I said, before I could stop myself. But I'd always wondered why and now seemed like as good a time as any to ask.

He laughed. 'Hangover from drama school. It's a sort of actor's uniform. Neutral. You can become anything you want to become.'

I nodded, suppressing a smile.

'Sounds a bit pretentious, doesn't it?' he said.

'Just a tad.'

'It's just that I haven't really been able to afford to buy a whole new wardrobe.' He glanced down at his jeans and shirt combo. 'I've had all this for about ten years.'

I'd always thought he was just playing me with his *I have to work all hours in a pub to make ends meet* routine, because it was clear from his accent that he came from money and hadn't gone to the kind of school I had. But who was I to judge? I knew very little about his family situation, except that he didn't get on with his dad and he rarely mentioned his mum, and just because he spoke like Benedict Cumberbatch (OK, he didn't, that was a massive exaggeration), it didn't mean he had Benedict's bank balance, did it?

'Right,' I said, scooching to the side to get past a couple who had parked themselves right in the middle of the only available thoroughfare. 'See you around at the flats.'

He looked like he was about to say something else, but then instead he raised his glass to me and made his way back to a scowling Nathalie.

I sat back down, desperate to look over at him, not quite sure why, and forcing myself to look at Val instead.

'Who was that?' she hissed excitedly. 'He's *very* hot. And he was looking at you really intensely like you were the most interesting woman on earth. He fancies you, I can tell.'

'Don't be daft,' I said, burying my nose in my drink. 'He's just my neighbour.'

'The one you went to the theatre with?' she shrieked.

I nodded. 'Did I mention we kissed the other day?' I said, throwing it casually in there.

Val slapped her hand on the table. 'You did *what?*'

'Yeah. It was no big deal. We were walking home from the station and went via the pub because it started tipping it down. One minute we were just sitting there and the next ... I don't know, we just sort of kissed.'

Val clutched her chest, all overexcited.

'He's the actor, right?'

'Hmmm. I was helping him run lines.'

'Sounds like it.'

'Stop it, Val. It doesn't matter, anyway, because now he's on a date with his gorgeous ex, Nathalie. So that's that, really, isn't it?'

For some reason the thought of Jack and Nathalie being back together annoyed me. They looked liked the world's most aesthetically pleasing couple, obviously, but now I'd got to know him better...I just wasn't sure they were right for each other.

'Is it a date, though?' She had a quick look over her shoulder. 'There's zero chemistry between them,' she announced confidently. 'And when I saw the two of you talking at the bar, well ... that was a whole different story. We're talking chemistry central,' she added dramatically.

I finally managed to veer Val off the topic of hot neighbours and onto the only thing I could come up with in the heat of the moment: ovulation cycles.

38

Jack

I walked from the station to the TV studios, taking my time. I'd been called for 10.30 and it was only 9.35. I hadn't been able to risk getting the later train out to Elstree, because if it had been delayed, I would have been cutting it very fine indeed. It was better, I'd thought, to arrive in a cool, calm and collected manner, even if it meant hanging around a bit. Besides, this way I'd get to spend longer in the green room. I might get to see some of the other actors, people I'd watched on TV myself since the show had started god knows how many years ago. I'd been a teenager, I knew that. I'd never managed to watch a whole episode, mind you, because my mum would generally sweep in and switch the channel to some boring documentary about art or fashion, the kind of thing that she felt I *should* be watching. The kind of programmes that her pretentious interior designer friends liked. She'd always say: *Get this rubbish off* and I'd protest that I was enjoying it, but to no avail. Dom had never stuck up for me, either, because he'd been in his room 24/7 playing FIFA on his PlayStation. He was obsessed with football, which, according to my dad, was what boys should be interested in. *Not dance or drama, Jack.*

I hovered around on High Street for about ten minutes, parking myself on a bench outside Tesco Extra so that I could read over my script again. I remembered how impressed Rebecca had been. I could do this. I knew the lines and I was confident that I was about to give the performance of my life. I thought that this was probably the point at which my career took a much-needed upward turn. I'd do well at this job and then the casting director would get me in for something else at the BBC. A bigger part. And then the next step, surely, would be the thing I coveted most: a series regular role. I'd be making serious money. I'd be doing interviews in the *Radio Times* and covers for *TV Choice* and I'd be part of something. I'd hang out with the cast and crew, we'd become close, I'd have everything I'd ever wanted. And my dad would have to eat his words, which would be the ultimate triumph.

I went through security, was ticked off a list and given a visitor's lanyard and then directed to one of the buildings I could see at the end of the driveway. As I walked along, I recognised sets I'd seen on other TV shows. A building I remembered from a drama series set in a school. A square I recognised from *EastEnders*. My heart started thumping in my chest. My mouth was dry, so I swigged at my bottle of water. I couldn't work out if I was nervous or excited. It felt like this was where I deserved to be. Now all I had to do was show them what I could do.

I was perched on a low sofa in the green room. There was a pool table in the centre of the room, a drinks machine and a smattering of chairs and cushions and lamps which made it look like a cosy, communal place to hang out. Presumably the regular actors had their own dressing rooms as well. God, I dreamed of having my own dressing room.

'Jack?' said a girl appearing next to me wearing a headset and khaki cargo pants.

I threw the script down on the sofa, looking up at her, attempting to exude a professional yet relaxed vibe. 'Hi. Yes,' I said, smiling inanely at her.

'We'll get you into wardrobe as soon as we can. We're running a little bit behind schedule, so bear with us, OK?'

I nodded vigorously. 'Sure, sure, no problem. Whenever you're ready.'

'Anything I can get you?' she asked.

Before I could answer, her walkie-talkie crackled and she began talking into her headset.

'I'll get it from his dressing room right now. Does he want the blue one or the grey?'

And then she was off without so much as a glance in my direction.

I spent the next couple of minutes fantasising about which actor had demanded something from his dressing room and wondering what this thing was in muted colours that he couldn't do without. I then extended my fantasy out, so that I was a well-known TV actor who could ask runners and production assistants to fetch me things (what things I didn't know) from my dressing room. I thought it might feel weird if it was something I was perfectly capable of getting myself.

I looked up as three actors I recognised tumbled into the room. I pretended to check messages on my phone whilst secretly listening in on their conversation. Something about a barbecue on Sunday. Someone – the actor who played Doctor Brian Keene, whose real name I couldn't remember – said the weather wasn't supposed to be good, that April was too early for barbecues. The woman said maybe she'd get catering in instead.

I dared to look at them. They were fully made up ready for set, stethoscopes round their neck. They all played doctors

276

and had done for years. They were older than me, mid-forties perhaps, and I thought that if I carried on as I was, I was bound to be in their position at some point. If I continued to work hard, then that could be me in a few years' time.

Several hours later, I was still perched on the sofa. I'd been to wardrobe and was now dressed in a red and white checked shirt and a pair of chinos. My hair had been flattened and brushed into a neater, teacher-like style with a side parting and was held in place with copious amounts of wax. I didn't dare move an inch for fear of creasing my costume, or brushing a hair out of place.

I'd watched various cast members waltz in and out, grabbing coffees, or the younger ones would have a game of pool. I'd overheard conversations about a script one of them had taken umbrage with, somebody's crap agent, somebody else's sick dog. Not one of the cast had even looked in my direction. So much for wanting to feel part of something: I felt completely invisible.

'They're ready for you, Jack,' said the girl with the headset. She looked even sweatier than she had several hours ago, presumably having spent the day rushing between the dressing rooms, the set and the green room. I smiled encouragingly at her, hoping she could feel my empathy, and stood up. I took one last look around. I was as good as these people. I could do this.

This was only my second job for a network show and as we walked along a series of corridors and up a flight of stairs towards the set, my heart began to race. As we rounded a corner to the set, I saw that there were more people involved than I'd remembered from my last TV gig, twenty or so of them, all immersed in important-looking tasks, like plugging in cables and adjusting lights. A group of them were gathered around the cameras; somebody else was rearranging the fruit on top of a bedside cabinet. The director, a cocky-looking guy in his mid-thirties, was reviewing something on a monitor and then barking orders at the lighting department. The girl who was presumably playing my half-dead pupil was lying on the bed connected to mock monitors. I got a sudden flashback to Clive and wondered what he would think of all this. And Rebecca. What would she say? Would she tell me I could do it? That this was what I was trained to do, that I was as capable as any of these people?

'Have we got the actor playing the teacher?' said someone whose job I didn't know but seemed to be the assistant director from what I could tell.

I raised my hand. 'Here,' I said, stepping forward, feeling as though I was facing a firing squad rather than a film crew. My character did have a name. Peter Walsh. Somehow that felt important.

'Can we have you in position?' the guy said, beckoning me over.

I said a quick hello to my 'pupil', who couldn't talk because she had a fake tube in her mouth. I ran my lines over in my head as they clipped a mic to the inside of my shirt and the make-up lady powdered my face and somebody waved a boom over my head. Nobody introduced themselves. And before I could focus, catch my breath, I heard the director say *Action*.

I imagined the smell of a hospital ward and, although it was completely silent, the sounds I might hear. I put myself in the shoes of Peter Walsh, a new teacher who had been distracted for a few minutes by a pupil misbehaving and hadn't noticed that somebody had fallen into the water and was in trouble. I took the girl's hand. My first line was on the tip of my tongue. I looked poignantly at the heart monitor to buy myself some time because my mind had gone completely blank. What was the fucking line? Panic flashed through me.

I shifted position, filling the silence by picking up her notes from the end of the bed and pretending to scan through them. I imagined myself in the pub, with Rebecca sitting next to me with her sweet, encouraging face. The line came to me immediately. I opened my mouth to say it—

'Cut!' shouted the director.

I coughed. 'Sorry,' I mumbled, shaking my head. Seriously, was I really doing this *now*? Messing up my one big break? Not managing to say the eight very simple lines I'd been assigned?

The assistant director came scuttling over. 'Do you need me to give you your first line?' he asked, looking worried.

'It's fine, I've got it,' I told him.

'Right, reset and let's go again,' said the director, looking pissed off.

Seriously, I felt as though I was being manhandled through some sort of cattle market for all the care and attention I was getting.

'Action!'

I took a deep breath, quietened my mind and channelled Peter Walsh.

'Your parents are on their way.'

Thankfully my ability to successfully say six words triggered something in me and once the scene began to flow, I relaxed, following my impulses, becoming the character. I thought only of the girl in front of me, of how she'd been in my care and I'd let her down, of how her parents were going to demand answers when they arrived and how that could spell the end of a career for a new teacher like me.

We did the scene three times in total, and eventually the

director said we'd got it and instructed the crew to reset. Nobody looked at me, already onto the next thing.

As I made my way back off-set, it felt as though something was pressing hard on my chest. I'd got what I wanted: a TV job, a decent amount of money. So why had the whole thing left me feeling so empty inside?

'Good job,' shouted the director, looking up briefly from his monitor as I walked past with my head down so as not to disturb him.

'Oh, right. Thanks,' I said.

I felt much better after that. He wouldn't have said it if he hadn't meant it, would he?

Striking whilst the iron was hot, as they say, I called Chad.

'Who is this?' he said, which was his usual response when answering his direct line. It always put me on the back foot. I let myself fantasise about how Alistair might answer my calls if I signed with him, which was becoming more and more tempting with each day that passed. Chad might have got me this role, but it was only because he happened to be going to dinner with someone from the show and I'd basically harangued him into putting me forward.

'It's Jack. Maxwell,' I said, in case he knew multiple Jacks, which he probably did. It was hardly an unusual name.

'Aren't you supposed to be on set?' he asked suspiciously.

'Just wrapped my scene,' I replied.

'How did it go?'

'Good. The director seemed pleased.'

'Excellent.'

'I was just wondering whether we could get some momentum going off the back of this,' I said, slipping my arms out of the polyester V-neck jumper they'd put over the shirt at the last minute. It had indeed looked very quintessentially teacher-y. 'Get me seen elsewhere in the BBC. Let them know I've just worked well on this.'

Chad hesitated.

I pulled the jumper over my head, trying not to move my phone too far away from my ear in case I missed what he said.

'Are you telling me how to do my job, Jack?'

Fuck. 'Course not. It was only a suggestion.'

Was my request really that unreasonable? And I knew, *knew*, that Chad would not make calls about me off his own back, no matter how much he might pretend otherwise.

'If I were you, Jack, I would focus on what you've got coming next. The whole point is that you'll be inviting people to see you perform at the Soho Theatre. That will have much more of an impact than me making a few phone calls.'

I sighed. 'Fine. Just thought I'd ask,' I said. I shouldn't have called him. I'd been on a high after a minuscule amount of praise from the director, as though I was craving his approval like a needy child, and then Chad – as usual – had gone and knocked me right back down again.

I made the decision there and then that I was going to email Alistair. It was time to take control of my own career instead of being at the mercy of Chad, who clearly couldn't give a shit.

I walked slowly up the stairs to the flat, stopping outside Rebecca's door. I wanted to see her, to tell her about my day, how badly it had gone at first, but then how I'd turned it around. Plus I'd offered to go through her presentation with her. Sometimes acting skills could come in very useful for actual real-life situations.

I was about to knock when I heard voices inside. I stopped, my knuckles inches from the door. I stayed perfectly still, listening. There was laughter. A man's voice, an American twang. Great. Mr Perfect was back on the scene, then. Seriously, what did she see in him (other than the money, the status, the smooth patter and the gym-honed abs, that was)?

I felt gutted. There, I'd said it. I'd thought there was something between us and even though it was unexpected and not something I'd necessarily wanted to get into, I'd been excited to see where it might go next. More than anything, I'd wanted to kiss her again, but clearly I should have known better. I wasn't good enough for someone like her. She didn't take me seriously. I wasn't relationship material. If I was a lawyer like Dom, I might have been.

I slunk back to my door, opened it and kicked it shut behind me, not caring if they heard.

39

Rebecca

I dialled Val's number. Why wasn't she here? I needed her calming presence more than ever today.

'Are you coming to the meeting?' I asked breathily, an air of panic in my voice.

'Yep,' she said. 'On my way.'

'See you in a sec,' I replied, going to put the phone down.

'Becs! Hold on. What happened last night? Did you-know-who come for dinner in the end?'

'Yep,' I said. 'Brandishing flowers. Charm personified. Problem was, I couldn't stop thinking about Jack. When he kissed me, I felt these little explosions in my stomach. You know the ones?'

'I can just about remember,' said Val. 'And you don't get that with Mr USA?'

'No,' I answered. 'So we had dinner and I told him I didn't think we should see each other again.'

'Becs! You heartbreaker.'

'Hardly. He was probably booty-calling someone in the taxi home.'

Val laughed. 'Good for you. I'll be up in a sec, OK?'

*

Mike Walbeck was sitting at the head of the table with his hands clasped in front of him, a stray grey hair on the lapel of his navy jacket.

'Morning, everybody,' he said.

There was a collective good morning before everyone dived into the plate of croissants in the centre of the table, leaving pastry crumbs splattered all over it.

I took one and picked at it, nerves rattling around in the pit of my stomach. I didn't know what exactly I was nervous about. So what if I hadn't gone for the job? So what if nobody knew that except Val and Freya? It was nobody's business but mine.

'May I start by saying how delighted myself and the rest of the SMT are with your hard work of late. I've had some excellent feedback about you all, particularly from Tyler Martin, who sends his apologies but had to fly unexpectedly back to New York this morning.'

I bit my lip, hoping I hadn't had anything to do with his urgent need to leave the country. Surely his pride hadn't taken that much of a bashing?

I noticed Amanda was scribbling worthily away in one of those posh Smythson notebooks. What was she writing everything down for, anyway? Mike's PA always sent the minutes round. She was particularly dressed up today in what looked like a Diane Von Furstenberg wrap dress. Her hair was loose and cascaded down her back and I wondered what time she'd had to get up to make it look that good.

The door flung open and Val came shooting through, throwing herself into the nearest chair. I caught her eye and she gave me a sneaky thumbs-up.

'I wanted to be at this meeting this morning to give you some very good news about the exciting management role we've created in the department,' Mike continued.

Everyone visibly relaxed (except me, that was). I had a last-minute panic that I'd been mad not to go for it, but it was too late now.

'As you all know, to help us build our profile even more, we have decided to appoint a head of press and marketing, who will oversee all the events, press and advertising for Kingsland Marketing.'

I took some deep abdominal breaths, trying to stay calm. I wondered whether that was something Jack did before going on stage. I'd ask him, if we ever had a proper conversation again. I was slightly worried I'd pushed him away after our unexpected kiss.

'We interviewed several extremely talented individuals for the position and have spent a great deal of time debating over who would be best placed to take things forward,' said Mike.

I fiddled with a stray thread of cotton on the sleeve of my shirt. *You've done the right thing*, I kept repeating to myself in my head.

'And ultimately we were all in agreement that there was one outstanding candidate. She brought some fantastic new ideas to the role, her presentation was exciting and boundary-pushing and we think she will be a wonderful addition to our senior management team.'

My heart hammered against my chest. Val winked at me and Freya nudged me in the ribs.

'I am delighted to announce that your new head of press and marketing is Amanda Hayhurst.'

There was a bit of a shocked silence all round and everyone sort of stared at me and then at Amanda and then there was lots of clapping, which I enthusiastically joined in with.

*

Afterwards, I sat back down at my desk and got on with my work. I had my interview at Children in Crisis at 6.30, so I needed to be out of here at 5.30 on the dot. It was good of them to see me out of hours as it was. How did everyone else slope off for daytime interviews? I mean, you'd basically have to lie, wouldn't you? Say you had a dentist's appointment or something. The fact that they'd offered me a realistic time because they said they knew it would be difficult for me to get out of work was extremely promising – imagine working for a company who actually genuinely cared about their employees.

Freya sat down opposite me.

'Are you OK?' she mouthed.

I nodded. I'd told her in the end because she was my friend and it felt like the right thing to do.

'Amanda, though ...' she said, screwing up her nose.

I shrugged.

It would have been nicer if the role had gone to an external candidate who perhaps could have brought something new to the role. But Amanda was great at talking the talk, at being gushy when required and at name-dropping her celebrity friends at every turn. In terms of doing the actual job, though, she annoyed everyone, so how she was going to manage us all, I had no idea. Fingers crossed I wouldn't be around long enough to find out.

Children in Crisis were on the fourth floor of a building just off Rosebery Avenue. When I stepped into the reception area, I immediately relaxed. It was lighter and airier than I'd imagined from the outside and homely, with a box of toys in the corner, a table housing an array of magazines and a wall adorned with colourful drawings and paintings, presumably the product of some of the children they'd helped over the years.

The middle-aged woman behind the desk was all smiley and warm, a stark contrast to the welcome you got when you entered Kingsland Marketing and Violet was the first person you saw.

'Hello! You must be Rebecca,' she said, standing up and offering me her hand, which I shook, smiling back. I liked it here already. 'Come with me. They're ready for you.'

Her name was Sheila, she told me, and she'd worked here for nearly thirty years.

'You'll be meeting the CEO, Katherine Grey, and the Head of Public Relations, Adam Clarke.'

'Great,' I said, swallowing hard. I tried to remember all the notes I'd written, all the responses to possible questions I'd memorised. My mind felt fuzzy with nerves; surely I'd retained at least some of it. I'd be fine once I got going.

Sheila knocked on the door and ushered me into the room ahead of her.

'This is Rebecca,' she announced before giving me a good-luck thumbs-up and disappearing off down the corridor.

Katherine and Adam were sitting in bright yellow arm-chairs, which I assumed were an attempt to make the room as unintimidating as possible so that the children didn't feel as though they were in a clinical environment. I wondered if some of them hated hospitals as much as I did. They both stood up and shook my hand.

'Thanks so much for coming in, Rebeca,' said Katherine, in the sort of tinkling, welcoming tone I warmed to im-mediately.

'Take a seat,' said Adam, who was young and quite trendy and nothing like Mike Walbeck or Paul from Accounts. 'I hope you found us all right?'

'Oh yes, it was no problem,' I replied, following their lead and sitting down, clasping my hands in my lap, trying to stop them shaking. I wished Jack had come to run through my presentation with me like he'd promised.

'Why don't you start by telling us a little bit about yourself,' suggested Katherine, sitting back in her chair. I felt more relaxed just looking at her. 'What made you apply for the position here?'

I thought about my mum and dad and how they'd always been helping other people, Mum with her social work and Dad had been a teaching assistant at a tough, failing comprehensive school in Luton. I'd always wanted to follow in their legacy but hadn't known how until now. And with that in my mind, I began to talk. In the event, I didn't need the notes I'd spent hours putting together, I just spoke from the heart, remembering how I wished I'd had somewhere like this to come when I'd lost my parents and how I was determined to help kids who were feeling as lost as I'd felt then.

40

Jack

Alistair pushed the contract across the table with a huge grin on his face.

'You're sure about this?' he said.

I nodded. 'Absolutely.'

I signed and dated two sets of contracts, a sense of calm and relief flooding through me. Everything about this felt right. Hargreaves & Kemp's offices weren't all shiny and pretentious like Star Management's were, they were smaller and messier, with lots of little nooks and crannies, where presumably phone calls and meetings took place. I clocked the wall of headshots. There was a decidedly smaller client list here, still with some names I recognised, but no A-listers. Just actors who were steadily working away, doing what they'd trained to do, doing what they loved.

'We should celebrate once you've let Chad know,' said Alistair. 'We'll have dinner and drinks somewhere. Get to know each other a bit more.'

'That would be really nice,' I replied.

'And so my priority is going to be getting casting directors to see you at the Soho Theatre. I'm going to spend this afternoon making calls and then I'll follow up with your Spotlight link so that they can see your showreel. It's really strong, Jack, so I'm pretty sure we'll get some of the big names in and a handful of the BBC guys.'

Was he for real? Alistair was doing more for me in five minutes than Chad had done for me in years. I'd been honest with him from the start, about my dyslexia (which he'd said was absolutely not a problem and that he would let the casting directors know on my behalf in advance if I wanted him to). I explained what had happened with Chad and what I didn't want to happen again.

'You can call me anytime, Jack,' he reassured me. 'Evenings, weekends, whatever. If I'm busy, I'll get back to you, but I *will* get back to you.'

I nodded, finding it hard to take in. I couldn't believe I'd suffered in silence for ten years when I could have done this ages ago and then my life might have looked very different by now.

'Right. Let's go and introduce you to the rest of the team, shall we?' said Alistair. 'You'll be seeing a lot of them. We're all about creating a family here – you'll be invited for barbecues and opening nights galore. We try to have a get-together at a big sporting event once a year, usually at Lord's, sometimes Wimbledon if we can get enough tickets.'

I got up, carefully sliding my copy of my contract into my bag. I finally had the acting family I craved. And I couldn't wait to get started.

I stood in a quiet side street away from the traffic and dialled Chad's number.

Alistair had some great ideas for my future. He wanted me to do pilot season in LA next February, for a start, and he'd already been in touch with Dax Delano from *Days of Our Lives*, who remembered me, apparently, and would be happy to get me in for a meeting if I did go out there. Alistair understood that money was tight and we thought about how I could manage it. Some TV guest roles, he suggested; a couple of well-paid commercials. Although Chad obviously had amazing contacts, they were always shrouded in secrecy so there was never any transparency as to what he was actually doing to get me seen for stuff (not much, I suspected).

Miraculously, after a few rings, Chad answered his phone.

'Chad speaking,' he said, in his usual offish tone, which I thought was very affected. It was something I reckoned he'd cultivated in order to sound busy and high-status, but actually he just sounded like a knob.

'It's Jack,' I said, going through the usual routine. 'Jack Maxwell.'

'What can I do for you, Jack?' he asked, sounding put out already.

'There's something I need to talk to you about.'

Chat sighed. 'What is it now, Jack? Because if you're going to complain about doing fringe again, I haven't got time to hear it. As I've explained before, it will—'

'It's not about the play,' I said, cutting in. 'So can you hear me out or not?'

God, I'd never spoken to him like this. Amazing what having other options could do for you. For the first time, I felt actual anger towards him, something I'd always suppressed before because I'd felt so grateful he'd chosen me in the first place. But how dare he make me feel crap about myself? He took fifteen per cent of my earnings and for what? Making me feel worthless? Making me doubt my abilities as an actor?

'I'm with a client on set. Whatever it is, just tell me now and let's get it over with,' he replied.

I shook my head; how the fuck had I put up with this for so long?

'It's time I moved on, Chad,' I said. 'Another agent wants to represent me and I've accepted his offer.'

Chad laughed. 'You're joking, right?'

'Nope.'

He was silent for a few seconds. I could hear him breathing heavily. 'I've nearly terminated our relationship several times, you do know that, don't you, Jack?' he said nastily.

'Well, no, because I'm not a mind reader, am I? You didn't share anything with me, that's part of the problem here.'

God, I was on a roll. If I'd felt any sense of loyalty before, it had all but disappeared now. I just wanted to get this done and get on with the rest of my life.

'Who is this mysterious agent you'll be signing with, then? Some two-bit agency working out of their conservatory in Kent, is it?' he sneered.

He really was a twat. 'It's Alistair Kemp from Hargreaves & Kemp.'

That shut him up. It was a good agency. They got excellent work for their boutique list of clients. There wasn't really anything negative Chad could say, although he was probably desperately trying to think of something.

'Right,' said Chad. 'Well, if you want to risk leaving one of the world's top talent agencies, that's on you.'

'Exactly. It's my choice. I don't want an agent that I can't communicate with, Chad. I appreciate you taking me on and everything you've done for me over the last ten years, but it's just not working out for me.'

I wasn't going to stoop to Chad's level and start hurling insults. My years at Star Management hadn't been all bad.

'Please put this in writing, Jack. And do remember that any money you make from work I found for you must continue to come through our books.'

'Of course,' I said. 'Alistair is aware and will be in touch.'

It was only fair. Besides, the play was hardly going to make me anything, was it? Any ticket sales would go towards covering expenses first; the venue itself probably cost a fortune.

'I sincerely hope you don't live to regret this, Jack,' said Chad, cutting off the call abruptly.

I won't, I thought to myself, already feeling as if this was the best decision I'd ever made.

I put my phone in my pocket and headed for the tube. This was the beginning of a new era. My career wasn't over yet; in fact, I had the feeling that it might just be properly beginning.

It was nearly 7.30 by the time I got home. In my hand was a carrier bag containing an M&S chicken tikka masala and their cheapest bottle of red. My dad would have a fit if he could see me now – he'd drummed it into me that I should never buy a bottle of wine that cost less than a tenner, but then again, my dad had never been skint, had he?

I bounded up the stairs, still high on everything that had happened. So much had changed in the space of a few hours. I'd dump my things in the flat and then I'd give Rebecca a knock. She'd be pleased for me, I knew she would be. Just because she was back with the American, it didn't mean we couldn't be friends. While I was looking for my keys, I somehow managed to drop the bag with the wine in it. I winced as it landed with an ominous smash. Red liquid seeped out from under the plastic bag, the burgundy pool growing bigger with each passing second. I swore several times before opening my door and stomping inside to get a towel. When I came back out, Rebecca was at her door looking worried.

'Is everything OK?' she asked, staring at the mess on the floor.

'I dropped a bottle of wine,' I said, crouching down to dab at it with an old towel. Stupidly, I'd chosen a white one.

She disappeared inside her flat, reappearing with a dustpan and brush, then she knelt down next to me, sweeping broken glass into the pan.

'I really fancied a glass of this as well,' I sighed, wondering whether I could stretch to another bottle. I probably couldn't. As it was, because of rehearsals for the play, I wouldn't be able to take on any extra shifts at the pub for the next few weeks. My money situation was looking more dire than ever.

'Bad day?' she asked.

'Actually, no. It was an exceptionally good day.'

She looked up, raising her eyebrows. 'What happened?'

I heard the front door downstairs open and then slam; voices floated up from the ground floor, a child and a woman.

'I signed with that new agent. And he's great. He's got so many ideas for me and he seems genuinely excited to represent me.'

'So he should be,' she said, smiling. 'What did Chad say?'

I rolled my eyes. 'He was an arsehole about it, of course. Which only proved to me that I've done the right thing.'

'I'm pleased for you,' she replied, standing up, brushing dust off her knees. 'I'm a bit on edge myself, actually. I had that interview for the charity job on Tuesday.'

'When will you hear?'

'They said by the end of the week, but it's Thursday now, so …'

'They've probably got other people to see before they can let you know.'

She shrugged. 'Yeah. Probably.'

'How did your presentation go?' I asked, feeling guilty. Perhaps I should have gone back another time instead of letting the fact I'd had a little knock to my ego put me off.

'OK, I think. I was a bit nervous, but I suppose that's to be expected.'

'Totally,' I said. 'And I'm sorry I didn't get a chance to run through it with you.'

She nodded. 'I was expecting you to knock.'

Shit.

'I was about to. On Monday, when I got back from shooting. But I think you had company.'

She looked confused. 'What do you mean?'

'I heard voices,' I said, cringing. 'So I assumed you were busy.'

What I really wanted to ask her was whether she was back with American boy. Whether she'd been thinking about me at all, about the fact that we'd kissed and it was great. Whether she in any way would like to do it again.

'If you want a new bottle of wine, I've got one here?' she said.

'Oh no, you'll want to keep that for yourself.'

She ducked into the flat, I heard a cupboard open and shut again, and she appeared in the doorway again. She handed me a bottle of Jacob's Creek Shiraz.

'Sorry, it's not a very good one,' she said.

I took it from her. The tips of our fingers brushed together for a second and I had this sudden desire to grip hold of her and not let go. Did that mean anything? Did I like her as much as it felt like I did?

'Thanks,' I said. And then, before I could overthink it: 'Would you like to come in and have a glass with me?'

She looked startled.

'Don't worry if you're busy,' I said, giving her an out.

'I have got some work to do,' she replied.

'Sure. Some other time, then.'

She was back with him then, probably. No doubt she

regretted what had happened between us and was trying to let me down gently.

'We'll have to do it before you move out,' she said.

I swallowed. Sometimes I managed to forget that I was only here temporarily. And that Tom would be back soon, with his wispy girlfriend in tow and I would be god knows where.

'When are you off?' she asked.

'Beginning of June.'

I picked the dripping, ripped carrier bag off the floor and folded it up into the towel, wiping up the remnants of heady red wine. If it tasted as bad as it smelled, perhaps it was a good thing I hadn't had a chance to drink it.

'Have you got somewhere else lined up?' she asked.

I shook my head. 'Better start looking for a house-share, I suppose,' I said. 'I can't afford much.'

She nodded, her hand on the door handle.

'Thanks for the wine. I'll replace it, of course,' I said.

'You don't need to do that,' she replied, smiling at me and closing the door.

41

Rebecca

I'd called in to see Clive, who was recovering on a rehabilitation ward. I'd accidentally called it a geriatric ward, which he'd been most upset about.

'I'm not going to be one of those old men who hobbles around on a Zimmer frame,' he told me indignantly. 'As soon as my hip mends itself, I'm going to be back doing my daily walks on the heath and going to the shops like I did before.'

I thought about the brochure in my bag and wondered when would be the best time to broach the subject of him potentially moving into a residential home. He'd had a heart attack brought on by the shock of the accident, plus there was the major surgery on his hip. It took ages to recover from those sorts of things, from what I could gather. He'd probably never get back to what he'd been, especially at his age, but of course I wasn't going to tell him that. I had to be subtle about it. Bring him round to the idea gently.

'So I went to see my nan the other day,' I said, waving over at the old guy in the bed opposite Clive's who was in with a broken knee amongst other ailments.

I'd noticed that each time I'd come to visit Clive it had felt easier and easier and I felt much less anxious now, and less convinced that somebody was going to die right in front of me every time I set foot on the ward.

'Oh yes?' said Clive, turning his head, which seemed to be a struggle. 'Where's she, then?'

'Just around the corner,' I replied, keeping it light. 'In a residential home called Greenhill Lodge.'

'I see,' said Clive.

'You'd like her,' I continued. 'She reminds me of you – really independent. Likes chatting to people and spending time outside when she can.'

'She can hardly do that in one of those homes, can she?'

'You'd be surprised,' I said, handing him the box of grapes and the Swiss chocolate bar I'd picked up at M&S on the way in and then slipping the brochure from the office at Greenhill casually onto his bedside table. 'They've got lovely grounds. I got you some information on it. Just in case.'

He tutted. 'You've been talking to those social workers.'

'I haven't,' I said. 'Jack mentioned something, that was all.'

Clive ripped open the box of grapes, stuffing three into his mouth at once. 'It's all because I haven't got any family at home to look after me. Ridiculous. I'm perfectly capable of looking after myself.'

I took a grape myself, twirling it between my finger and my thumb. 'Are you sure there's no one I can contact for you, Clive? A cousin, or something? An old friend? I'm sure there are people who want to know you've not been well, who would like to visit.'

He shook his head. 'There's no one, not anymore. Sure, I talk to lots of people. You're probably thinking: how can someone as chatty as Clive have nobody in his life …'

'Well, you are quite talkative,' I teased.

He looked at me with a serious look on his face. 'Don't end up like me, will you?'

I laughed lightly. 'Why wouldn't I want to be like you?'

'Because you might be all right now, while you're young.

But the friends I've had are gone now. Dead or in homes, or they've moved away to be closer to their families.'

I leaned forward, resting my elbows on his bed. I watched the monitor, flickering red to show his heartbeat, the beep of the machine that was making sure his oxygen levels were high enough. I swallowed, determined to keep the negative feelings at bay.

'That other young man of yours – Dan, wasn't it? – left a long time ago now, didn't he?' said Clive.

'Yeah,' I replied, wondering where this was going.

'And you haven't met anyone else since?'

I thought of Jack. 'Nobody serious.'

'There was that loud one in a suit.'

I laughed. 'Tyler. Yeah, that didn't go anywhere.'

Clive looked thoughtful. 'You know who I think would make a lovely couple?'

I narrowed my eyes at him, already predicting what he was going to say. 'Go on.'

'You and Jack get on very well, from what I can see. He's always talking about you when he comes to visit.'

I pulled at the hem of my blouse, running the satin fabric between my thumb and middle finger. 'Is he?'

'He said you went to the theatre together. That he had a good time.'

'He had a spare ticket, that was all. Anyway, his girlfriend was in it.'

Clive widened his eyes. 'What girlfriend?'

'Nathalie her name is. She's an actress.'

'No, no, no,' said Clive, shaking his head. 'I'd know if he had a girlfriend. You must have got the wrong end of the stick, my dear.'

'I don't think so. I saw them out drinking together the other night.'

'There's no rule against going out for a drink with some-one, is there?'

'Course not. But, you know, they looked ... together.'

'Oh, here we are. The man himself,' said Clive, looking eagerly over towards the entrance to the ward. 'Jack! Just the man we wanted to see!'

My heart immediately began thumping so hard it felt as though it was pulsating in my throat. What was he doing here at this time, he usually came much later? I'd thought a Saturday afternoon would be a safe bet.

'This is a nice surprise,' he said, looking as though it was anything but.

'I am honoured to have both of you here at the same time,' said Clive, chuckling. I hoped he wasn't going to say any-thing about what we'd just been talking about, the situation was embarrassing enough as it was. I hadn't seen Jack since he'd asked me to share the wine with him and I'd panicked and said no. I'd wanted to, more than anything, actually, but there was no point, was there? He had Nathalie, and I wasn't going to get caught up in whatever they'd got going on. We thought we had a connection, but maybe it was nothing more than a casual, neighbourly friendship. There was no reason we had to go and ruin it by turning it into something it wasn't.

'You're sitting up,' Jack smiled at Clive, pulling up a chair next to mine.

'Jack,' he said, looking maudlin. 'You need to get me out of here.'

Jack nodded sympathetically. 'It won't be long now, Clive.'

'I'm going crazy,' he added, lowering his voice. 'The noise is off the scale. Last night somebody died down there. One minute he was in that bed at the end, and the next they'd pulled the curtains round his bed and carried him out in a body bag.'

I swallowed, trying to get the image out of my mind. I'd been doing well up until now, but this new information was threatening to tip me over the edge.

Jack looked at me and smiled reassuringly.

'Ooh, what's this?' asked Jack, picking up the Greenhill Lodge brochure and leafing through it. 'Looks like a nice place.'

Clive tutted loudly. 'Haven't you two been listening to anything I've been saying?'

I squeezed Clive's arm before turning to Jack.

'I picked up some information for Clive. Just in case,' I said. 'No pressure.'

The last thing I wanted was to push Clive into anything. With Nan, it had been a process. It had taken her months to bring herself to open the brochure and even then she came up with every excuse under the sun as to why moving into a home wasn't a good idea. And then it had taken her ages to get used to things and settle in.

'We were having an interesting conversation just now, weren't we, Rebecca?' said Clive.

I shifted in my seat. He wouldn't.

'Were we?'

'We were wondering why you haven't got a woman in your life? Or a man,' he added quickly. 'If that's what you like. It doesn't matter if you do, of course—'

'I'm not gay, Clive,' said Jack.

'So why don't you have a girlfriend, then?' asked Clive.

'He does,' I said.

Jack looked confused.

I cleared my throat. 'Nathalie, right?'

I bit my lip. I'd said too much. It was probably early days. Perhaps they hadn't put a label on it yet.

'Rebecca seems to think you've been seeing some actress,' Clive added, fumbling with the wrapper of his chocolate bar.

'She's my ex,' replied Jack, looking put out. 'Believe me, I wouldn't go back there again.'

'See!' said Clive, triumphantly.

'Why did you think I'd been seeing her?' Jack asked me.

I could feel myself going red. 'I just assumed … when I saw you together at Somerset House.'

He shook his head. 'I did say that was about a job. That was all it was.'

A nurse came over to take Clive's temperature. He moaned and groaned as she fussed over him, rolling his eyes at me, but I could tell the nurse had a soft spot for him.

'This one's hard work,' she said to me and Jack, winking.

Once she'd gone, I thought I'd grab the opportunity to leave before Clive said anything else incriminating.

'I'm going to pop in and see my nan,' I said. And then, for Clive's benefit: 'They have a games afternoon in the garden at four o'clock, so she'll want me out of there by then. Apparently it's a right laugh.'

Clive looked at me with a flicker of interest. 'Do they have dominoes?'

'Think so,' I said. 'I'll check.'

'Hmm,' muttered Clive. 'Well don't go out of your way on my account.'

'Right then,' I began, my eyes flicking from one to the other, unable to settle on Jack, who was watching me, his hands over his mouth in the prayer position as though he was deep in thought. 'I'll get going.'

'Bye, love,' said Clive, who was seemingly completely oblivious to the fallout he'd caused.

I grabbed my bag and headed through the ward, thanking the nurse on the way out. I glanced over my shoulder at Jack, who had got up and was pouring Clive a plastic beaker of water. If he wasn't seeing Nathalie again, then why were things suddenly so awkward between us?

May

42

Jack

It was going to be the warmest day we'd had this year; twenty-eight degrees Celsius, apparently, according to the weather lady on *Good Morning Britain*. An ice-cream van was parked on the corner of Downshire Hill by the playground and excited kids were already queueing up, coming away with luminous lollies clutched in their hands. Over on the heath, the pond sparkled in the morning sun, the five-storey townhouses I coveted reflected on the water. The grass was littered with groups – teenagers on half-term break, families playing frisbee, dog walkers heading up to Parliament Hill. I breathed it all in. In a month's time, Tom would be back from LA and I'd be living in some shithole. I'd have to seriously start searching for a place this week. Get back on spareroom.com. Although they were sometimes snooty about letting to an actor; I didn't think that technically fell under the umbrella of 'young professional'. Sometimes I felt more like a professional barman, which had been fine when I was in my twenties but didn't feel quite so OK now.

I thought of Rebecca and how nothing ran smoothly, even when you had a decent job like hers. I'd barely bumped into her since I'd seen her at the hospital and she'd mentioned Nathalie. I'd spotted her getting off the bus at South End Green one night a few weeks ago – I'd been off to the hospital to see Clive and she'd presumably been coming home from work. She'd waved and I'd given her a thumbs-up for some bizarre reason, as though we were twelve and she'd just lent me her copy of *Beano*. I didn't know how to act around her anymore, now that I knew she wasn't with the American guy after all. At least I didn't think she was. Clive, who was clearly in matchmaking mode, had assured me it was over and she'd said she was single. I didn't entirely trust him to tell me the full story, since he was bizarrely obsessed with what a perfect couple we'd make. *Opposites attract*, he'd announced proudly, as though he'd coined the phrase himself. *You're like that Chinese saying: Yin and Yang.*

Anyway, today I wasn't going to think about Rebecca. Today I was going to concentrate on impressing Joe, the director of the play I was in. Despite it earning me no money, I thought this might actually have been quite a good move. We were performing in Soho, so casting directors could practically stagger out of their offices and into the theatre foyer. I just hoped they weren't going to be disappointed with what they saw.

We'd been running the same scene all morning and the atmosphere was tense. Joe wasn't easy to work with. He obviously had a clear vision in his head, but he seemed to find it difficult to translate that into something we all understood.

'Could you do that again but with more emotion?' said Joe, who was sitting on a director's chair with a pencil behind his ear and a clipboard in his hands trying to look all 'director-y'.

'By more emotion you mean …?' I queried, wanting to get it right.

'Less shouting, more feeling,' he replied.

I nodded. 'OK. Sure.'

We were halfway through our month-long rehearsal

period, and I was seriously worried. Joe didn't seem to like any of the character choices I'd made but couldn't actually help me come up with any better ones. We'd done absolutely no blocking, so the actress playing my wife just kept wandering aimlessly around the stage, barely staying still long enough for me to actually say my lines to her face instead of to the back of her head. The stage manager had quit on day two and we had a new girl who'd just graduated from Goldsmiths and who permanently looked on the verge of tears. The whole thing looked set for disaster and far from being the big success I'd hoped. I was sticking with it, though, because Alistair had lined up loads of people to come and see me and he was confident that it was going to be a brilliant opportunity to introduce me to the agency and effectively re-launch my career. I already trusted Alistair more than I ever had Chad. He'd rung me several times already to let me know who he'd approached, and what his plan of action was, and he'd even taken me for dinner at The Ivy, a place I'd always wanted to go.

We tried the scene again. This time instead of shouting at her (even if we were supposed to be having a blazing row, according to the script), I tried it in a calm and controlled way, as though I was desperately trying to suppress my inner feelings. Since my character was a law student who exuded confidence and loved the sound of his own voice, I wasn't sure this was a valid choice, but I'd give it a go. Sometimes things worked out better than you'd thought they would.

'Much stronger,' said Joe to me when I went to grab a drink of water. 'But can you stop moving around the stage so much? It's distracting.'

Once rehearsals were done for the day, I decided to walk up to Tottenham Court Road and jump on the No. 24 bus up to Hampstead Heath. I sat on the top deck, periodically checking my phone for non-existent messages and people-watching out of the window. I saw someone who looked like Rebecca coming out of Warren Street Station and I swivelled my head to look. I didn't think it was her. This girl was taller and was wearing trainers, which I'd never seen Rebecca wear unless she was going running. I'd missed her, although it had only been a few days. I'd heard her voice a few times on the landing and had been tempted to swing open the door, to casually ask how she was, what she'd been up to. Whether she might like to have that glass of wine sometime. Once, I'd even had my hand on the door handle, but something had stopped me. Nothing about it felt safe, and since everything else in my life felt new and a bit up in the air, I thought it was best to avoid throwing something else unfamiliar into the mix.

And yet the sound of her voice did something to me. I liked hearing her laughing into her phone, I imagined her listening intently to whoever was on the other end of the line.

The bus terminated at the Royal Free and I glanced up at the wards, making a mental note to pop in and see Clive later in the week. I crossed the road at South Grove, looked longingly at the cakes in Le Pain Quotidien, which each cost about as much as an hour's work at the pub, and walked up East Heath Road.

Just past Hampstead Heath Station, I saw Rebecca. She was walking down the hill in the opposite direction and she had her head down as though she was in a hurry. It was also possible, I thought, that she'd seen me and wanted to pretend she hadn't. I bit my lip, stepping out into the road, checking for traffic, intending to cross, but she was walking so fast she'd already passed me.

'Rebecca!' I called out.

She looked up and when she saw me, she looked genuinely surprised, so I deduced from that that she hadn't been trying to pretend not to see me. Funny the assumptions you could make about another person when really you had absolutely no idea what was going on in their head.

I waved, but somehow my feet were rooted to the spot. She stopped, too. One hand was holding onto the strap of her bag, the other was on her hip. She was waiting for me to say something else, probably. A car beeped its horn, which was hardly surprising when I was standing in the middle of the road. I put my hand up as an apology and jogged over to Rebecca. She looked lovely, all flushed from the walk, wearing a smart black dress belted at the waist and red lipstick.

'Hi,' I said, breathless. 'Not at work today?'

'I've got the day off, but I can't really talk,' she said, too quickly. 'I've got a second interview for that bereavement charity job.'

'That's brilliant!'

She smiled shyly. 'Wish me luck.'

I nodded. 'Course! Best of luck. I hope it goes really well.'

She twisted her body to move, but her feet stayed in the same place.

'We should go for a drink or something,' I suggested, trying to muster up a smile to make the situation less tense.

'Sure,' she replied. 'Before you go.'

There was less than a month until I had to move out and I hadn't done anything about finding somewhere else to live. I kept hoping that Tom would extend his stay in New York, but from the messages he'd sent, it didn't seem likely.

'Definitely,' I said, wanting her to stay but also not able to think of anything to say to keep her there. It hadn't been like that before, that was what had been so nice. I'd had no filter with her, I'd said whatever I wanted. Except how I felt about her; that I couldn't seem to say.

She turned and carried on down the hill. I watched her a for a few seconds, annoyed with myself for not being able to articulate my feelings and then started out for home, swerving to avoid a dog walker with at least ten dogs on leads, all splaying out in different directions.

'Jack!'

I looked around. Rebecca had stopped and was looking in my direction.

'If you want,' she shouted, 'come round later. I'll make cocktails or something.'

I smiled to myself. 'Sure,' I shouted back. 'Eight-ish OK?'

She gave me a wave and then she was off again.

I ruffled the back of my hair, wondering what it meant and then deciding that – for once – I was just going to go with the flow and not try to control how I felt. I'd taken a risk on my career, so maybe I could take a risk on this, too?

43

Rebecca

I'd dressed more casually than usual, in jeans and a white vest with spaghetti straps, my hair scraped up in a bun. I always seemed to be dolled up when I bumped into Jack; he probably thought I looked smart 24/7.

When I walked back into the lounge clutching a Negroni in each hand, Jack was standing in front of the fireplace, peering at the photo of me with Mum and Dad. I was about five and we were on holiday, at a caravan park in Great Yarmouth. I had sparkling eyes and ice-cream smeared around my mouth. Mum had a straw bag over her shoulder. I always remembered her with that. She had everything in there: her diary, a snack for me, a travel pack of tissues, her unnecessarily enormous purse, the shiny coral-pink lipstick she always wore.

'Your parents look lovely,' he said, running his finger around the edge of the frame.

'They were.'

'Do you still miss them?' he asked.

I nodded. 'Every day.'

I handed him a Martini glass full of brown liquid. It was as if we were both being very careful not to touch each other while we passed the drink from one hand to another.

'Sorry, these are in the wrong glasses. They should be served in an old-fashioned, apparently.'

'What's that?'

'It's a short tumbler,' I said.

'It smells good,' he said, inhaling the heady scent of bitter orange and vermouth. 'And who cares about the glasses?'

He went over to the window.

'You were right about how different your view is,' he commented.

It was still light, but the sky was turning a darker, duskier blue. Every so often the front door slammed; 7–8 was rush hour for Marlowe Court, with everyone arriving home from work.

'Do you know any of these people?' he asked, pointing to the flats opposite.

'I feel like I do. You get to know their schedules. What time they eat, whether they work, who's got a boyfriend, who's split up with theirs,' I replied, wondering if I was painting myself in the best light here.

'If I lived on this side, I reckon I'd spend the entire time nosing out of the window,' said Jack.

We actually had much more in common than I'd thought.

I went to sit on the sofa, squishing myself right up at one end so that when he sat down, there was a decent amount of space between us.

He had some of his Negroni and groaned, immediately taking another sip.

'This is amazing,' he said.

I shrugged lightly but was secretly pleased. All my practice had paid off.

I still couldn't believe I'd asked him over. I thought it was probably the thought of him leaving in a month. The fact that I'd been thinking about him all the time, even though I didn't want to. If he was only here for another four weeks, it was now or never really, wasn't it?

'How was your interview?' he asked.

'Good,' I said. It actually had been. 'I met the CEO again, who seems lovely. And the team I'd be working with. I think it went really well.'

He clinked his glass against mine. 'I knew you could do it,' he said.

'I've not done it yet.'

'I've got a good feeling about it.'

'Psychic, are you?' I teased.

I saw his eyes rest on my dirty running gear flung over the back of the armchair and wished I'd had time to do a proper tidy-up.

'It's nice in here,' he said.

I watched him drinking in every detail of the room, and I was aware, again, of how little it said about me.

'If I stick around much longer, I'll need to do something with it,' I said, feeling the need to explain. 'Look, I've even bought some interiors magazines for inspiration.' I pointed to the copy of *Elle Decoration* on the table.

'What are you thinking?' he asked, relaxing back on the sofa, crossing his feet at the ankle.

'I'd like a burnt orange wall,' I said. 'And some artwork. And some more bookshelves over there.'

He nodded enthusiastically. 'A pop of colour.'

I watched him running his fingertip around the rim of the glass.

'My ex – Dan – insisted on keeping it all white,' I said. 'He liked the minimalistic look.'

'This is the guy you used to live with?' asked Jack.

'Yeah. We moved in here together and then he moved out six months later.'

'Sounds like a wanker,' he said, and then looked like he wished he hadn't. 'Sorry,' he added. 'I'm sure he was very nice.'

I smiled, sipping delicately at my drink, even though I felt like taking massive gulps of it in the hope that I'd feel relaxed enough to act like my normal self instead of this slightly anxious, edgy person I'd suddenly become.

'It's fine. He was a wanker, ultimately. But for some reason, I always seem to fall for them.'

'Funny how we keep repeating the same old patterns, isn't it?' he said.

Our heads were both resting on the back of the sofa. He was looking up at the ceiling, at my lightshade with feathers stuck onto it, like a sort of lit-up swan. It was the first non-minimalistic thing I'd treated myself to when Dan had left.

'Nice lampshade,' Jack commented.

I tapped my fingertips on the sofa between us; I had the sudden desire to reach out and run my hand up the inside of his thigh but I was determined to hold onto the little bit of control over myself I still had. The problem was, when I was with Jack, my resolve seemed to go out of the window.

'I'm sorry I thought you were seeing Nathalie,' I said. 'I shouldn't have assumed.'

He put his hand over the top of mine. Our fingers slotted effortlessly together. Part of me wanted to move away because it felt too much, too intense.

'Well, I thought you were back with American boy,' he said.

I burst out laughing. 'Is that what you call him?'

'Ooops, did I really just say that out loud?' he grinned.

He put his glass down on the table and twisted in his seat to face me.

'You're really nice to talk to,' he said.

I nodded. 'I keep finding myself storing up things to tell you. You seem to be the first person I want to speak to about stuff these days.'

I couldn't believe I was being so open about how I felt. Warmed by the drink and more confident than usual, I reached out and stroked his cheek with my thumb, still holding my glass, which felt too heavy and clumsy in my other hand now.

'I enjoyed our kiss,' he said.

'Me too,' I whispered. 'So why has it taken us so long to do it again?'

Then suddenly we were kissing again, more urgently this time, so that I was breathing in short, sharp bursts. He put his hand under the hem of my vest, cupping my breast in his hand.

'One sec,' I said, fumbling to put my glass down, almost dropping it. We both laughed.

'Stand up,' he said.

Laughing lightly, I got to my feet.

He reached out and spun me around so that I was facing him and then he undid the top button of my jeans, very slowly sliding down the zip, pushing them down over my hips. I stroked the top of his head. His hair was so touchable, thick and downy; I buried my hand in it. Then I kicked off my jeans and sat on his lap, my legs straddling him. He helped me pull off my top, throwing it onto the floor.

'You're really beautiful, do you know that?' he said, kissing my neck. When he buried his head in my chest, I pressed him into me, quietening the voice in my head that was telling me I was going to get hurt, that I should play it cool, that I was going to like him too much after this. And then I thought briefly of the neighbours, that I ought to close the curtains, but I couldn't seem to stop for long enough to say.

Afterwards, I got dressed quickly.

'I hope nobody saw us,' I said, laughing lightly.

Jack was sprawled on the sofa, completely naked, his hands behind his head like he was sunbathing on the beach. 'I'm trying to work out how much I care.'

I perched on the edge of the sofa next to him. 'That was nice,' I said.

Which was an understatement, really, because I had never had sex like it before, not with Dan and certainly not with Tyler. I'd felt truly connected to him, like I could have done anything, said anything, and it wouldn't have mattered.

He pulled me into him, kissing the top of my head. 'An unexpected turn of events,' he said.

I watched him pick his T-shirt off the floor and put it on, then he did the same with the rest of his things. He sat back down, taking my hand and kissing it.

'Any more of those Negronis going?'

I swallowed, trying to steady myself. Panic had begun to kick in. I tried to tell myself that everything was fine. Just because I'd had sex with him once and it had been amazing and he was the first person I'd liked this much for ages (possibly ever) didn't mean I was going to lose my head and fall for him. I had lots of other stuff going on: possibly a new job, decorating the flat. And he'd be gone soon, moved out, going god knows where, and even though the thought of that was a tiny bit painful now, as long as I kept my distance from him between now and then, it would probably be bearable. I'd cope. I wouldn't feel lost or abandoned, I'd just be sad for a day or two and then I'd get over it.

'You know, I should probably get an early night,' I said. 'I don't do well at work when I've got a hangover.'

A look of disappointment crossed his face, which I thought was probably because he'd wanted to have sex again, rather than him having the sort of feelings for me that I, annoyingly, had seemingly developed for him. He was obsessed with his work, he'd told me as much; there's no way he'd want to complicate his life by getting involved with someone who lived across the hall.

'Oh right. Sure,' he replied.

I watched him get up, drain his glass. He pulled on his socks and found his shoes, which had somehow ended up at opposite ends of the room.

'Right, then,' he said, ruffling his hair at the back. I'd always thought he looked like a little boy when he did that. I almost crumbled then and thought: *Stuff it, let's have another Negroni*. 'We should do this again.'

I stood up.

'Yeah,' I replied, bending to pick a cushion up off the floor.

He put his hands on either side of my face and kissed me lightly on the mouth. 'You're lovely,' he said.

Don't go, I thought. Which meant I was in trouble. With Tyler, I hadn't been able to get him out of the door quick enough, desperate to have my own space back, to not have to put on an act. But I didn't have to do that with Jack, anyway.

'I'll walk you out,' I said.

He followed me down the corridor, his trainers squeaking on the floor. While I fumbled with the door, I could feel him breathing on the back of my neck, which almost finished me off. I could just turn around, throw caution to the wind; kiss him again.

I stood aside, shimmying into the kitchen. He dived

into his pocket for his keys, manically, as if he thought he'd dropped them.

'Thanks for the cocktails,' he said.

I put my hand on the door frame. 'Any time.'

He smiled. I looked at my doormat, laughing. He kissed me lightly on the mouth. And then I closed the door.

44

Jack

I was on the afternoon shift at the pub and my mind wouldn't settle. There was the usual slew of medical students and off-duty doctors dipping in and out, and a group of builders working on one of the exclusive properties surrounding the pub had commandeered the corner by the TV, their table scattered with crushed crisps and spilt beer. Luke shoved a plate of beef lasagne and salad at me and told me to take it to table five.

When I got back, he was looking at me, chucking me a cloth to polish the taps.

'Spill,' he said.

I pretended to concentrate on rubbing at a miniscule smear on the Amstel tap. 'Spill what?'

'Something's wrong.'

'It isn't,' I said.

'Are you not enjoying the fringe thing?' he asked, empty-ing some change into the till.

'Actually that's going much better. It's all coming to-gether, finally.'

And Joe seemed to have settled down and was starting to give constructive feedback rather than just barking orders. I was beginning to think we had something really good and was looking forward to actually performing it for whoever Alistair had lined up.

'Anything else bothering you?'

I sighed. 'If you must know, I've got myself into a bit of a situation with my neighbour. You know that girl I told you about? Rebecca?'

'Oh yeah, the one you've got a thing for?' he grinned.

'I wouldn't say I've got a thing for her,' I said defensively. Was it that obvious?

'Go on,' he said. 'What happened?'

A bell rang in the kitchen and I evaded his line of questioning by rushing off to deliver four portions of fish and chips to the builders, who then had me running back and forth from the kitchen to fetch various condiments. For once I didn't mind, because there was a good chance Luke would have forgotten what we were talking about by the time I got back.

He hadn't.

'You were saying ...?' he piped up, leaning against the bar with his arms crossed.

I pushed my sleeves up. 'Is it hot in here or is it me?'

Luke tutted. 'I'm waiting.'

'Fine. We slept together, all right?'

'Ha!' said Luke, doing an annoying sort of gun-slinging action in my direction. 'I knew it.'

'Pipe down,' I said, as one of the regulars looked over, an oncologist, he'd told me once, which explained why he was constantly in desperate need of a pint.

'So did you do something to mess it up, then?' asked Luke, looking serious all of a sudden.

I gave him a look. 'Why would you say that?'

He grabbed a damp sponge from the sink and removed fish and chips from the chalkboard menu; the builders had clearly polished off the last of it. 'Well, you've got that look about you,' he said. 'Sort of regretful. Like you did when you told me you weren't going to call that Janine girl you met at our dinner party.'

'I never promised to call Janine.'

'Well, she was under the impression you'd hit it off.'

I rubbed my eyes with the heels of my hands. 'I didn't feel like we did,' I said.

I didn't know why he was banging on about this again, the dinner party was ages ago and I honestly hadn't given Janine another thought. I had, however, been thinking about Rebecca constantly. The way I'd felt when I was with her, the way she'd clung to me and me to her as though for that short window of time, nothing else had mattered. I remembered the smell of her hair and the curve of the small of her back and the tiny, crab-shaped birthmark on her thigh.

'What happened, then?' asked Luke. 'Because it seems as though you really like this neighbour of yours. Didn't you tell her that?'

I examined my thumbnail to buy some time. 'There wasn't really an opportunity to.'

I thought I'd made it obvious how much I liked her, even if I hadn't exactly spelt it out. Part of me really, really wanted it to be the start of something, but then, of course, there was the other, darker side that thought she'd get bored of me having no money and no proper job and then she'd end it. Despite that, I thought I was ready to take a risk. To not run for the hills. She was worth taking a chance on, was how it felt.

'Fucking hell, Jack,' said Luke. 'You just got off, didn't you? Left the poor girl wondering what she'd done wrong?'

I groaned. 'No, that is not what happened, not at all. She was the one who couldn't wait to get rid of *me*.'

Luke looked positively shocked. 'Oh. OK.'

'It was like she instantly regretted it,' I said, remembering how it had stung to have to walk away. 'Her whole demeanour changed as soon as we'd finished you know ...'

'Did you ask her why?'

'No.'

'Jack, communication is the key here. You're assuming that she's not into it, but until you talk it through, you really don't know, do you?'

The thought terrified me. I didn't know why when I was clearly very used to rejection, on a professional level, at least.

'You're right. I'm going to talk to her,' I told Luke with conviction.

Even if it went badly, at least then I'd know.

I was still in a pensive mood at gone ten, when a familiar face came bounding over, all sparkly earrings and a blouse that flopped open when she leaned on the bar.

'Hello,' she said.

'Hello Ishanvi,' I replied, using her name on purpose to prove to her that I hadn't forgotten it, even if we hadn't repeated that one night. She'd made it clear that she'd like to, but my head just wasn't in it.

'How's things?' she asked, sliding onto a stool.

'Good. You?'

She laughed. 'Nice to see you're feeling less miserable tonight.'

'Thanks,' I said. That was nice to hear, actually, because I was sick of the melancholy, tortured-artist vibe. I finally felt as though things were on the turn. Alistair had already got me a casting for a Eurostar ad next week and we were going into previews for the play and I was feeling very positive about it. And there was Rebecca, who had made me momentarily very happy.

'What are you doing after?' asked Ishanvi.

'Um, heading home?'

'Want some company?'

I was going to have to be honest here. 'I'm in a bit of a weird headspace at the moment,' I said, keeping it light. 'Mind if I take a rain check?'

She looked a bit surprised, but not exactly disappointed.

'OK, sure,' she said.

She went back to her friends and I went back to work, wondering whether fate might be on my side and that when I got back to Marlowe Court, Rebecca might also be coming home from a night out. That she might be as pleased to see me as I would be to see her. I thought it was unlikely, but I fantasised about it anyway.

45

Rebecca

I slid into my chair at 9.15 when I should have been at my desk at 9. Of course, Amanda had noticed me skulking across the office the one time (OK, the second time) I'd ever been late. Within seconds, she sashayed over to my desk, bringing with her a cloud of perfume, one of those heady eighties scents that were marketed to powerful women who wanted to get ahead in business but just left everyone else gasping for breath.

'Rebecca, could I possibly have a word? Meeting room 2?'

'Sure,' I said, thrown off guard.

Had she dredged up something to bollock me for so that she could exert her newfound power over me? I grabbed my notebook and a pen (old habits died hard) and followed her into the meeting room next to the kitchen. She sat down with her legs crossed at the knee, her designer button-through maxi skirt revealing her calves and a hint of thigh.

I closed the door behind me and sat down.

'So I wanted to talk to you about something. It's a touch … sensitive,' she began.

'Right,' I said, unsure where this was going.

She took a deep breath. 'Tyler Martin and I have been seeing each other. And I've heard some rumours about the two of you and I wanted to ask you if they were true.'

'Wow,' I said, taken aback. This wasn't how I'd expected this to go. 'So what, he was seeing us both?'

I thought I saw Amanda's bottom lip wobble. God, was she really into him? Then again, I could imagine he was just her type.

'I haven't had a chance to speak to him,' she said. 'But it would seem so, yes.'

I sighed, feeling a bit bad. Amanda clearly really liked him and if I'd thought for a second he was involved with both of us, I would have ended things straight away, not that there was anything between us anymore.

'We only saw each other a couple of times,' I said, trying to reassure her. 'And it was nothing serious. It ended a while ago.'

Amanda was looking more flustered by the second. 'Can I ask how long ago? Was it before or after I caught you in the photocopier room?'

I wouldn't have put it quite like that. 'Before. Well, we went for dinner after, but nothing happened.'

She nodded. 'Right. Good. That's good.'

'I'm sorry if this has come as a shock,' I said.

Amanda took a deep breath. 'I should have known better than to get involved with someone in the workplace.'

I put my pen down. I hardly needed to write notes on this.

'I didn't feel comfortable with it myself,' I admitted. 'Which is why it's probably a good thing I'm leaving.'

Amanda did a double take. 'You're what?'

'Leaving.'

'When?'

'Well, I've only just handed my notice in to Mike. So a month from now, hopefully.'

Amanda looked decidedly put out, probably because now

she wouldn't get to lord it over me and boss me around like she'd planned. She'd have taken even more delight in it now, probably.

'Where are you going, then?' she asked.

It felt weird saying it out loud, but totally uplifting at the same time. They'd rung me late last night and I'd wasted no time handing in my notice. For possibly the first time in my life I was trusting my instincts and going after what I really wanted.

'Bit of a change of direction. I'll be working for Children in Crisis. It's a charity.'

She looked impressed for a second and then seemed to think better of it. 'Well. Good luck.'

I stood up. 'You too,' I said.

'Did you not go for the head of press and marketing, then?' she asked. 'Just out of interest?'

I shook my head, realising I'd shattered two of her illusions in the space of five minutes. She'd still beaten all the other candidates to the role – wasn't that enough for her?

June

46

Jack

Clive was looking perky when I arrived on the ward and was sitting up doing a crossword, which was lovely to see. He'd be asking me to sneak him in a rum punch next.

'Ah, Jack!' he said. 'Just the person I wanted to see.'

'How are you doing?' I asked him, pulling up a chair.

'Very good,' he replied. 'Did you bring my grapes?'

I dived into my bag, handing him a punnet. 'I think you've got a grape addiction.'

Clive laughed. 'There's nothing to do in this place except eat.'

'Give me some, then,' I said, ripping open the plastic and taking a handful for myself.

'Got anything interesting to tell me?' asked Clive.

'Missing your Marlowe Court gossip, are you?' I said, teasing him.

'Eh!' he said, batting me on the arm.

'I have got some news, actually. I dumped my agent. It happened a while ago. I meant to tell you but I didn't want to make it all about me when I came to see you.'

Clive looked surprised. 'This is the most exciting thing I've heard since I've been in here – you should have told me sooner. What are you going to do now, then?'

'It's OK, I've got another one. I need a change, Clive. This new agent really believes in me. He thinks I can do much bigger and better things.'

Clive patted my hand. 'Good boy. You're taking the bull by the horns, this is what I like to see.'

'Thanks, Clive.'

'I wanted to talk to you about something else, actually,' said Clive.

'Oh yeah?'

I wasn't sure where this was going, it could be anything with Clive. I really hoped he wasn't going to bring up Rebecca.

'They say I'll have to go into some sort of residential home.'

'So I hear,' I said, noticing the brochure for Greenhill Lodge was on the bed, next to the puzzle book. That was a good sign. He'd point-blank refused to look at it before.

'Rebecca says her grandmother is in there. That she has her own room and lots of people to talk to.'

'They'd love you in there,' I said. 'You'd be in demand with all those ladies, that's for sure.'

Clive looked off into the distance, deep in thought.

'Is there anything I can do to help?' I asked. 'To make it easier for you?'

He turned to look at me. 'It's funny you should say that. There is, actually. I want you to live in my flat in Marlowe Court.'

I nearly choked on a piece of grape skin.

'What do you mean?' I said, once I'd got my breath back.

'I own that place, you know. Outright,' said Clive.

I'd never really thought about whether he rented or owned it.

'And I have some savings,' he added. 'I had a successful business once, you know?'

I nodded. 'I don't doubt it.'

'I don't want to sell the flat, not yet. My whole life is tied up in that place. It would make me feel much better if I could hold onto it for now, but know that it was well looked-after.'

I patted his hand. 'Are you feeling all right, Clive?'

'Perfectly fine. And I've still got all my faculties, if that's what you're worried about.'

I shook my head. 'It wasn't.'

'Well then, what do you say? Will you live there, take care of the place for me? You'd be doing me a favour. There won't be any rent to pay, you'd just need to cover the bills and all that.'

I opened my mouth to speak, but nothing came out.

'Not like you to be lost for words,' teased Clive.

'Why would you do that, Clive?' I eventually managed to ask.

'Why do you think?' said Clive. If I didn't know him better, I'd think he was tearing up. 'You saved my life, didn't you? If it wasn't for you, I wouldn't be here at all.'

'It wasn't just me,' I replied.

'I know. But it was mainly you. Accept it, Jack. You saved me and I will be grateful for the rest of my days. So I hope you'll accept my offer.'

I rubbed my hands over my mouth. 'Is this some sort of joke?'

'It is not!' he said, roaring with laughter. 'So it's a yes?'

I swallowed, completely dazed. 'It's a yes.'

47

Rebecca

I grabbed a table near the back of Bar Monaco. A few minutes later, Val came over with the drinks.

'Are you still off wine, then?' I asked, glancing at her orange juice complete with straw.

'Yes …' she replied, looking enviously at my glass.

I'd wanted to tell her about Jack, but for some reason I'd needed to get it straight in my own head first. Other than at work, I'd barely seen her over the last couple of weeks and I was hardly going to tell her about my latest relationship disaster in the staff kitchen where gossipy ears lurked (i.e. Paul from Accounts).

'So something's happened,' I said mysteriously.

'Go on,' she said.

I cleared my throat. 'You know that guy Jack that we saw at Somerset House? My neighbour?'

'Uh-huh.'

Val got her compact out and reapplied her glossy red lipstick. She was going to be the most glamorous mum on earth when the time came.

'I invited him over for drinks.'

Val narrowed her eyes at me. 'You slept with him, didn't you?'

I put my head in my hands. 'Yes. And I wish I hadn't.'

'Why?' she said, looking at me and then in her compact mirror to check her lipstick hadn't smudged.

'Because I panicked and went all weird with him afterwards. And now it's a nightmare living opposite him. And also, I think I might actually have feelings for him.'

Val closed her compact, frowning. 'What do you mean you went "weird"?'

'I pretended I wasn't into it and practically pushed him out of the door,' I replied.

It was mortifying. I kept replaying the scene over and over in my head and I still didn't have a proper explanation, except that it had felt like I was doing the right thing at the time.

'Oh, Becs,' she said.

I shrugged. 'We'd had a really nice evening as well. We'd shared all this stuff about ourselves. He makes me laugh. It felt like we really connected.'

'What was the sex like?' asked Val. 'After months of timing it according to my cycle and having zero spontaneity, I'm desperate to hear how normal people do it.'

'It was amazing,' I said wistfully. 'He's really intense and kind of quietly sexy.'

Val fanned herself dramatically.

'Shame I've gone and messed it all up,' I added.

Val sat back and crossed her arms. 'Why don't you talk to him? Explain what happened?'

'I don't know …'

'Tell him how much you like him and see what he says.'

'I couldn't …'

'You have to,' said Val with her serious face on. 'The only way you're going to get what you want is by being open with people. Show that vulnerable side you've buried so deep.'

'But I'll be completely humiliated if he says it's too late and never wants to see me again.'

'You'll get over it,' replied Val matter-of-factly, sucking up the last of her orange juice.

I looked at her as though she was mad, but deep down, I knew she was right. I swung back and forth in my head: the worst he could say was no, and he was moving out soon anyway, so it wasn't like the humiliation would be sustained. And then I swung the other way and thought: what if he says he likes me too? It would mean starting over again, like I'd done with Dan. Trusting him; not being freaked out by the idea of letting someone into my life and then possibly having them leave me. Was it worth putting myself out there? And if I didn't, could I potentially be missing out on something that would make me happier than I'd ever been in my life?

48

Jack

I took my place on stage, nodding at Monty who was playing my father-in-law. He was a lovely guy and a brilliant actor; the whole company had really bonded in the end, once Joe calmed the fuck down and rehearsals stopped being so tense. I held my prop cup and saucer aloft and imagined myself into a living room in a house in Crystal Palace. I was a city boy (which was surprisingly fun to play, even if I couldn't stand them in real life) and I was trying desperately to find some empathy for this elderly man who had never been very nice to me but was beginning to forget who everyone was. I knew my character like the back of my hand; understood him. Liked him, despite his faults. And I was going to become him tonight and blow everyone away. I got my first line in my head as the house lights went down and the curtain went up.

Afterwards, the audience broke into a rapturous standing ovation. Well, as rapturous as it could be when there were only about eighty of them, but I loved it anyway. I actually felt a little bit emotional, which I reckoned was less about me and more about the fact I'd just spent the last two and a half hours playing a man who suppressed every single difficult feeling he'd ever had. We had a full house, apparently, which Joe assured us almost never happened on opening night. Word had got round, and Alistair had texted to say there was a handful of casting directors in and a good turn-out from the press. The play had come together in the end, and with the costumes and the music and the visual effects, I thought we'd created something really special.

As I took my first bow of the night, I spotted Alistair looking pleased and then, a couple of rows back, clapping manically and beaming proudly, my parents.

I blinked, not quite believing it. What were they doing here? I'd mentioned it briefly to my mum on the phone, but I'd never thought they'd come in a million years. This would have required them to book tickets, to arrange taxis (they didn't do the tube) and for Dad to have kept his diary free, which for some reason was always, *always* a problem. I felt a little bit teary when I thought about it. And then I felt even worse when, scanning the auditorium, I realised that the person I wanted to be here more than anything wasn't.

I'd dropped a note through Rebecca's door yesterday with one of the free tickets we'd been allocated. I'd been holding onto the fact that there'd been some sort of miscommunica-tion, that she'd been thinking about me as much as I'd been thinking about her, but clearly not. This was more galling than I thought it would be, but at least it had made me realise that I needed to move on and that she clearly wasn't interested. It would be hard, what with her living opposite, but I was just going to throw myself into my acting, like I'd always done. And perhaps, going on tonight, that wouldn't be so bad?

We took a final bow and filed off backstage to our shared dressing room. I changed into my own clothes and hurried out to the bar, where I was instantly surrounded by the familiar buzz of chatter and post-show excitement, reminding me of my drama-school showcase, when Chad had made a beeline for me and he'd been the agent everyone had wanted and my classmates had watched on jealously. I'd been on a high that night, convinced that it was the start of something huge. But tonight Alistair was here and I knew I felt safer in his hands than I ever had in Chad's.

I spotted Mum and Dad at a table near the bar. They looked out of place in this loud, slightly raucous bar. Dad looked hot in his too-tight suit and Mum took a sip of her wine and grimaced, as though it was cheap and sharp.

'This is a surprise,' I said, pulling up a stool and joining them at the table.

They both put their drinks down. Mum was smiling at me. 'Well done, Jack. You were brilliant.'

Dad cleared his throat. 'Yes, an excellent performance, Jack. I must admit, I didn't know you were this good.' He pushed a red wine in my direction. 'Hope this is what you wanted?'

I nodded, drinking a few large mouthfuls, touched by the fact that he hadn't forgotten me this time, but suppressing the urge to reply to his backhanded compliment about my acting skills.

'It was nice of you to come,' I said.

Mum nodded. 'Is your agent here? Chad, isn't it?'

'Actually, I've got a new one,' I replied, looking over my shoulder for Alistair. 'I should probably go and speak to him, actually. There might be some casting directors in he wants me to meet.'

'Well, I should think they'll be very impressed,' said Dad.

This was single-handedly the nicest thing he'd ever said to me. I actually felt quite choked.

Pulling myself together, I stood up. 'Will you two be OK here for a bit if I go and mingle?'

'We're going to head off soon, anyway,' said Mum. 'You go and enjoy yourself.'

I nodded, raising my glass to them. They raised theirs back, the three glasses clinking together.

I couldn't help smiling to myself as I walked over towards the bar where Alistair was chatting to two women I didn't recognise.

'Jack,' said Alistair, waving me over. 'There's some people I want you to meet.'

After an hour or so of schmoozing and talking non-stop and having Champagne pressed into my hands, I looked around the bar, which was emptying out now it was nearly eleven. I'd had lots of congratulations and handshakes from people I didn't know, and it had been a brilliant night. Everything had exceeded my expectations: the play itself, my parents turning up, Alistair introducing me to some really cool producers who wanted to arrange meetings for the following week. A casting director who worked closely with Sam Mendes making a beeline for me and giving me her card.

I popped to the loo, a bit overwhelmed by it all and wanting a couple of minutes to myself. I checked my phone for the first time that night. My heart thumped hard in my chest when I saw there was a message from Rebecca.

Hi. Sorry I couldn't make the show. I was planning to come, but my nan's in hospital. I've only just got back. Hope it went well.

I leaned against the sink, re-reading her message. Poor Rebecca. She'd be a mess, what with having to go to the hospital, which was difficult for her at the best of times, although she seemed to have got slightly better with it since

340

visiting Clive. And I had no idea what was wrong with her nan, but if it was something serious, she was going to be devastated. I knew what I had to do.

Walking out to the bar and keeping my head down so as not to get sidetracked, I grabbed my bag and made my way over to Joe and the rest of the cast.

'I'm off,' I said.

'Eh?' said Joe. 'You can't bail on us now.'

'There's someone I need to see,' I replied, feeling breathless. 'Thanks for everything, guys. See you all tomorrow, yeah?' I said, backing away.

'Don't forget I need you in at four o'clock for notes,' shouted Joe.

I waved at him to let him know I'd heard him and practically fell out of the bar onto Dean Street, where the air was strangely warm and the sky still not quite black.

49

Rebecca

I had a shower and put some comfy clothes on, shoving my hair up into a bun. My eyes still looked a bit red from where I'd been crying on the way to the Royal Free. Greenhill Lodge hadn't told me much on the phone except that Nan had been complaining of chest pains and that they'd called an ambulance to be on the safe side. They'd said it would probably be quicker for me to meet her at the hospital.

Just as I was looking in the fridge, deciding whether I could face having anything to eat, there was a knock on the door.

I looked at my watch. Who would be knocking at nearly midnight?

'Hello?' I said, peering through the spyhole.

'It's me. Jack,' said a muffled voice from the other side.

I opened the door.

'I got your message,' he said, looking worried.

I nodded. 'Oh, right.'

'How is she, your nan?'

'They think it's pneumonia. Hopefully they've caught it in time, though. Her temperature's come down already, so that's a good sign.'

'OK. That sounds positive. How are you?'

There was something about the concern in his voice, the

342

fact that he was here to check on me when he should be getting drunk at the theatre, that made me feel all warm and looked after and important. I'd been mad to shut myself off to him. It didn't come around often, this type of connection. We had something, I could see it now, and it was time to be brave and do something about it.

'Do you fancy coming to mine for a drink?' he said, before I had a chance to say anything. 'I've got some white wine chilling in the fridge.'

'Sounds good,' I replied, not giving myself time to think of all the reasons why I shouldn't. Anyway, I'd only sit around worrying about Nan.

I grabbed my keys from the kitchen and closed the front door behind me.

He let me into his and I walked down the hallway, barefoot because I hadn't thought to put shoes on. 'Shall I go into the lounge?' I asked.

'Sure,' he said. 'I'll get us a drink and I'll be right with you.'

I went over to the window, which he'd left open. I could hear the noise of the traffic snaking up East Heath Road and wondered if it would annoy me if I lived on this side. A breeze floated past me and I breathed in the scent of something floral. It was probably the bush with bursts of white flowers in the front garden that I didn't know the name of.

I went to sit on the sofa. His lounge looked different this time. There were boxes lined up against the wall and the bookshelves were emptier than they had been before. Of course, he was moving out. The photos had come down, too, and now the only hint that this was an actor's home was the script on the coffee table. It seemed to be for some sort of film and looked well leafed-through, with a coffee stain on its front cover. I couldn't help feeling a bit bereft that he'd be leaving soon.

He appeared in the doorway holding two glasses of white wine and came to stand next to me. I took one of the drinks from him, cradling it in my hands, enjoying having something to focus on. I swilled the glass, watching the liquid slop about.

'How did the play go?' I asked.

'I wish you'd been there,' he said.

50

Jack

'I was on my way to see you when I got the call,' she explained.

I nodded. 'I came back. As soon as I got your message. I didn't think you ought to be on your own.'

She smiled. 'You didn't need to do that.'

She looked so sweet and beautiful with her hair up and her fringe swept to the side and her clothes that looked like pyjamas. I wanted to kiss her right there and then, but I knew I shouldn't. She'd had a shock; it was probably the last thing she felt like doing. She had that perfume on again, the sexy, citrussy one. It brought back memories of the night we'd spent together. I remembered how I'd been able to taste it afterwards, when I was back at my own flat wondering what had gone wrong.

I gulped at my wine, trying to loosen my throat. Now she was here, how did I say what I wanted to say? I decided we needed some music on and got out my phone, flicking through my playlists.

'What do you fancy listening to? Are you into indie? Electronic?'

She shrugged. 'I don't mind.'

I put a bit of Bat for Lashes on because I thought she'd like it and I'd always found her stuff filmic, like it could be the soundtrack to the sort of deeply emotional conversation that I wanted to have but wasn't entirely sure I was capable of. The opening bars of their cover of 'Boys of Summer' blasted out of the speakers and I hurriedly turned the volume down, manically twiddling dials.

I turned to face her. It was now or never.

'I meant it when I said I had a good time the other night,' I said.

She looked uncomfortable. 'I did, too.'

I looked at the floor, willing myself to carry on. 'It's just that I didn't get that impression,' I added. 'I thought maybe you wished it hadn't happened.'

She shook her head. 'No. That's not it. It was the loveliest night I've had for a long time.'

I ruffled my hair. 'So what happened?'

She sighed. 'I know it doesn't make sense, but I acted strangely *because* I thought we'd had such a good time.'

I frowned at her. This sounded like an *it's not me it's you* style cop-out. 'What do you mean?'

'I'm scared of feeling things again. I'd shut all that off, I suppose, when I split up with Dan. It was easier to decide not to get close to anyone again. But then I met you and I found myself hoping I'd bump into you on the stairs. I started going out for runs thinking I might see you on the heath. I mean, I could have asked anyone to help me fix the lift, couldn't I?'

I laughed. 'Well, they wouldn't have done half as good a job, let me just say.'

I steeled myself. I was just going to have to man up and be honest about my feelings for her, too.

'I really like you,' I said, looking into her eyes. 'And I was the same as you, in a way. Not looking for anything. Thinking my career was enough, that a relationship would

346

just complicate things. But the thing is, when I'm with you, I have this sort of clarity. You let me be myself. You make me feel good enough, which sounds a bit wanky, but it's what I've always wanted to feel but never quite did before.'

She reached out and took my hand. 'You're more than good enough. Seriously, I don't think you realise how amazing you are.'

I laced my fingers through hers. 'I think about you all the time,' I admitted. 'Which is hard for me to say, because I'm basically battling this feeling that I'm going to make a fool of myself. That you'd never go for someone like me. I mean, I couldn't be more different from that American guy. And I thought that if that was the sort of person you liked, then I'd be kidding myself that you could ever feel that way about me.'

She hung her head, breaking eye contact. 'I can't believe we're being this honest with each other,' she said.

I laughed, reaching out to stroke her hair. 'Hard, isn't it?'

'Yes,' she groaned, 'but I'm working on it.'

51

Rebecca

'Let me get us a top-up,' Jack said, disappearing out to the kitchen.

While he was gone, I went over to the window and looked out at the view for what was probably the last time. If I lived on this side of the building, I'd miss the heath, the way the landscape changed right in front of your eyes. How the light was hazy and bright now and seemed to go on forever in the summer months. But what I was really going to miss was seeing Jack (or hearing him, at least) every day.

He came back and refilled our glasses.

'So,' he said. 'I know you can see boxes everywhere, but I'm not actually moving out as such.'

'You're not?' I asked, resisting the urge to whoop with joy. It wouldn't have been the same at Marlowe Court without him in it, but it was more than that. My life wouldn't be the same without him full stop.

'I'm moving into Clive's.'

I shook my head. 'Sorry, what?'

Jack smiled. 'Your PR campaign for Greenhill Lodge worked wonders. He's moving in there in a couple of weeks. He's asked me to live in his flat for the time being and only wants money for bills, or so he says. I'm going to sneakily find some way of getting some rent money to him, though.'

I swallowed. 'So you'll be living downstairs?'

He nodded.

'You do realise we'll have the same view, now?' I said.

'Yeah,' he replied, moving closer to me. 'And when I look out of the window, I'll be able to picture you, two floors above me, looking at exactly the same thing.'

I held my breath, watching him. He put his glass down on the windowsill and then he took my head in his hands. It felt as if everything was finally fitting into place.

'I got that job, by the way,' I said.

'I knew you would,' he said, kissing me.

I pulled off his T-shirt. He slipped his hands under my top, easing it over my head.

One advantage of being at Jack's was that this time I didn't need to worry about who might be watching us through the window, but, in truth, I didn't care anyway. All I knew was that I never wanted to let him go.

Afterwards, we finished the wine and sat around, him with his boxers on and me in just his T-shirt. I wasn't feeling the urge to bolt, which was promising.

'Haven't you got *anything* colourful in your wardrobe?' I asked, laughing.

'I don't think so,' he replied.

My stomach rumbled.

'You're hungry,' he said.

'I wasn't, but now I am.'

'Shall I make you something?'

'You'd really do that? For me?'

He nodded. 'Course. I love cooking. I've always got stuff going on in my head – other people's words, or regrets about stuff, or rehashing old auditions I've had and didn't get. Sometimes it's a bit much, but when I'm cooking, I forget all of that and just focus on the recipe, on following the method. And I love food, so …'

'I don't really cook,' I said.

'I thought not.'

'You've noticed all the ready meals, then?'

He looked sheepish. 'Sort of.'

'When I think of mealtimes, it reminds me of my parents. All of us together, laughing over dinner. I tend to get it over with as quickly as possible these days.'

He pulled me into him, stroking my hair. 'We can have nice meals together, sometimes,' he said. 'If you want.'

'I think that might be the sweetest thing anyone has ever said to me.'

'See, us Brits can be charming too.'

'Just to be clear, American boy turned out to be not charming in the slightest.'

'I knew it!'

He practically fist-bumped the air and I couldn't help but smile.

When Jack went out to the kitchen to make me a 'gourmet cheese toastie', as he described it, I tipped my head back, closing my eyes, listening to the beat of the music. I could hear him out in the kitchen, banging about, the clang of cutlery knocking together

'You are staying the night, right?' he asked, reappearing with some salt and pepper and an impressive array of sauces.

I reached up and brushed the hair off his face. 'Worried I'm going to do a runner?'

He laughed, crouching down and kissing me again.

'If it was up to me, you'd never leave,' he said, running his thumb across my cheek.

Which was good, because I didn't plan on going anywhere.

Acknowledgements

I wrote this book in the weirdest of times, mostly while the UK was in lockdown and I was confined to the four walls of my nice but small flat in London. And although this wasn't ideal for all the reasons you can imagine, one lovely thing about it was that I starting talking to some of the neighbours I'd previously only said a perfunctory 'hello' to. I think the idea of people from all walks of life living together under one roof - and the sense of community this can bring - became an important part of the novel, almost without me realising it. My first thank you is to the young woman whose lounge window is opposite my kitchen and whose name I don't know, but who gave me the initial idea for this story. Thanks also to Keith, my neighbour and inspiration for Clive, who was possibly one of my favourite-ever characters to write.

Many thanks to the team at Orion Fiction – firstly, my brilliant editor, Charlotte Mursell, whose vision for the book and never-ending enthusiasm made writing a novel during a pandemic surprisingly enjoyable, and to the other members of the 'dream team': Alainna Hadjigeorgiou, Lucy Cameron, Sanah Ahmed and everyone else who has worked so hard on this book. Thanks also to Victoria, who was the original sounding board for this idea. And I am forever grateful to the very lovely and hard-working Hannah Ferguson, who is everything I could have dreamed of in an agent and more, and to the rest of the fantastic team at Hardman &

Swainson. Thanks, too, to all the author friends I have made along the way and who have been so kind in taking the time to read, quote and talk about the book, especially the D20 Authors and the Debut21s. Thanks also to Dr Siobhan Leary for the medical advice and to Ora Dresner, psychoanalyst extraordinaire, for her help with character development – I must say, it's very useful having a friend who knows pretty much everything about how people's minds work!

And finally, thank you so much to all my family and friends – especially Mum, Matthew and Robbie – who have been so excited for me every step of the way. To my dad, who I know is supporting me from afar. And to Gabriel, for your love and enthusiasm – we survived home schooling, beautiful boy!

Credits

Lorraine Brown and Orion Fiction would like to thank everyone at Orion who worked on the publication of *Sorry I Missed You* in the UK.

Editorial
Charlotte Mursell
Sanah Ahmed

Copy editor
Jade Craddock

Proof reader
Clare Wallis

Audio
Paul Stark
Jake Alderson

Contracts
Anne Goddard
Humayra Ahmed
Ellie Bowker

Design
Tomás Almeida
Joanna Ridley
Nick May

Editorial Management
Charlie Panayiotou
Jane Hughes
Bartley Shaw
Tamara Morriss

Finance
Jasdip Nandra
Afeera Ahmed
Elizabeth Beaumont
Sue Baker

Marketing
Lucy Cameron

Production
Ruth Sharvell

Publicity
Alainna Hadjigeorgiou

Sales
Jen Wilson
Esther Waters

Victoria Laws
Rachael Hum
Anna Egelstaff
Frances Doyle
Georgina Cutler

Operations
Jo Jacobs
Sharon Willis

*Escape to Paris with Lorraine Brown's
unmissable and delightful romantic comedy …*

Could one split second change her life forever?

Hannah and Si are in love and on the same track – that is,
until their train divides on the way to a wedding.
The next morning, Hannah wakes up in Paris and realises
that her boyfriend (and her ticket) are 300 miles away in
Amsterdam!

But then Hannah meets Léo on the station platform,
and he's everything Si isn't. Spending the day with him in
Paris forces Hannah to question how well she really
knows herself – and whether, sometimes, you need to go
in the wrong direction to find everything you've been
looking for . . .